Missing
Quail Crossings

By Jennifer McMurrain

Missing Quail Crossings
By Jennifer McMurrain

Cover Design: Brandy Walker
         www.SisterSparrowGraphicDesign.com
Interior Design: Jennifer McMurrain
         www.LilyBearHouse.com

Published by LilyBear House, LLC
         www.LilyBearHouse.com

ISBN-13: 978-1517354329
ISBN-10: 1517354323

Also available in eBook publication

PRINTED IN THE UNITED STATES OF AMERICA

Dedication

To my sister, Brandy Walker. I wish you could see yourself as I see you. You are beautiful. You are intelligent. You are an artist. And to Jim Walker, thanks for making my sister smile.

Prologue

December 9, 1941

My Dearest Dovie,

I'm sure you've heard by now what has happened at Pearl Harbor. Let me start by saying I'm fine, but many aren't. I wish I could have written to you sooner, but it has been nothing but chaotic here.

It has been a couple of days since the attack, and we are still pulling soldiers from the ocean. I can't believe so much carnage happened in such a short amount of time. When the Japanese hit, it felt like all we could do was take cover.

I was lucky that I was in the barracks away from the coast when the bombings took place. My buddies and I ran to help, but there was nothing we could do. Some of our soldiers were able to take a few of the Japanese planes down, but it wasn't enough. I can't put into words how I felt, other than to say I felt helpless. We never expected this to happen on U.S. soil, and now that I've had time to fully digest what has happened, I am worried.

I am worried for our young men, men like Robert, Bill, and Elmer. I worry about our girls, that they will have to send their husbands, brothers, and fathers to war, knowing they may never see them again. I can't imagine all the families getting telegrams after this one attack.

With all of this suffering going on around me, I long for your embrace more than ever. All I can think about is getting home to you and Quail Crossings. Even on the island, that used to be paradise, I long for the peace of the Texas plains.

As much as I would love to come home now, I know it is my duty to stay and continue to train pilots. We cannot rest until evil is gone from this earth forever. We cannot let this attack on our country stand.

I pray that you, and the rest of the family, are doing well and will continue to stay safe during this uncertain time. Until we meet again, my sweet Dovie, and I know we will, I will be thinking of you and missing Quail Crossings.

With all my love,

Gabe

Chapter One

The buzz of Times Square was so contagious that not even the stoic Elmer Brewer was immune. He smiled and playfully slapped a sailor on the back of his shoulder before thrusting his fists in the air in triumph. The war was over. The Japanese had finally surrendered, and New York City seemed more alive than ever as cheers roared throughout the streets and ticker tape fell to the ground.

Elmer turned to pat another fellow soldier on the back and stopped in his tracks. *It couldn't be her. How was it even possible that the love of his life would be in the middle of Times Square at the same exact moment he was?*

Everyone called her Tiny, but she was his Mary. A smile filled Mary's face, and Elmer knew he wasn't hallucinating. His girl stood only a few feet away. Her red hair was fixed neatly in a bun but still shone brightly against her white nurse's uniform. Her blue eyes twinkled as she covered her mouth with one hand. Elmer could tell she was just as shocked to see him, and just as delighted.

Without another thought he marched right over to her and locked his arm behind her neck before dipping her into a long passionate kiss. It had been just over a year since he had seen his girl, and he wasn't wasting any more time to show her how he felt. He knew better than anyone that life could be taken away in the blink of an eye.

Dovie Grant hummed as she hung the clothes on the line in the backyard of Quail Crossings. It was going to be another hot day, but the temperature didn't stop laundry from piling up.

"Maybe once the war is over, I'll get me one of those electric washing machines," she said to Norman, the goose, who slept quietly under a tree. She looked at the bird with a bit of envy. "I wouldn't mind taking a nap about now. I remember when I could work all day without the thought of a snooze. I guess we're getting old, Norman."

"How old is Norman now?" asked Evalyn Smith as she carried over a basket of freshly washed diapers. She was followed closely behind by her almost six-year-old daughter Joy, who was pulling her seven-month-old brother, Caleb, in a red wagon.

Dovie rubbed her forehead. "I guess he's about fourteen. I think we had him a few years before y'all came into our lives."

Dovie looked over at Evalyn and the kids. Had it really been ten years since the Brewer clan came to work at Quail

Crossings? She could hardly remember a time without them.

"How long do geese live?" asked Evalyn as she started hanging the diapers on the second laundry line.

"That's a better question for Dad," said Dovie, "but I reckon Norman's got five or six more years with us. That is, if he doesn't try to take on any rabid dogs or boys with baseball bats."

Dovie reflected on Norman's life. He was ornerier than a cat in a yarn basket, but he had saved Evalyn's younger sister, Alice, from a rabid dog almost ten years ago and fought off some racist boys about five years ago. He'd suffered from dust pneumonia and broken wings but still was king of the crop at Quail Crossings.

"Who's that, Momma?" asked Joy as a black car pulled into the driveway.

"I'm not sure," said Evalyn. "Dovie?"

Dovie shook her head before yelling, "Bill, someone's here."

Evalyn's older brother, Bill, peeked his head out of the barn and watched the approaching car. He stepped out completely, letting the visitor see him. Even though Dovie knew Bill hated not being able to go fight the war against Hitler, she was glad he was there. She'd heard too many stories of women being taken advantage of by scams or worse while their husbands were away fighting the Axis of Evil.

She couldn't help but admit that the black patch he wore over his left eye made him not only look meaner but had made him stronger. Dovie marveled at how well Bill had adjusted to losing all sight in his left eye after being kicked by a horse during a tornado five years back. Thanks to Bill's hard work, Quail Crossings had continued running and remained profitable during the war.

She turned her attention back to the car. Goose bumps covered Dovie's body as she prayed it wasn't an unmarked government vehicle.

Evalyn grabbed her hand. "You don't think …"

Dovie squeezed her hand. "I hope not."

Dovie continued to pray that it wouldn't be their worst fears come to life. Evalyn's brother, Elmer, and her husband, Robert, still fought overseas in Europe, and Dovie had no clue where her dear love, Gabe Pearce, was currently training pilots. Too many families in Knollwood had received news via a long black car that their sons and loved ones would never be coming home.

The car came to a stop, and Dovie caught her breath as a uniformed officer stepped out briefly before bending back into the car to retrieve something.

She turned to Evalyn. "No matter what, we've got to be brave for the children. Understand?"

Tears had already started to form in Evalyn's eyes. Dovie gave her a quick hug. "We're gonna be all right. Everything's gonna be all right."

Dovie looked up just in time to see the car speed away, leaving an officer who was wearing a chocolate colored dress coat and tan pants. She looked at Bill who was smiling as he walked to the man. Dovie let go of Evalyn and took a step closer. Both hands flew to her mouth as she realized the officer was none other than her precious Gabe.

Unable to contain herself, she ran to him and wrapped him in a big hug. He swept her off her feet and swung her around. Stopping suddenly, he pulled her to him and kissed her. Dovie begged his lips to never leave hers again.

"Gabe," she said with a joyful sigh as they finally broke their embrace. "I'm so happy to see you."

"Not as happy as I am to see you," said Gabe before kissing her again.

Joy giggled, and Dovie, remembering she was in mixed company, took a step back. Gabe turned and picked up Joy, twirling her around as he had done with Dovie. Once he stopped spinning Joy, Dovie studied Gabe's face. His eyes still shown with the same kindness they always had, but there was something else mixed in … sadness. She could only imagine the horrors he had seen during his days at war. New gray hair mingling with the brown gave testament to the stress of the battles.

"Have you heard?" he asked.

"Heard what?" asked Bill as everyone else shook their heads.

"The war is over." Gabe smiled. "Japan has finally surrendered."

"Praise God," came a voice from the back stoop.

Everyone turned to see Dovie's father, James Murphy.

"Isn't it wonderful, Dad?" Dovie ran to her father and embraced him as he stepped off the stoop.

"Wonderful is an understatement," said James. "I can hardly believe this horrific war is finally coming to an end. When do you think everyone will be home, Gabe?"

"I've been doing my best to keep track of everyone," said Gabe. "I was able to locate Elm in New York. Since he's nearing the end of his four years, I reckon he'll be back soon. That is unless he decides to reenlist."

"Oh, I don't think he'd do that without talking to me," said Bill.

"Regardless, I'm sure he'll have some leave time and come home for that," said Gabe.

"And Robert?" asked Evalyn, twisting her hands.

For the first time since arriving at Quail Crossings, Gabe's smile faded. He gently took both of Evalyn's hands. "I'm afraid I have some bad news, Evie."

Evalyn shook her head as her tears began to fall. "Don't. Please. Don't say he's …"

"All I know right now," said Gabe, interrupting the words none of them wanted to hear, "is that he's missing in action."

Dovie wrapped her arms around Evalyn's shoulders. "We mustn't think the worst. I'm sure now that the war is over we'll hear from him."

"You'll stay here until he comes home," said James, placing a gentle hand on her shoulder. "You don't have to be alone."

"As if I have anywhere else to go!" Evalyn cried, shrugging his hand off. "We didn't have time to rebuild Rockwood after the tornado and before Pearl Harbor. Where else would I go?"

"Momma, where's Daddy?" asked Joy, her little lip quivering. "What's wrong?"

"I just meant …" said James searching for the words as he looked down at Joy.

Dovie's heart ached for both Evalyn and her father. She knew all too well what it was like to lose your spouse, whether it be by death or missing in action. Seeing her father struggle for the right words, when he used to be the voice of reason, made her heart ache. Even though she knew he was still as sharp as a tack, it hadn't gone unnoticed that he had to fight to find the right words on occasion.

Evalyn sighed as she brushed tears off her cheeks. "I know what you meant. I didn't mean to snap." She bent down and hugged Joy. "It's all right, baby. Momma is just sad that it's going to take Daddy a little bit longer to get home. I miss him so much."

"I do too, Momma," said Joy.

"We all do," said James.

Evalyn stood and hugged James. "I know."

"We've just got to keep the faith," said James. "I know the good Lord will bring him home."

Evalyn nodded. "I hope so and I appreciate the offer to continue to live here until Robert returns."

"Quail Crossings will always be your home," said James. "We'll always have room for you and your young'un's, even after Robert returns."

"Yay!" shouted Joy. "I love livin' with Papa James."

Dovie couldn't help but smile at the innocent little child. She was glad that Joy had no idea what was going on with her daddy. She leaned over and tweaked Joy's nose. "What am I? Chopped liver?"

Joy wrinkled her nose in disgust. "No, Mama Dovie, that's icky."

"I believe that's something we can all agree on," said Gabe.

"Dovie, would you mind watching the kids?" asked Evalyn. "I need to take a walk."

"Of course, honey," said Dovie. "Take all the time you need."

As Evalyn walked toward the orchard, Bill let out a grunt. "This wouldn't have happened had I been able to enlist."

"Now, you're just being foolish," said Dovie. "War is anything but predictable, and you don't know that you and Robert would've been fighting anywhere near each other. Besides, Quail Crossings would've fallen apart without you here. You have saved our hides more times than I can count. You ran the old rubber and scrap metal drives for the soldiers, and if that's not enough, just look at your brood headed this way."

Everyone turned to see Bill's wife, Lou Anne, walking across the pasture with their new four-month-old infant, Rose, in one arm, while holding the hand of their three-year-old daughter, Annabelle, with the other hand. Their five-year-old son, Dean, walked beside his sister.

Five years ago, Lou Anne was sure she was barren. Now she had a full crop of kids on her hands, and Dovie knew she loved every minute of it.

"Gabe," Lou Anne squealed as they approached the family. "I'm so glad you're home."

Bill took little Rose from Lou Anne, so she could give Gabe a warm embrace. "On leave?" she asked.

Gabe shook his head. "The war's over. Japan has finally surrendered."

"That's wonderful news!" cried Lou Anne as she hugged Gabe again. "So Elm, Tiny, and Robert should be home soon."

"Honey, Robert's missing," Bill said softly.

Lou Anne's hand flew to her mouth. "Oh no! Poor Evalyn." She looked around. "Where is she?"

"She's gone for a walk," said Dovie. "Hopefully, Elm will be home in a couple of months."

Gabe knelt down to talk to Dean. "How old are you now? Ten? Eleven?"

The boy laughed. "I'm five."

"Are you sure?" asked Gabe as he ruffled the boy's hair.

"I three," said Annabelle, making a huge effort to hold up the right amount of fingers.

"And the cutest three-year-old I know," said Gabe. The little girl giggled as Gabe stood.

Dovie heard the squeal of brakes and knew it was the school bus. "Sounds like Aunt Alice is home," she said to the kids.

Joy and Dean cheered and ran towards the front of the house to greet their aunt.

"Stay away from the road," Lou Anne shouted.

Within a few minutes Alice came around the corner, Joy and Dean hanging onto her like monkeys.

"Have you heard?" Alice asked, beaming. "The Japs surrendered! Everyone in town is dancing in the streets. I hated to leave but didn't want to miss the bus. It's like a big party on Main Street."

"I'm sure it is," said Gabe.

Dovie didn't think Alice's smile could get any larger, but it did when she spotted Gabe. "Gabe! Welcome home!"

She set the kids down and gave him a hug. Before she had time to ask, Dovie quickly told her about everyone else.

"Missing in action?" Alice tilted her head. "What does that mean exactly?"

"Just that they don't know where he is," said Gabe. "They lost track of him during a skirmish near the Polish border."

Alice furrowed her brow. "So he could just be working on gettin' home?"

Gabe nodded. "He could be."

"Any chance you know where Jacob Henry is?" asked Alice. "He used to write me all the time, but I haven't heard from him for a while now."

Jacob, a colored boy from Georgia, had found his way to Knollwood about a year before the U.S. entered into the war. Alice had found him beaten nearly to death by some local kids. After healing at Quail Crossings, he had gone to live in an all-colored town, Sweetsville some eighty miles away, but had remained pen pals with Alice.

Gabe shook his head. "I'm afraid not. Keeping track of all your kin was a job in itself. I'll be honest, I didn't think to check on Jacob before I left the base for leave. I'm sorry, Alice. I'll see what I can find out when I get back."

"I'd appreciate it," said Alice. "I've been writing to him and his wife, Blu, but neither have responded, and I'm starting to get worried."

"Did you say when you get back? You mean you're just on leave?" asked Dovie, trying to hide her disappointment.

"For now," said Gabe. He grabbed Dovie's hands. "I'm coming home as soon as I can, but the truth is, in order to find Robert, I have to stay contracted."

Dovie nodded as Gabe put his arms around her. "I understand," she said. "I just don't like it."

"Neither do I," said Gabe.

Norman the goose was not amused by all of the squealing that was taking place among the humans. He had been napping quite contentedly under the tree before the chatter had begun. As he waddled around the barn, he spotted the pink rump of Daisy the pig. Norman never missed an opportunity to torment the runt pig that had come to live at Quail Crossings five years ago, even though she was twice his size.

Norman lowered his head and toddled quietly toward his target. Each step was made cautiously as Norman snuck behind Daisy. Just as he was about to give the pig a rather large nip on her backside, Daisy quickly turned and nipped Norman on his wing.

Flapping back, Norman let out a surprised honk as Daisy trotted happily over to the huddle of people.

Chapter Two

Kathleen Wheaton barreled through the back door of Quail Crossings, set her pie on the table, and gathered Evalyn up in a huge hug. "What do you need? You just tell me and I'll get it done. I brought a pie, lemon meringue, your favorite, right? George is carrying in the roast."

Evalyn smiled slightly at Kathleen. Five years before, Kathleen's daughter, Evalyn's best friend, had died during a tornado. Since then, Evalyn had become Kathleen's surrogate daughter. Kathleen knew all too well about losing someone who held part of your heart.

"Thank you, Kathleen," said Evalyn. "You didn't need to do that. Everyone's been bringing food by, and it really isn't necessary."

"That's just our way of expressing our condolences," said Kathleen. "We can't fill your heart back up, but we can fill your stomach."

"I don't need condolences," snapped Evalyn. "Robert's not dead, and I wish everyone would stop acting like he was." Evalyn fought back the tears that were threatening to fall. "I'd know if he were dead. I'd know in my heart. He's coming home."

"Of course he is, sweetie," said Kathleen as she guided Evalyn to the sofa. "I didn't mean to imply otherwise. Sometimes my mouth opens before my brain has time to think about it. I just meant it's our way of showing you that we're here for you."

Evalyn nodded. "I know, and I appreciate the gesture. I really do. Thank you for the pie and the roast. And yes, lemon meringue is my favorite. It is Robert's favorite too. Did I ever tell you about the first time I made lemon meringue?"

Kathleen shook her head. "I'd love to hear about it."

Evalyn smiled. "I found a recipe in Dovie's old recipe box and decided I would try it. Most of the family had gone into town to the market, but Robert and I decided to stay here. Rarely did we get any time alone, and I figured it was the perfect time to bake Robert's favorite dessert. I've always been a pretty good baker, and the recipe seemed easy enough. Well, I put in corn meal instead of cornstarch."

Kathleen giggled and Evalyn joined her. "I pulled that pie out, and it was a soupy mess. I didn't know any better, so I figured it would keep cooking once I put the meringue on. I piled the meringue on and put the pie back in the oven. Robert came in right after I pulled it out of the oven, and he didn't even wait for it to cool down. He grabbed a knife and fork and cut himself a big ol' slice."

Evalyn hid her face behind her hand. "When he went to put that slice on his plate, it just leaked everywhere. It was a gloppy mess, and I dissolved into tears."

"Oh dear!" said Kathleen, hiding her own smile.

"And do you know what Robert did?" asked Evalyn. "That man grabbed a spoon and a bowl and ate a piece of it anyway. I know it had to be gritty, and it couldn't have tasted all that great, but you would've thought I fed him a blue ribbon pie."

"He really was a sweetheart," said Kathleen.

"Is," corrected Evalyn. "He is a sweetheart."

Tears refused to stay put as Evalyn laid her head on Kathleen's shoulder and wept.

Alice sat under the large cottonwood tree with her spiral notebook and tapped her pencil against her lips. She wondered what she could say differently in her letters to make Jacob or his wife respond. She didn't need them to write back with a novel's worth of words. She just wanted to know if they were doing okay. She needed to know that Jacob had made it home safely from the war.

Alice thought about Bud and Sara Clark, Tiny's parents, and the funeral she had attended for their son, Bud Clark, Jr. It had been a heartbreaking experience and had hit way too close to home. The dangers of war had never felt real to Alice until that day. She had assumed everyone she knew, family and friends, would come home safe and sound. She knew now that was a very naïve point of view, even for the thirteen-year-old she had been when the war had started. Now at sixteen, she knew better.

Events in her life should have made her a complete pessimist, but she wasn't. Things always seemed to work out for the best. Her mother had mistreated her when she was a small child and then both parents had abandoned her and her siblings. Bill struggled to support them, and then they found Quail Crossings. She had been caught in an open field during the worst dust storm in history, yet she managed to protect herself and Mr. Norman in a half-built house. She had survived a tornado, narrowly escaped an attack from a rabid dog, and saved a boy from a lynching. Things had always worked out, and she couldn't help but be an optimist.

She placed her pencil on the paper and started writing. Jacob would write her back this time. She knew it.

"Whatcha doin' out here?" asked Dovie, coming to the clothesline that hung from the large cottonwood. "It's hotter than a screeching kettle today."

Alice put her pencil and notebook down and started helping Dovie hang the laundry. "I was going to write Jacob and his wife, but I can't figure out what to say that I haven't already said. I just want them to write me back and tell me Jacob is okay."

"I'm sure there's a good reason Jacob hasn't written back," said Dovie, grabbing a wet shirt. "Maybe he's someplace where they haven't got their mail yet? It's not like the postman is driving up to his door."

"True," said Alice, hanging a pair of pants, "but why hasn't his wife written me back? As far as I know, she still lives in Sweetsville in the same house they shared after getting married."

"She could've moved," reasoned Dovie before biting her lip. "Look, Alice, Jacob and Blu got married really fast, as did a lot of couples when men started enlisting. It could be that she doesn't understand your relationship with Jacob, and therefore, is not responding to your letters."

Alice scrunched her face. "Like she's jealous? But she's never even met me!"

"That's part of the problem," said Dovie. "Some women fear what they don't know. You and Jacob have a special friendship. It would be odd under normal circumstances, but the fact that he's colored makes it even odder. I'm sure she just doesn't understand how a white girl could just be friends with a colored boy and not want something in return."

"Well, that's just stupid," said Alice, whipping another shirt from the basket. "I've never asked anything of either of them."

Dovie gently placed her hand on Alice's arm. "Not stupid, Alice. You have no idea what's happened in Blu's life. Not everyone treats colored people right, and you know that first hand. Being treated like a second class citizen can make you very leery of people. Keep writing her, but instead of badgering her about Jacob's whereabouts, ask her about herself."

Alice smiled. "Do you ever get tired of being right all the time?"

"It's exhausting," said Dovie with a wink.

Chapter Three

September 1945

Elmer sighed and looked over at Tiny. "Are you ready for this?"

"Jeepers, Elm, of course I am," said Tiny. "Do you really think they'll be surprised? Don't you think they've seen this coming for a while?"

Elmer nodded in agreement.

"Besides," Tiny continued, "they'll be so happy to see us, they probably won't give a lick about anything else we have to tell them."

Elmer nodded again, but this time he wasn't so sure. He remembered how upset Bill had been when Evalyn returned home, married and with a child, five years before. Of course Tiny was right about one thing, Evalyn's marriage had been out of the blue, whereas Tiny had been a part of his life since the moment he started school in Knollwood.

"I wonder how Evalyn's doing," said Tiny, looking out the window. "My ma didn't seem too hopeful that Robert would return."

"Mary, you can't say stuff like that," said Elmer, shaking his head.

"What? Evalyn's not here," said Tiny, looking around the truck to prove her point.

"We have to stay positive," said Elmer. "Once you put that kind of thought into the world, it has a habit of slipping out when you least expect it. Besides, I choose to believe that Robert is just having trouble making his way home. From what your pa said, he got separated from the rest of his unit, and he's probably having to fill out a mountain of paperwork just to get back to base, so they can get him home."

"Then why hasn't he written to Evalyn?" asked Tiny. "We still have POWs over there. You know as well as I do that there's a good chance he's in one of those camps."

Elmer pulled into the driveway of Quail Crossings. "Well, I certainly hope not, and we're not going to mention that either. Only happy stuff today, okay? I'll talk with Gabe and Bill to see if they have more information, but don't go upsetting Evie or her young'un's."

Tiny slid closer to Elmer and gave him a playful smile. "I do like it when you get all bossy, Mr. Brewer."

"That's a good thing, since you'll have to put up with it for the rest of your life, Mrs. Brewer," said Elmer, smiling back.

Elmer parked the truck and watched as his family started to gather around them. He had sent word that they would be in Knollwood the night before, staying with Tiny's family, and then making their way down the road to Quail Crossings the next morning. It was hard not coming straight to Quail Crossings the night before, but Elmer felt it was important to let Tiny's family receive their news first.

"Who's going to tell them?" asked Tiny.

Elmer smiled. "I guess it's my turn since you spilled the beans last night."

Elmer's door opened for him, and he was practically dragged out by Alice as she wrapped him in a huge hug. "Oh, Elm, I thought you'd never get here!"

"It's only 8:00 am," said Elmer, as he regained his footing. "We had to have breakfast with Tiny's folks. It was the right thing to do."

"The right thing to do would've been to come home last night, you ornery boy," said Dovie, hugging Elmer. "There was no reason to sleep on the Clark's sofa when you know we always have a bed for you here."

Elmer scratched his head. "Well, I didn't exactly sleep on the sofa, but I get what you're sayin'."

Evalyn squeezed in for a hug. "Glad to have you home, Elm, no matter where you slept last night."

"I'm glad to be home," said Elmer. He gave Evalyn another squeeze. "And I just know Robert will be home in no time. We're praying for him."

Evalyn gave Elmer a nod of thanks before retreating to let Bill, James, and Lou Anne in for hugs.

"So, Uncle Elm," said Joy, "if you didn't sleep on the sofa, where did you sleep?"

Elmer felt his face grow warm and knew his cheeks matched the color of his red hair. "Well, I ... um."

"Oh jeepers, Elm, just tell them we're married already," said Tiny, throwing her hands in the air before clamping them over her mouth. "Oh, Elm, I'm sorry."

Elmer smiled and grabbed Tiny's hand. "It's okay, Mary." He looked at his family who stared at him with open mouths. "Well, y'all heard her. Shouldn't you be saying congratulations or something?"

Lou Anne was the first to embrace Tiny. "Oh, we're so happy for you. Welcome to the family."

Soon the others followed suit, forgetting their surprise and showing their happiness. Everyone gathered for another round of hugs, except Dovie. As the crowd cleared, Elmer swallowed hard. Dovie stood with her arms folded, tapping her foot.

"You okay, Dovie?" asked Elmer, not sure he really wanted to hear the answer.

"No," Dovie shook her head, "I am not okay. You mean to tell me another one of you Brewers eloped without your family?"

"Oh, Mrs. Grant," said Tiny, "please don't be mad at Elmer. It was really the most romantic thing. I was in New York City for training when the war ended. I ran out into Times Square to celebrate with everyone else. Imagine my surprise to see Elm there as well. It was like a miracle. The atmosphere was electrifying, and we were both stunned to find each other. I knew he was stateside, but I had no idea where. Once we got a hold of each other again, after being at war all this time well, we vowed to never leave each other again and went straight to the courthouse."

"The courthouse?" Dovie gasped.

"And just what's wrong with the courthouse?" asked Evalyn. "Robert and I got married in a courthouse."

"That was different," said Dovie. "You two were in California and didn't know if you were coming back to Knollwood. These two did." She pointed to the couple. "And just what did your momma think about you getting married in a courthouse, Miss Mary?"

"She was happy for us," said Elmer. "Aren't you?"

Dovie sighed. "Of course I am, Elm. I just wish you two would've cooled your heels and waited until you got home to get hitched."

"I guess my ma was kind of upset," admitted Tiny. "She would've liked to have seen us get married in a church."

"Then that's settled," said Dovie.

"What is?" asked Elmer.

"Tomorrow, we're going into town to see when Pastor Spaulding can marry you two kids right." Dovie smiled at the crowd. "Go on now; it's okay to celebrate."

Evalyn smoothed the soft white fabric over the bed. It had been decided by both Dovie and Mary's mother, Sara, that Tiny should go ahead and wear white. Most of the town's people wouldn't know that Tiny and Elmer got married in New York, and they didn't want rumors to start.

She had been putting it off, and now she only had a week to make Tiny's wedding dress. It wouldn't be too much of a challenge since Tiny insisted on just wearing a nice dress, instead of a traditional wedding gown. Tiny had seen too many of her friends receive the sad news that they would never see their wedding days to want to go over-the-top with hers. Dovie and Sara may have insisted on white for the church ceremony, but Tiny didn't back down on the dress being something simple instead of an elaborate gown.

Evalyn sighed, dreading the task ahead. It wasn't that she was upset about Elmer's upcoming nuptials, or that she had to make the dress. Evalyn loved making dresses and hoped to open a little dress shop now that the war was over. But she found herself a tad bit jealous. She had always dreamed of making her own wedding dress for a large church wedding filled with family and friends.

As Evalyn turned to her dresser to find her measuring tape and scissors, she thought about her wedding to Robert. Immediately after Evalyn had said her vows in the courthouse, she had thrown the dress in the garbage.

Evalyn regretted that decision now, but at the time the dress had reminded her of what she thought she would never have: true love. But love had surprised her, and found her where she least expected it, in her marriage of convenience.

Robert had turned out to be the perfect husband and father to Evalyn's daughter, Joy. She loved him more than she ever thought possible, and now he was lost somewhere overseas. Was he lying in a hospital hurt? Or could he be in one of those horrible POW camps? Or worse?

She remembered him standing by the judge, eager to take her and her child on as his own. She didn't see it then, but as she looked back she knew he already loved her. She had no idea why. At the time she had no romantic feelings for him at all. In fact during the entire ceremony, she mourned the fairy tale romance she believed she'd never have, but it was as if Robert knew the whole time that theirs was a love that fairy tales were made of.

He would confide in her later that he had fallen in love with her on the bus that carried them both from California to Knollwood. After saving Evalyn from the attack of a fellow bus passenger during a bus stop, Robert had become her and Joy's chaperone. They were strangers before that bus ride, but by the time they got home to Knollwood, he had decided he needed both Joy and her in his life.

The tears slipped out before Evalyn could stop them. That kept happening to her. With just the thought of Robert, tears developed and refused not to fall. It didn't matter if she were washing the dishes, reading a book, or making a dress, Robert haunted her.

"I thought you'd never ask," said Bill as he gave his brother a sturdy hug. "Of course, I'll be your best man. I was afraid you were going to ask James."

Elmer smiled as he pushed his brother away and began to shovel some more hay into Poppy's stall. "I didn't realize it meant so much to you, big brother."

"I can't think of a more honorable thing to do than to stand up for my war-hero brother on one of the biggest days of his life," said Bill.

Elmer's smile faded. "I'm no war hero, Bill."

"Of course you are," said Bill. "You fought for our country. You saved a lot of people from Hitler and the Japs."

"Not enough," Elmer whispered.

Bill shook his head. "I can't know what you're going through or what you saw over there. We heard about those camps for all the Jews…"

"Camps?" interrupted Elmer. "More like prisons of torture. You're right, you can't know, Bill, but I was there. I saw it. They had rooms full of shoes. Shoes that belonged to people. People they murdered. There were thousands of shoes, Bill, one pair stacked on top of another all the way from the floor to the ceiling."

Bill tried to put his arm around Elmer.

"Don't," said Elmer. "I'm fine. I just want to forget, and if you start making a fuss about it, then I won't be able to." Elmer walked toward the barn door. "Just let me forget."

Lou Anne met Elmer coming in and gave him a friendly smile. Elmer mumbled something about taking a walk as he left the barn.

"Is he okay?" asked Lou Anne.

"Hard to say," said Bill. "He saw so much over there, and I can't help him deal with that 'cause I was here milking cows and chasing pigs." Bill kicked the dirt. "I should've been there. At least then I would know how to get him through this. He asked me to be his best man, and I'm nothing but a lowly farmhand. He needs someone who's done more. Maybe Gabe will step in."

"Bill Brewer, how dare you?" Lou Anne snapped.

"What?" asked Bill.

"You stand there and act like a kicked puppy when nobody's kicked you. You ought to be ashamed. Yes, Elmer, Robert, and Gabe went over and fought and you had to stay here, boo-hoo. As much as I hated that you lost sight in your left eye, I am so glad that you didn't have to go to war. You kept this place strong, so they had a good home to come back to. We both know James couldn't have done it on his own."

"Dovie would've been fine," countered Bill. "She's tougher than all of us, and you would've helped her."

"Sure, we would've survived, but you helped this place thrive during the war, and James would've worked himself to death trying to do what you did," said Lou Anne. She tapped her foot. "Now that is the last time I'm gonna tell you what an asset you've been to everyone. It's time for you to move on. The war is over, thank heavens, and it's your job to keep this place thriving so Elm has a place to get better. And he needs to know that you are there for him by being his best man."

Lou Anne headed to the barn door, then turned briefly. "And if all that doesn't stop your belly achin' about not being in the war, remember that if you had left we wouldn't have Annabelle and Rosey because you would've been overseas. Would you really want to trade that for being a target for the Nazis?"

Bill watched his wife leave, feeling like she had slapped him a dozen times for being selfish. Lou Anne was right. His griping about not being able to go to war wasn't doing anyone any good, especially Elmer.

He may not have gone overseas, but with Elmer's haunting memories, and Robert still missing, it looked like the war had come to him.

Chapter Four

Alice sat down at the kitchen table with a piece of paper and a pencil, causing Dovie to raise an eyebrow.

"Alice, honey, what are you doing? We've got to leave for the church in about twenty minutes for the wedding," said Dovie.

"I'm writing another letter to Jacob's wife," said Alice. "I need to know he's okay. Plus, he should be here to see Elm and Tiny get hitched."

"Well, it's a little late for that," said Dovie. "I don't think even the Pony Express could get that letter to Jacob before their wedding."

"I know," said Alice, "but if he knows they got married, maybe he'll come and visit. Or maybe he'll send them a note of congratulations. I guess I'm getting desperate."

Dovie twisted her apron. "Alice, exactly how long has it been since you heard from Jacob?"

Alice chewed on the end of the pencil as she thought about the question. "It's been a while, about six months, maybe more."

"You know Blu might not have good news for you," said Dovie. "We lost a lot of good men in the war."

Alice nodded. "I know, Mama Dovie, and I guess that's why I'm writing to her. I keep seeing Evie walking in the orchard, and I know what's hurtin' her more than anything is the not knowing part. She can't move on because she doesn't know if Robert's ... well, gone for good. I think I'd rather just know."

"Honey, maybe Blu doesn't want to talk about it," said Dovie. "If she's grieving, she may not have the strength to write and let you know he's gone."

Alice shook her head. "Wouldn't I know if he was gone? Wouldn't I feel it some way?"

"I didn't know anything was wrong with Simon and Helen until ol' Dr. Crowly pulled into that driveway and told me, and they were my whole heart," Dovie said with a sad smile. "I'm not trying to discourage you from finding out the truth, only trying to help you understand why you're not hearing from Blu."

"Then we should go to Sweetsville and check on her," said Alice.

Dovie shook her head. "We've never met Blu, and we're not about to go traipsing up to her door like the Spanish inquisition demanding to know the whereabouts of Jacob. When she's ready she'll write you back. Now get ready to go or we're gonna be late to Elm's wedding."

Daisy the pig rooted in the dirt beside three year-old Annabelle who sat playing with her dolly. Daisy watched the dolly go up and down, her yellow yarn hair bouncing like golden strings of corn silk.

"Annabelle Brewer, you get out of the dirt this instant," scolded Lou Anne. "We have to go see your Uncle Elm get married, and here you are getting all dusty."

Annabelle got up. "Sorry, Momma."

As soon as Lou Anne started brushing Annabelle's dress off, Daisy took her chance and grabbed the dolly.

"Momma!" Annabelle screamed. "My dolly. Daisy's got my dolly!"

Lou Anne took off after the pig. "Daisy, you daggum hog, stop! Give me the doll!"

But Daisy wasn't about to give up her new toy. She rounded the corner to the barn and met Norman face to face.

Norman hissed and raised his wings at the pig. Daisy tried to run around the angry goose but was corned between the barn wall and Norman's large gray wings. Norman hissed again and pecked at Daisy, nipping her ear.

Daisy squealed, dropped the doll, and ran off. Norman gently picked up the doll in his bill and waddled back to Annabelle as Lou Anne continued to chase the pig.

Sara Clark placed the last bobby pin in her daughter's hair and stepped back. "What do you think, Tiny?"

Tiny gasped when she looked in the mirror. Her red hair was arranged in a delicate bun that looked elegant and much too fancy for a country wedding, but Tiny loved it. "It's beautiful. Jeepers, Ma, I never knew my hair could do that."

"Well, with enough bobby pins you can make your hair do anything," said Sara with a laugh. "Just make sure you get them all out before you try to brush it, or you'll be in for a real surprise."

Sara stepped up to smooth Tiny's hair, and Tiny caught her hand. "Thanks, Ma."

"For what?" asked Sara.

"I know y'all wanted to move to Amarillo right after finding out about Jr, but stuck around because of me and Elm. It was really nice to come home even though I know it was hard on you."

Sara's eyes fell and Tiny knew she was thinking of her son, Bud Clark, Jr., who had died during the war. Tiny had been able to come home but had missed the funeral by a day. The folded American flag still sat on the mantle next to a picture of Jr. in his dress uniform.

Sara wiped the tears from her eyes. "Of course, Tiny, I know Knollwood will always be your home, especially now that you're married to Elmer. I'm happy that you're marrying into Dovie's family because I know you'll always be happy and safe among them." Sara cleared her throat. "Speaking of Elmer, are you ready for tonight?"

"Tonight?" Tiny cocked her head.

"Yes, your wedding night," Sara clarified.

Tiny knew her cheeks were turning as red as her hair. "Ma!"

"Listen," said Sara. "I know it's not really your wedding night, but I'm gonna offer some advice anyway. The act between husband and wife should always be one of love. If it ever feels anything other than that, talk to Elmer and tell him what you need. Men like to think they know everything, but they don't, and they aren't mind readers. Every morning when you get up think to yourself, 'How can

I make Elmer happy today?', and I pray he asks himself the same question about you every morning. Pick your battles. It's okay to let some things go in order to avoid a fight. Remember that men aren't as sentimental as women and sometimes those little things that you cherish will fly right past him. Try not to take it personally, but share why you cherish it. Remember you two are entering into a partnership of the most sacred kind, and that you should never take it for granted."

Tears pooled in Tiny's eyes as she wrapped her mother in a big hug. "Thank you, Ma. I love you."

"I love you, too, sweet girl."

Elmer shifted from side to side as he stood at the front of the church next to Bill. A considerable crowd had been meandering into the small sanctuary of the country house for the last twenty minutes, and he couldn't help but feel they were all staring at him. He absolutely hated being the center of attention, but he'd walk over hot coals for Tiny.

"You okay?" whispered Bill. "You're looking a little green. You're not getting cold feet are ya?" Bill gave Elmer a knowing smile.

"I just don't like everyone staring at me, is all," Elmer whispered back.

Bill smiled at his brother. "Don't worry, Elm. Soon no one will be looking at you. They'll all be looking at your beautiful bride, and they'll totally forget about you."

"Sounds good to me," said Elmer.

The organist took her seat and began to play. Elmer watched as James walked Dovie to her seat beside the rest of the family. Sara walked down the aisle carrying a single white rose in honor of Bud, Jr. and took her seat in the pew across from James and Dovie. Tiny's sister and maid-of-honor, Ruth, followed and took her place at the front of the church across from Elmer and Bill.

"Would y'all please rise," said Pastor Spaulding as the organist started playing *The Wedding March.*

Bill had been absolutely correct. All eyes went from Elmer to Tiny as she entered the sanctuary escorted by her father, Bud. It was no surprise to Elmer that everyone was looking at Tiny. She was stunning.

Her hair was swept up in a delicate bun with a few wisps escaping around her face, and the soft white fabric Evalyn had picked out for Tiny's wedding dress, made her blue eyes pop like the turquoise water Elmer had seen in a mountain lake in the peaks of the Alps. Tiny was breathtaking.

Elmer couldn't wait to hold her hands in his. It felt like it had been a lifetime since he had seen her, even though it had only been the day before. His wait was over quickly as Bud walked Tiny over to Elmer.

"We are gathered in our house of worship, in the sight of God, and in the presence of friends and family, to celebrate the beauty of love and unite Elmer and Mary in holy matrimony," said Pastor Spaulding. "Should there be anyone who has cause to why this couple should not be united in marriage in the eyes of the Lord, let them speak now or forever hold their peace."

Elmer held his breath. Even though he knew he was already legally married to Tiny, the thought that anyone would object to their love made his heart hurt. He was thankful for the silence.

"Very good," Pastor Spaulding continued when no one stepped forward. "Who is it that brings this woman to this man?"

Bud cleared this throat. "Her mother and I."

Pastor Spaulding gave a slight nod as Bud placed Tiny's hand into Elmer's.

"You take good care of her, son," said Bud.

"The very best, sir," replied Elmer. "I promise."

Bud stepped back as Elmer and Tiny stepped forward.

"I missed you," whispered Elmer.

Tiny blushed. "Jeepers, you just saw me yesterday."

Elmer smiled. "I know."

Twenty minutes later the service was over, and Elmer and Tiny were officially married in the eyes of the Lord. Everyone had gathered outside the church for a potluck dinner and cake and to continue the celebration of soldiers coming home. Since the Japanese had surrendered, three more soldiers from Knollwood had made their way home. Elmer couldn't think of a better way to celebrate his nuptials and their homecoming.

Elmer scanned the crowd and smiled. He had spent many days in the trenches during the war. It was good to feel the sunshine without dreading something terrible was about to happen. That's when he spotted her.

A woman stood in the middle of the crowded churchyard, a suitcase in one hand and the hand of a young girl in the other. Elmer's eyes were drawn instantly to the girl. She had bright red hair and freckles just like his. She stood with a slight slouch and her thin frame reminded Elmer of a time when food was hard to come by. His heart tugged as he noticed the flour sack doll the girl held tightly, as if her life depended on it. His eyes followed the woman with the girl. She was clearly looking for someone.

Reaching over, he tapped Tiny, who was talking with some friends, on the shoulder. She turned. "Yes, my husband?"

Elmer pointed to the woman. "Do you know them? The girl looks familiar to me, but I don't think I've ever seen the woman before."

Tiny shook her head. The woman caught Elmer pointing and started towards him. Elmer held his breath. Guess he was about to find out who they were, and he hoped he hadn't offended the woman by pointing her out to Tiny.

"Mr. and Mrs. Brewer?" asked the woman. Her voice was high and stern.

Elmer and Tiny smiled at the sound of their married name.

"Yes, ma'am, I'm Elmer Brewer and this is my wife, Mary," said Elmer, smiling at the way 'wife' felt on his tongue. It just felt right. "How can we help you?"

The woman pursed her lips. "My name is Colleen Waterman, and I'm from the United States Children's Bureau. I'm sorry to intrude on your special day, but the sheriff said you and your kin would all be here. Is your brother, Bill, here?"

"No need to apologize," said Elmer. He looked to his right. "Hey, Bill, could you come here? This woman needs to speak with you."

Bill walked over and Elmer made the introductions. Bill shook the woman's hand before scratching his head. "Did you say you were from the United States Children's Bureau?"

Colleen nodded. "I did. What I'm about to tell you may come as quite a shock, so I'm just going to come right out and say it." She gently pulled the girl in front of her. "This is your sister, Ellie Brewer."

"Did you say sister?" Dovie came up behind Colleen and joined the conversation.

"Yes, our records show she was abandoned at a doctor's office thirteen years ago when she was very ill. She's had an uneasy past. She was bounced from placement to placement before her file landed on my desk. Given her history, we at the bureau, decided it would be in her best interest if we could find her real family."

Elmer looked at the girl. She had hair as red as his and was the spitting image of Alice. Elmer knew Colleen was telling the truth, but he couldn't find the words to speak.

Dovie looked at the boys and clicked her tongue. "Shame on you both standing there like you've got roots for feet." She gave Ellie a smile. "Hi, Ellie, my name is Dovie. How old are you, dear?"

"I'm sorry but she doesn't speak," said Colleen. "She's thirteen."

"What's going on?" asked Evalyn as she and Alice walked up. "Oh my … Ellie? Could it really be you?"

"Ellie?" Alice raised an eyebrow at Evalyn.

"Do you know this girl?" Colleen asked Evalyn.

Evalyn shook her head. "I can't be sure since she was just a baby when my ma left her at the doctor's office." She looked to the girl. "But she looks just like Alice, except for the red hair."

"My research shows that she is indeed your sister, Ellie Brewer," said Colleen to Evalyn. "Is your mother around?"

"Our parents deserted us about six months after leaving Ellie at the doctor's office," explained Evalyn before turning to Ellie. "I used to take care of you when you were a baby. Then you got sick." A tear dropped on Evalyn's cheek. "It broke my heart when Ma came home without you. She said you were too sick to bring home, and that you'd not make it through the night. Oh, Ellie, I'm so sorry I didn't look for you."

Evalyn moved toward her for a hug, but the girl stepped back.

"I'm sorry," said Evalyn. "Of course, you don't know me, but I do hope you'll come home with us."

"This is our sister?" Alice asked, looking at her brothers.

Elmer finally found his voice and smiled at Ellie. "Yes, Alice, she is." He playfully slapped Bill, knocking his older brother out of his state of shock.

Bill smiled at Ellie. "Looks like we've got another reason to celebrate."

Chapter Five

Ellie glanced at the lady with curly brown hair tied up in a bun sitting beside her on the truck seat. She had a bit of grey, but nothing that spoke of being elderly. The others in the group had called her Momma Dovie which seemed strange since it was clear she wasn't their real momma, but they seemed to love her regardless. She turned her attention to the man who was driving. He was definitely older than Momma Dovie, having a full head of gray hair. His light blue eyes drew Ellie in. They were kind trustworthy eyes, but Ellie had been deceived by kind eyes before.

She hugged her doll tighter as she thought of the people Mrs. Waterman had called her brothers and sisters. They were obviously shocked to find out she was still alive. It was odd to Ellie that her mother had declared her dead to the rest of the family. Hadn't she even cared about her? Ellie had guessed she cared just enough to leave her with a doctor rather than just letting her die along some dusty highway. Many times Ellie wished she had died that day her mother abandoned her.

"Here we are," said the old man as the truck came to a stop. Ellie tried to remember his name, it started with a J and was either James or Jamie. It didn't really matter, she would never call him by it.

"I do hope you'll like Quail Crossings," said Dovie.

Ellie took in the two-story brown house. It was bigger than the other homes she had stayed in. She could tell it had a fireplace and wondered if she would be allowed to sleep by it in the cold months.

"We're packed in like sardines right now," said Dovie. "So you'll have to share a room with Alice. We've got a little cot up there that Joy was sleeping on, but you can use it now, and Joy can move in with her momma."

Ellie cocked her head. She would have her own bed? She couldn't remember a time when she hadn't slept on the floor.

She followed Dovie out of the truck and grabbed her suitcase from the truck bed before James could do it. She made sure her doll was safely tucked under her arm as she looked around. Quail Crossings boasted a large barn, which looked fairly new, with a large sliding window in the loft, a woodshop, smokehouse, large chicken coop, and stables which housed cows, pigs, and horses. She looked to the east and could tell there was a pond just a hundred feet away from the barn. To the north was an orchard that served as a windbreak, and Ellie wondered how much of the land beyond the orchard belonged to Quail Crossings.

"Come on upstairs," said Dovie. "You can rest awhile. I'm sure you're tired from your journey. When you get settled, I'll give you the dime tour. You'll be upstairs with Alice and Evalyn's bunch. Dad and I have rooms downstairs off the parlor. There's a washroom just on the other side of my room. We still use the outhouse for our needs, but the washroom has a sink for washin' up."

Ellie followed Dovie up the stairs and into the room she'd share with her sister, Alice.

"That's your bed," said Dovie pointing to a medium sized cot. "I figured you'd be more comfortable there than sleeping with Alice. Come winter you may change your mind, but Quail Crossings is pretty good at staying warm. During really cold spells, we'll have everyone down by the fire." Dovie let out a loud sigh as if trying to determine what to say next. "Ellie, we're happy you're here. Rest up and I'll let you know when supper's ready."

Ellie let Dovie's words sink in as Dovie exited the room shutting the door behind her. Ellie slid her suitcase under her cot, and then sat hugging her small, simple doll. The doll was made entirely of flour sack cloth with blue polka-dots and had no face or hair, but Ellie loved her, because the doll had been her only friend since birth, and the doll knew all her secrets.

"What do you think of that, Lovey?" she whispered to the doll. "Do you really think they're glad I'm here?"

She bent her head towards the doll as if listening and then replied. "You're right; it's a big place. They probably do need an extra hand with the chores. They do seem nice though."

Ellie nodded as she curled up in a ball. "Yes, they are all nice at first so I can't let my guard down. They'll be just like the others. Maybe this is where God will let me die."

Dovie let out a big sigh has she came down stairs. "I left her a plate, but I don't think she's coming down to eat."

"Maybe I should go talk to her," said Evalyn.

"Just let her be," said Elmer. "She's been through a lot. Maybe she just needs some time alone."

"Alone?" Alice raised an eyebrow. "If I finally found my family, I would want nothing more than to be around them, and how do you know what she's been through?"

"I don't exactly," said Elmer. "I'm just repeating what Mrs. Waterman said. We can be a lot to take on. Just give her time, is all I'm sayin'."

"Elm's right," said Bill. "Leave her be tonight."

"I wonder what all she's been through," said Lou Anne. "I've heard some pretty terrible stories about children that were on that Orphan Train during the 30's. They were beaten and abused. A lot of them died in the care of their adoptive families."

"But some found good homes," said Evalyn. "Maybe Ellie was one of them."

"Then she wouldn't be here," said Bill.

"But now that she is," said James. "We give her the time and space she needs to adjust to us, and we'll show her the kind of family we are. Now, bow your heads." Everyone did so. "Dear Heavenly Father, we have so many blessings for today. Thank you for blessing the union of Elmer and Tiny. We pray they have many years of happiness, and thank you for bringing Ellie into our lives. We can't know what she's been through, but help her to see you have placed her into a home of love and kindness and that we want nothing but the best for her. Bless this food to the nourishment of our bodies, and bless the hands that have prepared it. And, Dear Lord, thank you for this precious family, each and every one of them. We are truly blessed. Amen."

A chorus of "amens" echoed around the table as Dovie looked up the stairs. She hoped more than anything that Ellie had heard James's prayer.

Dovie scraped what was left of Ellie's breakfast into a bucket for the pigs. The girl had barely touched her dinner the night before and had only eaten a few bites of her breakfast. Dovie wondered if she might be sick. She looked healthy, but all she had done since she got there was sit on her cot and look at the wall. She tried to think of what she could say to make Ellie come out of her shell a bit. She wondered if the girl would ever feel comfortable at Quail Crossings.

A knock on the back door brought Dovie out of her thoughts as Kathleen let herself in.

"Good morning, Dovie. I brought you some bread," said Kathleen.

Dovie smiled at her friend as she took the bread. "Thank you, Kathleen, but you know you don't have to bring food just to come by and visit. Coffee?"

"Yes, please," said Kathleen taking a seat at the kitchen table. "I must confess, curiosity got the better of me this mornin', and I did figure you hadn't had time to make bread with the wedding and your new ward coming to stay. How is that going?"

Dovie placed a mug and the sugar bowl in front of Kathleen before pouring herself a cup of coffee and sitting across from her. "I'm not sure yet."

"What do you mean?" asked Kathleen as she stirred sugar into her coffee.

"She doesn't talk, and so far she hasn't left her room," explained Dovie. "Plus she's eaten very little. The poor girl's skin and bones. I'd like to fatten her up some."

"Oh, to be that young and not have to worry about getting 'fattened up'," laughed Kathleen. "She'll come down in time. Y'all have a way here at Quail Crossings. You'd make a badger feel welcome if they were family. Did the lady from the Children's Bureau give you her history?"

Dovie shook her head as she sipped her coffee. "She gave us very little information, but I'm not sure how much I want to know."

"Why is that?"

Dovie shrugged. "Because I want to know Ellie for herself, not for her past."

Ellie sat at the top of the stairs and listened to Momma Dovie and her friend chat about her. She felt a little pang in her heart and wondered if it was fear. She looked down at Lovey and nodded. Lovey was right as usual. It wasn't fear she was feeling ... it was hope.

Chapter Six

Alice sat across the kitchen table and studied Ellie. It was the first time Ellie had ventured out of their room since Elmer's wedding two days before. Alice shook her head. There was no way Ellie wasn't a Brewer, but Alice barely remembered Baby Ellie. She had been just under four-years-old when Ellie was born. The only thing she could remember was that Ellie cried a lot. Looking at the quiet Ellie now, it was hard to believe she used to be the child who wouldn't stop screaming.

"I'm glad you're here," said Alice, trying to welcome her sister. "I was mighty little when you were born, so I don't know much about you. Where have you been?"

Ellie just looked at the table.

"Have you been in Texas this whole time?" asked Alice. "We did a bit of traveling after Ma and Pa left for California. Went to Oklahoma and Kansas lookin' for work, but didn't find much. I just keep wonderin' how close we were to you, never knowing you were alive. Don't you have questions for us?"

"Alice, leave her be," said Dovie. "You heard Mrs. Waterman say she doesn't speak. Why are you askin' her all those questions?"

"I'm just curious," said Alice. "I hoped she would talk now that she's with family."

"Maybe she really can't talk," said Dovie. "Mrs. Waterman didn't know what ailed Ellie when she was taken to the doctor's office. Those records were lost in a fire, but for all we know she could've had an infection in her throat so bad that now she can't talk."

"I think that would be awful, not to be able to talk," said Alice.

"I bet you would," laughed Dovie.

"Ellie," said Alice, tapping on the table to get Ellie's attention. "Can you hear us all right?"

Ellie nodded.

"Okay," said Alice, "If you need anything, just get our attention. We'll figure it out somehow."

Alice got up and walked toward the door. "Guess I'll go milk Poppy."

Ellie bolted from her chair and pointed to herself.

"You want to milk Poppy?" asked Dovie.

Ellie nodded.

"You don't have to, you know." Dovie cocked her head. "We'll give you a set of chores to do at the start of the week. Until then you can just see how we do things around here."

Ellie shook her head and pointed to the barn.

"Fine by me," said Alice. "Come on, Ellie. I'll introduce you to Poppy."

Alice and Ellie walked out the back door as Evalyn walked in. "I'm so glad Ellie finally came down. Where are those two off to?"

"Ellie wants to milk Poppy," said Dovie.

"Did she say that? Did she speak?" Evalyn asked taking a step closer to Dovie.

"She didn't speak. She just pointed to herself when Alice said she was going out there," explained Dovie. "Like I told Alice, there may be a medical reason why Ellie can't talk. Even if there ain't, we can't force her to speak. Maybe once she gets settled in and comfortable with us, she'll start talking. Let's just be happy she's ventured out of the room."

Evalyn sat down. "I can't imagine what she's been through."

"What do you mean?" asked Dovie, grabbing some potatoes from a box beside the stove. "Here, help me peel these while we talk. I wanna get a jump on lunch since I have to go into town in a bit for my meeting at the church."

Evalyn got up and walked to the sink. "Mrs. Waterman said she'd been through a lot, and that's why they worked so hard to find her real family. That tells me that she's been in some bad situations, or they would've just found another family lookin' for a child. It had to be hard to track us down after all these years."

"Well, between Elmer's service records, and Bill getting married in town, it was probably easier now than it would've been ten years ago," reasoned Dovie.

Evalyn grabbed a potato and knife and started peeling. "She was just a little baby when Ma left her. How could they not find a good home for a little baby? I mean, look at Pastor Spaulding and Susan. They would've loved to have a child of their own, and they never could. Why couldn't that doctor's office find a family like them to look after Ellie?"

"Don't you think you're jumping the gun a bit here, Evie?" asked Dovie. "We don't know what Ellie's gone through. Maybe the people looking after her passed on? Maybe she was then bounced from family to family until she found her way to Mrs. Waterman. Sounds lonely, but not completely awful. Besides she's got us now."

"I feel guilty," said Evalyn. "I should've looked for her."

"How old were you when Ellie was dropped off at the doctor's office?" Dovie dropped a potato into the pan next to Evalyn and grabbed another potato out of the sink to peel.

"I was the age Ellie is now," said Evalyn, grabbing Dovie's just peeled potato and cutting it into chunks.

"And just how is a twelve-year-old supposed to search for her baby sister?" asked Dovie. "A sister she thought was dead, nonetheless?"

Evalyn shrugged. "I just feel like I should've done something which is why I'm going to do something now."

"Okay," said Dovie. "What do you have in mind?"

"I want to rebuild Rockwood," said Evalyn. "I've been thinking about it for a long time. Robert always wanted to rebuild, but we didn't have time before the war broke out. I want to rebuild it now, so Robert has a home to come back to."

"I think it's a wonderful idea to rebuild Rockwood. You and your kids need a home of your own," said Dovie. "I love y'all living here, but I don't think y'all, especially Robert, meant for it to be a permanent situation. We'll help you build it, get the things you need, and maybe your sisters can help you pick out fabric for curtains. We'll hit up some auctions and estate sales for furniture. We'll have you in ship shape in no time."

Evalyn smiled. "Sounds like a fantastic plan to me."

"Sounds like a fantastic plan to me too," said James from the doorway. "But maybe we should hold off for a little bit."

"Why would I want to do that?" asked Evalyn.

James took a few more steps into the room and ran his hands through his gray hair. Dovie remembered how it was peppered with brown hair when the Brewer children had first come to Quail Crossings. There was no sign of the brown hair now.

"Well," said James softly, "because we aren't sure when or if Robert is coming back. I hate the thought of you and the kids staying out at Rockwood alone. I was thinking it might be best just to build a few rooms onto Quail Crossings instead, now that Ellie is here."

Evalyn's mind flashed back to the day of the tornado and the dread she felt seeing Rockwood destroyed. Rockwood had taken a direct hit from the tornado, and the only thing left on the property was the old stone fireplace. They had found remnants of the house littered miles away, and nothing was salvageable. She hadn't cared much about the house, but the terror of thinking Robert may have been inside when the tornado barreled through raced through her veins. Her heart leapt as she remembered seeing him pull up and the relief she felt at knowing he was okay. She could almost feel his embrace as they touched each other to confirm it wasn't an illusion. The house they could rebuild, and both knew how lucky they were that both had survived the storm.

Evalyn wiped off her hands and went to James. She gave him a small smile, letting him know she knew he meant no harm with his concerns. "Robert is coming back. I just know it, and when he does, I want his home to be ready for him."

"Come on, Ellie," said Alice as she climbed the ladder to the loft. "I want to show you something."

Ellie hesitated and looked around the barn before following Alice up the ladder. Alice liked that Ellie seemed to have an adventuresome spirit. She figured Mama Dovie must be right about Ellie not being able to talk due to something physical. She figured most girls who were adventurous enough to follow someone who was practically a stranger into the loft wouldn't be afraid to talk.

Alice pointed to a huge stack of hay. "This is my secret place."

Ellie looked at the hay and raised an eyebrow.

Alice nodded. "Oh, I know it don't look like much now, but watch this."

Walking to the center of the stack, Alice reached down and grabbed some burlap that sat under a hay bale. She pulled and she thought she could hear Ellie gasp as the hay bale revealed a secret opening. Alice climbed inside and motioned for Ellie to follow.

Ellie pointed to the ladder.

"We can milk Poppy in a minute," said Alice. "She ain't goin' anywhere. Come on in."

Ellie looked at the ladder again and then slowly made her way into the middle of the hay bales. Inside the hay bale stack there was a small opening just big enough for the two girls to sit in comfortably. Alice had stocked the secret place full of her favorite books, paper, and pencils.

"This is where I come to write," said Alice. "I want to be a famous writer one day like J. M. Barrie. He wrote *Peter Pan*. Have you ever read it?"

Alice held the book up as Ellie shook her head.

"Do you want to read it?" asked Alice, holding the worn book out to Ellie.

Ellie bowed her head.

Alice bit her lip. "Ellie? Do you know how to read?"

Ellie didn't move.

"That's okay, Ellie." Alice smiled. "I taught my friend Jacob to read when he was sixteen. Lots of people don't know how to read. I just love it, and I love helping people read. I can teach you, if you'd like."

Ellie looked up, her face beaming with an ear to ear smile.

"I'll take that as a yes," said Alice. "It'll be a little bit of a challenge for me since you don't talk, but I bet you'll pick it up in no time. You don't have to talk in order to read. That's one of the reasons I like reading up here. I get just enough light to read, and no one bothers me until it's chore time. I have to be honest. This place ain't all that secret. They always know where to find me, but it's my space."

Ellie's smile faded a little.

"You know what?" said Alice. "It ain't my place. It's our place. You can use it whenever you'd like."

Ellie's smile returned and Alice met it with her own. She turned and started digging through her stacks of books until she found a book about the alphabet. "I never understood why I kept this ol' thing. Johnson's Drug Store was having a sale, and I bought it for a penny when I was about twelve. I was reading fine then, but I liked the pictures and I've hung on to it ever since. We can use it to help you. Want to start now?"

Ellie edged closer as Alice opened the book and began to recite the alphabet.

As disappointed as she was, Dovie was glad Elmer and Tiny had decided to stay with the Clarks for the time being. She knew they would visit, and as she looked at her kitchen table, she didn't know how she was going to fit one more place for Ellie around it.

Ellie had been a busy bee all day, volunteering for every chore Dovie mentioned. The girl had to be hungry after doing so much work, and tonight she would dine with the family. There would be occasions when she would have to sit at the kid table in the parlor, but tonight they had just enough room for her to join the adults.

Dovie turned and pulled a large ham out of the oven and placed it on the center of the table. Before she had time to turn around, Ellie had put the mashed potatoes, corn, and bread on the table as well.

"Girl, you're gonna spoil me if you keep helpin' like that," Dovie teased. "Thank you. You want to ring the dinner bell?"

Ellie nodded and stepped onto the stoop to ring the old iron triangle. Dovie's heart felt warm as Ellie seemed to find her place in their daily lives. She had been afraid that Ellie would waste away in her room, but it was like she had more pep in her step than a jackrabbit.

Coming back inside, Ellie stood in the corner as the rest of the family poured in from all directions. Evalyn and Lou Anne made plates for the little kids, Joy, Dean, and Annabelle, and then herded them into the parlor to eat at a smaller wooden table.

The men came in, hung their hats on nails, washed their hands at the sink, and then took their places at the table. Having the children settled in the parlor, Evalyn and Lou Anne came back in and took their places. Dovie and Alice were busy filling water glasses for everyone, and the room filled with the lighthearted tune of casual conversation.

With everyone seated, Dovie motioned to Ellie. "Come on over and get you a plate, hon."

Ellie looked around the table as if waiting for additional permission.

"It's okay," said Evalyn. "You must be starved."

Ellie slowly walked to the empty place and filled her plate as everything was passed around the table. Once her plate was full, she grabbed her plate, walked to the corner by the stove, and sat on the floor.

"Ellie?" Dovie stood and followed her. "Hon, family doesn't eat on the floor."

Dovie delicately touched Ellie's arm and could feel her tremble. "It's all right, sweetie. You'll always have a place at our table."

Chapter Seven

Ellie stared at the large grey and white goose standing in front of Evalyn's car. She had, until this day, been able to avoid the grumpy goose, but it looked as if there would be no avoiding it today.

She wondered if she should whisper a greeting to the bird named Norman or just scoot past him like she would any other chicken or fowl. Momma Dovie had warned her that Norman could be mean without notice, and you never wanted to turn your back to him, but Alice always spoke kindly of the goose. He had saved her from a rabid dog and a dust storm.

Ellie reminded herself that Norman was just a goose. She had never been afraid of geese before, and she wasn't about to start now. She took a step forward and Norman raised his neck, making himself look taller.

Holding her hands up in a peaceful pose, Ellie bowed her head. She wanted Norman to know that she knew he was boss, and that she didn't want any trouble. Her whole plan to stay at Quail Crossings was to work hard and not make any trouble at all, especially not with Alice's prize goose.

Ellie stepped forward again, and Norman raised his wings and hissed. Cocking her head, Ellie couldn't believe Norman's actions. She had been nothing but cordial, and now he was being aggressive. She was not going to let a silly ol' goose stop her from getting in the car as she was told.

She placed her hands on her hips and narrowed her eyes. She shook her head before raising her arms at Norman and hissed right back at him. Norman's neck jerked in confusion. He hissed again and waved his wings. Ellie hissed back and flapped her hands.

Norman tilted his head as he relaxed his wings. Then with a bit of a groan, he waddled around the car and headed to the pond. Ellie laughed at herself, proud that she had become the bigger goose. She also promised to feed Norman extra grain that evening. Today may have been a battle but she was determined to be his friend.

"Ready?" asked Evalyn, coming out the back door.

Ellie shrugged. She had never been to school before and was both excited and terrified.

"The first day is always the hardest," said Evalyn. "But don't worry, you're gonna love Mrs. Spaulding. You've probably seen her in church. She's the pastor's wife. You won't meet a kinder soul than her."

Nodding, Ellie got into the car hoping Evalyn wouldn't see her tremble. She was sure Mrs. Spaulding would be fine. It was the other kids that Ellie worried about.

"Mrs. Spaulding, I don't think I understand what you're saying," said Evalyn as she sat across from the pastor's wife. Susan Spaulding had been a teacher at Knollwood School for almost twenty years, and now she ran the place. She had welcomed every kid with open arms and always found a place for them. Now Evalyn couldn't believe her ears.

"Please understand, Evalyn, I'm not saying this to be cruel," explained Susan. "It's quite the opposite, in fact. Ellie is special, and because she doesn't communicate with us, I can't place her in the appropriate classroom. If I place her in with the younger children, then I feel I would be setting her up for ridicule. If I place her with the children her age, then I feel I'm setting her up for failure. I really think it's best if she's taught at home for the next couple of years. Find out where she is at academically, and then maybe she can attend high school and graduate."

"So she can't come to school?" asked Evalyn. She looked at Ellie and couldn't tell if her sister was relieved or disappointed.

"I'm saying she can't attend school now, but in the future, with enough hard work I believe we'll have a place for her," said Susan. "I have the utmost confidence that you and Alice can teach her at home. You, yourself, told me that she can't read or write. Or, that if she can, she won't. I just don't have the teaching staff to attend to situations like hers. And again, I'm afraid if I place her in a younger class than her peers, she will be teased. I would love to say that wouldn't happen in my school, but we both know children will be children."

Evalyn squared her chin. She could tell Susan was coming from a place of concern, but the words still stung. She was not upset for herself but for Ellie. "If that's what you think is best."

"I really do," said Susan. "Listen, I will have the grammar school teacher compile worksheets and assignments for Alice to pick up each day. That way y'all will have some material to work with. If you have any questions you can come to me."

Evalyn stood and Ellie stood with her. "Guess it will have to do, and we do appreciate your advice. I just can't help but think Ellie would gain ground faster around other children, but I respect your opinion."

Susan stood and turned to Ellie. "Work hard and you'll be in a classroom before you know it, and you know you're always welcome at Sunday school and at our youth meetings."

Evalyn held her tongue until they were back in the car, but she felt as if steam would come out of her ears at any time. "The nerve of her. Calling herself a Christian woman and even inviting you to youth meetings right after she said you weren't good enough for her school. All you need is to be around other children, and you'll loosen up in no time."

Evalyn looked at Ellie who stared at her feet.

"Oh, Ellie, it'll be okay," said Evalyn changing her tone. "This isn't the end by any means. Alice and I will get you all caught up, and then you can come to school. Besides I kind of like the thought of you being around more. That way we can get to know each other. We have a lot of lost time to make up for."

Ellie looked up and gave Evalyn a little smile.

"You're gonna be just fine, Ellie Brewer," said Evalyn starting the car. "And by the time we get through with you, you'll be smarter than the lot of them." She gave Ellie a wink. "I wouldn't doubt it if you were smarter than us all."

Ellie looked out the window as Evalyn pulled out of the school parking lot. As much as Evalyn didn't want to believe Mrs. Spaulding, Ellie knew she had been correct. Ellie had had no schooling. She didn't want to be placed with the little kids, even if that was where she belonged on an academic level.

She liked little kids and had always taken care of them, but it would be different if she shared a classroom with them. Ellie didn't really see it was necessary anyway. As long as Alice and Evalyn taught her how to read and write, and maybe some simple arithmetic, that was all she really needed.

Going to school could be a source of trouble for the family, and that was the last thing Ellie wanted. Coming to Quail Crossings and the way the family was treating her was like a dream. They treated her kindly, like family, and Ellie wanted nothing more than for that dream to continue.

Chapter Eight

October 1945

"Sure is hot for October," said Bill, wiping his face with his bandana. "I'm not sure we're gonna find any deer this evening. I bet they bed down until later tonight. I know I'd be lying in the shade right about now if I had the choice."

"We could check over by the north creek in the sand plum thicket," said Elmer, wiping the sweat from his brow with his shirt sleeve. "Lots of shade and plenty of water. That's where I'd go if I were a deer."

"Sounds good," said Bill as they started north. "So what are your plans?"

"Ummm ... I thought we were both going to the thicket," said Elmer, cocking his head. "Do you want to hunt that area alone?"

"Not hunting ... but as a married man," said Bill, shaking his head. "I'm sure you and Tiny are welcome to stay at the Clark's house as long as you need, but I figured y'all would want a place of your own," said Bill.

"We do," said Elmer, high-stepping over a yucca plant. "First, I gotta find a job."

"I figured you'd stay on at Quail Crossings."

"I think that job is taken," said Elmer. "We can't expect James to pay us both a living wage to split the work you've been doing alone while I was at war. That ain't right. You've been a steady hand to them for over ten years. There's no reason that should stop."

"I guess I just saw you stayin' on is all," said Bill, scratching his neck. "Got any leads?"

"Mary's dad wants me to take over their farm," said Elmer, "but we both know that place is a farmer's nightmare. There ain't enough water to farm it, and if you hadn't helped dig that new water well ten or so years ago, the house wouldn't have water either. It won't make us a decent living, but the land is paid for. I might be able to lease it out, and we'll be able to call it our own once the Clarks move to Amarillo."

"They're moving to Amarillo?" Bill stopped.

"Yeah, Mary's been pretty upset about it," said Elmer, stopping beside him. "But she doesn't want to live in the city and neither do I. They've promised to come back for holidays."

"When did they decide to move?" asked Bill, raising an eyebrow. "I can't imagine them living anywhere but here."

Elmer pursed his lips. "Bud has never been a good farmer. I'm surprised they've lasted out here as long as they have. You know he was an accountant before the Depression, and now he can get a job in Amarillo and make more money without the backbreaking work. Plus it was really hard on them to lose Bud, Jr. over in France. I think there are just too many memories."

Bill nodded and continued walking. "Yeah, when Sara Clark walked to her seat at your wedding carrying that flower in honor of Junior, I thought I was going to lose it. It was nice of Tiny to acknowledge her brother that way. I can't imagine how I would've felt had you not come back."

"You mean how Evie's feeling now," snapped Elmer.

Bill jerked like he'd been punched in the gut, causing Elmer to immediately regret snapping at him. He didn't even know where that hostility had come from. Everyone was worried about Robert, and they were all trying to stay positive. It was true Bill had not always liked his brother-in-law. He had been very clear that he hated the fact Evalyn got married in California without any family present. Heck, the family hadn't even known Robert was in the picture until the two returned home married with a child. But Elmer knew Bill had grown fond of Robert for two reasons, he made Evalyn happy, and he was a great father.

"I'm sorry," said Elmer, walking to his brother. "That came out wrong. I know what you were trying to say. I guess I'm a bit cranky today."

"We all get that way," said Bill. He pointed to the thicket area Elmer thought the deer might be bedding in. "We'll never get a good shot of them within those trees. I'll go around and try to flush them out this way. Watch out for that ol' water well out here. James used to have a stock tank out here until the well dried up. I don't know how many times I've tripped on those old boards. Get your gun ready."

Elmer nodded as Bill started to make a large circle around the area to try to spook the deer into running towards Elmer. Kneeling, Elmer readied his gun. Between the hot weather and the weight of the gun, Elmer's palms began to sweat almost instantly. He wiped them on his pants before lifting the gun an assuming a shooting stance, thinking Bill should be getting close enough to spook the deer.

Elmer heard a faint pop of gunfire behind him and quickly looked over his shoulder. He wondered if someone else was hunting in the area. Quail Crossings was private property, and all the locals knew it was off limits.

He heard two more shots, this time in front of him and swung back around. Suddenly his ears filled with the constant pops of gunfire, causing him to hunch over. Panic raced through Elmer's body. A single word ran through his head … *Thomas.*

He had to get to Thomas. He was out there somewhere. Everyone else was accounted for and Elmer wasn't about to leave a man behind.

He rose to his feet as two large bucks raced out of the trees, followed by a dozen or so does. Elmer raised his gun but hesitated as the deer turned into soldiers. He aimed at each one trying to determine if they were friend or foe, but they just barreled past him in a blurred mass of tans and greens. The ground rumbled beneath him as the stampede continued, and Elmer knew he had to find Thomas quickly before the German tanks did.

"Thomas!" Elmer cried out. "Where are you?"

The soldiers had gone, the rumble stopped, and silence filled the air.

"Thomas!" Elmer yelled again, swinging around trying to get his bearings. The landscape was all wrong. He wondered if he had been knocked on the head by some shrapnel and was having hallucinations.

"Elmer?"

Elmer paused. That wasn't Thomas's voice. He swung around, raising his gun at the enemy solider standing just a few feet away.

Bill dropped his own rifle immediately and flung both hands up in the air. "What are you doing?"

"Where's Thomas?" Elmer asked as the solider grew blurry. "What have you done with him?"

"Elm?" Bill said softly, "It's me, Bill, your brother. I don't know where Thomas is, but we can find him together."

"Bill?" Elmer shook his head and blinked as his eyes cleared to see his brother standing in front of him with his hands raised. Elmer put down his gun. "Oh, god, I'm so sorry, Bill."

Bill slowly picked up his gun and walked to his brother. "You okay? Who is Thomas?"

Elmer shook his head. "I just got confused for a minute. I'm okay now." He turned to head back towards Quail Crossings. "Were there any deer?"

"Elmer," yelled Bill as Elmer walked briskly to the house, "we should talk about what just happened."

"Ain't nothing to talk about," said Elmer, leaving Bill looking dumbfounded. "I bet dinner's 'bout ready and I'm starvin'. See you at the house."

Elmer knew Bill wanted to discuss what happened, but all Elmer wanted to do was forget. He just wanted to forget it all.

Norman hated the heat. It made him grumpy. Of course, most things made Norman grumpy, but it was October, a time when the leaves changed colors and the winds began to cool. There were no cool winds this evening.

Norman heaved himself onto his feet and started to waddle to the pond. He let out a low groaning honk as it seemed to be miles and miles away, even though it was exactly the same distance as it had been the day before.

"What's the matter, Mr. Norman?" asked Joy as she skipped in front of the grumpy goose. "You look sad."

Norman tilted his head at the child. Why was she standing in his way? All he wanted was a nice swim in the cool pleasant waters of the pond.

"Mr. Norman, do you want to play?" asked Joy.

Norman lowered his head at the girl. Joy did not take the cue that this meant she was to stand aside. She reached over to pat Norman on the head. Norman let out a loud honk. He had had enough of this child's foolishness.

Joy screamed and ran. Norman followed, his wings raised high. He was determined to teach the child a lesson about getting in the path of a hot goose.

Joy ran to the barn, Norman hot on her heels. Norman was just about to go in for a peck when he was barreled over by a large, pink blur.

Norman got to his webbed feet, feeling a bit dazed and hotter than ever. He looked around for Joy, and watched as Daisy the pig herded the little girl to the safety of the house. Norman narrowed his eyes at Daisy, but she just turned and gave him a loud snort.

Chapter Nine

"Any mail come for me today?" Alice asked Dovie as she sat at the kitchen table with Ellie.

"Afraid not," said Dovie, as she kneaded the dough for bread.

Alice folded her arms. "I swear, if I ever get my hands on Jacob Henry, I'm gonna chew him a new hide for not responding to my letters. It's just plain rude."

"Kind of like ignoring Ellie to complain about Jacob?" asked Dovie with a smirk.

Alice looked at Ellie. "I'm sorry. Where were we?"

Ellie pointed at the alphabet she had just written. Alice picked up the paper and smiled. "Very good, Ellie. Now that you know the letters, we can work on putting them together to form words. Do you feel ready for that?"

Ellie nodded and readied her pencil.

"First, I'm going to go over the sounds each letter makes again. Then we'll start on some small words," explained Alice, pulling a spelling list from the stack of work Mrs. Spaulding had given her for Ellie.

As she started going over the alphabet, a small rap on the back door interrupted them, and Kathleen let herself in carrying a large basket.

"How is everybody doing today?" asked Kathleen.

Dovie smiled at her friend. "I'm afraid to ask what's in the basket. It better be knitting."

Kathleen laughed and gave an apologetic smile as she removed the cloth covering the basket to reveal oatmeal raisin cookies. "I couldn't help myself. They're Joy's favorites. I was hoping to spend time with her and Caleb today. Give Evie a bit of a break."

"Kathleen Wheaton, my dresses are getting tighter every day from eating your delicious treats," proclaimed Dovie. "I've told you a hundred times, you don't have to bring anything over to come and visit. In fact, next time if I smell one baked good on you, I'm turning you away. The fabric in my waistline can't take it."

Kathleen crossed her heart. "I promise, I will not bring a single baked good next time." The ladies laughed as Kathleen sat at the table.

"How 'bout some coffee to go with those cookies?" asked Dovie.

"You know the only reason I bring you baked goods is because they go so well with your coffee," said Kathleen with a wink. "So is Evalyn here?"

"She and Joy are out gathering greens. They should be back soon," said Dovie, placing a steaming mug of coffee in front of Kathleen. "We're trying to get the last vegetation of the year before the cold weather takes hold.

Kathleen added sugar as she pushed the basket towards Alice and Ellie. "You girls want a cookie?"

"Thank you," said Alice, grabbing a cookie and giving one to Ellie. "Let's start with cat."

"What are y'all working on?" asked Kathleen.

"I'm teaching Ellie how to spell," said Alice.

"Oh, Ellie, did you know you have the world's finest speller teaching you spelling?" asked Kathleen.

Ellie shook her head.

"I'm not the world's finest speller," said Alice, blushing.

"Well, she's Knollwood's best speller," said Kathleen, "and I bet she'll win this year's spelling bee."

"I've got to beat Lawrence Dodson first," Alice said with a sigh.

"The grocer's son?" Kathleen waved Alice off. "Oh, you'll beat him with letters to spare."

"Don't mind her," said Evalyn as she came through the back door with a basket full of greens. "She and Lawrence compete over everything. I don't know how many times I've heard about Lawrence. Truth be told, I think our Alice has a bit of a crush on Mr. Dodson."

"I do not," snapped Alice.

"Nothing to be ashamed of," said Kathleen. "He's a good lookin' boy."

"And smart," said Dovie. "Always go with smarts over looks."

"Dovie is right," said Evalyn. "Marry a smart man so you don't have to go traipsing all over the pasture looking for eatable greens."

"Y'all need to hush," said Alice, hiding her face in her hands. "I don't have a crush on Lawrence, and I can't believe y'all are talking about me marrying anyone."

Ellie quietly picked up her notebook and spelling list and slipped away into the parlor. It was obvious Alice wasn't in the mood to concentrate on teaching her spelling when she was being teased about Lawrence. Ellie didn't mind that Alice was distracted, having the women clucking like chickens over Alice in the kitchen meant Ellie could journey into the parlor and whisper to herself the sounds the letters made.

She looked at her alphabet and started with the A, remembering the sounds Alice had taught her. Then she turned to her spelling list and started to sound out the words. After reading each word the best she could, she started to copy her spelling list into her notebook.

"Whatcha doing in here all by yourself?" asked Elmer.

Ellie jumped at the sound of his voice. She thought he and Bill were out hunting. Elmer walked around the sofa and looked at her paper.

"Spelling," he said with a sigh. "That was never my strong point, but I worked hard at it, and I'm a pretty decent speller now. What I really liked to do was draw. Can I show you a trick?"

Ellie nodded as she handed him the pencil.

"This won't work for every word, but it's a nice distraction from actually memorizing the spelling."

Elmer wrote cat. Then he made the c into a circle and drew eyes in both the circle and the a. He then made the top of the t into an ear drawing and connected it to another triangle over the c. He drew a circle around the whole word to connect the ears. Lastly, he added a nose and whiskers, successfully transforming the word "cat" into a cat.

Ellie clapped her hands in delight. Elmer handed her the pencil. "Now, you spell cat."

Thinking of what Elmer had done with the letters, Ellie spelled cat quickly and correctly.

"There you go!" said Elmer, a big smile on his face. "You're as smart as a fox, you are."

Ellie's heart swelled with pride as she looked down at the first word she'd ever spelled on her own.

Chapter Ten

Tiny was thankful October was almost over. She hoped the coming of November would mean an incoming of fall weather. She usually didn't mind the heat of an Indian summer, but lately she was just feeling exhausted and light-headed all of the time. As far as she could tell she wasn't sick, so she decided it was just the heat getting to her after her years on the tranquil islands of Hawaii.

She knew how fortunate she had been to be stationed at Pearl Harbor after joining The Army Nurse Corps. Her instructors had quickly realized that she was an organizer at heart and had assigned her to logistics instead of medical. Tiny appreciated that they had realized she was better at paperwork than surgeries. She wanted to help and so she did by making sure all the nurses had a way to get to their ordered destinations.

Tiny had grown to love Hawaii and her co-workers. She was going to re-enlist until she was politely informed by an Army superior that her job position was needed for a soldier coming back from overseas, and she would be sent home since her enlistment was fulfilled. She could re-enlist if she still wanted to, but she would be put in the secretarial pool and be stationed stateside.

She decided it was fate that she and Elmer had found each other in Times Square during the celebration of the war's end. God had a plan and it was for her to return home, a place she had missed even in the tropical paradise of Hawaii.

Tiny sat with Lou Anne and Evalyn as the children waded in the cool water of the pond. It was hot enough to get their feet wet, but none were brave enough to actually take a real swim.

"I just love this weather," said Lou Anne. "I wouldn't mind if it stayed this way all winter long."

"Then we wouldn't get to make a snowman," whined Dean at his momma.

Tiny laughed at her nephew. "Like we get enough snow around here to actually build a snowman. Now snow angels, that's the way to go."

Tiny could think of nothing better than to lay in a cold bank of snow right about now.

"We've had our fair share of snow and ice," said Evalyn, giving an involuntary shiver as she picked up Caleb who had been playing in the dirt and started to brush him off. "I'm with Lou Anne on this one. Regardless of the snow, I wouldn't miss the cold north wind that never seems to stop. Chills you right to the bone and makes you think you'll never get warm."

"Come on, kids," said Lou Anne, taking a cue from Evalyn. "It's time to wash up and help with dinner. Besides I bet little Rosey is up from her nap 'bout now and probably looking for something to eat."

A chorus of groans escaped from the children as Evalyn and Lou Anne stood. Annabelle started to cry. Lou

Anne swept her up. "Now, now, Annabelle, there's no need to cry. We'll come back to the pond tomorrow."

"But I want to play," cried little Annabelle, her toddler mind feeling as if tomorrow was a lifetime away.

"Here let me take her," said Tiny as she went to stand. Before she could make it to her feet, her whole world went dark, and she fell back into the dirt.

Tiny woke up to a circle of faces looking down at her. She blinked and tried to get her bearings. It was cooler and shadier than it had been outside. She felt the soft cushions of the sofa under her. Someone must have carried her inside.

"Mary, are you okay?" asked Elmer.

Tiny rubbed her head and tried to remember the events leading up to her blackout. "I think so. I guess I was just a little light-headed from the heat."

"Give her some room," clucked Dovie, making her way into the parlor. "My lands! I leave for a second, and y'all crowd over her like cows to a freshly filled grain trough."

Evalyn, Lou Anne, and Joy all took a step back. Elmer was the only one who stayed put. Tiny tried to sit up.

"Just lay still a second and get your thoughts together," said Dovie. "There's no rush."

"What happened?" Tiny asked.

"The girls said you fainted out by the pond," said Elmer. "Joy was running to the house to get help when she saw me coming out of the house. I ran to the pond and carried you back."

Tiny smiled. "You always were my hero."

Her smile grew as she watched Elmer's cheeks turn a light shade of red.

"Do you remember any of that?" asked Dovie, helping Tiny into a sitting position and giving her a cup of water.

"I remember I was going to help with Annabelle, and then I got really dizzy and everything went black," said Tiny.

"Did the heat get to her?" asked Evalyn. "I didn't think it was that hot outside, but maybe we were out too long."

Dovie shook her head. "No, I don't think it's that. Tiny have you had any other problems lately?"

Tiny shrugged. "I've been exhausted and a bit light-headed. But I'm sure it's just the heat and getting used to the dry Texas Panhandle weather again. Jeepers, my ma used to say that we Clarks were not cut out for the heat of panhandle summers. She'd go on and on 'bout how we belonged on the coast, right next to the ocean, even though she's never even seen the ocean. Between you and me, I think she was a tad bit jealous when I went to Hawaii. I keep tellin' her I'll take her …"

"You've been stateside for months," interrupted Elmer, his eyes full of concern. "I think you've gotten used to the weather, no matter what your ma says."

"Have you been feeling nauseous?" asked Dovie.

"A little," said Tiny, "but usually I just eat something and it goes away."

Dovie smiled. "Honey, when was the last time you had your monthly?"

This time it was Tiny's turn to blush as she felt the heat rush to her checks. She couldn't believe Dovie had asked that question in front of Elmer. Even if he was her husband, that was personal information, and Dovie had no right bringing it up in mixed company. Tiny was just about to open her mouth and give Dovie a stern lecture on bluntness when it dawned on her what was happening.

"I haven't since before our church wedding," said Tiny as the corners of her mouth curved up. "Do you think?"

Dovie nodded. "If you're that late, then yes I do."

Elmer looked from Tiny to Dovie and back to Tiny as they sat smiling at each other. He heard both Evalyn and Lou Anne let out squeals of delight.

"Could someone please tell me what's going on?" he asked, flabbergasted.

Tiny turned to him, her smile wide. "Elm, I'm pregnant!"

Elmer wrapped her up in a hug. "Really? So soon, I mean we just got married."

"All it takes is once," said Dovie, giving Elmer a wink that caused his cheeks to flare red again.

"So is she okay?" asked Elmer. "You know with the fainting and all?"

Dovie nodded. "She probably just needs to eat a little more, now that's she's eating for two. No more skipping breakfast like you did this morning even if you get down with morning sickness. You've got to feed yourself and your baby."

"Yes, ma'am," said Tiny, giving a salute. She reached down and gently caressed her belly. The only reason she had been skipping breakfast was because her dresses were fitting a bit tight and now she knew why. Little butterflies fluttered around in her stomach, and she wondered if that was the baby or just her excitement. She needed to tell her folks right away. Maybe they wouldn't move. "Will you drive me to see my parents?"

"Of course," said Elmer, bouncing up from the sofa. "We can go now and then come back in time to tell everybody else at dinner."

"How far along are you, do you think?" asked Evalyn giving Tiny a hug as she stood.

"Six weeks, maybe two months," answered Tiny.

Lou Anne counted up on her fingers. "A June baby, how sweet."

"And hopefully you'll have the little one before the summer heat gets unbearable. Nothing worse than being pregnant through the hottest part of summer," said Evalyn.

"We better get going," said Elmer, "if we plan to be back for dinner."

"Can we have fried chicken, you know, to celebrate me getting an aunt?" asked Joy.

"You're getting a cousin, you silly goose," said Dovie, giving Joy a playful pinch on the cheek. "But yes, we can fry up some chicken."

Joy stuck her lip out and folded her arms.

"What's the matter, Joy?" asked Dovie. "I said we could have fried chicken."

"I don't want any more baby cousins," pouted Joy. "All the little ones do is cry and poop. I want more aunts like Alice and Ellie. They know how to play tea party with the dolls. All Annabelle does is knock everything over, and Dean wants to put dirt in my tea set."

"Joy Smith, you stop that whining this instant," demanded Evalyn. "Tiny's gonna have a baby and that's a wonderful thing. You're being mighty selfish thinking about yourself."

"Besides," said Tiny, "all these babies will be grown and be playing tea party with you before you know it. You won't just have tea parties, but huge parties with all your cousins."

"You mean like a princess?" Joy squealed. "Aunt Alice has been reading me a book about a princess, and she just had a huge tea party with all of her friends."

"Just like a princess," said Tiny. She felt another swirl in her belly and knew she was having a girl.

Ellie hurried upstairs while everyone was congratulating Tiny and Elmer on their wonderful news. She crawled onto her cot with Lovey and gave her a hug.

"Tiny is going to have a baby," Ellie whispered to Lovey. "Can you imagine?"

Ellie looked at the doll. "Of course I'm too young for a baby now. I just think she's gonna be the best mother."

She nodded at Lovey. "You're right. I don't have much experience with that, and I do wonder what our mother was like."

Ellie's eyes grew wide. "I can't do that, Lovey. I can't ask Alice or Evie. I have to keep my mouth shut and do my work. I can't cause any trouble, or they'll make me leave."

Ellie hugged Lovey. "But it sure would be nice to have a mother like Tiny, or Evie, or even Alice, even though she's not that much older than I am." She leaned and whispered in Lovey's ear. "What I'd really like is for Momma Dovie to be my momma. She's such a wonderful momma to everyone else. Maybe one day I'll prove that I'm good enough to be her child too. One day."

Chapter Eleven

The family sat around the ever growing table in the Quail Crossings' kitchen. Ellie, Joy, Dean, and Annabelle ate at their small table just inside the parlor, while the younger children, Caleb and Rosey sat on a blanket by the pantry, having already been fed. Dovie kept saying she was going to replace the sofa with a large dining table but never did. Everyone enjoyed the closeness. Dovie hated to admit that once Rockwood was finished Evalyn, and her bunch would be eating there. Bill and Lou Anne already ate at their house most nights. Soon Elmer and Tiny would be moving permanently into the Clark's place, and her table would be mostly empty.

Dovie's heart ached at the thought of her friend, Sara, moving away. They had struggled through the Great Depression together. They had gardened, canned, sewed, and quilted together just trying to feed their families and stay sane during a time so uncertain, many couldn't handle it.

Dovie thought of the way Sara handled the news of Bud, Jr.'s death. Dovie remembered the day well. Even now, almost a year later, Dovie felt ashamed at how she had debated going to see Sara at all after the news spread that

Bud, Jr. had been killed in action. All Dovie could think about was her own little Helen who had died in a car accident at the tender age of six, along with her husband, Simon.

Bud, Jr.'s death had stirred up some awful emotions Dovie had thought were long gone. But she had put on her best front and gone to see Sara. As they sat on Sara's old sofa together, Sara looked Dovie right in the eyes and said, "You don't have to say anything, I know you, of all people, understand."

It had gone unspoken that Sara meant she knew the pain of losing a child. Dovie felt a familiar pang in her chest as her eyes began to tear. She looked at everyone around the table and knew Helen would've loved each and every one of them as her own siblings. Of course, had Simon and Helen not passed away, would the Brewers even be here?

Dovie shook the thought away. She would not choose. There was no reason to. Helen wasn't coming back. She wouldn't see her daughter again until they embraced at Heaven's gates.

"Dad, how is Rockwood coming along?" Dovie asked, trying to get her mind off heavy subjects.

"Really well," said James. "The boys and I have the foundation done and most of the walls are framed. The plans you ladies drew up were pretty simple, efficient, but simple. We should be able to get it done before the cold takes hold. We're very thankful for this glorious October weather. Lord knows we could be building in snow right now. We've gotten blizzards in October before."

"Aunt Evie says we don't get no snow," Dean hollered from the kids' table. "She said so today right before Aunt Tiny fell."

"Tiny fell?" James looked at Tiny with concern. "You okay?"

"Better than okay," said Tiny. "I'm … "

"… going to have a baby," Elmer finished for her with a big smile.

"Elmer Brewer," snapped Tiny, with an ornery smile, "I was going to tell them."

"Just like I was gonna tell them that we were married?" Elmer winked at his wife.

"Fair enough," said Tiny.

"Well, that's wonderful news," said James, reaching out to shake Elmer's hand.

"I'd get up to hug you," said Bill, "but once I get out of this chair, I may never get back in and this is the best fried chicken. Dovie, did you do something different?"

"It wasn't me," said Dovie. "Ellie insisted on cooking the chicken, so I let her."

"You mean you watched over her like a hawk," chuckled Lou Anne.

"No one wants to eat raw chicken," said Dovie. "I was just making sure it was cooked through."

"Well, it's delicious," said James looking at Ellie.

Ellie had integrated well at Quail Crossings. Whenever there was work to be done, she was the first to volunteer. Everyone spoke of what a wonderful work horse Ellie was, but Dovie wondered if it wasn't something else. Something she hadn't quite put her finger on.

"I've got some news too," said Gabe, clearing his throat.

Dovie cocked her head at her love. She couldn't imagine what he had to announce. Her heart raced as she thought about the possibility of Gabe finally proposing to her. Their love affair had been going on for the better part of five years. She knew Gabe wanted to spend the rest of his life with her, but he had insisted on waiting until the war was over to get married. Dovie had to admit, the war was over, and she was ready for a proposal.

"I leave for Europe tomorrow," said Gabe.

Dovie's face dropped. "But … you just got here."

"I know," said Gabe, "but my leave time is up. We all knew I was going to have to go back."

"I just didn't think it was going to be so soon," said Dovie, trying to hide her pout.

"Honey," said James softly, "he's been here almost three months."

"Still not long enough," said Dovie. She knew she was being selfish, but she wished Gabe had told her in private that he was leaving.

"The good news is, they're letting me go to Europe," said Gabe.

"And how is that good?" asked Dovie.

"So he can search for Robert," said Evalyn, barely above a whisper.

Dovie's heart sank. She had been so foolish. Of course Gabe was still looking for Robert. He had been reaching out to every source he had over the past few months searching for word on Robert's whereabouts.

"Of course," said Dovie, shaking her head at her own nonsense. "Please forgive me. I've sounded more foolish than a dog trying to meow."

"How is it that you got three months of leave anyway?" asked Elmer.

"As you know, I was out of the Air Corps when I found myself in Knollwood," explained Gabe. "When they asked me back to train pilots, I insisted on a specific contract, so I'm more of a retired veteran working within the military system. That's why I only trained and didn't fly in combat. Once the war ended, I was guaranteed six months of leave time regardless of what was left on my contract."

"Then you have more time," said Dovie, hope escaping in her voice.

Gabe nodded. "But I called in a favor to allow me to go to Europe and look for Robert. Once I find him, I can use the remaining three months of my contract for leave and never have to go back."

"So you do think you'll find him?" asked Evalyn as she twisted her napkin.

"I'm doing everything I can, Evie," said Gabe.

He reached down and grabbed Dovie's hand, then looked at her with promising eyes. "As God is my witness, Dovie, when I come back with Robert, it'll be for good. I'm never leaving you again."

Chapter Twelve

November 1945

Evalyn walked through her new house. Rockwood now boasted a large kitchen area, including a custom wooden table made by Elmer. A small sofa and soft beige chair sat in front of the large fireplace in the parlor. Two small rooms sat just off the parlor on the south side for the children, while Evalyn's larger room sat on the other side of the fireplace on the north side.

She, along with the help of Dovie, Lou Anne, Alice, and Ellie had spent the last week putting up wallpaper to give the structure a homey feel. Bill and Elmer finished moving in the furniture that Evalyn had purchased at an estate sale. She still needed to add some cozy decorations but knew those things would be added over time. Living at Quail Crossings she had been able to put most of the money from Robert's military pay into a savings account. She was thankful that she had been so frugal and could afford to build and furnish a house.

She was grateful Dovie offered to keep the kids for the night. She seemed to understand that Evalyn needed to be alone in order to adjust to not only a new house but to being back at Rockwood without Robert. In the morning the children would be back, and they would be staying at Rockwood full time.

Evalyn entered the bedroom she would share with Robert when he returned. It looked very similar to the original master bedroom that was destroyed by the tornado, except that the fireplace had been moved to the other side of the room where it would heat both the living area and the bedroom.

Evalyn pictured the old house and saw Robert sitting on the bed singing, *Back in the Saddle Again* by Gene Autry, to baby Joy. Even though he wasn't her real daddy, he had loved her from the beginning. Evalyn's secret that Joy wasn't her biological child either and had been adopted was never revealed.

The song Robert sang, danced through her head in his strong baritone. Robert's voice matched his stature as he towered over most men and had the muscles of a bull. Evalyn couldn't imagine him being taken out by a Nazi solider. But then again, being such a tall and stocky man may have made him a huge target.

Evalyn sat on the bed for a moment before letting herself fall back onto the pillow. She turned to the side where Robert would sleep and traced the edge of the empty pillow. They had had so little time between acknowledging their true feelings for each other and the war. Theirs had been a marriage of convenience that turned into a marriage of love and commitment.

She remembered the day that he broached the subject of signing up for four years in the army in order to not only fight for their country but also to protect Elmer.

"Robert, please don't go," she had begged. "We've just barely begun to live our lives together. We don't even have a home right now."

"But you do have a home," said Robert. "You can stay here at Quail Crossings. I already talked to James about it and he thinks it's best. Truth is, Evalyn, we can't afford to rebuild Rockwood unless I enlist. All our money was tied up in those pigs."

"I'm sure James would loan you the money to rebuild," said Evalyn.

"I know he would," said Robert. "James would give you Brewers the shirt off his back if you asked, but I'm not going to ask him. It ain't right. Not when I can join the Army."

"But what about your job at the feedlot?" asked Evalyn. "Don't they need you there with all the younger boys going off to fight?"

"They'll get along just fine without me," said Robert.

Evalyn felt her blood boil. "Why are you doing this? What about Joy? What about me? What if you go over there and get yourself ..."

She broke down in sobs and Robert hugged her tight. "Evalyn, I don't want to leave you and Joy. Y'all are my life. I would like nothing more but to rebuild our lives here and forget about this war. But I can't. I can't sit back and do nothing. Not after what they did to us ... to Pearl Harbor. They attacked us on our own soil, and I have to stand up for our country. It is my duty. Please try and understand. I'm going over there, and I'll do whatever I can to win this war because if those Japs or Germans find their way here ...." He shook his head. "... I can't imagine what they'd do to you and Joy. So I'm going over there to stop it, so it doesn't come over here."

"Why now?" cried Evalyn. "You didn't rush to sign up right after Pearl Harbor. It's been two months since the attack. Why not give us some more time together and then go over? Maybe it will be over soon, and you won't have to go at all."

"Because Elmer and Bill are signing up," said Robert softly. "Bill's not going to make it. There's no way they'll let him in with that eye. Someone's got to watch over Elmer. He's just a boy."

Evalyn finally understood. There would be no stopping Elmer. He had wanted to join the minute they had heard about Pearl Harbor, and Bill had agreed to sign the parental waiver letting him join at sixteen. Robert was doing what he had always done. He was protecting his family.

Evalyn caressed Robert's pillow and wondered what life would have been like for them had the war not broken out. Rockwood would have been rebuilt years before and they would probably have a thriving pig farm. Evalyn wrinkled her nose at her husband's choice of livestock. They were smelly and rude and noisy, but she'd take on a thousand pigs if it just meant having her husband back.

She had seen him once since the war broke out. He was able to get leave two years before, and the result of that homecoming had been Caleb. Robert learned of her pregnancy and delivery through letters but had never even seen his son.

Turning into the empty pillow, Evalyn wept. She wept for the marriage they'd yet to live and the fear for the marriage they might never get to have.

Elmer helped Bill patch up a hole in his chicken coop. He had to hand it to his brother. Bill had not only kept Quail Crossings running, but he had managed to take on some livestock of his own. Bill's barn now held a couple of milk cows, a handful of pigs, and a nice flock of chickens.

"Are you ready to talk about it?" asked Bill.

"Talk about what?" Elmer cocked his head at his brother.

"What happened in the field a few weeks back," said Bill. "Who is Thomas?"

Elmer tried to hide his annoyance. It was clear from Bill's face that he was really worried. He had every right to be since Elmer had turned his gun on him.

Elmer sighed. "Thomas Pope was a member of my platoon and a good friend of mine. We were both kids. Of course I didn't realize how much of a kid I was until I got over there, and Germans started shooting at me. But in a lot of ways Thomas was younger. He claimed he was sixteen, but I'm betting he was closer to fourteen."

Elmer concentrated on the wire he was attaching to the coop, hoping his concentration would make the story easier to tell. "We were in a really rough battle with the Germans. They had some huge tanks, and they were knocking us out by the handfuls. We were buried in the trenches for days. We couldn't move due to the tanks, and they wouldn't move and give up the line. So it was kind of a stalemate until our tanks got to us."

"So what happened to Thomas?" asked Bill.

"We just all kind of waited for something to happen. Then Thomas and some other fellas got it in their heads that they could sneak across enemy lines and steal one of them German tanks." Elmer yanked at the wire. "Stupidest idea on the planet and I told them that. I tried to talk some good sense in them and thought I had, until the next morning."

"They left, huh?" Bill shook his head.

"Yep," said Elmer. "Four of them, including Thomas. 'Bout that time we were ordered to advance. So we did. We ran out in a hail of gunfire, and all I could think was that I had to find that dumb kid, Thomas."

"I can't imagine," said Bill.

"You don't want to," said Elmer. "Trust me; don't even try."

Elmer remembered advancing on the enemy, the smell of blood and mud assaulting his nose as he high-stepped over his fallen fellow soldiers. Enemy soldiers came at him from the trees, and he fired without hesitation and watched them fall. He felt the earth rumble under his feet and knew the tanks were close. He just needed to find Thomas and get back to the trenches. Tears welled up in Elmer's eyes and he quickly brushed them away, the call of the retreat echoing in his ears.

"You never found Thomas," Bill stated more than asked.

Elmer shook his head. "I found him, but ..." Elmer couldn't finish, too choked up to speak.

"You're home now, and it will get better," said Bill. "I'm really sorry about your friend."

"Me too," said Elmer as he finished attaching the last wire on the coop. "Can you finish up without me? I have to go."

"Sure," said Bill, taking the pliers.

Elmer stood and walked toward the pasture.

"Hey, Elm," Bill hollered.

Elmer turned and looked at his older brother.

"I'm so thankful you're home, and I hope you know this is a safe place for you. I pray you never experience that kind of terror again, and though I may not have been there with you, I'm here for you now."

"Thanks, Bill." Elmer forced a smile before turning back to the pasture. It was true he was safe. If only he could have done the same for Thomas.

Elmer was thankful Bill hadn't pushed further for more of the story. He had accepted that Elmer had found Thomas already dead, and Elmer wished that was the truth. But he couldn't tell Bill what really happened. He couldn't tell anyone about the horrific end to that day. If he said the words out loud, he'd probably lose the shred of sanity he was barely clinging to.

Elmer tried not to sigh as he watched Tiny walk towards him. He knew that wasn't the attitude he should have toward his wife, but she would notice something was wrong, and he was done talking about it. He hoped it wouldn't spark a fight.

"Whatcha doin' walking out here, handsome stranger?" said Tiny playfully.

"Just getting some air," said Elmer.

Tiny's face fell. "You've been 'getting air' a lot lately, Elm. One would think you'd forgotten how to breathe."

"Some days it's harder than others," said Elmer walking toward Quail Crossings.

"Do you want to talk about it?" asked Tiny.

"Rather not," said Elmer.

"Jeepers, Elm," Tiny sighed. "I'm your wife. You're supposed to talk to me."

"I talk to you all the time," said Elmer, knowing full well that wasn't what she meant.

Tiny stomped her foot. "Elmer Brewer, don't play dumb with me. Tell me what's wrong. Let me help you fix it."

Elmer stopped. "That's just it, Mary. It can't be fixed."

Chapter Thirteen

Alice bolted up in bed. Something had startled her, but she couldn't figure out what. She listened to the silent house and waited for the noise to sound again. After a few minutes, she laid back down.

She looked over at Ellie who was sleeping in the small bed on the other side of the room. There was just enough light from the moon to make out Ellie's troubled face. Alice knew without a doubt that Ellie was having a nightmare. Alice wondered if she should wake her but shook the thought away and looked at the ceiling. There was no reason Ellie should have to be awake just because Alice couldn't seem to go back to sleep.

"No! Please stop!"

Alice again bolted up just in time to see Ellie fighting off some imaginary creature. Alice hurried out of her own bed and went to Ellie.

"Ellie, wake up," she pleaded. "It's just a dream."

Ellie slapped Alice's hands away as she continued her screams of protest.

"Please, Ellie, it's Alice. Wake up!" cried Alice, grabbing Ellie's wrists so she wouldn't get hit again.

Ellie opened her eyes in horror, fists raised to defend herself. She looked at Alice, then scrambled out of the bed and into a corner. Ellie brought her knees to her chin and started rocking back and forth.

Alice sat for a moment on Ellie's bed trying to keep her heart from racing right out of her chest. That same heart ached for Ellie and what must have happened to her to warrant such a nightmare. Slowly, Alice rose from the bed and walked to Ellie.

"Ellie," she said softly. "You're okay. It's just me, Alice. No one is going to hurt you here."

Alice kneeled in front of Ellie. Her breath caught as she saw tears cascading down Ellie's face. Nightmare or not, whatever Ellie was dreaming about was very real to her.

"I used to get scared a lot," said Alice, "but it was about silly things. I was terrified of the cellar until Mama Dovie made me go down there one day to fetch some apple cider. I begged her not to make me go down there alone, but she wouldn't hear any of that nonsense."

Alice remembered how her legs had trembled as she walked down the cement stairs. "I just knew there was a monster down there, but I also knew Mama Dovie was serious and she was teaching me how to bake a pie. It was the first time anyone had ever taken a minute to teach me how to do anything. They always just did it for me. I was grateful for her lesson and didn't want to let her down. So, you know what I did?"

Ellie shook her head.

Alice smiled. "I sang *Jesus Loves Me* all the way down those creepy steps. I know it seems silly, but just reminding myself that Jesus does love me and He was watching over me, made me feel better." Alice inhaled deeply. "I can't know what you've been through, but I do know Jesus is watching over you, too."

Alice slowly crawled to the side of Ellie and sat down. She placed her arm over her sister's shoulders and pulled her close, somewhat surprised that Ellie didn't pull away. She could feel Ellie's body quiver, still shaken from the nightmare. In a very soft voice, Alice began to sing the song that comforted her as a child, *Jesus Loves Me*. She didn't know how many times she repeated the verse before Ellie's body relaxed into slumber, but she kept singing until her own body gave into sleep.

James watched Alice let out a huge yawn at breakfast the next morning.

"You keep yawning like that you'll catch flies," said James with a smile. "Did you stay up too late reading?"

"Not this time," said Alice, shaking her head as she played with her oatmeal.

Dovie hurried over and placed her palm on Alice's forehead. "What's a matter, child? You feeling ill? You don't seem warm."

"It was Ellie," said Alice, sitting up a little taller. "She had a nightmare, and I was up half the night singing to her. We ended up falling asleep in the corner on the floor."

James frowned. "How do you know she was having a nightmare?"

Alice gave him a sideways look. "Because she screamed 'no' and then tried to fight me off when I went to wake her."

"She talked?" asked Dovie sitting down.

Alice nodded. "She only said 'no' and 'please stop', but it was clear as day. Even after she was awake, she was tremblin' with fright. So I did what I used to do when I was a kid and sang *Jesus Loves Me*. I probably should have moved her once she was asleep, but I was afraid she'd get upset again. I think someone hurt her real bad before she came here." She looked to James. "Is there something we can do? We gotta help her."

"Let me think on it a bit," said James.

"Better think fast," said Alice with another big yawn. "I'm not sure I can take too many nights like that. I don't know how Evie and Lou Anne do it, getting' up with the babies all the time."

"Oh, honey," said Dovie, patting Alice's shoulder. "I'm so glad you were there for her. Why don't you go upstairs and lay down."

"What about school?" asked Alice. "I'm supposed to help Mrs. Spaulding teach the younger ones to read."

"I'll take you in late. I'm sure Mrs. Spaulding will understand," said James. "Go on up. Better you get some rest than fall asleep while trying to teach the young'un's."

Alice nodded and headed up the stairs, leaving most of her oatmeal untouched.

"I can't believe Ellie talked," said Dovie as she removed Alice's oatmeal bowl from the table. "I wonder why she won't talk now."

James ran his hands through his hair. "Maybe she got in trouble if she talked before."

"Do you really think that's it, Dad?" asked Dovie, sitting next to him. "I can't even imagine."

"I've heard stories of some pretty awful things people do," said James. "I never wanted to believe them, but I think we have to figure out what actually happened to Ellie before we can help her."

"How are you going to go about that?" asked Dovie. "Guess we could try asking her now that we know she can talk."

James shook his head. "Not sure that's the right way to go about it. Could give her more nightmares, or make her scared that we'll send her away if we know what really happened."

"Then what are we going to do?" asked Dovie.

"Well, we're coming up on the holidays so nothing right away, but I think I'll go down to Amarillo and visit the Children's Bureau in January. Maybe a conversation with Mrs. Waterman will shed some light on what's happened to her," said James.

"But she said she didn't know," said Dovie. "We asked her when Ellie arrived. Seems like an awful long trip to take when she's already told us she knows nothing."

James nodded. "I'm not sure she was being completely honest with us then. I'm hoping that she'll have some more information now that she sees Ellie isn't going anywhere."

"I can't believe she'd lie to us," said Dovie. "What would be the purpose of that?"

"She didn't know us," said James. "She might have thought we'd turn her away if Ellie had a troubled past. People do that. We may not want to think about it, but people don't want the trouble."

Dovie got up and walked to the sink. "I don't know, Dad, you could be chasing gnats."

"Guess those will be my gnats to chase then," said James as he got up and walked out the back door.

As James walked to the barn, he thought about Ellie, sure that Mrs. Waterman had withheld crucial information regarding Ellie's past. There were more people than he cared to admit that would reject a child simply due to a troubled past, even if that past was not of the child's doing.

Looking around for Bill and Elmer, James stopped in his tracks. He didn't know which way to go. The barn layout confused him. As he tried to get his bearings, the barn began to tilt. James grabbed for Poppy's stall, but he was unable to hold on. It was as if his fingers forgot how to grasp onto things.

James fell to his knees before leaning over and falling into a loose stack of hay. He tried to call out, but his mouth wouldn't form the right words. He knew what he wanted to say, but all that escaped from his lips were words he didn't recognize. As he looked at the ceiling, he prayed to God that his time wasn't done.

Chapter Fourteen

Norman waddled into the barn to see if he could steal some of the morning grain Poppy received during milking. Once he spotted James lying in the hay, he immediately started honking. Norman toddled over to James, quieted his honk, and nudged his arm. When James could barely turn and look at him, Norman went into full alert mode. He honked even louder and raised his wings, flapping wildly as he moved toward the exit of the barn.

Norman ran straight out of the barn and into his nemesis, Daisy the pig. Norman narrowed his eyes at Daisy and honked out his alert. With wide eyes, Daisy began to squeal and charged toward the house. She ran up the stairs and rammed the back door.

"What in the world?" asked Dovie as she stepped onto the stoop to investigate. Daisy ran down the stairs to Norman who was still frantically honking around the barn door.

"What is going on?" asked Bill, coming around the corner due to the commotion.

"I don't know," said Dovie. "Daisy rammed the door, and I came out here to see Norman acting like a fool by the barn. Do you think there's a fox in there?"

Bill grabbed a hoe that was leaning against the house. "I'll go check it out."

Norman let out another loud honk and flung his wings up as he ran into the barn. He stood by James and continued to honk until Bill entered the barn.

Dovie watched Bill creep into the barn before throwing the hoe down and calling for her. Recognizing the panic in his voice, she ran down the steps and followed Bill inside, knowing it was much more than a wild animal. It took a moment for her eyes to adjust and fall on her father lying in the hay.

"Oh, God, no! Dad!" She rushed to James's side, pelting him with questions. "Dad, can you hear me? What's wrong? Did you fall? Where does it hurt? Can you talk?"

James opened his mouth to speak. "Imma dibbersh ksigh."

"What's he saying?" asked Bill.

"We don't understand, Dad," said Dovie. She looked at Bill. "Help me get him in the house. Then run into town and phone for the doctor."

"Is he going to be okay?" asked Bill as he placed James's arm around his shoulders.

Dovie did the same on the other side. "I don't know." She looked at her father. "Dad, we're going to stand you up now. Try to walk with us, okay?" She looked to Bill. "On the count of three."

When Dovie said "three," she and Bill rose together and lifted James. Dovie was glad that, although unstable, James remained standing and, with clumsy feet, walked with them toward the house.

"Mr. James," Alice gasped from the doorway, "are you okay? I heard Mr. Norman and Daisy making a fuss out here and had to see what was going on."

"Not sure yet," answered Dovie. "We need to get him to bed, then Bill's gonna fetch the doctor. Get him some water please, Alice."

Alice held the door open before rushing to the sink and getting some water in a tin mug.

The moment James was safely on his bed, Bill rushed off to get the doctor. Dovie silently cursed herself for not getting a phone installed at Quail Crossings when the phone lines went in. She couldn't stand the shrill sound of it ringing in Johnson's Drug Store all the time. She hardly ate lunch there anymore due to its constant interruptions. But right now she'd give anything to hear its high-pitched noise.

Alice walked over with the water as Dovie placed her head on James's chest.

"How is he?" whispered Alice.

"His heart is beating really fast," said Dovie, "but that's to be expected with all this excitement. Hush now, and let me listen to his breathing."

She laid her head again on James's chest and was relieved to find his breathing wasn't labored. Her heart leapt as James's hand fell on her head. She looked up and gazed into her father's eyes. "Say something, Dad."

"I ...," he took his time as if searching and forcing the right words to come. "I ... okay."

Dovie could see the relief in her father's eyes as the sentence came out correctly instead of in gibberish. She grabbed his left hand. "Can you squeeze my hand, Dad?"

His eyes fell to their entwined hand. She could tell he was trying, but his fingers remained limp.

"It's okay, Dad," she said softly. "The doctor will be here soon, and we'll figure out what's going on. You just rest."

"Alice, could you get me a wet cloth, please," asked Dovie and to her surprise, Ellie handed her one immediately. Dovie looked at Ellie. "Thank you."

Ellie nodded.

Dovie noticed the lack of color in Ellie's skin and how she trembled when she handed her the cloth. "Are you okay, Ellie?"

Again Ellie nodded and then pointed to James.

"We're doing all we can right now," said Dovie. "Please try not to worry."

Ellie gave one more slow nod, but Dovie could tell she was still worried. She couldn't blame the girl, Dovie was more than concerned for her father.

"What can we do?" asked Alice, her voice cracking.

"We keep him comfortable until the doctor gets here," said Dovie. "Ellie, would you mind starting some chicken broth?"

Ellie hurried into the kitchen without hesitation.

"I think I'll help Ellie," said Alice.

"I … okay," James repeated again, giving Alice a small crooked smile.

"How 'bout I turn on the radio, Dad," said Dovie. "Give us something to listen to until the doctor gets here."

James gave her a single nod as she went into the parlor and searched the radio stations for some country music. Finding *Oklahoma Hills* by Jack Guthrie, she turned it up just enough for her father to hear it. She loved the western swing almost as much as her father did and prayed the upbeat song would put them all at ease.

Dovie watched her father as he lay motionless on the bed. She had never seen him so still. As thankful as she was that he was resting, she wished he would tap his foot, or even just a finger, to the music. She longed to hear him say her name and start up a conversation. Dovie looked to the ceiling and said a silent prayer that her father would pull through and make a full recovery. She wasn't sure what exactly ailed him. This was beyond anything her mother had taught her about natural remedies and patching folks up. She had never felt so helpless.

It felt like a million songs had played when Bill finally came in with the doctor. She looked at the clock and saw that less than an hour had gone by.

"Thanks for coming so quickly, Dr. Hushton," said Dovie.

"Thankfully the Richards have a telephone," said Dr. Hushton. "My nurse was able to catch me there, so I wasn't too far away." He looked down at James. "So what have you gotten yourself into Mr. Murphy?"

"He's had some kind of spell," answered Dovie.

James raised up on the bed into a reclining position with Dovie hovering by his side.

"Not … sure," James said slowly, but Dovie could tell he had some confidence in his words again. "Went to … barn looking … don't remember … but … confused … dizzy. Tried to grab stall … fingers wouldn't work."

Dr. Hushton nodded. "Did you holler for help? Could you talk?"

"He tried to talk once we found him, but it didn't make sense," said Dovie. "I couldn't understand it, and he's still not talking like normal, although it's a load better than before."

"How so?" asked the doctor. "Were the wrong words coming out or was it all gibberish."

"Gibberish," answered Dovie. "They weren't really words at all."

"Can you squeeze my hand now?" asked Dr. Hushton. "How did you get inside? Did you walk or did someone carry you?"

"Bill and I were able to walk him inside," said Dovie. "He held some weight, but it was a bit clumsy. I don't think he could've walked in on his own."

Dovie watched as James attempted to squeeze the doctor's hand with his right hand and then his left. Dr. Hushton continued to test James's motor skills before shining a small light into each of James's eyes.

"What happened right before you went out to the barn?" asked Dr. Hushton.

"Talking about …." James looked to Dovie, confusion in his eyes.

"Ellie," Dovie clarified. "Ellie is part of the Brewer family, and she's only been with us a short time. She had a nightmare last night and Alice had to calm her down. We were talking about how we could help her."

The doctor tilted his head back and forth. "So a stressful conversation then? Adding another mouth to feed can be a burden to bear, especially one that's keeping you up at night."

"No," said Dovie. "I mean, we want to help her know she's safe, and Dad talked about going to Amarillo after the holidays to see if we could find out more about her past. Then he went to the barn."

"Well, Mr. Murphy," said Dr. Hushton as he wiped his hands on a handkerchief. "I believe your daughter was right.

You did indeed have a spell. From what I can tell it was a pretty small one, but we'll need to keep an eye on you for a few weeks. For now I want you to rest and let your body heal. I'll be back tomorrow to check on you."

"Thank you, doctor," said James, as he started to get out of bed.

"Hey now," said Dr. Hushton. "I told you to rest. Your daughter can see me out."

Dovie walked the doctor out to his car. "I'll be back tomorrow to check on him. Just keep him resting, with plenty of fluids and food to help him get his strength back."

"So will he really get back to normal?" asked Dovie, wringing her apron.

Dr. Hushton pursed his lips. "You know, we really don't know much about these types of spells except that they seem to happen without much rhyme or reason. He could have another one, a stronger one that causes paralysis, or he could live out the rest of his days without any problems. I can't say for certain."

Dovie bit her lip, fighting the tears that began to form. Dr. Hushton put his hand gently on her shoulder. "Mrs. Grant, I don't see cause for too much worry. His speech is back. He'll still be a bit slow coming up with the right words, but I believe it will get better. Also, he can still grasp with his left hand. It's weak but the movement is there. These are all good signs. Just keep him rested." He gave her a reassuring pat. "I'll check in tomorrow."

"Would you like some lunch?" asked Dovie, remembering her manners. "I asked Ellie to start some chicken broth for Dad, and I swear she made a feast for the rest of us while the soup was cooking."

Dr. Hushton shook his head. "Thank you, but I have other patients to check on, so some other time." He rubbed his jaw. "Let me ask you about the girl."

"Ellie?" Dovie cocked her head.

"Yes, you said she's experiencing nightmares?" asked the doctor.

Dovie nodded. "She had one last night. Quite a doozy to hear Alice tell it."

"Have you asked the girl what happened to her?" asked Dr. Hushton.

"She doesn't speak," said Dovie. "Well, I guess she does. She did in her sleep last night, but she doesn't normally."

"Interesting," said Dr. Hushton. "What did she say?"

Dovie shrugged. "You'd have to ask Alice, but from what I reckon it was just 'no' and 'stop'. Why?"

"I'm just curious. You know a lot of kids had it very rough during the Depression. Some never get over it and have to be institutionalized. Has she acted out otherwise? Caused any problems for you and your family? There are places that will take children like her. I can arrange it for you, if need be."

Dovie narrowed her eyes. "Doctor, Ellie's been the picture of helpful around here. She always does what she's asked, and we've never had any problems. I don't like where you're going with your questions. She's family and we're not sending her anywhere."

The doctor raised his hands in surrender. "Okay, I understand and was just trying to help. All I was saying is if she's a source of stress, it's stress Mr. Murphy doesn't need right now."

"Dad only wants the best for Ellie," said Dovie, "as we all do. Besides sending her away would only cause him more stress. He wouldn't like it."

"All right then, I'll see you tomorrow."

Dovie watched the doctor drive away and steadied her breath. As thankful as she was he had come to Quail Crossings, she didn't appreciate him acting like Ellie was the cause of James's episode.

Turning toward the house, she stopped short as she saw Ellie standing on the other side of the screen door. She didn't know how long Ellie had been standing there, but from the tears streaming down Ellie's face, she knew it had been too long.

Before Dovie could comfort the girl and explain, Ellie barreled out of the door and ran into the barn. Dovie started after her.

"Mama Dovie," said Alice from the doorway. "Mr. James is asking for you."

Dovie reluctantly turned away. Ellie would have to wait.

Ellie ran into the barn, thankful she had hidden Lovey there that morning after her nightmare. Now that Alice knew she could talk, she had to be more careful about where she spoke to Lovey.

She climbed into the loft and crawled into the secret spot in the hay bales. Digging through the hay, she found the shoebox she was looking for, quickly opened it up, and hugged Lovey.

"They mean to send me away," she cried. "They think I'm too much for James to be around."

Ellie rocked as she listened to her doll. "But what if they do? Alice knows I can talk, and what if they think I'm not right in the head and send me away with him. I can't go. I can't go with him."

Taking a deep breath, Ellie nodded. "You're right. Momma Dovie said she wasn't sending us anywhere. I just need to be extra helpful and make sure they know I'm a good girl." Ellie continued to rock back and forth whispering. "I'm a good girl. I'm a good girl. I'm a good girl."

Chapter Fifteen

Elmer stared at James lying on the bed and concentrated on the rise and fall of his chest. As long as James's chest continued to rise and fall, then everything would be okay. Soon Elmer's own breath seemed to match James's and muffled voices began to fill the air. Elmer's eyes grew wide as James's bedroom morphed into rows of makeshift hospital beds.

The groans of men with various wounds grew louder as doctors shouted orders at nurses. The nurses ran back and forth, trying to get all the necessary supplies needed to save the lives of the soldiers lying in the cots.

Elmer walked the row and covered his mouth with his hand as he witnessed missing limbs and craters in men's stomachs. They reached out to him, begging for medicine, for their mothers, and some even for death.

Rubbing his face, Elmer hurried back to James's bed.

"Doctor, it looks bad," whispered a nurse as she leaned over James to speak confidentially to the doctor. "Looks like he's taken a direct hit to the chest. He's lost so much blood. I don't think we can save him."

Elmer shook his head. James hadn't been shot. He had collapsed in the barn, so why were they in this hospital? The doctor had come and gone, expecting James to make a full recovery.

Elmer took a step towards James and watched as James's face was replaced with the face of Thomas Pope.

"No!" shouted Elmer. "What did you do?"

"Elm?"

A gentle hand touched his shoulder, and Elmer swung around to see Tiny. She looked so worried and concerned.

"Just look what they're doing to him," he cried, thrusting his arm in James's direction. "They're gonna kill him. He was doing fine and now he's bleeding, and they don't think they can stop it."

Tiny rushed to James's bedside to see about the bleeding. "Elmer, he's not bleeding."

Elmer rubbed his eyes and the military hospital disappeared, leaving only James's bedroom. "I'm sorry," said Elmer. "I thought I was somewhere else, I guess. Maybe I fell asleep."

"On your feet?" asked Tiny. "Elm, please tell me what's going on."

Elmer shook his head. "I just get lost sometimes, Mary. I think I'm in one place, but I'm really in another. I guess it's hard for me to forget being over there."

"Over there?" Tiny stepped closer to Elmer. "You mean the war. Sometimes you still feel like you're fighting the war?"

Elmer nodded and fought the tears that threatened to give away exactly how scared he was, not just for himself, but also for James.

"Forget it," said Elmer. "I didn't sleep well last night, and I'm just worried about James. I'm not thinking straight. I just need some coffee." He turned and left James's room.

"Elmer, we should talk about this," said Tiny as she hurried after him. "If you're seeing things that aren't there, we need to speak to the doctor, or maybe someone down at the veterans' hospital."

"I don't need to talk about it at all," said Elmer, as he skipped the coffee and walked right out the back door. "I just need some air. I'm fine."

"What's going on?" asked Alice, looking up from her notebook.

"Just your brother being stubborn," said Tiny. "What are you doing? School work?"

Alice shook her head. "I'm writing to Jacob and letting him know what happened with Mr. James. I think he'd want to know, and maybe he'll come home or at least respond."

"I like that you keep writing to him," said Tiny.

"You do?" Alice raised an eyebrow. "You're the first person who hasn't tried to get me to stop."

Tiny shrugged. "I like Jacob and I hope he's doing well. There could be a million reasons he hasn't responded, and since I worked in logistics for the Nurse Corps, I also know all those letters could be sitting in a warehouse somewhere."

"You mean the military isn't delivering them?" Alice's eyes grew wide.

"It was hard enough to get mail as a white service man," said Tiny. "Pretty sad that all those colored boys were risking their lives, fighting for our country, and they couldn't even get mail. We had this woman who cleaned our offices named Jamella. She was sharp as a tack. I remember one night I was working late trying to get a unit of nurses closer to the battle lines. I had a whole corkboard devoted to it. I thought if I could get the nurses closer to the wounded, maybe we wouldn't lose as many men. She came right up, studied the board for a minute, and then asked why they couldn't come in on the same landing crafts as the soldiers."

Tiny laughed at the memory. "And you know what? It made perfect sense. Have the landing crafts drop the soldiers and then go back for the nurses once the battle had died down. And that's exactly what the Army started doing. But did Jamella get credit for it? No, cause she was colored. Neither did I, for that matter, as the suggestion moved up the lines, I was left out of the credits. But at least I wasn't having to mop floors just because I was colored. Every time I had a tough assignment, I stayed late and ran over options with Jamella."

"So what happened to her?" asked Alice.

"Oh, she's probably still there mopping floors," said Tiny. "But you keep writing Jacob. Who knows? One day maybe Jamella herself will deliver them."

"Ellie, are you up here?" asked Dovie as she climbed the loft ladder. "We need to talk about what you heard."

Ellie climbed out of the hay bales as Dovie reached the top. Dovie's heart ached as she saw Ellie's face, red and swollen from crying. She wished she could have come sooner to talk to Ellie, but her dad had needed tending to. Dovie walked over and gestured for Ellie to sit beside her on the bales.

"Look, Ellie," said Dovie. "I don't know what all you heard when I was talking to the doctor, but you need to know we would never send you away. You've been nothing but an asset to this farm and to our family. We don't ever want to see you leave. Understand?"

Ellie bowed her head.

"You need to understand that you are not a burden on our household. I'm not sure how I got everything done before you came to live here. If you were to leave, that would be a burden to Quail Crossings. Honey, we want you here. Don't ever think anything else. You're family and this is your home. That's never gonna change."

Dovie wondered if she should hug Ellie. She wanted to with all her might, but she was concerned how Ellie would take it. Dovie chastised herself for overthinking the situation and wrapped Ellie in a big hug before the girl could react. To her relief, Ellie's arms wrapped around Dovie and squeezed her tight.

"Right then," said Dovie, breaking the embrace. "You okay now?"

Ellie nodded.

"It's lunch time, and I don't know about you, but I could eat a horse," said Dovie. "So Tex just better watch out."

Dovie playfully tweaked Ellie's nose and her heart leapt as Ellie giggled.

Chapter Sixteen

Evalyn paced the room, bouncing a fussy Caleb on her hip as everyone else ate the supper that Ellie and Alice had prepared.

"This is all my fault," she said, biting her lip.

"What is?" asked Dovie with a tilt of her head. "Caleb? Nonsense, ten-month-olds get fussy all the time. He's probably just teething."

"No, James." Evalyn gestured to James's bedroom door where he was resting. "I shouldn't have insisted on Rockwood being rebuilt right now. We have enough on our plates just waiting to hear from Robert. Why do I have to be so selfish? I do this all the time. I get a thought in my head, and then I just go for it without thinking of anyone else. I did it when we first got here when I tried to get Bill fired so we could go to California."

"Which was never gonna happen," said Bill.

"I did it again when I married Robert without talking to y'all," continued Evalyn, "and then with Rockwood. I just had to have it built so we could move in. Sure we're happy living there, and I'm glad we did it for Robert, but it could've waited."

"Could it?" Lou Anne asked gently.

"Of course it could," snapped Evalyn. "No one was rushing us out of here."

"Evie, look around," said Lou Anne.

Evalyn took in the controlled chaos that was a typical meal time at Quail Crossings. Joy, Annabelle, and Dean squabbled in the parlor at the kids' table as Ellie sat quietly, while the adults sat elbow to elbow at the long kitchen table. Even with Evalyn, Robert, and James missing from the table, it was a tight fit.

"We will always love Quail Crossings," said Bill. "And this will always be our home away from home, but you have to admit we've outgrown the place."

"Now who's talkin' nonsense?" said Dovie, throwing her napkin down before standing. She picked up her plate and walked to the sink. "Our flock has grown large, that's true, but you all will never outgrow Quail Crossings. I don't care if we're walking around bumping elbows, we'll make room. Besides, it does Dad's heart good to see this house full. It's something we thought we'd lost when Simon and Helen died."

A hush fell over the room as Dovie paused at the sound of her own voice saying the names of her lost family. It wasn't often she said their names out loud. Evalyn watched her take a deep breath and felt herself breathing with her. Evalyn had never known Dovie's husband and child whose untimely death had rocked both Dovie and James to their cores. But over the past ten years, after hearing many stories of their lives, Evalyn felt she knew them and also felt the pain of their loss.

"It's the truth," continued Dovie. "Y'all think we saved you by giving y'all work and a home. But y'all saved us right back. So I don't want any of you to ever feel like you're a burden on Dad or me, you hear?"

Everyone nodded.

"That being said," countered Lou Anne. "Maybe we should take turns bringing the little ones around. Just until James feels better. I know he wants to see them but maybe not all at once right now. It's a lot of noise, even for a healthy soul."

"We can also take turns bringing dinner over, so y'all don't have to worry about all the cooking," said Evalyn.

"And then have a potluck on Sundays," Alice suggested, "where everyone comes. I'm gonna miss not seeing y'all every day."

"We're right across the pasture, Alice," said Bill.

"Evie's not. Rockwood is a good five miles from here," said Alice, "and it won't be long till Elm and Tiny move into the Clark's place on their own and will be too busy to visit."

"Alice, it's not forever, and you and Ellie can come to Rockwood any time," said Evalyn. "I may need you to watch the kids while I run into town. Would that work?"

Alice nodded with a smile.

"All right." Dovie said as she wiped her hands on a towel. "That sounds okay for now, but if y'all start becoming strangers I'll hunt you down like a hawk on a rabbit."

Everyone laughed as Dovie grabbed a clean plate from the cabinet and started to fill it for James.

"Do you think he'll eat that?" asked Evalyn. "Wouldn't broth be better?"

Dovie smiled. "You know what Dad says, 'You can't be healthy without a healthy soul, and nothing feeds the soul better than good food.' So I think he'll appreciate this a lot more than chicken broth." She looked at Alice since Ellie was in the other room. "You girls did a mighty fine job."

"It was all Ellie," said Alice. "I just helped her a bit."

"Well, I think she's earned a seat at the big table, don't y'all?" said Elmer. "Ellie, come on in here and eat with us, will ya?"

As Ellie brought her plate in, wearing a big smile, Evalyn couldn't help but notice Tiny's slightly green face. Evalyn walked around the table to her sister-in-law, bent over, and whispered. "You okay?"

"I walked in here starving, but now I'm feeling kind of sick," confessed Tiny. "You don't think it's the food do you? I mean, I love meat loaf, but right now, the smell of it ...," Tiny wrinkled her nose. "I think it's bad."

Evalyn smiled and shook her head. "The food is just fine. Come on. Caleb needs a walk, and I could use the company." Evalyn looked at everyone else. "We're gonna take a walk. Save me a plate, will you?"

Bill smiled at his sister. "You know better than to leave food around these folks and expect there to be any left."

"You mean, I know better than to leave food around *you* and expect there to be any left," teased Evalyn.

"Are you okay, Mary?" asked Elmer.

"She's fine," said Evalyn. "I just don't want to walk alone, and it seems Tiny could use some fresh air."

They had no sooner gotten outside, when Tiny ran to the shed and threw up in the pig slop pile.

Joy watched Ellie enter the kitchen as her mom and Tiny left out the back door. As soon as the door shut behind them, she leaned in and whispered to Dean and Annabelle. "Let's go see Papa James."

"We ain't supposed to," said Dean. "He's restin'."

"Papa James needs us," said Joy. "When Momma gets all sad about Daddy being gone, I give her a hug, and she says it's the perfect cure for what ails her. So if Papa James is sick, then all he needs is a hug from all of us."

Dean scratched his head. "I don't wannna get in trouble."

"You won't," said Joy. "Once Papa James is all better, they'll be happy we went in there to hug him."

"I don't know," said Dean. "Still sounds like I'm gonna get in trouble, and you don't want to see my ma mad."

"Aunt Lou Anne wouldn't hurt a fly," said Joy.

"You ain't seen her when she's mad," emphasized Dean. "And I've seen her kill flies, lots of 'em."

"Fine, you sit there like a scaredy cat," said Joy, taking Annabelle's hand and tiptoeing towards James's room. "We'll go, and you can stay here. Just don't tell."

"I ain't no tattletale," said Dean, hurrying over to join the girls. "And I ain't no scaredy cat."

Joy gently pushed open James's door and all three of them scurried inside before she pushed it closed with a small click.

"He ain't movin'," whispered Dean. "Is he dead?"

"I don't think everyone would be laughin' in the kitchen if Papa James was dead," Joy whispered back.

"They would be if they don't know he's dead," snapped Dean before clamping his hands over his mouth.

Annabelle's lip started to shake.

"Now you've gone and done it," scolded Joy before turning to Annabelle. "It's okay. Annabelle, please don't cry."

"I don't want Papa James to be dead," Annabelle wailed.

James rose to his elbow. "Anna ... belle, ... hon - come ... here."

"He's a mummy!" Dean cried before bolting from the room.

"Dean, you dummy, he ain't a mummy because he was never dead," yelled Joy.

Annabelle ran to James's bedside and scrambled up beside him as fast as her three-year-old legs would allow. She hugged his neck tightly, causing James to fall back on his pillow.

"You okay?" Annabelle asked as her tears fell on her rosy cheeks.

James managed a small nod. "Don't worry."

"What in the world is going on in here?" asked Dovie, one hand on her hip while the other held James's freshly filled plate. "Dean almost made me drop Dad's plate. You kids aren't supposed to be in here while Dad's resting."

"Dean said Papa James was dead," wailed Annabelle.

"Shh ... Annabelle," said James. "Don't cry."

"I just don't want you to be dead like Uncle Robert," said Annabelle through her tears.

"Uncle Robert?" Dovie walked to Annabelle, setting James's plate on the bedside table.

"That's a lie!" screamed Joy. "My daddy's not dead."

"Everyone simmer down," said Dovie as Bill entered the room holding Dean by his shirt collar.

"What is going on?" asked Bill.

"Tell her to take it back," cried Joy.

Dovie hurried to Joy and wrapped her in a hug. "Annabelle is just a baby. She doesn't know what she's saying. We are praying every day for your daddy's safe return."

"I'm not a baby," said Annabelle, pouting her lips. "I'm big and Dean told me that Uncle Robert is dead like those people on that radio show."

"What radio show?" Bill asked Dean.

"I heard it on the news while you and Papa James were listening," Dean mumbled. "They said that most of the missing soldiers were dead."

"Billy Dean Brewer, I can't believe you would tell Annabelle that," said Lou Anne from the doorway.

"Tell your cousin you're sorry," demanded Bill.

"For what?" asked Dean. "I didn't do nothin'. It was her idea to come in here."

Bill narrowed his eyes at his son. "Unless you want a whoopin' you will apologize to Joy for telling Annabelle that her daddy is dead. We don't say things like that, especially when they ain't true. Your Uncle Robert went to war to fight for our great country and you will respect his name, you hear. Now apologize to your cousin."

Dean turned to Joy whose cheeks were still wet with tears. "I'm sorry I said your daddy was dead. I didn't mean it."

Joy buried her head in Dovie's shoulder as she nodded an acceptance of the apology.

"Good, and tomorrow you can clean out both chicken coops," said Bill.

"I didn't do nothin'," whined Dean.

"You sassed me," said Bill, "and for that sass you'll be cleaning the coops for the rest of the month."

"But …"

"Son," said Lou Anne pushing through the crowd. "Learn when to stop talking. Now give Papa James a hug and let's go home. It's time for Annabelle and Rosey to go to bed."

Dean and Annabelle gave James hugs before leaving with their parents. Evalyn and Tiny entered as Bill's family left.

"What did we miss?" asked Evalyn, eyeing the situation and spotting Joy's swollen tear-streaked face. "Baby, what happened?"

"She's okay," answered Dovie. "They were concerned about Dad, and Annabelle said something she shouldn't have. It's all settled now."

Joy ran to Evalyn. "Momma, I miss Daddy."

Evalyn handed Caleb to Tiny and bent to hug her daughter. "So do I, baby girl, so do I."

"He's coming home, right?" Joy asked, eyes wide with hope.

"You can bet your bottom dollar that he is doing everything in his power to get back to us," said Evalyn firmly. "Don't stop believing that Joy, not even for one minute, no matter what anyone says." Evalyn pulled Joy in for another hug. "He's coming back, baby girl. He's coming back."

Chapter Seventeen

"Dovie!" cried James. "Dovie, get in here right now!"

Dovie rushed into her father's room, concerned he might be having another spell. It had been just under two weeks since his fall in the barn. He was gaining strength in his left hand but still had problems walking very far without feeling fatigued. Of course Dovie's main problem was that James kept trying to do everything as he normally had, and he just wasn't ready yet. It was hard to convince James of that.

"What's wrong?" asked Dovie, feeling slightly out of breath after running from the back stoop.

"Everything," snapped James, rummaging through his dresser. "Where are my pants? I've checked in my drawers and closet. I haven't got one pair, not even my Sunday suit."

Dovie tried to swallow her smile. "You can have them when the doctor gets here. Until then, I've hidden them so you will rest."

"Now you listen here," said James. "I've got to talk to Bill and I need my pants. I can't be walking all over Quail Crossings in my skivvies."

"No, you listen," said Dovie, placing her hands on her hips. "The doctor has told you repeatedly to rest. Orders which you have failed to follow on a number of occasions. Just yesterday I found you walking to the chicken coop to fetch the eggs. We've got a dozen people here fetching eggs, not to mention that it's Dean's chore for being so ugly to Joy."

"That boy did nothing wrong," said James. "He was just repeating what he heard on the …"

Dovie sighed as James searched for the right word. "Radio, Dad. The word you're looking for is radio, and this is exactly why you need to rest. Dr. Hushton said the more you rest the better your chances for a full recovery. Don't you want that?"

"Of course I do," said James. "But it's very important that I talk to Bill. We have the cattle sale coming up."

"Fine," said Dovie. "Get back in bed under the sheet and I will send him in."

"Dovie Grant, you are my daughter, and I'm ordering you to give me my pants," said James with a huff.

"Well, father dear, I guess if you want them you'll have to come out here in your skivvies and find them," said Dovie. "I'll let Bill know you need to speak with him right away, so you might want to go ahead and crawl back in bed."

Dovie left James's room and headed into the kitchen. She couldn't help but shake her head at her father's persistence in trying to work when he was supposed to be resting.

"Can I go see Mr. James?" asked Alice, as she placed her breakfast plate in the sink. "I just want to tell him good-bye before I go to school. Not seeing him walk around the farm makes me feel lost."

Dovie gave Alice a sympathetic smile. "Of course, dear. I know it's been hard watching him go through this, but hopefully all this rest will result in a full recovery. I know he's actin' like he's got ants in his pants."

Alice laughed. "If only he could find his pants!"

Dovie laughed with her. "Don't you go telling him where they are either, young lady. He'll never think to look in the pantry behind the sauerkraut. He can't stand the stuff."

"I promise," said Alice.

Dovie watched Alice walk towards James's room before she turned to walk outside. It was still really nice for November. She couldn't believe their luck. Maybe they would have a mild winter. Life had been so hard on folks, a nice mild winter would be welcome.

Before Dovie could make it to the barn, Dr. Hushton pulled up in his dark gray car. As happy as she was to see Dr. Hushton, she knew James wouldn't be happy about her not getting Bill like she said she would. But the doctor's visit trumped anything James might need to say to Bill.

"Dr. Hushton, how nice to see you," said Dovie, shading her eyes from the bright morning sun. "Would you like some coffee?"

"Thank you, Mrs. Grant," said Dr. Hushton. "That would be lovely. I'm afraid I got called out very early this morning, and Annette's Café was closed when I drove through town."

"I hope your early call turned out okay," said Dovie, opening the back door for the doctor.

"Just a case of indigestion, but Mr. Harlow was sure he was having a heart attack," said Dr. Hushton.

Dovie gestured for him to have a seat at the table. "Let us get you some breakfast too, then." She turned to Ellie who stood in the corner. "Ellie dear, would you mind frying Dr. Hushton a couple of eggs?"

Ellie hurried to the stove immediately and started the eggs.

"We've got a bit of bacon left over and some biscuits," said Dovie. "I'm sorry we haven't any gravy left, but I've got some homemade apple butter and Ellie can fry a mean egg."

"Thank you much, Mrs. Grant," said Dr. Hushton. "How are things going with young Ellie? Any words spoken yet?"

Dovie handed the doctor a mug of coffee. "No, but we communicate just fine. Her sisters, Alice and Evalyn, are schooling her here at home. Unfortunately, she's not quite ready for traditional school, but she'll get there soon enough."

"Perhaps a boarding school would be the way to go," said Dr. Hushton. "Something that specializes in situations like hers. She could really benefit from that type of institution."

Dovie placed fresh silverware and a cloth napkin on the table and then sat across from the doctor. "I think she's benefiting quite nicely here, being able to spend time with the family she never knew. I do have some concerns about Dad though."

Ellie quickly set the finished plate of bacon, fresh eggs, and biscuits in front of the doctor, then hurried and stood in the corner.

"Ellie, dear, why don't you go outside and see if Bill needs any help," said Dovie. She could tell Ellie didn't care for the doctor. Of course, why would she? Dovie was certain Ellie had heard the doctor suggest she be sent away. Even now he was talking about sending her away to boarding school. "Thank you for breakfast. I'll get the dishes."

Alice walked into the kitchen.

"Boy are you in trouble." She smiled at Dovie. "He is not happy about the pant situation."

Dovie blushed as Dr. Hushton chuckled behind his napkin.

"I hid his pants," she confessed, "because he wouldn't rest."

"Well, that is one way to do it," said Dr. Hushton.

Alice grabbed her jacket and book satchel. She gave Dovie a kiss on the cheek and hurried out the door to meet the bus.

"So let's talk about Dad," said Dovie. "I have a few questions."

Dr. Hushton smiled. "Of course you do."

Dovie found herself blushing again. "I'm afraid you'll have to excuse me. Dr. Crowly was used to my questions. Of course, usually I was asking so I could learn."

"Have you nurse training?" asked Dr. Hushton.

Dovie shook her head. "My ma was the local healer until she died, and then I just kind of inherited the reputation for knowing what to do in a bad situation. It was hard to get a doctor up here from Tucket before Dr. Crowly and yourself, so we just kind of had to fend for ourselves."

"Well, you need not do that any longer," said Dr. Hushton. "In fact, I must insist you don't. Since you don't have proper medical training you could be doing more harm than good."

"I assure you doctor, I know when I'm in over my head," said Dovie, trying to keep the conversation light. "That is why you were called when Dad had his episode, but I've tended many a person through influenza, chicken pox, and broken bones without incident."

Dr. Hushton wiped his mouth and placed his napkin on his plate. "I believe you've been lucky up till now. Just call me and I'll see to the medical treatment from now on." He got up before Dovie could respond. "Now, let's see about your father."

Chapter Eighteen

Thanksgiving Day, 1945

"Mama Dovie!" squealed Joy as she rushed through the back door.

Dovie opened her arms and swallowed the little girl up into a hug. "Sweet Joy, girl it feels like it's been a month of Sundays since the last time I saw you."

"It's only been a week," said Evalyn, carrying in two pumpkin pies. Ellie walked in behind her, carrying two more and giving Dovie her customary greeting of a silent smile. "Sorry, to miss Sunday's potluck, but Ellie and I were up to our elbows in pumpkin."

"Did you get all your deliveries made?" asked Dovie.

Evalyn nodded as she placed the pies on a long dresser the men had moved into the parlor to use as a serving line during their Sunday potlucks. It worked a lot better than everyone trying to crowd around the table to fill their plates.

"Who knew the women around here would be so keen on buying pumpkin pies instead of making them themselves?" said Dovie.

"When I lived in California, people bought pies all the time. A lot of people didn't have big kitchens like we have, so they ate out," said Evalyn, taking off her coat. "So I thought I'd try it here, and we did all right, if I do say so myself."

"Well, I'm glad to hear it," said Dovie. "How much do I owe you for ours?"

Evalyn gave Dovie a playful slap with her apron before tying it on. "Don't insult me, Dovie. I'm happy to make pies for the family. Just don't make me stuff the turkey." She laughed. "I've always found that process to be disgusting. Maybe it's because I know too much about fowl."

"You've got a deal, especially since it's already in the oven" said Dovie.

"How's James doing today?" Evalyn pulled three jars of green beans from the pantry as Ellie busied herself folding some dish towels from the clean laundry basket.

"He's doing really good," said Dovie, before laughing. "So good I think he's bored. There's only so much he can read and so many card games he can play alone before he gets all fidgety and starts taking short walks to the barn looking for something to do. Thankfully, Bill and Elm have everything running like a finely oiled machine, so Dad can't find anything too strenuous to work on. Let's just say all the tools in the shed are fixed, as well as my squeaky cabinet doors." Dovie opened and closed one to demonstrate.

"So he's getting around okay?" asked Evalyn.

"He's still very slow, but he's lifting that left foot further off the ground," answered Dovie. "He's not gonna win any races, but he's made a lot of improvement."

"I'm so glad he is feeling better," said Evalyn as she seasoned the green beans. "These are ready to go when we're ready to put them on."

"Good," said Dovie. "Do you mind helping me with the potatoes? I swear we'll need a whole bag to feed this brood."

Ellie picked up a paring knife and started peeling. Evalyn placed a gentle hand on her sister's shoulder, getting her attention. "Ellie, I'm really thankful for all your help with the pies. But it's Thanksgiving, and I really want you to have fun today. I know you're thirteen but go play dolls with Joy or climb trees with Dean."

Ellie shook her head and turned back to her potatoes. Evalyn tapped her again. "I insist."

Dovie nodded eagerly. "So do I."

Ellie's face fell as she put the knife down. Dovie gave Ellie a small smile. It was amazing that even though Ellie never said a word, they had all learned to not only communicate with her, but know exactly how she was feeling without a single word being spoken.

"Ellie," said Dovie, "you don't have to work your fingers to the bone to be a part of this family. You know that right?"

Ellie gave her a half shrug with a noncommittal nod.

"Even more of a reason for you to go do something fun," said Evalyn. "You need to trust us and trust that we want you here because you're family."

"We could read in the barn. It's a nice day for November, and we won't be cold if we sit in the sun by the loft window," said Alice from the stairs. "Is that okay, Mama Dovie?"

"More than okay," said Dovie.

Ellie's face lit up as she grabbed her coat and hurried out the back door.

"Guess she's good with that," said Alice. "Y'all sure you don't need our help? Thanksgiving is a huge meal."

"Oh, don't worry," said Dovie with a sly smile. "You girls can do the dishes after dinner."

"Or you could have the boys do it," said Alice, rolling her eyes. "They never help in the kitchen."

"Fine," said Dovie. "I'm sure the boys wouldn't mind helping in the kitchen if you muck out all the stalls, feed the chickens, slop the pigs, and milk Poppy."

"Okay, okay," said Alice with a sigh, grabbing her own coat. "I'll do the dishes afterwards. I'm going to go read with Ellie now. See what I get for helping my sister learn to read? Dish duty."

"Life is so hard at that age," said Evalyn with a sarcastic laugh. "What I wouldn't give to be a teenager again." Joy ran through the house squealing, followed closely by Dean. Evalyn leaned toward Dovie. "Or better yet a five-year-old." She turned to the children. "Y'all take that nonsense outside. No running in the house."

The children flew out the back door.

"I wouldn't mind having their energy." Dovie stretched her back. "I remember when I could fix up Thanksgiving dinner without breaking a sweat. Now my back aches and my feet hurt. Getting old ain't for the weak, that's for sure."

"I hear you. I wouldn't mind their energy and I'm half your age," said Evalyn.

"Evalyn Smith, just how old do you think I am?" scoffed Dovie, as she flicked water from the potato pan on Evalyn, who squealed out a laugh.

"Oh, I don't know." Evalyn giggled. "How old is Moses? I hear you two were sweethearts in school."

Dovie gasped as she flicked more water onto Evalyn, who let out another squeal before splashing Dovie right back. In the blink of an eye, both Dovie and Evalyn had dropped their paring knives and were splashing handfuls of water onto each other, laughing up a storm.

"Hey now, what's going on here?" came a voice from the door.

Dovie turned, water dripping down her face. "Gabe!" She hurried to him and wrapped her arms around his neck. "What a wonderful surprise!"

"I was hoping you'd see it that way. I sure have missed you," he said before bending down and giving her a passionate kiss.

Evalyn cleared her throat, reminding them they were not alone. Gabe gave her a winning smile. "Happy Thanksgiving, Evie."

"Happy Thanksgiving," said Evalyn as she twisted a towel in her hand, worry etched on her face. "Can't say we expected you back so soon, October seems like yesterday."

Dovie walked to Evalyn and gently took the towel before walking back to Gabe. She began to dab at his uniform, which she had gotten wet. "Not sure I need this anymore, pretty sure all that potato water that was on me is now on you." Dovie bit her lip. "Any word on Robert?"

Gabe slowly shook his head as he looked at Evalyn with sad eyes. "I'm sorry, but no."

Evalyn turned back to the sink and bowed her head.

"But I'm not done searching," Gabe said quickly. "I'm only here because a buddy of mine was flying to Amarillo Air Force Base and asked if I could co-pilot. I couldn't pass up the opportunity, especially since my plane was being stored near there. I was able to fly up this morning, and Pastor Spaulding was kind enough to drive me out here."

"You must have been colder than a lizard on ice flying up there," said Dovie. "Here, come sit by the stove. The turkey is roasting, so it's nice and warm." She looked toward the door. "Is Pastor Spaulding out there talking to Bill? Hope you invited him to dinner."

"I did," said Gabe, "but he and Susan had already accepted an invitation to eat with the Wheatons so he had to rush off."

"I should've asked them to join us weeks ago," said Dovie, walking back to the sink to help with potatoes. "I just wasn't sure where we'd put everyone. I'm thankful it's nice out, so the children can play outside, and we aren't tripping all over each other."

"Speaking of being nice out," said Gabe. "I know you have a big meal to tend to, but do you think we can take a short walk?"

"Go ahead," said Evalyn. "I'll finish the potatoes and start on the yams. Lord knows I'll get more done without you splashing me in the face." She put on a small smile.

Dovie could tell that Evalyn was saddened by the lack of news regarding Robert and hated to leave her.

"Are you sure?" asked Dovie.

Evalyn sighed. "Truth be told, I could use a minute alone, just as much as you could use a minute with Gabe."

Dovie nodded as she took off her apron. She gave Evalyn a little pat on the shoulder. "Okay then, I'll be back in a bit."

Gabe grabbed her hand and led her quickly out the back door and toward the orchard. He didn't slow down until they were among the trees, where he swung her around and kissed her again. "I cannot even express how much I've missed you."

"I missed you too," said Dovie, breathlessly. "I'm so glad you're here. I didn't expect to see you for a minute this Thanksgiving. I had hopes for Christmas but never Thanksgiving. If only you had found Robert, what a joyous Thanksgiving this would be."

Gabe nodded as he walked toward the old bench that had sat in the orchard for decades. James had installed it many years before for Dovie's mother who had loved to watch the birds. They sat.

"I came close," said Gabe. "I traced Robert to a POW camp in Poland."

"And, was he …?" Dovie squeezed Gabe's hand, not sure if she wanted the whole story.

"He could've been there. That area was the last place he was seen by his unit. But all the prisoners were moved right before the end of the war," said Gabe. "The Germans destroyed all the files regarding the prisoners. I can't find any trace of where they might have taken them."

"Oh no," said Dovie. "Sometimes not knowing is harder than knowing. What now?"

Gabe shrugged. "I have to keep looking as long as the army allows me to. I have to know I did everything I could to bring Robert back to his family … our family."

"So you're leaving again," Dovie said, more than asked.

"As soon as I get any type of lead, I'll fly up to Nebraska and catch a transport back to Germany out of Lincoln," said Gabe.

"How much time do you think until you have a lead?" She leaned her head onto Gabe's shoulder, taking in his scent. He smelled of leather with a hint of mint.

"I'm not sure," said Gabe. "Could be tomorrow, could be a month from now."

"Well, that doesn't give us much time," said Dovie, looking up into Gabe's molasses-colored eyes. She loved his eyes. Every time she looked at them, she melted like hot butter. She gently caressed his stubble-covered cheek. "But I'll take all I can get."

Evalyn watched Dovie and Gabe walk toward the orchard and demanded her tears not to fall. It was Thanksgiving Day, and the last thing she needed to do was start feeling sorry for herself because there had been no word about Robert. Gabe could have just as easily come home with bad news.

Evalyn couldn't help but chuckle out loud when she thought of Robert's first Thanksgiving at Quail Crossings. Evalyn had asked Robert to look after Joy, who was just over a year old and getting into everything. Even though he had been to many a family dinner at Quail Crossings, the chaos of cooking the huge meal, mixed with the banter of the men, had really thrown Robert for a loop.

His family had always been small and kept to themselves. They never really celebrated any holiday except for attending special church services on Christmas and Easter.

They hadn't been there an hour when he rushed into the kitchen saying he couldn't find Joy.

"What do you mean, you can't find Joy?" asked Dovie. "She didn't go outside did she?"

"I think we would've noticed the door opening, don't you?" said Evalyn. "She has to be in the house."

Soon everyone was calling for Joy and looking under beds and in closets. It wasn't until Evalyn opened the pantry that she found the little girl, sitting on the floor, with one hand in a large jar of lard, while the other hand poured salt into the jar. As Evalyn looked around the pantry, she saw salt and lard covering the floor and smeared on every jar and shelf that little Joy could reach. It was beyond a mess.

"Oh, Joy," Evalyn said with a sigh.

Robert had peeked over her shoulder and smiled. "There you are, pumpkin!" He looked at Evalyn and kissed her on the cheek. "I'll be right back."

He grabbed some old newspapers and spread them out in a corner of the kitchen. Then he sat Joy on the newspapers and gave her a large dollop of salt lard to play with and looked at Evalyn. "Go back to workin' on dinner. I've got this handled."

He then proceeded to clean the pantry from top to bottom before carrying a giggling Joy at arm's length into Dovie's room to carefully clean her up.

Everyone had been amazed that when Evalyn and Alice offered to help, he had refused stating it had been his fault for letting Joy out of his sight, and he never said an ugly word about the entire situation.

Evalyn wasn't sure what made her love him more, the fact that he hadn't gotten angry with Joy who hadn't known any better, or that he had cleaned up the mess.

She turned back to her potatoes and their current Thanksgiving preparations. When she had first met him she had very much been a mess of lard and salt, but his love had washed that mess away too.

Chapter Nineteen

December 1945

Tiny walked into the kitchen at the Clark Ranch, hugging a bucket as if it were her favorite teddy bear. Elmer buttered some bread and set it in front of her. "Feel like eating?"

Tiny shook her head and sat down. "The very thought of it, makes me want to vomit."

Elmer pulled out the chair across from Tiny's. "Mary, you have to eat for the baby."

"I know what I have to do," snapped Tiny, before resting her head on her arm. "I'm sorry, Elm. It's just I feel so darn lousy. What's the point if I'm just going to throw it all up again? It's not like the baby's getting any of that food."

"We need to talk to the doctor," said Elmer. "Let me drive you to Tucket."

"I can't make it to Tucket," said Tiny, into the wood table. She picked her head up and looked around her childhood home that she now shared with Elmer. "I wish my ma was here."

Elmer knew that Tiny's family moving to Amarillo had been hard on her. Even with all of his family, she still felt lonely and longed for her mother. Elmer couldn't help but think if Tiny would just bond with Dovie the way Lou Anne did, she wouldn't miss her mother so much.

"Let's go talk to Dovie then," said Elmer. "She's bound to have a remedy."

"I don't want to bother her," said Tiny. "She's dealing with James's health and Ellie."

"James is just fine," said Elmer. "In fact, knowing him as well as I do, he's aching for some work to do. He can't hardly stand all this restin'. And what about Ellie?"

Tiny rolled her eyes. "Elm, she's dumb. She ain't said a word since she got here."

Elmer fought the urge to narrow his eyes at his wife. He knew she was struggling with the pregnancy which made her grumpy, but going after Ellie was a hard thing for even the most patient man to swallow. "She's not mute. She spoke while having a nightmare. Alice heard her. And even if she was, it doesn't make her a burden. She's been nothing but helpful to Dovie. She cooks and cleans without ever being asked." Elmer raised his eyebrows. "And let's not forget one important fact."

"What's that?" asked Tiny with a hint of annoyance.

"She's family," said Elmer. "Ellie's my sister and I won't have anyone talking bad about her, not even you, Mary."

Elmer got up and took the toast to the sink.

"Jeepers, Elm," said Mary. Elmer could hear the sob in her voice and immediately felt bad for getting onto her, right or wrong. "You're right. I shouldn't have said anything about Ellie. I'm sorry. I hate to keep blaming the baby but carrying her is just making me a grumpy old bear."

"That's because you're not getting enough to eat," Elmer said as he turned around and scratched his head. "Come with me to Quail Crossings and talk to Dovie while I'm helping Bill with the herd. Knowing Dovie as well as I do, she's aching for some work to do as well, since Ellie's doing everything."

"I'm just gonna stay here and try not to vomit," said Tiny.

"Mary," Elmer said softly, "I don't like you being this sick and here all alone. If you don't come with me, I'm sending Dovie here. You can't keep going on like this. I'm worried about you."

"Fine," said Tiny, standing with her bucket. "Let's go. But try not to hit every bump between here and there, will you?"

"I'll try my best," said Elmer as he followed her out the door.

Elmer helped Tiny climb into the truck and then walked around to the driver's side.

"Before you get in," said Tiny as he opened the driver's side door. "Would you mind running back in and getting me some pickled okra from the pantry?"

"I thought you weren't going to eat anything," said Elmer with a raised eyebrow. "You turned down bread and butter and now you want okra?"

"I thought you wanted me to eat!" snapped Tiny.

Elmer held up his hands.

Tiny covered her mouth with a hand. "Oh, Elm, I'm so sorry. I didn't mean to yell. It just came out before I had any time to think about it."

"It's okay," said Elmer. "How many okras do you want?"

"The whole jar, please" said Tiny, folding her hands in her lap. "Your baby girl has a thing for the salt and vinegar."

Elmer wrinkled his nose. He couldn't stand pickled okra. He'd rather have it battered and fried any day of the week, but he tapped the roof of the truck and said, "A whole jar it is then." He gave her a wink. "And it could be a boy."

A few minutes and six okras later, Elmer pulled into Quail Crossings and helped Tiny out of the truck. Her fingers were sticky from the pickling juice. "I can't believe you like those slimy things."

"They ain't slimy, Elm," said Tiny, licking her fingers. "They're crunchy. Plus it's a vegetable. It's good for me and the baby, so I can eat as many as I want."

"Hey, what my baby likes, my baby gets," said Elmer kissing Tiny on the forehead as he placed a hand on her growing belly. "Please talk to Dovie about your sickness. I really think she'll be able to help."

"I will," said Tiny, cradling her bucket and jar of okra as she walked toward the house.

"It's good to see Tiny," said Bill as he approached Elmer. "She hasn't been around much since Thanksgiving."

"She hasn't been feeling well," said Elmer.

"Morning sickness?" asked Bill.

"I guess so," said Elmer, "but it happens morning, noon, and night. I'm worried she and the baby aren't getting enough to eat."

Bill nodded. "You know Lou Anne was saying just the other day she thought Tiny was carrying small. I'll admit I didn't rightly know what she was talking about at first, but now that you mention it, she hasn't gained as much weight as Lou Anne and Evalyn did when they were pregnant."

"Hopefully Dovie can get it straightened out," said Elmer. As a cold wind swept over the brothers, Elmer buttoned his coat. "What are we doing today?"

"I think we'll move the cattle to the south," said Bill. "They keep grazing north of the tree break, and I'm afraid if we get a winter storm they'll freeze out there without shelter. Plus I want them closer, just in case the weather does blow in."

"Are we expecting a hard winter? Seems like it's been pretty mild so far," said Elmer, looking at the sky. "They'll probably be all right."

"Well, let's go see what James has to say about it," said Bill. "You know I like for him to be in on all the decisions. I know he gave me free reign after his incident, but I think he's having trouble not being in charge."

Tiny sat at the kitchen table, eating her ninth piece of okra as the boys came in and walked through on their way to see James in the parlor.

"You might want to be careful with that pickled okra," said Dovie. "Too much salt can make your ankles swell."

"I'm not worried," said Tiny. "I've always had thin ankles. My ma used to say that if my ankles got any thinner, I'd have to tie sticks to my legs just to hold my body up. Besides, it's a vegetable." Tiny's face turned the shade of her okra. "Oh no," she said, right before puking in the bucket.

"Oh, bless your heart," said Dovie, grabbing a wet wash cloth from the sink and hurrying towards Tiny. "I wondered what the bucket was for. I'm surprised this hasn't let up this far into your pregnancy."

"I'm not even halfway through this pregnancy," wailed Tiny. "By my count I'm only about four months in." Tiny started blubbering. "Dovie, I don't think I'm gonna make it. All I do is throw up. I'm afraid to eat anything, and then I get walloped by a food craving that I can't make go away, like the pickled okra. So I eat it and then I throw up again. It's a vicious cycle. I think there's something wrong with me."

Dovie gave Tiny a small smile. "Tiny, honey, there's nothing wrong with you. This is just part of the process."

"Am I a bad person for hating the process?" asked Tiny. "'Cause I'm just miserable. My back and belly hurt all the time. And Dovie," Tiny hushed into a whisper, "I'm snapping at Elmer for no reason. I'm being just awful to him and he's being sweet as sugar. It ain't fair."

Dovie patted her hand. "All normal I'm afraid, but I can help you feel better."

Dovie walked to the pantry and pulled out a jug of apple cider vinegar and a jar of honey. "Go and get you a mug of hot water out of my tea kettle."

Tiny did as she was told and met Dovie back at the table. Dovie placed the honey, vinegar, and a brown paper bag on the table.

"What are we doing here?" asked Tiny.

"Add a tablespoon of the vinegar and a teaspoon of honey to your water, stir and then drink," said Dovie. "It'll help your sickness."

Tiny wrinkled her nose. "You want me to drink that?"

"Says the girl eating a jar of pickled okra," retorted Dovie. "Trust me. It ain't that bad. Your ma had horrible morning sickness when she was pregnant with you. This helped."

"She never told me that," said Tiny.

"Why would she?" asked Dovie. "When she got pregnant with your brother and sister, she didn't have any problems. Sometimes those first babies just throw our bodies for a loop."

"Fine, I'm willing to try anything," said Tiny as she poured the ingredients into the water as Dovie had instructed. She stirred vigorously before pinching her nose and downing the entire mug.

"Tiny, you'll burn your tongue," gasped Dovie.

Tiny wiped her mouth with the back of her hand. "It wasn't that hot and it wasn't that bad. Tastes a lot like my okra juice."

"Good," said Dovie. "Drink it once a day and then suck on these as needed."

"What is it?" asked Tiny, eyeing the bag. "Do you have some eye of newt and thistle leaves in there?"

"Well, aren't you just all sass," said Dovie, taking her bag and shoving it in Tiny's hands. "It's peppermint candy."

Dovie got up to go back to finish the breakfast dishes. Tiny grabbed her hand. "See what I mean, I'm opening my mouth before my brain has time to pull on the reigns. I'm sorry, Dovie, I really appreciate your help. Do you have anything to help with my temper?"

"Sorry, honey, only you can control that," said Dovie, patting Tiny on the shoulder as she went back to the sink.

Evalyn sat in her parlor at Rockwood and enjoyed the quiet. Caleb was finally down for his nap, and Joy had fallen asleep looking at a book. It was a very rare occasion.

Normally, Evalyn hated the quiet because it gave her too much time to think, but today she needed it.

She looked down at the letters sitting in her lap. She didn't know what had prompted her to read Robert's letters again. He had been very good to write her weekly while he had been away. When weeks started to go by and she didn't receive letters, that should have been her first clue that something bad had happened. But there had been other weeks that went by with no letters and then she'd get two or three at a time. She knew well enough that the mail was not a priority during war time.

She shuffled through the stack and took out the last letter Robert had sent. Robert had horrible penmanship, but Evalyn had learned to decipher his handwriting over the years he was away. She joked in letters back to him that he could tell her all the Army's secrets, and the Germans would never know because even if they did intercept the letter, they wouldn't be able to read his handwriting. Evalyn smiled at her joke as she started reading the last letter she had received:

My Dearest Evalyn,

How are you? How are Joy and Caleb? I still can't believe I have a son. My heart just leaps when I think of him, and I can't wait to meet him. Honestly, I can't wait to see the lot of you. Every time I think of how much I miss y'all, my legs just want to turn tail and run for home. The past few weeks have been quiet here. It's given me time to take in my surroundings and this forest is beautiful, even in its war-ravaged state. The trees are tall and sometimes so thick you can't even see the sun, but then you'll come to a hill just covered with wildflowers or a lake with water so blue it puts the sky to shame. But it's the meadows that really get to me. The green grass is the same shade as your eyes, and I just get lost. I'm coming home to you, Evie. I'm coming home to you and our children. I swear.

All my love,
Robert

Evalyn read the last three lines of the letter again. *I'm coming home to you, Evie. I'm coming home to you and our children. I swear.* She cradled the letter to her chest and whispered, "You better."

Chapter Twenty

"Moving the cattle south of the wind break is never a bad idea in December," said James as he sat in the parlor at Quail Crossings with Elmer and Bill. "That's a good call, Bill."

"Thanks," said Bill. "How you feelin' today?"

"Pretty good," said James.

"I'm really glad to hear that," said Elmer. "Since I've got you both together, I'd like to talk to y'all about something."

"Okay," said James.

"I have an opportunity I'd like to take. It would mean less time here, but I could still help out early in the morning and in the evenings some," said Elmer.

"Oh yeah?" asked James as Bill stared at Elmer in confusion.

"I went to see Butcher Davis a few days ago, and he told me he's leaving for Florida," said Elmer. "You know he got wounded in the war, and when it gets cold I guess his leg bothers him something terrible. Plus he can't stand as long as he used to. He said he remembered me being a hard worker when I worked for him before the war, and that I really took to the job. Anyway, he offered to sell me his shop, and I'd like to take him up on it."

"But what about your work here?" asked Bill.

"Let's be honest," said Elmer. "The only time you really need me is on a day like today when we move cattle. I told you before, Bill, that I was looking for something permanent to take care of my family. I think this is it. Knollwood will need a butcher after Mr. and Mrs. Davis leave."

"That sounds like a mighty fine plan," said James. "Congratulations, Elm. You know I worried about our town not having a butcher when Butcher Davis left for the war, but Mrs. Davis took it over like she was born to do it. And now I think it's your turn."

"But we need him here," argued Bill, looking at James. "He can't just leave. Not with your condition."

"I'm fine," scoffed James.

"Bill," said Elmer, softly, "I'll still help around here, but I can't continue to let James and Dovie support my family. This is your job, always was. Now let me find my way for my family like you did for us so many years back."

Bill shook his head. "It's not going to be the same not seeing you every day, and Evie's already keeping her distance."

"Bill, I'm not moving away," said Elmer with a smile. "I'll just be working in town. We live right up the road. You didn't think we'd all live at Quail Crossings forever, did you?"

Bill shrugged. "I guess I had hoped."

"Have you got the money to buy the butcher shop?" asked James. "I'd be more than happy to go to the bank with you and help you secure a loan for the rest."

Elmer smiled. "I have some, but I would rightly appreciate your help with the bank. Tiny usually handles our accounts, but for this, I'd like to be the one."

"So this is really happening?" asked Bill, looking like a kicked puppy.

James let out a little chuckle. "I remember thinking the same thing when my daughter, June, moved away with her husband to New York. It's been really hard, especially since I never see her or the grandkids. Just count your blessings that everyone is staying close by."

"We don't hear you or Dovie talk much about June," said Elmer.

James's eyes fell. "She never really took to the farm, so she spent her entire life begging to get out of here. Since Dovie and her mom seemed to thrive here, they became really close but June was kind of left out. None of us ever planned it that way, it just kind of happened. When June said she was marrying David Banner and moving to New York, we had a fallin' out. I refused to bless the marriage knowing she just wanted a way out of Knollwood. The Banner family had a reputation for running moonshine. I was afraid she'd find herself in trouble." He paused and looked at the ceiling. "I gave her a choice, us or him. When she chose him, I cut her off thinking she would come back. It's been one of my biggest regrets."

"She doesn't ever come around?" asked Bill.

James shook his head. "I have three grandbabies I've seen only once. I went and found her in New York after

Sylvia passed. June didn't even come to her own mother's funeral. I had hoped to mend bridges, but she turned me away. I saw the kids as they peeked around their mother's legs trying to see who was at the door. She didn't even tell them I was their grandfather. Called me a salesman. Told me she wasn't interested in anything I was selling and closed the door right in my face."

"How could she do that?" asked Elmer, shaking his head.

"Hurt runs deeper in some people," said James. "I write her a letter once a month hoping one day I'll get a post from her."

"What about Dovie?" asked Bill. "Does June talk to her?"

"Dovie was devastated when she didn't show up for their momma's funeral. She was even more devastated when June didn't come for, or even after, Simon's and Helen's funerals, even though we sent a telegram. I know Dovie has forgiven her, since she won't say a bad word about her sister, but she hasn't forgotten and doesn't go out of her way to speak to June. Like I said, hurt runs deeper in some people."

The three men sat in silence thinking about James's story and long lost daughter.

"Well," said James breaking the silence, "you boys best get those cattle moved, so Elm and I can go to the bank after lunch."

"Bill," said Elmer, weakly, "you're okay with me doing this, right?"

Bill nodded as he patted his brother on the back. "I couldn't be prouder."

Evalyn looked around the house for something to do. She had already washed the dishes, scrubbed the floors, oiled the wood furniture, done the laundry, and made curtains for every room in the house. Rockwood was spotless, and Evalyn had time on her hands.

Having nothing to do was Evalyn's worst enemy. When she wasn't busy, she thought about Robert and when she thought about Robert, her heart ached so painfully she was sure it was going to stop beating altogether. After the pain subsided she would just be plain mad. She would be mad at Robert for going and leaving her. She'd be mad at the Army for not finding him. She'd be mad at the Germans for being so evil and starting the war in the first place. She'd be mad at Gabe for not trying harder to find Robert. But most of the time she would be mad at herself for not cherishing the time she had with Robert before he left.

She had been so angry at him for signing up to go to war. She had given him the cold shoulder for a week, finally coming to her senses only a few days before he left for basic training. She ached to have that time back. To savor those moments with him, moments she may never have again.

"Stop it!" screamed Joy.

Evalyn swung around, jarred from her thoughts. "What's going on?"

"Caleb keeps taking my little Mr. Norman and trying to chew on his head," whined Joy.

Evalyn looked down at the wooden figures Elmer had made Joy right before his deployment. Joy had loved them from the moment she laid eyes on them. Not only because her Uncle Elmer had made them, but also because her Aunt Alice had a matching Mr. Norman.

Evalyn smiled. "Well, at least he's not sticking Mr. Norman's head up his nose which is what you used to do."

"Did not," pouted Joy.

Nodding, Evalyn sat on the floor by her children. "You did. In fact, the day you turned two you started sticking things up your nose, and it took everything I had to get you to stop. Don't you remember? Mama Dovie had to use needle-nose pliers to get a metal nut out of your nose."

"That's yucky," said Joy, wrinkling her nose at the wooden Mr. Norman. "I wouldn't do that to Mr. Norman. I love him."

"I know," said Evalyn, "but at the time you didn't know any better, just like Caleb doesn't know any better now."

"Well, make him know better," snapped Joy.

Evalyn raised an eyebrow at her daughter, who immediately looked to the floor. "You best mind your tongue, Joy." Evalyn picked up the rattle sitting beside Caleb and gave it to him. "If you don't want him to chew on your toys, make sure he has his toys."

She brushed her hands together and looked at her children. "Everyone happy?"

Caleb gave her a big toothy smile which made her heart both leap and sink, since it reminded her of Robert's winning smile.

"Momma, you want to play with us?" asked Joy. "We can play *Little House on the Prairie.* Aunt Alice's been telling me about it and I really like it. Can you imagine living out there on the prairie like that?"

Evalyn laughed. "Oh, honey, we do live on the prairie. We're a living picture of what Laura Ingles Wilder is writing about."

"You got that right!" said Joy with a rush of excitement. "We even get to use an outhouse! I just love those stories. I can't wait for her to read them to me. She said I needed to be a little older."

Evalyn's face lit up. She suddenly knew exactly what she was going to do for Christmas. She would sew Caleb some farm animals of his own, and she would make Joy some dolls that resembled Laura, Mary, and Carrie Wilder from the fabric in her scrap basket. In fact, she could make all the cousins a little stuffed toy, make the women new aprons, and the men new handkerchiefs, all from her spare fabric.

"We'll play for a little bit, then Momma's got to do some sewing," said Evalyn, thankful she finally had a project. She wished her project had to do with getting Robert home, but she knew her most important mission was making sure her kids remained healthy and happy until their daddy's return.

Alice checked the mailbox after getting off the school bus and felt her heart sink at the emptiness. She knew it was possible that Dovie had already gotten the mail, but she also knew that the odds a letter from Jacob had come were slim to none.

She had continued to write Jacob and his wife, Blu, every month and still hadn't gotten a response. She was beginning to think she'd never hear from them again.

Norman waddled up to her and bumped her hand with his head. Alice patted the goose on the head. "I'm really worried about Jacob." She sighed. "What if I never know what happened to him? Short of going to his house and banging on his door, I don't know what else to do."

She walked toward the house, Norman walking with her, and wondered if she could convince Elmer to drive to Sweetsville with her. Before she knew what was happening, Daisy the pig, bumped the back of her knee, causing her to stumble. The pig grabbed the handle of Alice's lunch pail.

"Get back here, you nasty pig!" yelled Alice. "I still have a piece of cake in there that I intend to eat."

Alice got to her feet and ran after the pig who rounded the corner to the back side of the house. She heard a loud squeal. Turning the corner Alice saw Ellie brushing her dress off as Daisy shook the dirt off her back. Ellie held up Alice's lunch pail and smiled.

"Oh thank you, Ellie," said Alice hurrying over to grab the pail. "I know it's silly, but I've been thinking about this piece of cake all day." She motioned to the stoop as Daisy grunted and waddled off. "Sit down, and I'll share it with you."

The sisters sat on the stoop, and Alice tore the piece of apple cake in half, giving some to Ellie. "You had another nightmare last night."

Ellie nodded as she took a bite of the cake and then shrugged.

"Are you sure you don't want to talk about it?" asked Alice. "You have to know by now that we won't hurt you."

Shaking her head, Ellie took another bite of the cake.

"I'm worried about you," Alice said softly.

Ellie looked at her and cocked her head.

"I hate that we don't know what you've been through and that you still don't feel safe," explained Alice. "I know you aren't getting much sleep, and I just want to help change that."

Ellie popped the last bit of cake in her mouth and then patted Alice's shoulder. Alice could tell Ellie appreciated the gesture, but she wasn't going to talk about it. Ellie stepped off the stoop and headed to the barn.

Alice felt as if she'd hit one dead end after another. She couldn't help Jacob and she couldn't help Ellie. There just had to be a way to help them both, she just needed more information.

Chapter Twenty-one

"Dad, what are you doing out here?" Dovie stood, hands on her hips staring down at James sitting on the milking stool. "It's freezing."

James laughed. "You're right. By the time I get this milk inside, it'll be ice cream, and we won't even have to crank the handle."

Dovie stomped over. "You're supposed to be inside by the fire, staying warm."

"Dovie, honey, I'm fine," insisted James.

"Scoot, let me finish," said Dovie giving James a small nudge. "What if you had another episode? I didn't even know you were here. You could've froze to death."

James looked up at his daughter from the stool, his eyebrows furrowed. "Now you listen here, young lady. I appreciate you being worried. I can only imagine how it must've felt to find me in the barn talking gibberish. But enough is enough. I'm fine and I can milk a dang cow. I've been doing it all my life, and a spell I had months ago is not going to keep me from doing it. You've been coddling me like a newborn since then and I'm sick and tired of it."

He got up and grabbed his bucket of milk. "See, I'm done anyway. Now stop your fussin' and tend to your own chores."

"Well, I can't," said Dovie with an exasperated sigh.

"Why not?" asked James.

"'Cause Ellie's done them all," said Dovie, as she started to pace. "She's up at dawn making all the bread and biscuits. Then she cooks breakfast. She cleans the entire house before I'm finished with my morning coffee and then rushes in to do the breakfast dishes. I've told her she doesn't have to do all these things, but she seems to enjoy doing the household chores. At first, I enjoyed all the help and the rest I was gettin', but now I'm bored."

"Well, find something to do," said James. "And fussin' over me ain't your something."

Dovie watched her father exit the barn. He was right. She had been coddling him since the incident. He seemed to be fine, other than walking a bit slower and sometimes having trouble finding the right words he wanted to use.

He'd had no trouble finding the words to use this morning and he was right. As long as Ellie was around, she was going to have to find a hobby. The rumble of two cars got her attention. She was expecting Evalyn but not a second vehicle. Her heart pounded in her chest as she rushed outside the barn. It could be news of Robert.

As she cleared the door she saw Gabe reach out and shake the hand of a man who had just gotten out of a green utility truck that read "Bell Systems" on its door.

Evalyn walked to Dovie. "I didn't know y'all were having a telephone put in."

"Neither did I," said Dovie.

She walked over to Gabe and the telephone service man who seemed to be sharing war stories. "Excuse me," said Dovie, interrupting their talk.

Gabe put his arm around Dovie. "Hey, Dovie, this is my old friend, Albert Wabber. When I learned he was working for the Bell Telephone Company, I just knew it was time."

"Time for what?" asked Dovie.

"To have a telephone installed," said Gabe, beaming. "I know it's early, but Merry Christmas, my love."

"You're going to install a telephone here at Quail Crossings?" Dovie asked slowly as if trying to understand the concept.

Gabe nodded. "Talked to James, and he thought it would be a wonderful idea, so we went in town and filled out the paperwork."

"And you didn't think for one minute that asking me my opinion on the matter was a good idea?" Dovie crossed her arms.

"Excuse us a minute," Gabe said to Albert, who gave him a smirk.

Gabe grabbed Dovie's hand and led her back to the barn. "Look, Dovie, I couldn't ask you because then it wouldn't be a surprise. Besides you said yourself that you wished we'd had a phone out here when James had his spell." Dovie opened her mouth to speak, but Gabe held up his hands. "Also, I want to be out here with you, not waiting for the phone to ring at Johnson's with news of Robert. I'm getting a gut drinking all that Root Beer."

He poked his belly which resembled nothing close to a bulging gut, and Dovie couldn't help but smile.

"So will you accept my gift?" asked Gabe.

Without a word, Dovie turned and exited the barn. She marched right up to Albert and said, "Come on, let's figure out where to put this thing."

Alice watched Dovie march inside, the Bell service man hurrying behind her. Joy and Dean hurried behind the man, and Alice knew she had to distract them. If she didn't, they'd be in the way, and Dovie might just change her mind about letting Gabe install the phone.

Alice's stomach fluttered with excitement. She couldn't believe they were getting a telephone at Quail Crossings. They'd be one of the first farm families to actually have one. The Wheatons were the first, but the Wheatons were the first to get everything.

"Joy. Dean. Y'all come here," hollered Alice. "And bring Annabelle."

"But I wanna watch the telephone man," said Dean.

"Dean Brewer, you march yourself right over here," said Alice.

Both kids groaned but did as their aunt instructed, with Joy grabbing Annabelle's hand and leading the way.

Alice kneeled so she was eye level with the children. "Do you know what time it is?"

"Time to get a telephone?" answered Joy, with a cock of her head that indicated she wondered if Alice was asking a trick question.

Alice shook her head. "We have to leave the telephone man alone so he can do his job. And while he's doing his job, we can do ours."

"But I already gathered the eggs," whined Dean. "Momma said I was done with my chores."

"Not that silly," said Alice, tweaking his nose. "It's our job to find this year's Christmas tree!"

"Yay!" squealed Annabelle, clapping her hands in excitement. "I wanna find a Christmas tree and eat popcorn."

Alice laughed. "I can't believe you remember that, Annabelle. You were so little last year when we made popcorn garland."

"Can't we watch the telephone man and then find our tree?" asked Joy.

Alice stood. "Like I said, we have to stay out of his way. We don't want Mama Dovie to change her mind, do we?"

The children all shook their heads.

"All right then, let's look for a tree," said Alice. "Do you remember what we're looking for?"

"Just an ol' tumbleweed," said Dean kicking the dirt. "It's not even a real Christmas tree. I seen pictures in a magazine, and everybody's got green Christmas trees and ours is just yucky yellow."

"Let's go sit on the hay," said Alice. "I want to tell you a story."

The children followed Alice to the outside haystack, and everyone sat down to listen to Alice's story. "Once upon a time about ten years ago, before y'all were even a twinkle in your parents' eyes, there was a sadness about the land. It was a dark time, filled with hunger, sickness, and lots and lots of dust. During this dark and dusty time, people had to work hard just to find something to eat. There wasn't a lot of money, and there were even less plants."

"I'm not sure what this has to do with Christmas," said Dean, crossing his arms.

"Just wait, I'm gettin' there," said Alice. "During this time there were four children who didn't have any parents to look after them. These four children had a really rough time. In fact they had to sleep in a truck because they didn't have a home. They would go days and days without any food to eat or a warm place to sleep. The oldest child tried his best to find work, but during that time there just wasn't much work to be found. Until one day when the four children went into a small café to order a glass of milk. A kind man saw the children and knew he had to help, so he hired the oldest child to work on his farm and allowed the other children to come along as long as they helped out."

"This is a long story," Joy whispered to Dean.

"Okay, we'll move ahead, but it's a really good story if y'all would just listen." Alice rolled her eyes. "So the children came to live on the farm and worked really hard for the man and his daughter. Come Christmas time, the youngest child desperately wanted a Christmas tree, but the man who owned the farm said they couldn't afford to cut any trees down just for decoration. The trees needed to stay in the ground to help break the ferocious winds that blew during this dark time."

"What happened?" asked Annabelle sitting up on her knees, fully involved in the story unlike the other two children.

"Well the little girl was very sad, but instead of crying about not having a real Christmas tree, she vowed to find something that would work in its place. Something they wouldn't have to chop down or hurt in order to use. The farmer promised that if the little girl found something suitable, he would see to it that it was decorated." Alice stood in front of the children to act out the rest of her story.

"The little girl looked for days and days for a Christmas tree. She braved the cold winds and even fell into the creek scraping her knee something awful. The family begged her to stop looking. They were all afraid she was going to get sick, but the little girl refused."

Alice smiled. "And then she found it. The very thing that she had been looking for and it was perfect. Wedged between the barn and the shed was the largest tumbleweed she'd ever laid her eyes on. It was just about as big as she was, but the little girl didn't care. She grabbed the tumbleweed's stem and worked hard to get it untangled from the rest. Thorns bit into her soft hands, making them bleed, but she didn't care. She had found her tree. Once she pulled it free, she drug it to the house and the family rejoiced, decorating it with paper and popcorn garland, red bows, and a silver foil star."

"Just like our tree!" squealed Annabelle.

"Yes, just like our tree." Alice smiled.

"Wait," said Joy, with a knowing smile. "Was the little girl you?"

"It was," said Alice. "When I found that old tumbleweed, I never thought it would become a tradition here at Quail Crossings, but Papa James said that it fit the spirit of Christmas better than any evergreen tree because it showed that you don't have to have a lot to make a priceless and wonderful memory. So we've been doing it ever since."

"I guess that is kind of a neat story," said Dean, before puffing out his chest. "And if Papa James likes it better than a real tree then so do I."

"Now are you ready to find our tree?" asked Alice.

The children all bounced up, screaming with excitement as they ran around the north side of the barn where the tumbleweeds collected.

Chapter Twenty-two

Ellie sat by the loft window and watched Alice and the smaller children run around the barn. She had carefully watched Alice gather the children up after the telephone man had arrived, tell them a story, and then they all ran to the north side of the barn.

Wondering what Alice had told the children, Ellie continued to look out the window until no one was in sight. None of the Brewers had really talked about their real parents, and it wasn't like she had asked. She wondered if their mother had been like Alice, smart but fun. Or if she had been like Evalyn, firm but kind.

Ellie shook the thought away. Their mother couldn't have been any of those things. Their mother gave her away. Only a mean nasty mother would give her child away and then tell the rest of the family that she had died. Their mother had then left the rest of her children to fend for themselves. No kind mother would do that to her own children. They were lucky they had Bill to look after them.

She found herself jealous of the lives her siblings had lived. If only she had ended up with Dovie at the very beginning, her life would have been totally different.

Ellie got up and crawled into the secret place in the middle of the hay bales. Digging through the loose hay, she found the shoebox she'd hidden there that contained Lovey.

"I don't have long, Lovey," Ellie whispered to the doll. "But I wanted to say hi, and let you know I haven't forgotten about you. I'm sorry you have to stay in the box, but I don't want any of the other kids to take you from me like *he* did. I never thought I was going to see you again. He told me he'd burned you with the trash."

Ellie hugged her doll. "Remember how happy I was when Missus brought you back to me. She told me to keep you a secret, or you'd be taken away again. So I have, just like she said. And I'm doin' everything I'm supposed to do here even before they ask. I don't want them to make me go away. I like it here. I want to stay. So I have to be good and do the chores. You understand, right, Lovey?"

She leaned against the haystack and twirled her doll in little circles. "I know you love to dance. I'm sure it feels good to stretch your legs. It would feel good to talk to everyone like I used to. But talkin' always got me into trouble, so it's best I keep my mouth shut. That's what *he* always said. I have to do it, Lovey. I can't leave here. They'll send me back to *him*. I know they will and I just can't go back." She hugged Lovey again, forcing the tears to remain hidden. "I just can't."

Evalyn and Dovie sat by the fire knitting as the children decorated the tumbleweed Christmas tree they had found earlier that day. It wasn't as big as the tumbleweed Alice had found that first Christmas, but it had a lot of branches and worked well for decorating.

Evalyn longed to be decorating the tree with the children but forced herself to concentrate on the socks that Caleb needed. There were enough hands tending to the tree.

"The tree does look nice," said Dovie, filling the silence. "I can't believe we're still using those old tumbleweeds, but every time I think of getting a real tree I can't bear the thought of not having a tumbleweed tree."

"It's a nice tradition," said Evalyn. "Something our family can call their own."

Ellie walked in with a fresh batch of popcorn, and Evalyn and Dovie put down their knitting to string more popcorn garland.

"Thank you, Ellie," said Dovie. "Now sit down and relax. You work harder than a mule on plow days."

Ellie walked to the tree and started to help decorate.

"I swear that girl is a chore-doing fool," said Dovie. "I haven't done my regular chores in months. She's making me lazier than a cat in summer. You know I actually took a nap yesterday? A nap! I haven't had a nap since I was a child. I just couldn't think of anything else to do, so I took a nap. I have to find a way to get her to do less without hurting her feelings."

"Or you could help me," said Evalyn, pouncing on the opportunity. "I need to make the children's Christmas gifts, but they're under my feet practically all day, and in the evenings I'm busy mending and making dresses for the ladies in town."

"So you need me to take care of the kids?" asked Dovie.

"Would you?" asked Evalyn. "You could come to Rockwood for a change of pace, or they could come here."

"That would be nice, and I'm sure Ellie wouldn't mind some time to herself. She seems to be taking to her studies well. She acts like she's reading anyway, and Alice has her writing complete sentences now," said Dovie.

Evalyn watched Ellie help Annabelle tie a red ribbon on the tumbleweed tree. She smiled as Annabelle exclaimed, "How pretty!"

"You know," said Evalyn. "I think Ellie's just trying to make y'all happy the only way she knows how."

"By doing chores?" Dovie raised an eyebrow.

"When I was younger, I used to rush to do all the chores so Ma wouldn't have to," said Evalyn. "She always seemed happy that she didn't have to do the household duties, and the last thing any of us wanted was to see Ma unhappy."

"How do I get her to realize her being happy, makes me happy?" asked Dovie.

Evalyn shrugged. "I don't know. I never got that far with my ma."

The ladies sat in silence, each lost in their own thoughts as they continued to string popcorn garland.

"I'm sorry," whispered Dovie.

"What on earth for?" asked Evalyn.

"I just can't imagine having a mother that was so …" Dovie searched for the word. "… discontent, I guess. You kids shouldn't have had to live that way, and I just get so angry at your parents for hurting y'all the way they did."

Evalyn laid a hand on Dovie's knee. "Don't ever apologize for my parents. They made their choices, and you made yours. You could've turned us out that first day. Lord knows I gave you every reason. But you didn't. You not only took us in, you loved us. When your heart was hurting the worst kind of hurt, the kind of hurt that would make most people close their hearts forever, you still found room for all of us."

Evalyn sighed. "Even if they would've stayed we would've never known that kind of love. I wouldn't change our lives for the world. Don't ever say you're sorry, Momma Dovie, especially not for them."

Tears escaped Dovie's eyes. "Oh, Evie, you've got me all leaky." She grabbed Evalyn's hands. "Thank you for that."

"Momma Dovie, what's a matter?" asked Annabelle climbing into Dovie's lap and gently wiping the tears off her cheeks. "You okay?"

"Don't worry, Annabelle," said Dovie. "These are happy tears."

Chapter Twenty-three

Christmas Day, 1945

Three short rings bounced through the air causing Dovie to jump as she prepared the ham for roasting. "For Pete's sake … I will never get used to this shrilling contraption." She picked up the phone and heard a conversation already in progress on the line.

The conversation stopped. "Dovie, is that you?"

Dovie sighed. She had done it again.

"Yes, Kathleen, I'm sorry. I keep gettin' it mixed up," Dovie shouted in the receiver.

"It's okay, Dovie," said Kathleen Wheaton, "and you don't have to yell. We can hear you just fine when you're using a regular tone. Since you're on the line, Merry Christmas. Ben, tell Mrs. Grant Merry Christmas. Ben called us from Montana. Can you believe that, Dovie? Montana! Aren't these telephones just the best?"

"They sure are something," Dovie started to shout but then lowered her tone. "I'll let you talk to your son. Sorry I interrupted. Merry Christmas."

Dovie hung up without waiting for a response, hoping her Merry Christmas sounded genuine. She was sure Ben calling from Montana was costing them a lot of money in long distance charges. She was just glad she hadn't picked up the line before Kathleen, or Ben might not have gotten the chance to tell his parents Merry Christmas. Ever since the telephone had been installed, Dovie couldn't remember if their ring was two or three short rings or long rings. She was so afraid of missing a call for Gabe that she just answered it every time.

"Was that the phone?" asked Gabe, coming in the back door and stomping his boots.

"Yes, but it was Ben for Kathleen," said Dovie, going back to her ham.

"And you answered it?" asked Gabe with a big grin on his face, walking over and giving her a peck on the cheek.

"You know I did," said Dovie. "I can't ever remember which ring is ours."

"Two long rings," said Gabe. "We've told you. I even wrote it on the notepad by the phone."

"Who has time to look at those things?" said Dovie waving him off. "What's going on in town today?"

"Nothing," said Gabe. "Everything is closed, it being Christmas. I couldn't even get coffee at Annette's, and I live above the café."

"There's some left on the stove. Help yourself," said Dovie. "You know you could stay upstairs. We have an extra room now that Evalyn is at Rockwood. Ellie still sleeps on the cot in Alice's room. I don't think she likes sleeping alone."

Standing behind Dovie, Gabe wrapped his arms around her waist. "We've talked about this. I will not move in here until we're married. If I did the whole town would be talking about it. Can't have scandal at Quail Crossings."

Dovie leaned her head back on Gabe's chest and looked to the ceiling. "Let's see, we took on four orphan kids during a time when no one had any money. One of those kids terrorized the community with her pranks, and then came back married with a child to a man who most thought had left the town for good. We harbored a black boy that the town wanted to lynch and married a couple who was already married. I think the scandal ship has sailed."

Gabe kissed her cheek. "If you like scandal, then I can think of some other things that will have the whole town talking."

Dovie turned around and threw her arms around Gabe's neck. "Why, Mr. Pearce, you are being mighty feisty today."

He leaned down. "I'll show you feisty."

Dovie closed her eyes and met his advance. His kisses still sent lightning bolts through her body. She held his neck tightly, begging him not to stop.

"Ummm, children, why don't you play outside for a minute?"

Dovie gasped at the sound of Lou Anne's voice, and Gabe took a step back.

"But, Momma, it's cold," whined Dean.

"Yeah, Momma, it's cold," repeated Bill as he walked past Lou Anne who was cradling little Rosey close to her chest to keep her warm.

Dovie knew her cheeks flared red as Bill surveyed the scene.

"Well, now, what have you two been up to?" Bill asked with an ornery smile.

Dovie had no time to answer for Annabelle let out a loud scream as Daisy the pig ran into the house.

"What in tarnation?" asked James as he walked toward the kitchen and was met by a squealing pig. He leaned into the wall as Daisy ran into the parlor.

"Bill, you've let the pig in," yelled Lou Anne. "Go get her."

"Me?" said Bill. "You were the one holding the door open."

"I was just trying to give Dovie and Gabe some privacy," said Lou Anne. "They were having a moment, and I didn't want the kids to see."

Dean ran inside after the animal. "I'll get Daisy."

"Daisy," hollered Annabelle as she ran quickly after her brother. "Come here!"

"Come on," said Gabe. "Looks like we've got some herding to do. Lou Anne, will you stand by the door and open it when she comes your way?"

Lou Anne propped the screen door open with her foot as Rosey began to cry. "I know little one. I'll get you some food as soon as I can."

Everyone entered the parlor.

"How do you want to do this?" asked Dovie. "Should we all surround her and then pounce?"

"Daisy's like a dog," said Bill. "Maybe we could just sit and call her to come over for a good ear scratch."

Dean sat on the floor and started calling for Daisy while patting his thighs. Annabelle did the same. Daisy looked at all the children as if she wanted to go to them but knew better.

"Looks like we're going to have to pounce," said Gabe.

The adults began to circle the pig. As they closed in, she bolted between Bill's legs and ran back into the kitchen. Lou Anne shoved a dustpan under the screen door to hold it in place and started to chase Daisy around the kitchen table, clutching Rose tightly to her chest.

The air filled with the sounds of squealing pig, screaming baby, and the war cries of Dean and Annabelle as they barreled around the kitchen table after Daisy. Then the phone started to ring, adding a mix of shrilling to the already chaotic chorus.

"Was that two long rings?" asked Gabe. "I can't hear anything."

"Lou Anne," said Dovie, "go on upstairs and feed Rosey. Gabe answer that God-forsaken contraption. I don't care how many rings it was. And children please stop yelling!"

Lou Anne nodded and hurried up the stairs as Gabe plugged one ear and answered the phone. Dean and Annabelle continued to scream as they chased Daisy from one room to another.

Alice and Ellie stood on the stoop, staring through the open door with their collection of eggs and milk. Norman stood a bit behind them with his head cocked.

"What's going on?" asked Alice.

"Daisy got in the house," answered Dovie as Dean chased Daisy back into the parlor. "Put down your stuff and come help, will ya?"

"Hello? Hello?" said Gabe into the phone. "I'm sorry there's a bit of a ruckus right now, you'll have to speak up."

Alice and Ellie did as they were told, placing their milk and eggs on the counter and entered the parlor to get Daisy.

"Have you tried just callin' her?" asked Alice. "She's more dog than pig."

"We tried that," said Bill. "She knew it was a trick."

They tried to surround Daisy once more and this time she got by Ellie, knocking her to the ground before running back into the kitchen.

"You okay?" asked Dovie as Ellie nodded holding her elbow.

"Where's Elm?" asked Bill. "He's the one who's won prize money for pig wrestling."

As Daisy ran back into the parlor, everyone stopped in their tracks. There sat Norman by the fire with his head resting on Daisy's back. If a person just walked in they would have thought the two animals had been resting there all along.

"When did Norman come in?" asked Dovie. Everyone shrugged.

"Awww … that's so cute," said Annabelle, causing a round of laugher.

"You said Paris?"

Dovie turned to Gabe who was still on the telephone and was scribbling wildly on the pad.

"Are you sure it's him?" Gabe asked as the whole room stood still.

"Robert?" Dovie whispered.

"Do you think?" Alice whispered back, a smile of hope tugging at her lips.

"No, I understand," said Gabe. "I'll take the next transport out. Don't let them move him until I get there. It might take me a while since it's Christmas. Thank you, thank you so much."

Gabe hung up the telephone and turned to meet the eager faces. But before he could speak, a voice came from the back door.

"Why is this door wide open? It's colder than an Eskimo's house outside. Y'all are letting all the heat out." Evalyn closed both the screen door and winter door after Joy entered and found all faces staring at her. "What's going on?"

Gabe walked to Evalyn and led her to the kitchen table. He gestured for her to sit down and then sat beside her. Evalyn pulled Joy close under one arm while hugging Caleb like a security blanket on her lap with the other. Everyone crowded around, wanting to hear what Gabe had to say.

"Now I don't know anything for sure," said Gabe, folding his hands. "It could be nothing."

"Just tell me," said Evalyn, raising her chin as she tried to put on a brave face.

"They think they found Robert."

A burst of happy gasps sprang from the family as James said, "Praise God."

"Is he okay?" asked Evalyn, showing no emotion.

"Yes."

With that one word, Evalyn broke down into tears. A roar of cheers rang out as Lou Anne made her way back down the stairs to see what was going on.

Gabe held up a hand. "Not so fast, everyone. They found a man that meets Robert's description at a boarding house in Paris, but he doesn't have his tags and he's suffered memory loss. The man can't tell them who he is or if he even served in the military. The owner of the boarding house said he was brought in with a bunch of men, so at first he didn't notice he was American. The man never spoke and when he did, he told the boarding house operator he wanted to go home, but he didn't know where that was. So the boarding house owner took the man to the hospital and they contacted the army."

Evalyn sighed. "So it might not be him."

"Momma, it's him," said Joy. "You told me Daddy was coming home, and I've been praying to Jesus every night that Daddy would come back. Jesus heard me. Daddy's coming home!"

Tears ran down Joy's face as Evalyn hugged her and Caleb. Evalyn looked at Dovie. "Is it wrong to hope?"

Dovie hurried over, kneeled beside Evalyn, and joined in her tears. "Never."

Chapter Twenty-four

Tiny nudged the bottom of Elmer's boot as he laid on his belly and played with Dean and Caleb. He had made them new wooden animal figures. A group of prissy dolls had just wrangled all their wooden cows and they were on a perilous mission to get them back.

"Elmer Brewer, why didn't you tell me you had a hole in your boot?" Tiny asked, eating her second piece of apple pie. "I could've gotten you new ones for Christmas."

Elmer shrugged as he rolled over and sat up. "The hole ain't bothering me, so I didn't think about it. I hardly know it's there unless I'm lookin' at the bottom of my boots and how often do I do that?" He held up his boot. "Plus, it's kind of neat."

"What's neat about a hole in your boot?" asked Tiny. "It's only gonna get colder outside and you need good work boots to help Bill. Can't have you getting sick because you're too stubborn to get new boots."

"But it looks like a crescent moon," said Elmer, as he scooted closer to Tiny. "You know, at night while on the battlefield, I used to look at the moon. It gave me comfort."

"How so?" asked Tiny.

"Well, because even though I was so far away, I knew we were both under the same moon. So, as long as I could see the moon, I felt a little closer to you."

Tiny felt her cheeks glow. "Elmer Brewer, you are just a big ol' sap. I should tap you and make some syrup."

"Now who's being sappy?" asked Elmer as he lifted up and gave Tiny a little peck.

"Ewww," said Dean.

Elmer turned and winked at Dean. "You say 'ewww' now, but one day you'll be singing another tune."

"Not me." Dean wrinkled his nose. "Girls have cooties."

"Well," said Elmer, "if girls have cooties, then I guess I just got them from your Aunt Tiny..." He raised his hands. "... and now I'm gonna give them to you!"

Dean let out a yell and started to scramble to his feet, but Elmer caught him and began to tickle him. "You've got cooties! Annabelle. Joy. Come over and give Dean girl cooties. He'll love 'em."

Evalyn watched as Joy and Annabelle ran over and joined in with Elmer tickling Dean causing the whole family to start giggling. She wanted to laugh too, but her mind was on Robert. She watched as the children all smiled and laughed. Even Ellie was playing contentedly by the fire with her two new dolls. She wondered what Ellie had done with the doll she had arrived with, realizing she hadn't seen it in a while. For a brief moment, she wondered if Joy had possibly taken it as her own, but she hadn't seen it in her bedroom or at Rockwood. She shook the thought away. Knowing Ellie, it was someplace safe.

She looked over and saw Alice staring out the window. She walked to her sister.

"What are you doing?" asked Evalyn.

Alice sighed. "I guess I was hoping Jacob would show up and surprise us. I wrote him a letter and told him he was always invited at our table, and we'd love to have him."

"I understand," said Evalyn. "I guess I was coming to the window hoping Robert would show up by some miracle. I guess neither one of us got what we really wanted for Christmas, but hopefully he'll be home soon."

"I'm sorry, Evie," said Alice. "I shouldn't complain. I didn't mean to be insensitive. I miss Robert too."

Evalyn smiled. "You weren't. I came over here and asked what you were doing, not the other way around. I'm sure Jacob's okay. There are probably a hundred reasons why he's not responding. I personally believe he's just moved and hasn't gotten them."

"You really think so?" asked Alice.

"I can't see any other reason why he or his wife wouldn't get back to you," said Evalyn. "If he died during the war, I think Blu would've been kind enough to tell you, if for no other reason than to get you to stop writing."

"But what if she moved after he …" Alice couldn't finish her sentence.

Evalyn shook her head. "Don't think like that and don't give up. You'll get your answers."

"Thanks, Evie." Alice hugged her sister. "Hopefully we both will."

Alice left the embrace and walked over to sit with Tiny. Evalyn took her spot by the window, sitting in an old wicker chair. She leaned her forehead on the cool window and looked up at the sky to stare at the stars. She had heard what Elmer had said to Tiny about the moon making him feel closer to her while they were so far away. Evalyn pictured Robert looking up at the same stars.

"Merry Christmas, my love," she whispered and closed her eyes as she heard his voice say, "Merry Christmas."

She looked around and found herself in a beautiful meadow with a crystal clear blue lake and beautiful wild flowers. Robert had been right. It was greener than anything she had ever seen and the blue of the lake did put the sky to shame.

"I wondered if you would come," came a voice from behind her.

Evalyn sucked in a breath. *It couldn't be him. I couldn't be ...*

She swung around and fell right into the warm embrace of Robert. She wrapped her arms around his neck and hugged him tight. "I know this is a dream, but don't let me go."

"Never," he whispered.

She looked up and gazed into his warm eyes. "I miss you so much."

"I miss you too," he said. "Remember what I told you before I left?"

"You promised you'd come back," said Evalyn, a tear dropping to her cheek. "It was a stupid promise. You shouldn't have made it."

"But I did make it," said Robert, gently kissing the tear away. "And I intend to keep it."

Evalyn met her lips to his, eager to taste his love.

"Momma."

"I've got to go," said Robert. "But remember, I keep my promises."

"No, please stay," sobbed Evalyn.

"Momma!"

Evalyn's eyes snapped open as Joy tugged on her shirt sleeve. She quickly wiped her eyes. "What is it, Joy bug?"

"I just wanted another Christmas cookie, and Momma Dovie said I needed to ask you," said Joy. "You okay, Momma?"

"Yes, baby," said Evalyn. "I'm fine and of course you can have another cookie. Get one for your brother too, okay?"

Joy nodded before skipping to the dresser where the desserts still sat. Evalyn turned back to the window and smiled at the stars. She couldn't help but hope the man in Paris was Robert, but even if it wasn't, she felt an odd sense of peace. It might have only been a dream, but she couldn't help but feel her Christmas wish had come true, even in that small way.

"I'm holding you to it," she whispered to the sky. "I know you're coming back to me."

Chapter Twenty-five

January 1946

Dovie tightened her grip on Gabe's hand as they sat on the bench in the orchard outside Quail Crossings. "Do you think Robert's still there? I can't believe there weren't any flights going to France until now. These two weeks have felt like a lifetime."

"I don't think they moved anyone during the holiday," said Gabe. "The war is over. Everyone wants to spend the holidays with their families, not flying overseas."

"I just know this waiting has been hard on Evie," said Dovie. "And now when we're so close to having the answers, I'm sure the time spent waiting is even harder."

"I know," said Gabe. "Part of me wishes I hadn't told her about the man they found. I feel like I'm giving her false hope. What if it isn't him?"

"We can't think like that," said Dovie, lacing her fingers with his. "Sometimes false hope is better than no hope."

Gabe shook his head. "She'll be devastated if it's not him. This is it, Dovie. I can't come back without giving Evalyn some answers. It's not fair to her."

"What are you saying, Gabe?" asked Dovie, her heart beating faster.

Gabe grabbed both of Dovie's hands and squeezed. "I'm not coming back without knowing, one way or another, about Robert. If this man is not him, I'll keep looking even if it's for a grave, and when I come back, I'm never leaving you again."

"How long?" asked Dovie in barely a whisper.

"I've thought long and hard about this. If I can't find him in the next ninety days, chances are he's been killed in action and buried by the Germans or Italians. At that time I'll request a death certificate for him so Evalyn can get her insurance settlement and any back pay," explained Gabe.

"Three months is a long time," said Dovie.

"And to Evalyn it won't be nearly enough if this man doesn't turn out to be Robert," said Gabe.

Dovie bit her lip. "It just has to be him."

"Dovie, there are a lot of men who fit Robert's description. You have to be ready for the worst because you're gonna have to be the one who gets Evalyn through it. Having lost Simon, you're the only one in her life that truly understands what it means to lose a husband young." Gabe hugged Dovie tightly.

"No more talk about Robert. I have to leave in an hour."

"Maybe I'm talking about Robert, so I don't have to think about that," said Dovie. "I know you have to go, and part of me wants you to leave so you can see if that man is Robert, but I hate for you to go." Dovie sighed. "I sound more mixed up than a bag of salt sitting with the sugar sacks."

Gabe smiled. "You sound how I feel." He leaned down and kissed Dovie gently. "As I said, when I come back it will be for good, and then I want you to marry me."

He let go of Dovie's hands and fished around in his pocket. Dovie gasped as Gabe slid off the bench, got on one knee, and held up a gold wedding band for Dovie to see. "Dovie Grant, please say you'll marry me and be my wife when I return."

Dovie nodded as Gabe slipped the ring onto her right ring finger.

"That's the wrong hand," said Dovie with a giggle.

Gabe shook his head. "Wear it on the right hand until I return. When we get married, I'll make sure it goes on the appropriate finger. And promise me you'll never take it off. Promise me you'll wear it forever."

Dovie smiled. "I do."

"Has anyone seen Dovie and Gabe?" asked Evalyn as she looked out the kitchen window at Quail Crossings. "We better cut Caleb's cake now. Gabe has to leave soon."

Tiny looked at Elmer, who looked at Bill, who looked at Lou Anne. They all shrugged and shook their heads.

"How long can they stay outside?" asked Alice. "It's freezing out there."

Ellie brought the carrot cake, along with a long knife for cutting to the center of the table. Little Caleb reached for the cake with his chubby one-year-old hands, and Ellie quickly moved it further from him, right before giving him a little peck on the check.

Caleb let out a squeal before yelling, "Cake! Cake!"

"Will someone please go find them?" asked Evalyn, pulling Caleb from the chair. "It's okay, birthday boy, we'll have cake real soon. Also someone will need to wake James from his nap. He said he didn't want to miss this part. And get the other kids. They're upstairs playing games. Never mind, I'll just holler to them."

Evalyn walked to the stairs, but no one else moved.

"What's a matter?" asked Evalyn, stopping at the foot of the stairs. "Y'all got roots for feet?"

"Just let them have their time," said Lou Anne. "Who knows when Gabe will be back, and James can sleep until then. He needs his rest."

"I don't want to go look for them," said Elmer, his cheeks turning red. "Last time I caught them kissing in the orchard."

"That's probably where they are now," said Alice, walking to grab her coat. "I'll go see about them."

"They act like a couple of teenagers," said Bill before pulling Lou Anne closer with a smile. "I remember those days, always sneaking away to steal a few moments."

Lou Anne laughed. "And now we have kids, so we still have to sneak away to steal a few moments."

"Ain't that the truth," said Bill as everyone laughed.

"What's so funny?" asked Dovie as she and Gabe entered through the back door. She noticed Alice putting on her coat. "Where you going, Alice? We have Caleb's birthday cake to cut before Gabe leaves."

"I was going to find you," said Alice with a smirk. "And that's funny too, the fact that you two are acting like teenagers."

Dovie covered her face with her hand to hide her blush.

"Dovie Grant, what is that on your finger?" asked Evalyn, hurrying over with Caleb.

"I wondered when you were going to ask her," said James, as he walked into the kitchen with a smile. "You asked for my blessing weeks ago."

"Oh Dovie!" squealed Lou Anne, jumping up to give Dovie a hug. All the women joined in the hug as Bill and Elmer stood with smiles on their faces.

Bill shook Gabe's hand. "It's about time."

"Does this mean we call you Papa Gabe?" asked Elmer with a smirk as he shook Gabe's hand.

"There's only one Papa in this family," said James, taking his turn to congratulate Gabe. "I'm very happy for you."

"When's the big date?" asked Alice.

"That depends," said Dovie, "on when Gabe comes back with Robert. Then we'll get married right away."

"That doesn't give us much time to plan," said Evalyn with a big smile. Evalyn had asked Gabe when he was coming back with Robert before and had never gotten a clear answer. She hoped with the engagement, he'd finally give her a timeline. "Since Gabe's going to get Robert today … what do you think, Gabe? A week?"

"Three months," said Gabe. "If it's not Robert at the Paris hospital, I'll give it three months."

"That's not very long," said James in a soft voice.

"Don't you think you oughta look longer," said Elmer. "We can't just leave him behind."

"You gotta keep looking," said Bill.

"What are you guys fussin' about?" asked Evalyn. "Leave Gabe alone."

Everyone turned and stared at Evalyn with open mouths. She knew what they were thinking. If it wasn't Robert in the hospital, she would want Gabe to look forever and that was true.

"It's him," she said bluntly. "I know it's him. I feel it in my heart and soul."

She looked down at Caleb. Here he was, already a year old and had never seen his daddy. Evalyn knew without a doubt that Caleb would be the spitting image of his daddy when he got older, with his black hair and his eyes the color of warm molasses. They were dark and rich and more than anything else, kind and loving.

Every day she looked at her son, she saw Robert's kind, loving eyes staring back at her. The man in the hospital not being Robert was not an option. There was no question in Evalyn's mind that Robert was coming home with Gabe.

Evalyn looked at Joy who had started down the stairs. If Robert was the man in the hospital, would he remember his daughter? How would Joy feel if the daddy she loved so much came home and didn't know who she was? Would it break her heart? Of course it would.

Would Robert remember her, his wife? And if he didn't would he want to stay married to her? Would the little family she had longed to have together again, be torn apart even if he came home?

Evalyn shook the thoughts away. "I'll make your dress, Dovie. I have this blue cotton fabric that would look fantastic on you. Lou Anne can make the cake. What do you say, Lou Anne?"

Lou Anne nodded slowly. "Yes, I'd be happy to do that."

"All right, y'all," said Evalyn. "Now let's give this birthday boy the celebration he's been waiting for."

Evalyn bit back her tears as she focused on her son's birthday. She could not dwell on all the things that could go wrong. She had to stay strong and continue to hold on to hope. Robert was coming home, and even if he did have memory loss, their love would remind him of who he was and how much he loved them. His love for Joy would remind him, as well as his new love for Caleb. Everything would be better than it was before.

After everyone had cheered and giggled at Caleb eating his cake by the fistfuls, Alice pulled James into the parlor so she could speak with him privately.

"I think we need to go to Amarillo," said Alice.

"Why?" asked James, cocking his head.

"Ellie's nightmares are getting worse," said Alice, wringing her hands. "She screamed so loudly last night, I'm surprised it didn't wake y'all up down here. I just feel like if I knew what she were dreaming about, I could help her."

James nodded. "I've been thinking about that too. In fact, I told Dovie back in October that I was going to visit Mrs. Waterman after the holidays."

"Well," said Alice, a hopeful smile twitching at her cheek, "the holidays are over."

Bowing his head, James sighed. "Dovie will never allow us to go to Amarillo without her. She's been tending to me like I'm on my deathbed, and she's far too busy planning that all-day ladies circle to go with us now. We'll just have to wait a few weeks."

"Or we could just leave her here," said Alice.

James raised an eyebrow, and Alice held up her hands in a peaceful gesture. "Just listen. She's busy and that's fine, but I think this is the perfect opportunity for you to show her that you're doing just fine, and you don't need all this coddling. I'll be with you to help drive. We'll leave early before she gets up and plan on being back before dark. It's just a day trip.

If you're feeling up to it, let's just leave Momma Dovie out of it and go."

"She won't like it," said James.

Alice folded her arms. "Well, I don't like not knowing what happened to my sister. If you don't take me, I'll ask Elmer."

"Elmer doesn't need to be taking time away from his new business," James said quickly. "I'll take you but not a word to Dovie. This is a situation where it's better to ask for forgiveness than to ask for permission."

Alice hugged James's neck. "Thank you, Mr. James. I just know we can help Ellie once we know the truth."

James laughed. "But who will help us once Dovie learns the truth?"

Chapter Twenty-six

Alice chewed on her thumbnail before stopping herself and sitting on her hands. "How long do you think it'll take us to get to Amarillo?"

"About four hours," said James.

"How mad do you think Momma Dovie will be when she reads your note?" asked Alice. "You didn't even tell her why we were going to Amarillo."

James looked at his watch. "I'm sure she's spitting nails about now. I didn't tell her why because I'm pretty sure Ellie will get to the note first and since you taught her how to read, I didn't want her to get worried about what we're doing."

"Makes sense. Do you need me to drive?" asked Alice, hoping he would say yes. She had learned to drive while helping Bill with the chores, and running errands for Dovie and James while Elmer was away at war. Since everyone had come back, she seldom had a chance to get behind the wheel.

James pulled over to the shoulder and, as if reading Alice's thoughts, said, "Why don't you drive the next stretch, then I'll drive us on into the city."

"Sounds good to me," said Alice, beaming.

As James got out and walked around the truck, Alice slid over on the bench seat and got herself situated behind the wheel. As soon as he closed the door, she hit the gas and popped the clutch, causing the pickup to sputter to a stop.

"Whoa now," said James. "Don't make me regret my decision when we're not even a mile up the road."

"Sorry," said Alice with a small smile. She restarted the truck and eased out onto the road. "I was a little too excited. Thank you for agreeing to do this … and for letting me drive. Since Elmer's been back, I haven't gotten in much practice."

"You're a fine driver," said James. "Also I thought we'd stop by Sweetsville on the way home and see about Jacob. We'd do it now, but I don't want to miss our appointment with Mrs. Waterman."

"Really?" asked Alice, wanting to hug James but keeping both hands on the wheel.

"I know you've been writing letters to his wife and haven't gotten a response. I just thought we'd drop by and see what the locals know. It's only about twenty miles off the main highway. I figured if we were on a fact-finding mission, it should be about all our friends and family."

"Oh, thank you, Mr. James." Alice beamed as she kept her eyes on the road.

She knew Jacob had been in the Pacific. His last letters spoke of how wonderful it would be to live on one of the islands in the Pacific if there hadn't been a war going on. She hadn't been too worried until after the atomic bombs were dropped. Once Japan surrendered, there was no reason for Jacob not to return home. Of course, his letters had stopped coming months before the bombs destroyed Japan.

"Alice," James said softly, "you do know this could be a hard trip?"

Alice nodded. "I know something bad happened to Ellie. She has nightmares all the time, and she's trying to get someone to stop hurting her. I've tried to ask her questions while she was sleeping. You know, trying to get her to tell me in her sleep what happened, but it never works. All she ever says is 'no' and 'stop'. I'm surprised she even knows those words. I mean I think I'd forget how to speak altogether if I never did it."

"Well, I for one, am glad that she hasn't completely forgotten how to speak," said James. "I still have hope that one day she'll feel comfortable enough around us to talk to us, but I wasn't talking about Ellie. We know how her story turns out in the end. She's with us now, and we'll do our best to make sure she's never hurt like that again."

"You were talking about Jacob," said Alice, biting her lip. She wouldn't let herself cry now. Jacob just wouldn't stop talking to her. Something bad had happened to him.

"A lot of good men never made it back," said James. "We have to prepare ourselves for the possibility of Jacob being one of those men."

"I know," said Alice, with a slight bow of her head.

"I want him to be okay as much as you do," said James. "I just don't want you to be unprepared for bad news."

"Is anyone ever really prepared for bad news?" asked Alice. "No matter how much we're warned about Jacob, or Robert, and even yourself, we already know it's gonna happen sometime. And when it does happen, having warning is not gonna make it easier. So let's enjoy what time we have."

Alice sucked in a breath. She had never spoken to James that way. They sat in silence for a long time, and Alice worried that she had seriously hurt James's feelings.

"You're right," said James, after what seemed like an eternity of silence. "I got really scared after my incident. I've been trying to prepare y'all for me going to my heavenly home, when I should leave it to God. And so far He has seen fit for me to get better, so you're right. Instead of seeing everything that could go wrong, I'll focus on what could go right. Now pull on over. We'll be in the city soon. I better drive from here."

Ellie was surprised when she woke up just before dawn, and Alice was not in her bed. She hadn't thought Alice was going to the ladies Bible study, and even if she was, she wouldn't have to get up before dawn to be prepared for it. Maybe Alice had decided to sleep in the other room. Ellie had half expected Alice to move into the empty room after Evalyn moved to Rockwood, but Alice had stayed, stating she wanted Ellie to know she wasn't alone.

After braiding her red hair in two long braids that rested on her shoulders, she walked down the stairs and into the kitchen. There was a note on the kitchen table. Ellie picked it up and worked hard to sound out the words:

Dear Dovie,
I've taken Alice to Amarillo. We'll be back before dark.
Love,
Dad

Ellie wondered why they had gone to Amarillo. Of course, it was a large city and there were many things they could be doing. She supposed it had something to do with the livestock. She wondered even more how Momma Dovie was going to react once she read the note. She didn't have to wait long as she heard Dovie shuffle into the kitchen.

"Good morning, dear," said Dovie.

Ellie turned and handed the note to Dovie before going to the stove to start the coffee.

"What in the world does he think he's doing?" Dovie yelled at the note. She looked at Ellie. "When did they leave?"

Ellie shook her head and shrugged.

"Why, I oughta call the sheriff right now and have him track Dad down. He can't be going to the city in his condition. I'm gonna tan that Alice's hide when she gets back."

Even though Ellie knew Dovie wasn't being literal when she said she'd tan Alice's hide, it still made her cringe. She couldn't bear the thought of anyone laying a hand on Alice, nor could she bear the thought of Momma Dovie striking a person.

Ellie walked over, grabbed the pencil James had left on the table, and took the note from Dovie. She squinted her eyes as she tried to remember how everything was spelled:

Leave them be. He will be OK.

She handed the note to Dovie with shaking hands. This was the first time she had used her writing skills to communicate with anyone. She worried Dovie might take it the wrong way. She worried she might get herself in trouble, but she worried more about Alice getting into trouble.

Dovie read it as tears pooled in the corners of her eyes. "Oh, Ellie honey, thank you for this. It means a lot that you'd talk to me, even without speaking." Dovie wiped her eyes. "I know that doesn't make sense but hopefully you get it. I'll leave them be because you've asked me to."

"Are you sure you'll be okay?" asked Lou Anne.

"Lou Anne, I think I can handle three children," said Bill, rocking baby Rose in the rocking chair. "See Rosey is almost asleep. Annabelle is playing with her dolls in their room, and Dean will be a while collecting the eggs. Once he's done here, he's walking to Quail Crossings to gather the eggs there. Of course, by the time he dillydaddles around and gets there, Ellie will have it done. But he'll be busy for a while regardless."

"I feel like a bad momma leaving my babies for the day," said Lou Anne, brushing the fine baby hair off Rose's forehead. "What if she gets hungry?"

"Of course she'll get hungry," said Bill. "You're gonna be gone all day. And when she gets hungry, I'll grab the goat's milk from the ice box and warm it on the stove with a low flame, just how you showed me last night, and then put it in a bottle." He grabbed Lou Anne's hand. "We'll be fine. You go have a day of devotion with the ladies. It'll do you some good to get out of the house and go to town for a while. You've been cooped up either here or at Quail Crossings since Rosey was born."

Lou Anne bit her lip. "You're right, but if anything happens …"

"You'll be at the church," said Bill, standing with Rose, cradling her in his arms, and giving his wife a peck on the forehead. "I know. Now go or you'll be late picking Dovie up."

"If you're sure," said Lou Anne as she grabbed her coat.

"For the hundredth time, I'm sure," said Bill, giving Lou Anne a final kiss before practically shoving her out the door. "Have fun."

Bill watched Lou Anne get in their car and drive toward Quail Crossings. He looked at Rose. "Your momma sure is a silly goose. Thinking I can't handle you for one day."

"Daddy!" came a blood-curdling scream from Annabelle's room. The scream startled Rose, making her wail. Bill's heart thudded as he cradled baby Rose in one arm and raced down the hall to see what was wrong with Annabelle.

Ellie watched from the chicken house as Dovie came outside to meet Lou Anne at the car.

"Ellie," said Dovie. "Hon, we talked about this. Now get out of that chicken coop and let Dean do his own chores. You do your chores and let everyone else do theirs, okay? We have to work together around here. It's not fair for you to do everything."

Ellie bowed her head. She had been worried when Dovie sat her down to have a talk about only doing her own chores and not all the chores. She loved Dovie and feared every day that Dovie would send her away for being a curse on the family. She had to make sure Dovie knew she wasn't a curse, that she was helpful and quiet and never got in the way. Those were the things she had been taught at her last home.

Once Dovie and Lou Anne had disappeared down the road, Ellie finished gathering the eggs, leaving a few for Dean. After she had put the eggs up, she went from room to room at Quail Crossings looking for any chore that might need to be done. It was the first time she had been left alone at Quail Crossings and though she found the silence comforting, she also felt very lonely.

After realizing there wasn't anything to be done that wasn't someone else's chore, Ellie made her way to the barn. She brushed Poppy, the milk cow, and the horse, Tex, before going into the loft and sitting in her secret spot. She dug up her shoebox and opened it exposing Lovey the doll.

"Hi, Lovey," said Ellie, giving the doll a hug. "Everyone's gone, and I'm kind of lonely, so I thought I'd come see you. I bet you've been lonely."

Ellie listened to the doll before answering. "I know it's nasty in that box. I was thinking maybe I could take you inside the house now. I don't think anyone will take you from me. All the other children have toys. Dovie and Alice made me dolls, but they're not like you. They don't talk to me."

Ellie cradled Lovey in her arms as she crawled out of the haystack. "Maybe you and the other dolls could be friends? Would you like that, Lovey? I've never had any friends."

Ellie looked at the doll. "You're right; Alice is like my friend. But she's my sister so I'm not sure it counts." She looked around the loft. "You know what I did today? I wrote Dovie a note."

Holding Lovey tight, Ellie climbed down the ladder. "I can't talk to them, Lovey. I have to be silent so I don't upset anyone. Writing the note was a big risk, but I didn't want Alice to get into trouble. I have to do everything I can to stay here with them, Lovey. I can't go back to that other place."

"Whatcha doin'?"

Ellie let out a scream and hid Lovey behind her back as she came face to face with Dean.

"Were you talkin'?" asked Dean. "I thought you didn't know how, and what's behind your back?"

Ellie shrugged and slowly showed Lovey to Dean. She held her breath and waited for his response.

"Oh, it's just a doll," said Dean, waving it off. "I don't play with dolls."

Ellie let her breath out as Dean ran toward the chicken coop to scare the chickens away from the door. Lovey was safe, but would Dean tell everyone he heard her talking?

Chapter Twenty-seven

Elmer hung the last pig on the hook and then walked Mr. Dustin back to his truck. "I'll have these hogs processed for you by Monday."

Elmer pulled a receipt pad out of his pocket and began to scribble the order.

"Thank you, Mr. Brewer," said Mr. Dustin. "Seemed to take Butcher Davis twice that long. I appreciate the rush job since I've got a buyer already waitin' for a whole hog."

"That's good," said Elmer, handing Mr. Dustin the receipt. "Happy to help. I'll see you Tuesday."

Elmer waved goodbye as Mr. Dustin drove away and then turned to go back into the meat cooler. If he was going to process six hogs of Mr. Dustin's and tend to his other duties, he was going to have to start immediately to get everything done in two days. He hoped Tiny wouldn't be angry about the long hours, but knew he'd probably hear about it. He had tried without success to get her to go to Dovie's ladies circle, but she had refused, not trusting her morning sickness to not attend as well.

Elmer was more thankful than ever that Butcher Davis had a little apartment attached to the shop. Tiny was currently in there taking a nap and not home alone. He always worried about her when she was home alone and knew she wouldn't eat if he wasn't around. The pregnancy had not been kind to Tiny, and they fought constantly about her meals, or lack thereof.

Elmer entered the meat cooler and the lights flickered. Furrowing his brow he walked to the light switch and flipped it off and then back on again. It seemed fine. He walked toward the hog hanging at the far end. That pig was the biggest and Elmer wanted to tackle it first thing. As he grabbed the boar, the lights flickered again, and Elmer found himself not holding the hog, but the body of Thomas hanging from the hook.

"No," he cried, letting go and stumbling backwards into another hog. He turned around to steady himself, only to be confronted by another body of Thomas. "No!"

He looked down the line of hogs, all of which had transformed into Thomas hanging gruesomely on meat hooks. Elmer ran through the bodies and towards the door. The bodies reached out to him and called his name. They begged for help and for Elmer not to leave.

Elmer screamed as he ran out the door, slamming it behind him. He slid to the floor, head in his hands. "It isn't real. It isn't real."

"Elmer?" Tiny slid down beside him and put a gentle hand on his arm. "Are you okay? Should I fetch the doctor?"

Elmer looked at Tiny, tears in his eyes. "I'm seeing things, Mary. Things no man should see."

"Let me fetch the doctor," said Tiny. "This happens after war. I heard some of the nurses talking about it. Some men never really leave it."

"I'm going crazy," said Elmer.

"No, Elm," whispered Tiny as she wrapped her arms around his neck, "you've always been sensitive towards the needs of others and quick to help out. That's why you're still seeing things from the war."

"I never saw that in the war," said Elmer. "I never saw anything as terrible as that."

"It wasn't real," said Tiny. "It was your mind playing tricks on you because it's having a hard time forgetting what happened over there. Let me get the doctor. He may be able to give you some medication to help."

"No, you're right, I just have to tell myself it's not real." Elmer shook his head. "There's nothing a doctor can do for me. I just have to forget."

He stood, took a deep breath, and opened the door to the meat cooler. He flinched, expecting to see the bodies of Thomas. Releasing his breath, he was relieved to see only hogs.

"Are you okay?" asked Tiny. "Is everything as it should be, or are you still seeing things?"

"Everything's as it should be," said Elmer, walking slowly to the last hog. "Just stay in the door a minute, please. Just 'til I know it's okay."

"Elm, honey, do you want to talk about it?" asked Tiny. "Maybe you should lie down or have some coffee?"

Elmer held his breath as he touched the pig. The lights stayed on and the pig remained a pig. He sighed. "I'm okay, Mary. I've got lots of work to do. I'll meet you for lunch in an hour."

Elmer continued to take deep breaths as he started his work. He knew Tiny was in the doorway, but he wouldn't look her way. If he saw the concern on her face, he was liable to lose it again. He had to work. He had to finish the job he had contracted because he had to take care of his family, and he would no longer let the war stand in his way.

"Mrs. Grant, do you have a moment?" Dr. Hushton asked as Dovie was helping Kathleen unload the lunch the ladies circle would be sharing.

"Of course, doctor," said Dovie, "but we'll have to walk and talk. The ladies circle is due to start in about ten minutes, and we've got to get this food inside."

Dr. Hushton grabbed a large pan filled with smoked ham. "I was just checking in on James. How's he feeling?"

Dovie let out a grunt of annoyance. "I guess he's feeling like a spring chicken since he and Alice took off for Amarillo this morning without telling me."

"Amarillo?" The doctor's eyes widened. "Whatever for?"

"He didn't say," said Dovie, "but I reckon he went to speak to Mrs. Waterman about finding out more details on Ellie's past. I've got to tell you, doctor, I'm worried about her. Her nightmares are getting worse. I know Alice thinks if we know Ellie's past then we can help her get over it, and maybe even see that some justice is done."

"I'm not sure they'll find the answers they're looking for," said Dr. Hushton as Dovie opened the church door for him.

"Why?" Dovie led the way to the church's kitchen.

"I'm afraid the folks at the Children's Bureau have a bit of an agenda," explained Dr. Hushton. "As long as there are extreme cases of child abuse, then they have a job. It has been my experience they tend to exaggerate the circumstances in order to keep their employment. You really can't believe half of what they tell you."

Dovie set her pan of cornbread down and frowned at the doctor. "We feel very grateful that Mrs. Waterman brought Ellie home. She took the time to find us, and she didn't have to do that. She could've just as easily placed Ellie in one of those institutions you keep telling me about. I don't think she would exaggerate about Ellie's past. In fact, I'm not sure Dad and Alice will get much out of her at all. She was pretty firm that the past should remain in the past, and it would be in Ellie's best interest to move forward."

Dr. Hushton nodded. "Well, let me know what you hear."

"Thanks, doctor," said Dovie. "I will. Now please excuse me, the circle is about to start.

The doctor tipped his hat as Dovie watched him leave. She wondered if he had had a bad experience with orphans in the past. He seemed to have such a skewed view of what should become of them. She couldn't shake the feeling that Dr. Hushton wouldn't be satisfied until Ellie was no longer in the picture.

Dovie pushed the thought away. He was just trying to look after them as a good doctor should. But as Dovie walked into the fellowship hall for the ladies' gathering, she was happier than ever that James and Alice had gone to Amarillo. Answers would be the best for everyone, especially for Ellie.

Alice's mouth dropped open when they began to enter the city of Amarillo. "I don't remember it being so big."

Alice stared up at all the skyscrapers. She couldn't imagine actually going into one of those tall buildings. She had slept on the second floor of Quail Crossings for over ten years, but as she looked at the towering Santa Fe Building with its thirteen stories, she wondered how it didn't all crumble to the ground.

"Just wait until we get to Polk Street," said James. "There will be more people walking on the street than live in all of Knollwood."

"Oh, I remember that," said Alice. "There was a soup kitchen just off Polk that Bill did some work for before we traveled back north to Knollwood. I liked the city because there was always something exciting going on, but Bill wasn't too keen on it."

"Well, I agree with Bill," said James as he turned onto Polk Street.

He hadn't exaggerated. People of all kinds were walking the sidewalks and running their daily errands. Alice figured some were headed to lunch since it was going on 11:30 in the morning. Her stomach rumbled as she thought about food. They had an 11:45 am appointment with Mrs. Waterman. There would be no time for lunch before the meeting.

James pulled into a parking spot in front of a tan five-story building and turned off the truck. "Here we are. Mrs. Waterman's office is on the fifth floor."

James and Alice quickly exited the truck and soon found themselves sitting in front of Mrs. Waterman in her tiny office. Alice had been grateful for the elevator for two reasons: it was the first time she had ever been in one and was beyond excited, and she couldn't stand the thought of James trying to climb five flights of stairs when he hadn't been able to climb to the second story of Quail Crossings since his spell.

"What can I do for you today, Mr. Murphy?" asked Mrs. Waterman. "I hope there's no problem with Ellie?"

"Ellie's doing just fine," said James. "She's fitting right in at Quail Crossings. She's quick with her chores and always polite. She's about to drive my daughter crazy because she's so efficient." James laughed, but stifled his laugh and continued when Mrs. Waterman didn't even break a smile. "Really, she's doing great."

"So why are you here?" Mrs. Waterman looked at Alice. "She's a bit old for you to drop her off. I'm not sure I can find placement for her."

"No," said James holding his hand up, "I'm not here to drop off Alice. Alice is Ellie's sister. We're here to find out more about Ellie's past."

"Well, that's good, because frankly I don't have time for one more homeless child. Especially one that's practically grown," said Mrs. Waterman.

Alice cringed at Mrs. Waterman's crass attitude. She was supposed to be helping children, but she was acting like they all were a nuisance and not worth her time. Maybe she was the reason Ellie was having nightmares.

"So, can you tell us about Ellie?" asked Alice, needing to get to the bottom of Ellie's past. "We want to help her, and we think knowing what she's been through will help us do that."

Mrs. Waterman folded her arms. "Rehashing the past never helped anyone. Why don't y'all just continue what you've been doing if that's already working out for you?"

"Mrs. Waterman," said James, his voice turning from friendly to firm, "we have a right to know what Ellie's been through. I promise on the word of God that no matter what you tell us today, Ellie will always have a warm home at Quail Crossings. We just want to help her."

"I don't think you really want to hear it," said Mrs. Waterman. "You think you do, but you might become biased against the young girl once you know her history. I feel keeping the past in the past is what's best."

"I'm not leaving until I know," said Alice, grabbing the arms of the chair. "I will sit in this office and wait until you tell me. She is my sister. I've heard her scream in the night like the devil himself is attacking her. I have to try to understand, so I can try to make it better. I can't fight a battle without knowing the enemy. Now are you going to tell me what I need to know, or should I have Mr. James go get our lunches out of the truck and picnic right here on your floor?"

"Well, I'll just call the police and have you removed," said Mrs. Waterman. "This is a government office, and I am an agent of the government. This will not end well for you. I will not be badgered."

"She's right," said James. "Let's just go on down to the newspaper and tell them our story. I'm sure they'd be interested to know how the Children's Bureau is hiding your own sister's history. I believe Becky Johnson works there now." He turned and looked at Mrs. Waterman. "She's the daughter of the owner of the drugstore in Knollwood. I've known her since she was knee-high to a June bug. I'm sure she won't mind writing us up a story about Ellie and getting it published."

"Or we could just call up Officer Jones," said Alice. "Didn't Momma Dovie take his family eggs and milk during the Depression? I'm sure he'd be interested to know how people who helped tend to his family are now being treated. Isn't he married to the mayor's niece?"

"There is no need to do that," said Mrs. Waterman, pursing her lips. "I'm doing this in Ellie's best interest."

"Why don't you let us decide that?" said James. "We aren't here to cause you any trouble. We help our own; that's what families do."

"Fine," said Mrs. Waterman. She turned and shuffled through a tall stack of files, before pulling out a large file. "But don't say I didn't warn you. I won't give you the names of the people who cared for her, but I will give you a general overview of her history. Will that get you out of my office?"

"We'll see," said James. "Depends on how general you get."

Mrs. Waterman cleared her throat as she opened the file. "Ellie Brewer was born on January 31, 1932, in Tucket, Texas. In May of that same year she was taken to the local doctor's office with an unspecified illness. As you know, her mother abandoned Ellie there. A former nurse went to the Brewer residence once Ellie had recovered from her illness to let the parents know that their child was fine but was turned away at the door."

"So Ma knew Ellie was alive?" gasped Alice with wide eyes. "She told us all that Ellie had died."

James grabbed Alice's hand and gave it a supportive squeeze as Mrs. Waterman continued.

"Ellie was then put up for adoption. We have the adoption papers for the first family that took her in as a child. They never changed her name, and there are no documented incidents during the stay with this family. When both of Ellie's adoptive parents were killed in an automobile accident in 1936, Ellie and the other children of the house were split up among the remaining family. Ellie was sent to live with the uncle of her adoptive father."

Mrs. Waterman scanned through her papers. "From here it's all hearsay, but from what I can tell, Ellie was bounced around from family member to family member. The members of this family all thought she was cursed. Strange things would happen at each of their homes while she was in residence."

"What kind of strange things?" asked Alice.

"Most of the family blamed Ellie for her adoptive parents' accident, even though Ellie was not even in the car," said Mrs. Waterman. "They also blamed her for dead chickens, cows dying, dust storms, water wells that dried up, and illness to name a few,"

"Those things happened to everyone during the Depression," said James.

Mrs. Waterman nodded. "But Ellie was blamed. One of the cousins confessed that she thought Ellie was beaten severely on a number of occasions by a number of different family members. The cousin stated that it was beyond any reasonable punishment a child should receive. At around eight years old, she stopped talking. The cousin said it was due to her last guardian's insistence that she never speak. That only the devil's words came out of her mouth and if she did speak, she was beaten."

"Poor Ellie." Alice covered her mouth with her hand, trying not to imagine the horrible beatings Ellie had to endure. "No wonder she has nightmares."

"We have hospital records for Ellie documenting that she had three broken arms and a broken leg over this time period. The hospital also stated that Ellie had a number of bruises, busted lips, and black eyes during these visits. Each time the family stated that Ellie had fallen or been trampled by a horse, and since they were a respected family in the community, no one ever questioned their explanations." Mrs. Waterman cleared her throat. "Then there was the fire."

"Fire?" James's eyes widened.

"To hear the family tell it, Ellie set the house ablaze after getting into trouble. To hear the cousin tell it, Ellie was trying to cook dinner and accidently started a fire. The final beating occurred after the house went up in flames. The family lost everything, but thankfully no one was hurt in the fire. That is when Ellie was brought to me."

Alice was surprised to see tears on Mrs. Waterman's cheeks. "She was a broken little girl when I got her. I took her straight to the hospital, and she spent a week there recovering from her injuries. I filed a complaint with the local authorities, but they never did anything. Said if they were gonna charge the family with beating Ellie then they'd have to file charges on Ellie for starting the fire."

She brushed the tears from her cheeks and closed the file. "I've never thought for one moment that Ellie started that fire. It was clear to me that Ellie had been abused since her adoptive parents' death. I would've taken her home myself, except I've already raised my children. My husband died in the war, and it wouldn't be prudent for me to raise a girl on my own while trying to support myself. That is why I worked so hard to find her family, and I've been protective of her ever since. I knew telling you about the abuse and fire could open a door to suspicion of her, and she doesn't deserve that."

Alice got up and hurried around the desk, wrapping Mrs. Waterman in an unexpected hug. "Thank you for getting her out of there," said Alice, "and for finding us. Thank you."

"Can you tell us who the family was?" asked James. "I'd like to see about making that right."

Mrs. Waterman let Alice go and shook her head. "I won't tell you because I don't want Ellie to have to relive what happened to her, and I don't want her to be charged for a crime she didn't commit."

"Where did this happen?" asked Alice, her voice weak.

"Just south of the city," said Mrs. Waterman. "So having her in Knollwood, so far from where all this took place is very fortunate. It was my hope that this vicious lie wouldn't follow her through life. That no one will know except the parties involved. That is why I hesitated to tell you."

James nodded. "Tears me up inside not to be able to bring those awful people to justice."

"Me too," said Mrs. Waterman as Alice went back to her seat. "But again, I think it's best for Ellie if we all forget the past and move forward."

Chapter Twenty-eight

"Ant!" cried Annabelle to her daddy as he ran into her bedroom. "There's an ant on my Posey doll. Get it off, Daddy! Get it off!"

"Annabelle Brewer, you mean you screamed like a wild goose over a tiny black ant," scolded Bill as he plucked a small ball of black fluff off Annabelle's beloved doll while balancing a wailing Rose in his other arm. "Don't scream like that unless there's a real problem. You scared the life out of me. It wasn't even an ant. We don't have ants this time of year."

"Daddy!" came a cry from the front door.

Bill knew it was Dean. "You okay, Annabelle? I need to see about Dean."

"Daddy!" screamed Dean again.

"Dean!" screamed Annabelle as she ran out of the room. "Do you have an ant on you?"

Bill hurried out of the girl's room to see what was going on with Dean. He stopped in his tracks as he saw blood dripping down his son's arms. Annabelle began to cry at the sight of her injured brother which only made Rose cry louder.

Bill tried to bounce Rose in one arm as he ran to Dean. "What happened?"

"I ... I ..." cried Dean, trying to catch his breath. "Then ... mud ... rooster ... Norman."

"What?" asked Bill, leading the injured boy into the kitchen. He pulled a chair from the table over to the sink and then helped Dean to step on it. "Keep your arms over the sink. Stay right here. I'm gonna put Rosey down."

"What's wrong with Dean?" cried Annabelle.

"He'll be fine, just a little scratched up is all," said Bill. "Come with me and help me look after Rosey."

He grabbed Annabelle's hand and took the girls into the parlor. He laid Rosey on a large quilt and gave her the stuffed rabbit Evalyn had made her for Christmas which seemed to settle her some. "Annabelle, I need you to stay in here and watch your sister. Don't let her roll towards the fireplace, and if she does, holler at me."

Bill knew it would take Rose four to five rolls and a turn for her to get anywhere near the fireplace and giving Annabelle the big job of watching her sister would keep her occupied while he tended to Dean.

Walking back into the kitchen, Bill grabbed a washcloth and started to gently wash the blood off Dean's arm to see how bad the wounds actually were. "Now that you've got your breath, tell me what happened to your arms."

"I was gathering the eggs," said Dean, still sniffling. "I think Ellie got them already 'cause there were only three. As I was trying to leave, I was pretending to be a brave war spy, and I wanted to kick the Germans, but I accidently kicked one of the hens and slipped in the mud." The sniffling grew louder as Dean started to cry again. "Before I knew it that big red rooster was on me, and he started pecking my arms and getting me with his spurs. I couldn't get him off. Then Mr. Norman came flying at the gate, making all sorts of ruckus. Daddy, he just kept flying at the gate, honking. All the hens ran inside the coop, but that rooster wouldn't stop. Then Ellie came out and grabbed the rooster, so I could get out."

"What happened to Ellie?" asked Bill.

"I don't know. I just ran home," said Dean. "I'm not a brave war spy at all. I just left her there. A brave war spy wouldn't have done that."

"It's okay, Dean," said Bill. "I'm sure Ellie's all right. We'll go see 'bout her in a bit. Let's get you cleaned up."

Bill wondered how he was going to get his injured son and two young daughters the mile distance to Quail Crossings to check on Ellie. He knew Dovie was gone and wanted to make sure Ellie wasn't hurt. He knew his sister well enough to know she wouldn't bother James with anything, no matter how painful, and Alice had told him she was spending the day researching her term paper in the library, which meant she went into town with Lou Anne and Dovie. He should have just asked Ellie to come over, but he was being stubborn and wanted to prove to Lou Anne that he could handle his own children, plus he didn't want James to be alone.

"Daddy!" Annabelle screamed from the parlor. "There's an ant, and it's gonna get on Rosey!"

"Annabelle, for the last time there are no ants this time of year," hollered Bill, still dabbing at Dean's many scratches, trying to assess the damage.

"Daddy, it's a big ant!" screamed Annabelle. "And Rosey's gonna grab it."

"Well, stop her," yelled Bill. "Dean, I'll be right back. Stay here. I have to see what's wrong with your sister."

Bill hurried into the parlor just in time to see Rose grab a large black beetle. He ran over, prying the beetle from Rose's fat little fingers. With her new toy gone, Rose started to cry again.

"Where in the world did that come from?" Bill asked, trapping the beetle in his fist. He went to the fire.

"Don't kill it, Daddy," whined Annabelle.

"Fine, I'll take it outside," said Bill, knowing full well the beetle would die outside in the cold. "Try and calm your sister."

"Daddy, I'm bleeding again," cried Dean from the kitchen.

"It's okay, sister," said Annabelle patting the baby's belly as Rose continued to scream.

"Daddy, it's getting on my shirt," yelled Dean. "It ain't stoppin'!"

"Daddy," cried Annabelle, "Rosey won't stop cryin'."

The noise was getting to Bill. It was too loud. How did Lou Anne manage three young kids all day, every day? Seemed like he'd get one settled and then another one would get wound up. He tightened his fist around the beetle as the noise from his children echoed in his ears.

Pulling the door open with a tug, he lifted his fist ready to pound the stupid beetle like he wanted to pound out the noise but was met with the wide eyes of Ellie.

She quickly fell to her knees and covered her head as if waiting for Bill's blow. Bill dropped the beetle, which promptly ran back inside, and kneeled down to Ellie.

"Oh, Ellie, I'm sorry," said Bill. "I wasn't going to hit you. I was throwing a bug outside. I'm sorry I scared you. It's okay. I promise. You're okay. No one's gonna hurt you here."

"Ant!" screamed Annabelle, seeing the beetle run towards her. "Daddy!"

Ellie looked up, her body trembling. Bill grabbed her hand and helped her up. He could see she was carrying Dovie's doctor's bag, and that she or James had already tended to a cut on her cheek, probably from the rooster attack.

"Daddy, the ant! The ant!" yelled Annabelle. "It's gonna get me!"

"I'm glad you're here," said Bill. "I could really use some help. Beetle duty or Dean duty?"

Ellie handed Dovie's bag to Bill and hurried over to swoop up the beetle before it got any closer to Annabelle. Bill let out a sigh of relief and went back into the kitchen to clean the rest of Dean's wounds.

"Do you still want to see about Jacob today?" asked James. They were about an hour outside the city limits of Amarillo. Both had been silent after leaving Mrs. Waterman's office.

Alice nibbled on the sandwich she had taken from a brown paper bag. They had decided to eat their sandwiches on the road instead of the park after the meeting with Mrs. Waterman, since neither felt very hungry after the news.

"Yes," she said softly. "Putting it off 'til we feel better won't help with any bad news we might get. We might as well just get it over with while we're already feeling down."

"No need to be gloomy," said James with a small smile.

"How am I not supposed to be?" asked Alice. "All those awful things that happened to Ellie, and she won't see any justice for it. Instead they are accusing her of setting the fire. How many times has she cooked a meal for us, never even once burning the food, much less the house? It ain't fair."

"You're right," said James. "It's not fair, but life isn't fair. We know that all too well. We saw it when we took in Jacob, and that mob wanted to kill him just because he's colored. We see it with the fact that Robert is missing when so many boys got to come home. We feel it when Dovie talks about Simon and Helen. And you've experienced it first hand, like when

Harriet Wheaton died in the tornado a few years back, and when Tiny's brother, Junior, died in the war before he was old enough to vote. Both kids not that much older than you and gone too soon. Life is not fair, but don't you see the difference in all of that and Ellie?"

"Not really," said Alice, throwing the sandwich back into the bag.

"We have a chance to make things right in Ellie's life," said James. "We might not be able to give her justice, but we can give her happiness." He pulled the truck over. "You drive. I wanna eat my sandwich. I'm starving."

Tiny held her nose and looked away from the meat counter. "Elm, I think you're gonna have to hire someone to help you in the store. I don't think I can handle the smell."

"What smell?" asked Elmer as he checked the temperature gauge inside the display area.

The door chimed as Kathleen Wheaton walked in to collect her order. Tiny dashed out to get some fresh air. The winter had been mild, but Tiny was thankful for the brisk north wind that caressed her face and made her head stop spinning. She laid her cheek against the cold red bricks of the building and tried to get her stomach to stop churning.

"Tiny, dear, you don't look so good," said Kathleen as she exited the butcher shop. "Do you need me to take you home? Elmer said he didn't mind and that he would handle things at the shop."

"Thanks, Mrs. Wheaton," said Tiny. "That would be nice, but I should really stay with Elmer. I really do want to help him, but I can't handle the smell."

Kathleen smiled. "Oh, I used to get so sick with every child. You know what did it for me? Green beans. Every time I opened a jar of canned green beans it would send me running for a bucket. The funniest thing is, I'd crave them all the time."

"I'm craving pickled okra," said Tiny.

"Isn't that funny?" said Kathleen. "Come on, my car's just right over there." She pointed to across the street to her '43 Packard. "Have you spoken with Dovie? Did she offer any remedies?"

"I have, and they've worked for the most part," said Tiny, following Kathleen mostly for the conversation. She really didn't want to leave Elmer, no matter how bad she was feeling. "In fact, I bought a bag of peppermint candy yesterday, but I left them at home. They usually help settle my stomach."

Kathleen made a tsking noise. "Don't eat too many peppermints. All that candy will make the weight harder to get off later. Just ask my poor Charlotte. She hasn't had a baby in five years, and she's still hanging onto all that baby weight."

Tiny nodded that she had heard and heeded Kathleen's warning, but she wondered if one could still call it baby weight after five years. She stood beside Kathleen's car.

"You probably have nothing to worry about," said Kathleen. "Looks like you could stand to put on a few more pounds. How far along are you?"

"About five months," answered Tiny.

Kathleen gasped. "That's it. We're going to Annette's Café right now and getting you some food. Get in the car, young lady. I won't take no for an answer."

"I don't want to leave Elmer," said Tiny. "I really don't think I can eat, anyway."

"Well, we're gonna try and Elmer's a grown man. He'll be all right alone. Tonight they're having chicken fried steak as their special. George is at the feed store. We'll stop by there and tell him I ain't cooking and to meet us at Annette's. I didn't feel like cooking anyway."

"Really, Mrs. Wheaton, I shouldn't," said Tiny.

"Nonsense," said Kathleen. "It will be my treat, and we'll bring Elmer a plate so he can eat. He said he had a big order to cut for tomorrow, and that he might be late. I'll take you home after we eat." Kathleen sighed. "Truth is, Tiny, Charlotte doesn't come around much now that they've moved to Perry, and with Harriet gone, I could use some woman conversation."

"Weren't you at the ladies circle with Dovie and Lou Anne today?" asked Tiny.

Kathleen smiled. "Here is the most important lesson anyone will ever teach you, as a mother and as a woman, you can never have enough time with the girls."

Chapter Twenty-nine

Lou Anne surveyed the scene. Annabelle sat on the floor with her back to the door playing with her dolls as Rose slept on the large quilt beside her. Bill and Dean laid together on the sofa, both fast asleep. She heard a noise in the kitchen and went to see who was there.

"Ellie," said Lou Anne softly.

Ellie jumped in surprise and then smiled as she touched her chest.

"Sorry," said Lou Anne, "Didn't mean to scare you. I just didn't know who would be in the kitchen." Lou Anne noticed Ellie's bandaged cheek. "What happened to your cheek?"

"Momma!" squealed Annabelle, walking into the kitchen and reaching up, gesturing for her mother to pick her up. "She saved me from an ant!"

"Is that how she got that ouchy on her face?" asked Lou Anne.

"No," said Bill, coming up from behind and giving his wife a big hug. "She got that from that big red rooster."

"What?" asked Lou Anne shaking her head. "How'd that happen?"

"It's a long story, involving Dean being a war spy in the chicken coop," said Bill. "I'll tell you all about it, later. I'm really glad you're home."

"Is Dean okay?" asked Lou Anne, turning to see her boy still sleeping on the sofa and seeing all the bandages for the first time. "Oh my goodness, Bill!"

"Shhh," said Bill, "Don't wake them. He's got a lot of cuts from the rooster's spurs and scratches from his claws, but he'll be okay." He looked to Ellie. "Thanks to his Aunt Ellie."

Lou Anne gave Annabelle a kiss on the cheek. "Honey, go play with your dolls while I talk to your daddy, okay?"

Annabelle nodded as she scrambled out of her mother's arms and ran into the parlor.

"Look," said Bill, "Dean was horsing around in the chicken coop and accidently kicked one of the chickens, so the rooster attacked him. Norman made a ruckus and Ellie heard, ran out and got the rooster off Dean. While I was trying to tend to Dean, a beetle, probably from the firewood, started walking toward Rosey and caused Annabelle to get upset. Thank goodness, Ellie showed up at that time with Dovie's medical bag. She tended to the girls while I cleaned up Dean. There was one large cut on Dean's inner arm that needed stitched and low and behold she just stitched him right up. It was like she'd done it her whole life." Bill looked at Ellie. "Had I not seen her do it, I would've thought it was Dovie's handy work."

Ellie put a large platter on the table.

"And now it appears, she's cooked us dinner." Bill laughed and looked at Ellie. "Let me guess, we owe Dovie a rooster?"

Ellie shrugged as she grabbed a chicken leg and Dovie's medical bag and walked out the door headed back to Quail Crossings.

James and Alice sat outside the small house that carried Jacob's address. Alice chewed on her thumbnail as she took in the broken window, shutters, and a porch railing that had seen better times. A rusty bicycle sat on the porch next to three dead potted plants and five forgotten coffee mugs were lined up on the windowsill. One lonely kitchen chair sat next to the door, looking as if it would send the next person to sit in it crashing to the ground.

"Are you sure this is the right place?" she asked. "Seems like Jacob would take better care of his house and stuff."

"It's the right address," said James. "Doesn't mean he didn't move after the war, or that his wife didn't move them while he was away. She might have found a better place for them while he was gone."

"Hope so," said Alice as she opened the truck door. "Guess we should go see."

James and Alice approached the door slowly. Alice could feel eyes on her, like the neighbors were watching from their windows. She wondered if this was how Jacob felt when he walked around Knollwood. After all, they were probably the only white people in Sweetsville, just as he had been the only colored person in Knollwood.

The steps creaked as James walked up them, and Alice wondered if the porch would hold both of them at the same time. She stayed on the walkway while James knocked, not wanting to chance putting a hole in someone's porch floor.

"Hello?" came a voice from the other side, but the door remained closed.

"I'm looking for Jacob Henry," James yelled through the door. "I'm an old friend of his."

"Jacob Henry ain't got no friends," came the voice.

Alice's blood boiled. Who was this person to claim that Jacob had no friends? She marched right up onto the porch, not caring if she put a hundred holes in it.

"Now, you listen here," she said through the door, loud enough for the whole neighborhood to hear. "Jacob Henry is my friend, and I will not have you talkin' bad about him. Now do you know where he is or not?"

"Alice?" came the voice.

"Jacob?" Alice cocked her head. "Jacob is that you? Open the door."

"Go away," said the voice. "Jacob's not here."

"Jacob," said James, "we know it's you, son. No one else would know Alice's voice. Please let us in. We just want to see how you're doing."

"I'm fine," said Jacob.

"I'm not leaving until I see that for myself," said Alice, "and you know I'll sit on your porch in your rickety ol' chair all winter if I have to."

Alice listened for a response but heard only silence for what seemed like forever. Then she heard a huge sigh, then a groan. She could hear someone walking toward the door, but the footsteps were odd, like a *thunk*, then a *slide*.

Jacob cracked the door open and flashed his perfect smile. "Nice of y'all to check on me. Now you see I'm fine. Please go."

"Not yet," said James as he pushed the door further open.

Alice gasped as she saw Jacob leaning on a crutch. As her eyes traveled down, she clamped her hand over her mouth as she noticed his pant leg pinned up at mid-thigh and his missing right leg.

Walking through the door, Dovie stopped in surprise as she watched Evalyn put a meatloaf in the oven.

"I'm surprised Ellie didn't beat you to that," said Dovie.

"Me too," said Evalyn. "Actually, I haven't seen Ellie since I got here 'bout an hour ago."

"She's probably just out walking," said Dovie, taking her coat off.

"How was the ladies' circle?" asked Evalyn, going to the pantry to gather some potatoes. She held them up. "I figured I'd fry these tonight, that okay?"

Dovie smiled. "Have I ever turned down fried potatoes? The circle was good. Wish you could've been there."

"Me too," said Evalyn, "I just wasn't up for all the sympathetic looks and questions about Robert."

Ellie walked in the back door, still gnawing on her chicken bone with Dovie's bag in her other hand.

"Well, there you are," said Dovie. "We wondered if you'd run off with the coyotes." Dovie stopped and hurried to Ellie. "What happened to your cheek? Are you okay? Where have you been? Is that my medical bag?"

Ellie pointed toward Bill's house and gave Dovie the okay gesture.

"Let me see that cheek," said Dovie. "I want to see what's going on under that bandage. If there was ever a time to talk, now's it."

Ellie walked to the notepad by the phone and pointed to the note she had left before going to Bill's house. Dovie walked over and read the note. "Well, we need to work on your spelling, but I believe it says a rooster got Dean and you went to Bill's to help."

Ellie nodded.

"So I guess the rooster got you too?" asked Evalyn.

Again Ellie nodded.

"Big Red?" asked Dovie.

Once Ellie confirmed Dovie's suspicion, Dovie sighed. "What are we gonna do with that bird? He's a mean spirited thing all right."

Ellie held up her chicken bone and gave Dovie an apologetic smile.

Dovie smiled back. "I would've done the same thing. Now get over here and let me see that cheek. I won't take no for an answer."

Ellie did as she was told and sat in a chair in front of Dovie. Dovie carefully removed the bandage. "Well that's a nasty cut all right. Who cleaned it up?"

Ellie pointed to herself.

"Didn't it hurt?" Evalyn gasped.

Ellie shrugged.

"Maybe I should call the doctor," said Evalyn. "I don't want her to get an infection."

Shaking her head, Ellie bounced out of the chair.

"She's fine," said Dovie. "Ellie, I'm so proud of you. I know that had to have hurt something terrible, but you did a wonderful job cleaning it. I don't think it'll need stitches. We'll keep an eye on it and I don't think she'll have much of a scar at all."

Ellie smiled as she started to gather the plates and set the table.

"Just five of us tonight," said Dovie. "Don't think Dad and Alice will be here before dinner, and it appears you already fed Bill's brood."

"Where are Alice and James?" asked Evalyn.

"They ran off to Amarillo," said Dovie. She looked over her shoulder to see if Ellie was within ear shot, then whispered. "I think they're talking to Mrs. Waterman about Ellie's past."

Evalyn nodded. "Will you come over tomorrow and tell me what they've found out?"

"Of course," Dovie whispered, then picked up her voice. "You know, Evie, you're gonna have to face the town's people at some point. You know they're just trying to be helpful when they ask you about Robert."

Evalyn grabbed a jar of pickled beets from the pantry and carried them to the sink. "Half are just being nosy, and the other half act like he's already dead." Evalyn paused and looked out the window. "How did you do it, Dovie? How did you ever get over Simon? I start to think about Robert not coming back, and I just double over it hurts so much. I'm talking physical pain, like my heart is just going to explode into a thousand pieces, and I'll never be able to breathe again."

Chapter Thirty

Dovie's eyes fell as she felt Evalyn's heartbreak. She knew it all too well. Simon might have died almost eleven years ago, but some days the pain hit her like a train at full speed. Dovie sat, wanting to comfort Evalyn but feeling unsteady on her feet.

"You don't really ever get over it," said Dovie.

Evalyn turned, looking surprised. "But you have Gabe now."

"I do, and I love him very deeply, but there will always be a spot in my heart that belongs to Simon, and that spot aches. Now sure the achin' doesn't hurt as much as it used to. Gabe's love seems to tame it, but there are times when even Gabe's love can't drown out the loss of Simon."

"What am I gonna do, Dovie?" asked Evalyn, coming over to Dovie and kneeling before her. She laid her head in Dovie's lap and began to sob. "I'm not sure I can bear it."

"You can," said Dovie, placing her hands on Evalyn's back. "Listen, I hope that Gabe comes home with Robert, and y'all get the life you've longed to have. That is one of my greatest prayers for your family. But if it does turn out that Robert is no longer with us, then you'll hang on. You'll hang on for your children. There will be days that you'll need help holding on, and you've got us. You see, grief is like a boulder at first. So heavy you can't possibly hold it alone. That's when you'll need us the most to help you shoulder the weight. As time goes by, that boulder will get a little smaller. Day after day you'll find that weight easier to carry, until one day it'll be like carrying a pebble in your pocket. Easy to carry but always there."

Tears slipped down Dovie's cheeks as she felt a hand gently rubbing her back. She looked up and gave Ellie a thankful smile.

James and Alice sat in chairs facing Jacob who slouched on his sofa.

"Tell us what happened, son," said James. His eyes were soft, but there was a firmness in his voice that Alice knew meant he wanted the truth and wasn't leaving until he knew exactly what was going on with Jacob. She was glad because she wanted to know too but hadn't been able to find her voice since noticing Jacob's missing leg.

Jacob chuckled and put on a sarcastic smile. "It's a short story really. Them Japs threw a grenade at my platoon and when I went to kick it away from us, it went off. The docs said it's a miracle I wasn't killed instantly and only lost my leg. They sent me home about a year ago to an empty house. Turns out my wife left me for another man while I was overseas. She left me a note on the table, next to a jar of her sand plum jelly. Like leaving a jar of my favorite jelly was going to ease the pain of learning my wife ran off."

He shook his head. "Guess that was my fault. I sent her a picture of me eating a fresh coconut. The women who brought us the coconuts were in the picture. They weren't even Japanese, not that my wife would've known the difference. I just wanted to show her something positive from the war, the fact I got to try a real fresh coconut. Guess she thought I was telling her something else."

"Sounds like she couldn't handle being married to a soldier," said James. "It happens more often than people realize."

"You've been home for a year," said Alice, finding her voice and folding her arms. "Didn't you think for one second to get a hold of us? I've been writing you and your wife for months."

Jacob's smile faded. "And tell you what, Miss Alice? My sob story of how my wife left me and I lost my leg? What are you gonna do about it?"

"I was worried about you!" yelled Alice, jumping to her feet. "Even if you didn't want to tell me what happened, you could've at least said you were alive."

Jacob thrust out his hands. "'Cause this is living?"

James stood. "All right, that's enough. Let's stop this argument before it even gets started." He looked at Jacob. "I'm not gonna stand here and tell you I know what you're going through, but I'm glad we came because we can help you."

"How?" asked Jacob. "You gonna fix my windows and find a job for a one-legged man. 'Cause let me tell you, no one wants to hire a colored boy with one leg."

"You're coming with us," said James. "Back home to Quail Crossings."

Jacob shook his head. "Oh no, your townfolk made it quite clear I'm not welcome there."

"Knollwood's changed," said Alice. "We have two colored families that live just outside of town, and no one gives them any trouble. Once the Kelley's moved, no one really cared about the colored folks one way or another."

"Jacob," said James, softly, "I can't promise you there will never be bias against you, not even in Knollwood. Alice is right that we do have two colored families living just outside Knollwood, and they haven't been given much grief, but there are some people who still harbor ill will towards coloreds. What I can promise is we'll help get you going again. Find you a job and a decent place to stay. You'll be around family which is what you need now. You don't have to do this alone."

"What if I want to do it alone," said Jacob, now folding his arms. "Y'all are just offering because you feel sorry for me."

"Of course we feel sorry for you," snapped Alice. "You're family and you're suffering. I also feel sorry for Evie and the fact that Robert's missing, but she ain't sitting around pouting about it."

"Robert's missing?" Jacob's face fell. "How long? Where was he last seen?"

"Hopefully he's been found in Paris," said James. "There's a man with memory loss at a hospital there that fits Robert's description, but it's been months since anyone has heard from him."

"You would've known that had you read my letters," said Alice.

Jacob rubbed his face with his hands. "I just didn't want y'all to see me like this, and I knew the minute I opened your letters Alice, I'd want to respond. So I just pretended they weren't there. Just like I pretend that window ain't broke, and that I haven't eaten in two days."

"Why haven't you eaten? Doesn't the army give you money for being injured?" asked James.

"I was told they would," said Jacob. "But I ain't got a check yet. Seems like every time I get to the Vet Center to ask about it, they close down. They won't even come to the window. I've stood there for hours. So I've been living off what wages I did get during the war. But it ain't easy gettin' to the store."

"Then it's settled," said Alice. "You need to come with us."

"How about," James started before Jacob could refuse again, "you spend the rest of the winter with us? It's bone freezing cold in here. Then come spring, we'll all come back and get your house in order and things straightened out at the Vet Center. Everyone would be mighty happy to see you."

"I don't want to be any trouble," said Jacob. "Y'all already have a housefull."

Alice sighed but softened her voice as she walked over and sat next to Jacob. "Again, if you would've read my letters you would know that Evie moved out after we rebuilt Rockwood. Elm and Tiny live over on the Clark's place since her parents moved to Amarillo. So it's just Ellie and me, and we share a room, so there's an empty room upstairs that I'm sure Dovie won't mind moving into until spring, so you can have her room on the ground floor."

"Who's Ellie?" asked Jacob.

"I'll tell you all about her in the truck," said Alice as she grabbed his hand. "Jacob, please say you'll come."

Jacob looked at Alice who put on her best begging face and then at James who was also giving him a hopeful look. "Fine, I'll come along with you, but only for the winter, and I'll be doing my part. I can still milk a cow and slop the pigs, and even do the dishes if I need to. I won't just be sitting around."

Alice tilted her head from side to side. "We'll see how Ellie feels about that."

"Again, who is Ellie?"

James and Alice laughed as they started to gather Jacob's things.

"We'll tell you all about her," said James. "Now let's get moving and pack what you need. I'd like to get home before midnight."

"Oh, Jacob," cried Dovie, before wrapping him in a warm hug as he stood just outside the pickup door, leaning against the truck frame. "What a wonderful surprise! I'm so glad you're here. Y'all hungry? I've got some leftover biscuits and honey."

"It's good to see you, Miss Dovie and how can I pass up one of your biscuits," said Jacob. "I hope you still appreciate me being here that after you hear what these two have cooked up."

Dovie looked to her dad. "So this is why you went to Amarillo? Why didn't you say that in the note?"

"We went to talk to Mrs. Waterman and see about Jacob," said James. "He's gonna stay with us until winter is over. You don't mind moving upstairs until then, do you, hon?"

"Of course not," said Dovie, walking toward the house. She looked at the three bags Alice and James carried. "Is this all you brought?"

"This is all I need, Miss Dovie," said Jacob.

Dovie nodded. "Come on in, y'all. Let's get out of this cold."

"Surprised you're still up, Momma Dovie," said Alice with a yawn.

"I couldn't go to bed without seeing y'all were home, safe and sound," said Dovie. "Especially since y'all left without even a hint of a goodbye this morning."

Alice bowed her head. "Sorry, Momma Dovie, I should've asked you if it was okay, but I just knew you'd say no."

"You're right," said Dovie. "I would have, so I'm glad you didn't ask because I'm as delighted as peaches on ice cream that Jacob is here. So happy you're safe and sound. We were all worried about you when you didn't return Alice's letters."

"Aren't you gonna ask?" Jacob said, still standing beside the truck. He stared at Dovie, who turned to face him. "You haven't said one word about where my wife is or where my other leg is for that matter."

Dovie cocked her head. "I figured you'd tell me when you were ready."

Jacob gave Dovie his widest grin as he shook his head. "God love you, Miss Dovie. God love you."

She walked up to him and returned his wide smile. "God loves you too, Jacob. That's why he's brought you home. Now come on. Let's get inside."

Jacob took his crutches from James and grimaced as he started toward the door.

"What's wrong?" asked Dovie.

"I'm just fine, Miss Dovie," said Jacob.

"Don't you lie to me, Jacob Henry," said Dovie. "Is it your underarms or your leg that hurts?"

"Never could get anything past you," said Jacob as he labored up the stairs. "I'll show you in the house."

Once inside, Jacob sat at the kitchen table and unbuttoned his coat. Dovie took it and hung it on a spare nail by the door along with all the other winter coats. She wasn't surprised when Jacob didn't stop there and took off his flannel shirt, sitting only in his white sleeveless undershirt.

"Alice, go get my kit, please," said Dovie before turning to Jacob. "Show me."

Jacob raised both hands and Dovie stifled her gasp. Both of Jacob's underarms were rubbed raw and bore sores. His right armpit was oozing puss with tints of yellow. Dovie felt Jacob's forehead. "You're running a fever, probably due to infection. Your left isn't as bad, but it's not good either. We'll clean them both tonight, and then call the doctor in the morning. How long have they been this way?"

"This time, a couple of weeks," said Jacob. "I get sores like this all the time. Usually I just stay off my crutches for a while and they heal up, but then I use my crutches again and get the sores again."

Alice walked in with Dovie's bag and gasped. "Oh, Jacob, why didn't you tell us?"

"Well, Miss Alice, I knew once you saw this you'd fuss over me the entire trip home," said Jacob. "I just need to stay off my crutches for a few days. It'll get better."

"A few days?" Dovie shook her head. "More like a few weeks, Jacob."

Jacob shook his head. "I already told these two, I won't just be sitting around. I'll earn my keep."

"Of course you will," said Dovie. "But first, you have to let your underarms heal, and you will see the doctor in the morning. I won't have you dying from infection on account of being stubborn. Alice, dear, get me some fresh bandages from the hall closet while I put on some water to boil. Let's get this cleaned up, so we can all go to bed." She looked to her father. "Dad, you go on to bed. You need to rest so you don't have another spell."

"A spell?" Jacob looked at James.

"Again, if you had read my letters you would know this," Alice said playfully.

"I had an incident a few months back," said James. "I'm okay. I might not walk as fast as I used to, and sometimes I forget words but regardless of what 'Mother Hen' here says, I'm fine."

Jacob grabbed Alice's hand as she turned to get the bandages. "Miss Alice, I'm real sorry I didn't read all your letters. But I brought them with me, and I promise I'll read every word while I'm healing up. I shouldn't have made you worry like that. I should've told you I was okay. I'm really sorry for making you worry."

Alice gave him a smile before patting his hand. "Just don't let it happen again, 'cause now you know: we'll come lookin' for you."

Chapter Thirty-one

Ellie stared at the colored man standing at the stove cooking breakfast. He wasn't supposed to be there, and he definitely wasn't supposed to be doing her job.

Trying not to make a sound and alert the interloper that she was there, she hurried to Dovie's room. She was surprised to see the door open with Dovie nowhere to be seen. Panic raced through Ellie's body as she raced up the stairs to get Alice. The man had done something to Dovie. She didn't want to bother James, just in case the excitement of it all made James have another spell. Maybe if she woke Alice, they could both run to Bill's house to get help.

She shook her sister awake. Alice groaned. "Ellie, we got in really late. Let me sleep, I'll just skip breakfast."

Alice closed her eyes to go back to sleep. Ellie shook her again.

"Ellie, what's wrong with you?" snapped Alice.

Ellie started pointing downstairs and then grabbed Alice's arm and tried to pull her out of bed.

"Fine, I'll go downstairs. Just stop pulling on me," Alice growled as she got to her feet and pulled on her housecoat.

Ellie put her finger to her lips.

Alice looked at the window. "Ellie, the sun ain't even up yet. What's going on? Why do I have to be quiet?"

Ellie pointed toward the stairs and again put a finger to her lips.

"Fine, lead the way," said Alice with a sigh.

Ellie tiptoed down the stairs, careful to avoid the third stair from the bottom since it squeaked when even little Annabelle stepped on it. When they reached the bottom, Ellie pointed at the man, put her finger to her lips again, and then pointed to the door.

"Morning, Jacob," said Alice, shuffling past Ellie to the table and sitting down.

The man turned with the help of the back of a kitchen chair he had scooted next to the stove and gave Ellie and Alice a smile. His grin was ear to ear, and Ellie instantly wanted to like him.

"Good morning, Miss Alice, didn't expect to see you up this early. You must be Miss Ellie," said Jacob. "My name's Jacob Henry."

Ellie searched her memory. The name was familiar to her, but she couldn't place it.

"Miss Alice and everyone here at Quail Crossings, your family that is, they helped me out a few years back and now they're doin' it again. I hope that we can be friends, Miss Ellie. Would that be okay with you?"

Ellie looked at Alice who sat dozing with her cheek on her fist. Alice seemed to be fine around the man. Ellie wondered if this was the colored boy they had helped after the townspeople tried to lynch him. Alice was always writing him letters. Ellie slowly nodded that she would try to be his friend, but that was going to be hard if he kept doing her chores. What if they liked him better? Would they ask her to leave?

"Good," said Jacob. "Now I hear you're a mighty hard worker, and I'm gonna take a guess and say that you work hard to earn your keep here at Quail Crossings."

Again Ellie nodded. Jacob already seemed to understand her more than anyone else at Quail Crossings.

"I'd like to make a deal with you," said Jacob. "I wanna earn my keep too, so I was hoping that we could divvy up the chores. Some I can't do yet on account of my leg and some healing my body needs to do, but if you've got any shoes that need shined or potatoes to peel, anything I can do while sitting, would you allow me to do those things, so I feel like I'm not just in the way?"

Ellie nodded and pointed to the stove. She could smell the sausage burning. Jacob seemed nice and she knew exactly where he was coming from because she felt the same way. She decided she'd allow him to help. How much could a one-legged man do anyway?

Jacob used the chair to turn back around and flip the sausages. "I used to be a pretty good mess cook. Guess I'm out of practice."

"Ellie, can I go back to bed now?" asked Alice, walking back toward the stairs.

Ellie half-nodded as she walked to the pantry and started gathering the ingredients to make biscuits. If there was sausage, James was sure to want biscuits and sausage gravy.

"You read my mind," said Jacob, surveying her ingredients. "Nothin's better than biscuits, gravy and sausage. And I know it's one of Mr. James's favorites." He gave Ellie another winning smile. "You and me, we're gonna get along just fine."

Ellie couldn't help but smile back.

Dovie pushed her plate away and leaned back in her chair. "That was the best breakfast this side of the Mississippi, Ellie, great job."

Ellie pointed to Jacob before heading outside to gather eggs.

Dovie cocked her head. "Jacob Henry, you're supposed to be resting until the doctor gets here to look at you."

"Truth be told, Miss Dovie, I woke up hungry," said Jacob. "I figured if I was gonna fix something for myself, I best fix something for everyone else. Ellie came down a few minutes after I started, and she did the majority of the work. I just cooked the sausage. I might have eaten a few before they made it to the table. I only used my crutches to get to the kitchen then I just balanced using a kitchen chair."

"I'm just glad you have an appetite," said James. "Running a fever, I wouldn't expect you to be hungry."

"I'm feelin' pretty fine, to be honest," said Jacob, rubbing his belly. "I think I'm finally full. First time I've felt full in I don't know how long."

"I do wish you would've come to us," said Dovie. "Breaks my heart to hear 'bout you going hungry and being all alone. No one should have to endure that."

The back door opened and Elmer stood in the doorway looking as if he'd seen a ghost. "Jacob?" he gasped.

"Mr. Elmer," said Jacob, flashing another grin. Dovie wondered if Jacob had stopped smiling since he got to Quail Crossings.

"I told you years ago to stop with that mister stuff," said Elmer, hurrying around the table to shake Jacob's hand. He stopped when he saw the empty, limp pant leg.

"Forgive me for not standing, Elmer, my leg's a little tired from cooking breakfast," said Jacob.

Remembering his manners, Elmer averted his stare and grabbed Jacob's outstretched hand. "I'm just glad you're back. Where's your wife? I'd love to meet her." Elmer looked around.

Jacob shook his head. "I'm afraid my leg wasn't the only casualty of the war. She left me while I was in the Pacific."

Elmer scratched his head as a bit of red flushed his cheeks. "Sorry to hear that. Is this just a visit or are you stayin' for good?"

"Through the winter," said Jacob, "and then back to Sweetsville to find a job."

"I'll take care of that," said Elmer, as he sat in the chair next to Jacob. Then he noticed the food. "Is that biscuits and gravy? Can I have some?"

"Help yourself," said Dovie. "How's Tiny feeling this morning?"

"I think most of the morning sickness is gone, but she still ain't up for making much more than toast in the morning," answered Elmer, filling his plate. "I tell you what, if Ellie didn't make us bread every week, I'm pretty sure that Mary, the baby, and I would all starve."

"You're gonna be a daddy?" Jacob slapped Elmer on the back. "And you married that sweet girl, Miss Tiny? Congratulations!"

"I thought you knew," said Elmer.

"Well, he would have if he'd read my letters," said Alice walking down the stairs and giving Jacob an ornery smile.

"Now, Miss Alice, I thought we were past that," said Jacob, acting as if he were hurt.

Alice sat across from Jacob and started filling her plate. "I reserve the right to throw that into any conversation I see fit until you're up to speed and have read my letters."

"Okay, I deserve that," said Jacob, regaining his smile.

"What time will the doctor be here?" asked Alice.

"His nurse thought he could get here around 9:30 this morning," said Dovie, "so any time really."

"Doctor?" mumbled Elmer, with a mouth full of biscuits and gravy before looking at James.

"I'm fine," said James. "We just need him to take a look at Jacob's underarms. His crutches have rubbed them raw with sores, and Dovie wants to make sure the infection hasn't spread."

Elmer looked around and saw the crutches sitting against the wall in the corner. He pointed to them, and Jacob gave him a nod of approval. Elmer walked to the crutches and picked them up to examine them closer.

"Jacob, these come all the way to my chin," said Elmer. "I know you're taller than me, but no wonder they're rubbing. And this padding is all shot." Elmer flipped the crutch over. "Where are the pegs to adjust the height?"

"How do you know so much about crutches?" asked Alice, ladling gravy over her biscuits.

"A buddy of mine was on them after he twisted his ankle something bad over in Poland," explained Elmer. "Where'd you get these? They look like they were just thrown together."

"That's what they gave me when I left the hospital," said Jacob.

"Mind if I fix them?" asked Elmer. "You're gonna need to be able to get around when you come to work after you get all healed up."

Jacob squinted his eyes. "You know I thought you said something earlier before we got to talking about Miss Tiny, but I decided I must've heard wrong. What do you mean when I come to work?"

"I bought the butcher shop from Butcher Davis at the first of this month, and I need some help," said Elmer. "Tiny can't help 'cause the smell of the meat makes her sick … well everything makes her sick. But I can't have her running out of the store every five minutes to get fresh air. In fact, I'm on my way there now, just stopped to find out why they went to Amarillo yesterday without tellin' anyone." He smiled at Jacob. "I guess now I know."

"Elmer, you can't give me a job," said Jacob. "I appreciate the offer, but hiring me would only cause you trouble in this town. You could lose business. I won't do that to you. You've got a child to think about now."

"So you're saying you won't help me out?" asked Elmer.

"You know I'd help you anyway I could," said Jacob.

"Then it's settled," said Elmer. "In fact, you can live in the back of the shop if you want. Butcher Davis had a small apartment in the back for when he worked late or when the weather got bad. He'd just go to sleep there. It has a little stove for cooking and everything."

"I won't do it," said Jacob. "That wouldn't be helping. People won't come if they know I'm working and living there."

"Look," said Elmer, holding up his hand, "you're my friend and all returning soldiers deserve jobs, in my opinion. If anyone has a problem with that, I'll let them know exactly what they can do with their business."

Jacob looked at his hands.

"Just think about it, okay," said Elmer. "I'm going to go to work now, but I'll be back later to work on those crutches. Dovie, do you mind if Tiny and I eat dinner here?"

"That would be fine," said Dovie as she heard a car pull into the driveway. "How long do you think it'll take you to fix the crutches?"

"A few days," said Elmer.

"Sounds good," said Dovie.

"We also talked to Mrs. Waterman," said James.

"What did you find out?" asked Elmer as he walked back to the table.

"I'll tell you the short version since you need to be gettin' to the shop," said James.

Dovie looked out the kitchen window. "Oh good, the doctor is here." She cocked her head. "He's talking to Ellie. What could he be saying to her?"

Not liking the look on Ellie's face, Dovie grabbed her coat and walked out the door. With the approach of Dovie, Ellie ran towards the barn. "Everything okay, out here?"

Chapter Thirty-two

Dr. Hushton flashed Dovie a smile as he walked toward her. "Good morning, Mrs. Grant. I was just asking young Miss Brewer about her cheek," said Dr. Hushton. "She, of course, didn't answer. Everything still going okay?"

"Absolutely, Dr. Hushton, I've told you before that Ellie's a good girl and a hard worker," said Dovie as she walked with the doctor. "She had a run-in with our nasty rooster and got a little cut on her cheek. But she's doing fine and we're happy to have her here."

James and Elmer came out the back door, and Dovie knew James was telling Elmer about Ellie's story by the look of concern on James's face and the look of disgust on Elmer's. "So we can't do anything, or they'll send Ellie away for the fire?" confirmed Elmer and James nodded.

"Morning," said James, shaking the doctor's hand. "Please excuse us for a minute."

As Elmer and James walked away, Dr. Hushton turned to Dovie. "What fire?"

Dovie waved him off. "Happened a while back at Ellie's last home. It's a long and sad story, but the family had it in their minds that Ellie started the fire when the facts point to it being an accident." She lowered her voice. "They beat her something severe; it's just awful. We can't press charges against the family, or they'll sic the law on Ellie for the fire."

"Do you know who the family is or where the fire took place?" asked Dr. Hushton.

Dovie shook her head. "Only that it happened south of Amarillo. Mrs. Waterman wouldn't give Dad the name of the family. She's trying to protect Ellie, but we're heartbroken to hear what happened to her."

Dr. Hushton rubbed his jaw. "So what do you intend to do?"

"Not sure if there's anything we can do," said Dovie. "Just make sure she knows nothing like that will ever happen to her again."

Dovie put her hand on the door, ready to open it when Dr. Hushton stopped her. "Mrs. Grant, be careful. I've heard of similar situations where the child was actually to blame. These kids without homes, something happens in their minds, and they lose control. There was a family over in Stapleton who all became gravely ill after their adopted daughter dissolved rat poison in their tea and another case down by Temple where a boy who had been staying with the family tried to murder the father of the family while he slept. Thankfully the boy was not successful, but the family was sure he was about to murder them all."

"Ellie's not like that," said Dovie, narrowing her eyes. "I will not have her lumped into a category simply because of some bad apples."

Dr. Hushton held up his hands in a peaceful gesture. "I just don't want to see your family hurt, is all. We know something is wrong with Ellie because she chooses not to speak. That's not normal. Just be careful."

Dovie bit her lip. She had a slew of words for Dr. Hushton's warning but was afraid if she let them all out, he wouldn't tend to Jacob. "How 'bout we see to Jacob?" She pulled open the door and let the doctor in. "I cleaned the wounds last night, the best I could, and put on some ointment we had on hand. But I wanted you to look at it and make sure the infection hadn't spread further."

Dr. Hushton hesitated. "You didn't say he was colored on the phone."

Dovie smiled at the doctor. "Why would I? Will that knowledge help you better tend to him?"

The doctor shook his head. "I'm just surprised because you said he was a family friend."

"He is a family friend," said Dovie, pretending she didn't know what the doctor was trying to get at. "Do you want to examine him here or in a bedroom?"

"Here is fine," mumbled Dr. Hushton.

Dovie watched Dr. Hushton tend to Jacob's underarms and then glanced out the kitchen window. Ellie stood in the doorway of the barn, eggs cradled in her coat. Dovie wondered why she didn't come in since it looked as if she was trembling. She shook the thought away. Knowing Ellie, she just wanted to stay out of the way and being it was a crisp winter day, she was probably just shivering and would come inside when she got cold enough.

There was nothing wrong with Ellie, Dovie reminded herself, but she would be asking Ellie later exactly what Dr. Hushton had said to her. She hadn't known Dr. Hushton for very long, but he always seemed like a gentleman. He had come to be their country doctor when Dr. Crowly retired. She had wanted to like the doctor, but something about him unnerved her. She was sure it was just because he wasn't Dr. Crowly, who had been their family doctor since Dovie was a baby.

"All right, Mrs. Grant," said Dr. Hushton, giving her a smile. "You did right by his wounds. Jacob seems like a strong boy, and I think he'll fight off the infection just fine. If his fever spikes, take him to the hospital in Perry immediately. They'll get him stable, then transfer him by ambulance to the Veterans' Hospital in Amarillo. It's a good thing y'all caught this when you did, or he could've lost his arm as well as his leg. Keep the wounds clean and dry, and he'll be fine in a few weeks." He turned to Jacob. "You need to stay off your crutches completely until the wounds are healed. Don't go being stubborn and using them before then, or you'll just wind up in the same situation. Take aspirin for any pain."

"Thanks, Doctor," said Jacob as he started to put his shirt back on.

"Thanks again, Dr. Hushton," said Dovie. "What do we owe you?"

"Walk me to my car, Mrs. Grant," said the doctor.

Dovie grabbed her coat and pocketbook and walked Dr. Hushton to his car.

"This visit is on me," said Dr. Hushton. "I overstepped earlier and for that I apologize. I won't lie, I'm still concerned with Ellie Brewer's mental state, but I trust she'll turn out just fine."

"Doctor, you don't have to do that," said Dovie. "I know you were just coming from a place of concern. Let me pay you for your time."

"Again, not necessary," said Dr. Hushton as he got in his car. "I'll be back in a week to check on that boy's underarms."

Dovie watched the doctor drive off before turning toward the barn. Ellie was no longer in the doorway. She scanned the area for her father, who had never come back inside after walking Elmer to his truck. She went towards the barn in search of her missing family members.

She slowed as she heard her father talking and then peeked around the corner. James sat on the milking stool while Ellie sat in the hay and listened as James told her the story of the large tornado that had taken out the barn. Ellie watched wide-eyed as James finished the story with how he had found Bill and Lou Anne in the partially caved-in dugout.

"The doctor's gone," said Dovie once James had finished. "Not sure who y'all are hiding from out here, but it's just us chickens now."

"We're not hiding from anyone," said James as he used the stall post to help himself up. "I was just tellin' her about the tornado of 1940 and how lucky we all were."

"God was lookin' out for us, that's for sure," said Dovie. "Ellie, run on into the house and put up those eggs before you get sick. You've been out in this cold long enough."

She waited for Ellie to exit the barn before turning back to her dad. "Did she give you any hints on what the doctor was saying to her?"

James shook his head. "No, but I got the impression she's not too fond of him. I reckon she's not too fond of doctors in general after all her times in the hospital. I'm sure she thinks of the pain and suffering she went through when she sees a doctor. Why?"

Dovie rubbed her hands together. "When I saw them talkin', I got the feeling she was scared. Then I saw her in the barn trembling or shivering. Either way, it was as if she wouldn't come inside while he was here." She bit her lip. "You know Dr. Hushton has warned me about Ellie several times. Says her refusal to speak means she's mentally unstable, and he's seen cases where orphan children have tried to hurt their caregivers."

"But that's not our Ellie," said James.

"That's what I said." Dovie hugged herself. "We've not known Dr. Hushton very long. You don't think he said something bad to Ellie do you?"

James shook his head. "Ellie's not gonna trust people easily after everything's she's been through.

I'm sure Dr. Hushton was just being friendly. Now let's get inside; it's freezing out here."

Chapter Thirty-three

February 1946

Dovie stared at the letter she had just received from Gabe. Evalyn was due to arrive any minute, and Dovie would have to tell her. Tears fell onto the paper, and Dovie quickly wiped them off the letter and her cheeks. She had to be strong. Gabe had been right when he said she was the only person who really understood what it was like to be a young widow, and Evalyn was going to need her more than ever now.

"Momma Dovie!" Joy squealed as they entered through the back door, announcing their arrival. She barreled into Dovie and gave her a large hug. Dovie barely had time to set the letter down before Joy crashed into her.

"Hey there, Joy, watcha been up to this morning?" asked Dovie, putting a pep in her voice she didn't quite feel.

"Just the usual," said Joy. "I helped Momma with the dishes and then she sewed and sewed and sewed while I played with Caleb. I wanted to go outside, but Momma said it was too cold."

"'Cause it is," said Evalyn, walking in with Caleb.

"She's right. It's a might cold outside," said Dovie. "You should listen to your momma. She doesn't want you to get sick."

"Where's Ellie?" asked Joy, changing the subject. Dovie guessed it was because she was agreeing with her mother.

"In the parlor, playing with the dolls by the fire. Why don't you go join her?" suggested Dovie. She walked to the parlor. "Ellie, be a dear and keep the children busy for a bit, I need them to stay out of the kitchen."

Ellie nodded as Evalyn put Caleb down by the fire. "Y'all mind your aunt, now."

"Everything okay?" asked Evalyn, walking back into the kitchen with Dovie and shedding her coat before placing it on a nail beside the back door.

Dovie swallowed hard and cleared her throat. "I got a letter from Gabe today."

Evalyn stood still for a moment as if digesting the words. "And?"

"Maybe you should sit down," said Dovie.

"So it wasn't him," said Evalyn, sinking into a chair.

Dovie shook her head. "I'm sorry, but Gabe is certain the man in the Paris hospital isn't Robert."

Evalyn stood and grabbed an apron. "Shall we get started on the muffins for church tomorrow?"

"Sit down, Evalyn. We don't have to start on that now," said Dovie. "Take a minute to think about what you just heard. Talk to me about it."

"What is there to talk about?" asked Evalyn, walking to the pantry. "We knew it was a long shot that the man was Robert."

Dovie stood. "So you're just okay with it?"

Evalyn slammed the flour sack onto the table. "Of course I'm not!" she said dissolving into tears.

Hurrying over to her, Dovie wrapped her up in a hug. Evalyn wilted into her as Dovie helped her to sit. She pulled a chair close to Evalyn and continued to hold her as she wept.

"It's all right," said Dovie, hugging her tight. "You just let it out."

Dovie held Evalyn until her weeping slowed. "Now look, this isn't the news we wanted, but Gabe is traveling to London on another lead."

"What's the point, Dovie?" asked Evalyn. "We both know how much time has passed and each day that goes by, we know the chances of Gabe finding Robert alive are smaller. I need to face the fact that he's not coming back."

Dovie rubbed Evalyn's back. "A while back you asked me if you should give up hope, and I told you never. I still feel that way. Let Gabe finish his three months and with every lead, you allow yourself hope because sometimes that's all that keeps us going."

"I'm so scared, Dovie," said Evalyn. "I'm so scared I'll never see him again. That Caleb will never know him, and Joy will forget him as time goes by. She was so little when he left. I think she's more in love with the thought of him. I don't think I can do this alone."

"It's normal to be terrified," said Dovie. "I'd be concerned if you weren't scared, but you know you've got us to help you out with the kids and with the memories. You're not alone, Evalyn. You'll never be alone."

With the jingle of the bell, Jacob closed his book and looked up at the customer walking into the Brewer Meat Market. His heart raced as he slid off the tall stool Elmer had placed at the cash register for him and grabbed the nearest crutch. Elmer had outdone himself making Jacob new crutches out of a nice pine and Jacob was glad he had a solid weapon nearby.

"What can I do for you today, Mr. Kelley?" asked Jacob, trying not to let his fear be heard in his voice. He gripped his crutch and tried to make himself look taller.

He knew Frank Kelley's face the minute he laid eyes on him. He would never forget the face of the boy, now a man that beat him to near death and then tried to kill him during a tornado. Frank Kelley was the worst kind of racist, the kind that didn't mind hurting those who bore a different colored skin.

Frank took off his hat and fingered the rim. "I heard Elmer had bought this place, and you were working for him."

"I heard your family had moved from Knollwood," said Jacob. He wished that Elmer wasn't taking a late lunch at Johnson's Drug Store up the street, but if Frank came to fight, he'd be ready this time, unlike the last time when Frank and his friends caught him from behind.

Frank smiled and nodded. "Yes, 'bout four years ago, but I still keep in touch with some of my old friends from 'round here."

He took a step forward, and Jacob lifted his crutch to where it sat in both hands. He wanted Frank to know he had a weapon and wasn't afraid to use it.

Frank held up his hands. "I'm not here to cause you any trouble, Jacob."

Jacob flinched at the sound of his name coming out of Frank's mouth. It was the first time he'd heard Frank use his given name and not called him 'colored boy' or worse. "Then why are you here? Just doing your shoppin'?"

Frank let out a low chuckle. "No, my wife would never allow me to do the grocery shopping. I tried it once and came home with all the wrong stuff. I work in insurance now and had an appointment with a client not too far from Knollwood. I couldn't pass up the opportunity to stop by." Frank took another careful step toward the counter. "Jacob, would you please put the crutch down? It would be a lot easier to talk to you. I know you have no reason to trust me, but I have something I need to say, then I'll leave. No trouble, I promise."

Jacob slowly lowered the crutch, barely able to believe his ears. Frank Kelley was talking to him in a kind manner, using words like "please" and "promise".

"Thank you," said Frank. "I don't know if you know this, but I joined the Navy after the attack on Pearl Harbor. My ma just about had a heart attack thinking about this Texas Panhandle boy surrounded by water, but I just knew it was right for me. Anyway, we had a few colored men on board the USS New Jersey. I didn't think much about them most of the time. As far as I was concerned they were in their place. They served us food and cleaned our messes, and that's how I thought it was always supposed to be. Then one day we were taking some hard hits from the Japanese. Everyone was ordered to take cover when this colored boy tackled me to the ground."

Frank swallowed hard. "At first I was so angry at him. I yelled at him to get off me and called him deplorable names, but then I noticed he wasn't moving. When I got myself free of him, I realized when he tackled me, he had saved my life by sacrificing his own." Frank looked at his hat. "I never even knew him, but he took a bullet for me ... he died for me."

Jacob loosened his grip on the crutch as he watched Frank fight back tears for the man who had saved his life.

"I couldn't sleep that night," Frank continued. "I just kept thinking about that sailor sacrificing his life for mine, and it didn't take me long to realize that it wasn't the first time a colored man had saved my life. I didn't want to admit it back then, not even after Paul told me how you got me in the closet during the tornado. You saved my life and I never once admitted it, much less said thank you. So I'm saying it now. Thank you for not leaving me in the storm. You had no reason to risk your life to save mine, especially after everything I'd done to you."

Frank reached into his pocket and pulled out a war medal attached to a purple ribbon. "After that sailor saved me, I was able to get to one of our Oerlikon's and bring down three Jap planes while the rest of the ship rallied, and the Japs retreated. Because you saved me from that tornado so many years ago, I was able to save all those men on the ship, and Lord knows I didn't deserve saving once, never mind twice."

He put the medal on the counter and slid it toward Jacob. "They gave me the Legion of Merit award for my outstanding service to my country and my fellow sailors during that attack, and now I'm here to give it to you for outstanding service in the name of humanity and bravery during the tornado of 1940. It might not have been a war, but I made it a war zone."

Frank turned, put on his hat, and started for the door. As soon as he reached it, he turned and tipped his hat at Jacob. "Thank you, Jacob, I promise the life you saved will not be one that lives in hatred."

Chapter Thirty-four

James fought to catch his breath as he sat on the milking stool. He thought about what Dr. Hushton had told him about taking deep breaths whenever he felt winded or dizzy. James shook his head. He couldn't even give Poppy and Tex a little hay without losing his breath. His incident in the barn seemed like a decade ago, but James still felt like a helpless old man.

"James, are you okay?" asked Bill, putting a hand on James's back. "Do you need me to go get Dovie?"

James waved him off. "I'm fine," he said slowly, trying not to pant. "Just need to catch my breath."

"What are you doing out here, anyway?" asked Bill. "That north wind is not playin' around today. I won't be surprised if we get snow."

"Too cold for snow," said James, taking a deep breath. "I just wanted to give Poppy and Tex some extra hay on account of the weather."

"Then ask me to do it," said Bill. "You know I don't mind."

"Why should I have to ask you to throw in a couple of extra forks of hay?" asked James, frustration building in his voice. "I should be able to do that." He took another deep breath. "You've got enough to do out here by yourself since I'm about as helpful as a rock."

"I know how you feel," said Bill, grabbing the pitchfork and continuing the job James couldn't finish.

"How so?" asked James.

"During the war, I felt like I was nothing but a bump on a log," said Bill. "All these men my age were going over to fight and I was just here, doing what I'd always done. Even though I knew I was helping this farm stay afloat, I felt helpless the entire time. It wasn't until Elmer got home that I realized it was a good thing for me to have stayed here. I saw to it they had a home to come back to. Not saying you wouldn't have kept Quail Crossings going had I gone to war, but I knew God's reason for having me stay. As you always say, we may not see the reason in the beginning, but there's always a reason in the end."

"Well, I can't say I see it like that yet," said James.

"Maybe your job now is to enjoy all those grandkids you've got running around. Maybe God wants you to slow down and spend your time remembering what it was like being a child, instead of being the responsible one. Maybe God needed you to step down, so I could step up and feel useful. I can think of a lot of reasons," said Bill, finishing with the hay and putting the fork down. "Would you like me to continue?"

James shook his head.

"We need you, James," said Bill. "We don't need you to fork hay, move cattle, or even slop the pigs. We just need you."

Annabelle watched as Dean gathered the eggs. She wanted to go inside the coop with him and help him gather the eggs, but he had told her she was too little. She could tell her brother was still scared to go in the chicken house after the rooster attack, but he put on a brave face and did it anyway.

Annabelle wanted to be brave like her brother. If he weren't scared of the roosters, then she wouldn't be either. She looked around the farm wondering what other brave thing she could do and spotted the open cellar.

Momma Dovie had been going in and out restocking the pantry inside. She could be brave by going into the cellar and helping Momma Dovie bring up the canned goods. Annabelle hurried toward the open cellar. She wanted to bring a jar up before Dovie came back outside.

She was almost there when a squeal came out of nowhere, and Daisy the pig, blocked her path.

"Move, Daisy," said Annabelle. "I'm helpin' Momma Dovie."

Annabelle tried to skirt around the pig, but Daisy wasn't having it.

"Daisy, stop it!" cried Annabelle.

Again she tried to get around Daisy, but Daisy blocked her path.

"Daisy," Annabelle whined as she heard something walk up behind her. She was sure it was her brother, but when she turned she was surprised to see Norman.

"Mr. Norman, Daisy won't let me by," she cried to the goose.

Norman waddled past Daisy and sat by the open cellar door. Daisy turned to keep an eye on Norman and Annabelle took the opportunity to run toward the cellar. She had just reached the door when Norman raised his wings and hissed.

Annabelle screamed, causing Bill to race out of the barn, followed quickly by James.

"Mr. Norman's gonna bite me," cried Annabelle, running into her daddy's arms.

"What's going on?" cried Dovie, running out of the house.

"Norman attacked Annabelle," said James.

"What on earth for?" asked Dovie.

"What happened, Annabelle?" asked Bill.

"I was going to help Momma Dovie in the cellar," cried Annabelle. "But Daisy blocked me, and then Mr. Norman hissed at me."

Dovie looked over her shoulder and saw the two animals still guarding the cellar door. "I think they were trying to keep her from the opening," said Dovie. "Annabelle, honey, I appreciate you wanting to help me, but you gotta be careful around the cellar. The stairs are steep, and if you fall, you really could get hurt. I think Norman and Daisy were just trying to protect you."

"Really?" cried Annabelle, her head resting on her daddy's shoulder.

"Really," said Bill. "Momma Dovie's right. You can't play around the cellar because it's dangerous. You hear me?"

Annabelle nodded.

Dean walked over with the eggs cradled inside his coat. "What's going on?"

"Nothing," said James. "We were all about to go inside and get warmed up. Ready?"

"Can I get down?" asked Annabelle, and her daddy set her on her feet.

"Come on, Annabelle," said Dovie, holding out her hand, "You can help me close up the cellar."

Holding Momma Dovie's hand, Annabelle approached Daisy and Norman. Letting go of Dovie, she got on her knees and wrapped her arms around Norman's neck. Daisy hurried over and nudged Annabelle with her snout. Annabelle kept one arm wrapped around Norman's neck as she hugged Daisy with the other. "Thank you. You're my best friends."

Alice walked down the stairs in a light blue dress with pink ribbon that Evalyn had made for her. Her blonde hair rested in curls on her shoulders with the sides elegantly pulled back and secured with pins.

"Oh my, you do look grown up," said Dovie. "Such a beautiful young woman."

"Thank you," said Alice, giving a little curtsy.

Dovie blotted her eyes with a dishtowel and turned to the sink.

"You okay?" asked Alice, hurrying over to Dovie.

"You just remind me so much of Helen," said Dovie. "You always have, and I can't help but think of the fact she'd be going to that dance with y'all if she were still here."

"We don't have to go if you don't want us to," said Alice. "I know this is a hard day for you."

"You'd think after all these years, it wouldn't be so difficult," said Dovie. "But I miss them terribly."

"We won't go," said Alice. "I'd rather stay here with y'all anyway than go to a silly Valentine's Day dance. I don't even have a sweetheart."

Ellie walked down the stairs in her hunter green dress with gray ribbon. Her hair was pulled up into a ponytail that Alice had obviously curled.

"Oh, Ellie, you look wonderful," said Dovie, quickly drying her tears. She hollered into the parlor. "Bill, grab the camera, and y'all come in here and take a look at your sisters. We need to get a picture before they head to the dance."

"Momma Dovie, we're gonna stay here with you," said Alice.

"Nonsense," said Dovie. "I've got a house full of people who love me and can keep me company tonight. Y'all go to the dance and have fun. Who knows, maybe you'll find your sweetheart tonight."

"Doubtful," said Alice as her family members started pouring into the kitchen with their "ohs" and "awes". "All the boys in Knollwood are like my brothers."

"Sounds good to me," said Bill, holding the camera up. "No sweetheart, no problem in my book. Where do you beautiful ladies want your picture taken?"

"By the stairs, just under the light," said Dovie. "Just wish the pictures were in color, so we could see the lovely work Evalyn did on your dresses better."

Alice and Ellie stood in front of the staircase and smiled as Bill took their picture.

"Wish we'd had one of these when I took Lou Anne to the dance," said Bill.

"Oh, that would've been a great picture," said Lou Anne with a laugh. "We could've gotten Charlotte Wheaton as she draped herself over you while Peter and I stood beside y'all looking uncomfortable."

"Sounds 'bout right," said Bill with an ornery smile before turning to the girls. "Y'all ready to go?"

Alice gave a noncommittal nod while Ellie shook her head.

"Well, aren't you two just as excited as a couple of slugs," said Dovie. "If you go to the dance expecting to have a bad time, then you will. How about you two give it a chance, before already deciding it's a waste of your time?"

"I would like to see what it's like," said Alice turning to Ellie, "and I don't want to go alone. Maybe Bill could wait in the car for a half hour, and if we don't like it, we'll just come back out."

"One hour," said Bill.

"You can't sit in the car for an hour, Bill," said Dovie. "You'll freeze."

"I wasn't plannin' on it," said Bill. "Mrs. Spaulding won't mind if I come in and chaperone for an hour. Once I see the girls are fine, I'll head on to Annette's Café or go keep Jacob company and wait until the dance is over."

"Oh great, my brother is escorting me to the Valentine's dance." Alice rolled her eyes. "You can't do that, Bill, I'll be the laughing stock of the whole school."

"No one except Mrs. Spaulding will even know I'm there," said Bill. "It's not like I'm going out onto the dance floor."

Alice grabbed her coat. "Let's just go, so we can get back home."

"That's the spirit," Dovie joked as she gave them one last hug and watched them go out into the night. She prayed a silent prayer for their safety, that they had a good time, and that Alice didn't kill Bill before the night was over.

Chapter Thirty-five

Alice laid their coats on the bleachers by the door and looked around the gymnasium for people she knew. Ellie stood so close to her that Alice wondered if it looked like they were attached. The dance committee had done a good job with the decorations. Pink, white, and red paper hearts hung from the ceiling over the makeshift dance area while four large paper mache hearts flanked the band that played a lively number on the stage overlooking the gym floor.

The dance floor was already crowded with couples doing a lively jitterbug to the band's swing tune. Alice watched Bill slide in, staying close to the wall and in the shadows. She appreciated him staying but wished he had found another place to wait. He could have just gone to Elmer's shop and then come back in an hour. Alice highly suspected he was worried about Ellie finding her place among all the school kids. She couldn't blame him. She was worried about it too. Ellie was at least a year younger than the kids there, but Mrs. Spaulding had said it would be okay for her to come as Alice's guest.

Alice spotted a group of girls from her class and grabbed Ellie's hand to lead her over to them.

"Hey, Alice," said Virginia. "Love your dress."

"Thanks, Virginia" said Alice. "My sister, Evie, made it. Do y'all remember my sister, Ellie? Ellie, this is Virginia Evans, Shirley Manders, Doris Beller, and Jean Fisher."

Ellie gave them all a little wave.

"Oh yeah," said Shirley, "She's the dumb one."

"She ain't dumb," snapped Alice. "She talks when she wants to. She just doesn't want to talk to you."

Shirley held up her hands. "I didn't mean nothin' by it. I was just makin' an observation."

"Look," said Alice, "sorry I snapped. It's just she's my sister, and I don't want nobody saying mean things about her. You don't know what she's been through."

"So tell us," said Doris.

Ellie squeezed Alice's hand and, Alice shook her head. "It's not my story to tell. Besides we got better things to do tonight than to talk about Ellie. Y'all been dancing?"

Alice felt Ellie's hand release and looked over her shoulder. Ellie had taken a few steps back, separating herself from the group. Alice motioned for her to come back up, but Ellie just shook her head. Turning to get her sister, Alice felt a small tap on her shoulder.

She turned back around and blushed as she came face to face with Lawrence Dodson.

"Hi, Alice," he said in a soft voice. "Would you like to dance?"

Alice noticed the band had selected a slow song. She looked at her friends who all encouraged her to go with nods and smiles. She then looked back at Ellie who gave her a wave of encouragement.

"That would be nice," said Alice.

Ellie watched Alice on the dance floor and felt happy for her sister. Alice never really talked about boys, but occasionally Lawrence's name would come up since he seemed to enjoy reading as much as Alice did.

Ellie scanned the sides of the gym and relaxed a little to see Bill standing in a corner with Mrs. Spaulding drinking punch and talking. She had turned to make her way toward Bill when she was surrounded by Alice's friends.

"So if you can talk, why don't you?" asked Shirley.

Ellie shrugged.

"Maybe she just doesn't have much to say," said Virginia. "You know like Jean."

"Hey, I have stuff to say," said Jean.

"I know," said Virginia, "but out of all of us, you're the quiet one."

"Hard to get a word in with you, Shirley, and Doris yappin' all the time," said Jean, folding her arms.

"I don't talk that much," countered Doris.

"Honestly though, Alice said you could talk if you wanted to, so say something," Shirley said to Ellie, ignoring the conversation between Jean, Doris, and Virginia. "Prove to us that you aren't dumb."

Ellie turned to walk towards Bill when Shirley grabbed her arm. "Don't walk away. If you leave Alice will be mad. Just say one word, and I'll leave you alone."

"Why don't you just leave her alone?" said Virginia.

"Cause I want to know if she's faking it," said Shirley, still holding onto Ellie's arm.

"Faking what?" asked Doris. "Alice said she talks when she wants to. What's she faking?"

Panic ripped through Ellie's body as Shirley's grip grew tighter. She had to get away. If she didn't get away now, the hitting would start. She looked at Bill talking to Mrs. Spaulding as he watched the dance floor. She desperately wanted to cry out to him, but she'd lost her voice in her panic.

"She ain't like us," said Shirley. "There's something wrong with a person who won't speak just 'cause they don't want to. My ma said the devil's got her tongue and that she'll probably kill her entire family while they sleep, or burn the house to the ground."

"No!" cried Ellie as she slapped Shirley's hand off her arm and ran out of the gymnasium.

Alice and Lawrence had danced the last three songs together, and he didn't let go when the band broke into an upbeat two-step. Lawrence spun Alice around with the grace of a professional dancer, and Alice laughed with delight.

A firm tap on her shoulder interrupted her fun as Lawrence stopped with wide eyes. Alice turned to see Bill frowning at her.

"Bill, what are you doing?" snapped Alice, her cheeks hot. "You said you'd leave after an hour, and we'd never know you were here."

"I'm sorry, Alice, but Ellie ran out of here, and I can't find her," said Bill. "I need your help to look for her. She didn't grab her coat, and it's awfully cold out there."

"Oh no," gasped Alice, "what happened? I looked over and she was talking to my friends. I thought she was okay."

"All I saw was Ellie slap Shirley's hand off her arm, and then she took off," said Bill. "I didn't stop to ask what happened. I just went after her, but she was gone by the time I got to the door."

"I'll help you look," offered Lawrence.

"Thank you," said Alice, "but first I need to know what happened."

Alice marched over to Shirley. "What did you do?"

Shirley shrugged. "Nothing. Your sister just went crazy and ran out."

"You grabbed her arm," said Virginia. "You were badgering her to say something."

"How could you?" Alice was on the verge of tears. "I thought you were my friend. How could you be so awful to my sister?"

Alice turned to Doris, Virginia, and Jean and wiped away the stray tears that had fallen. "We need your help looking for her. She didn't take her coat."

"Of course," said the girls.

"I can help too," said Shirley.

Lawrence narrowed his eyes at her. "You've done enough, haven't you? Let's go, Alice."

Alice looked at Lawrence and gave him a thankful nod.

"Where should we look first?" asked Jean as she buttoned her coat.

"We should split up," said Bill. "Alice, you and Doris check inside the school. Jean and Virginia check behind the school, and Lawrence and I will check in front of the school and the parking lot. Meet back here in half an hour. If we don't find her by then, we'll need to get the sheriff involved."

Everyone nodded and started toward their designated areas. Shirley ran up behind Alice and Doris. "Let me help," she cried. "I know I was awful, but I didn't mean for her to run off in the cold. I'm worried about her too."

"Fine, come with us," said Alice. "You can apologize to her when we find her."

The girls started up the stairs to look on the second floor of the school house.

"She spoke you know," said Shirley.

"She did?" Alice looked at Shirley with wide eyes.

"She only said no, but it was clear as day," explained Shirley.

"You were being pretty awful," said Doris. "Saying the devil had her tongue and that she was going to burn down Quail Crossings."

"Shirley!" cried Alice as they reached the top of the stairs. "She was accused of starting a fire at her last home, and then they beat her something horrible. She was in the hospital for a week recovering from her injuries, and everyone knows the fire was an accident."

"How do you know?" asked Shirley. "She could've set that fire and made it look like an accident."

"No."

The voice came from the end of the hallway on the second floor where there was an old storage closet. The door was recessed into the wall, and if a person didn't know it was there, they wouldn't think to look.

"Ellie," said Alice, she turned to her friends. "Stay here a minute, okay?"

She walked slowly to her sister who sat hugging her knees to her chest in front of the storage room door. She looked at Alice, tears running down her face. "I didn't do it."

Alice gave her a loving smile. "I know, Ellie. I never once thought you did."

Chapter Thirty-six

Elmer ran. Sweat dripped off his brow and his sides burned as if they were about to explode, but he wouldn't stop running. He couldn't. If he stopped, he would die.

He jumped into a trench and looked at his fellow soldiers. They all stared at him with terror in their eyes. "What do we do, Brewer? We're surrounded."

"Has anyone seen Thomas Pope?" Elmer asked. The soldiers shook their heads.

"I saw him last by the barbed wire," said one of the soldiers, "Before the tanks."

"Was anyone with him?" Elmer asked as an explosion of dirt rained on them, and everyone hit the ground.

The soldier shook his head as the dirt storm stopped. "I don't think so."

"We can't leave him," said Elmer.

"We can't go back, Brewer," said the soldier. "It's suicide."

"We don't leave a soldier behind," said Elmer. "Thomas is one of us."

"I'm not dying for him," said another soldier. "We've got to retreat."

"Go back to the line," ordered Elmer. "I'm going to the wire to look for Thomas."

Elmer left the trench just as another explosion rocked the ground. Elmer's ears rang, and he cried out, falling face first into the mud. Turning he saw the bodies of the soldiers he had just been with, their faces twisted with the horror of death.

"No!" cried Elmer as he looked around the battlefield. Everywhere, he saw broken, bleeding soldiers, each bearing Thomas's face. He turned back to the trench, and those soldiers, too, had Thomas's face. "No! I'm sorry. I'm so sorry!"

"Wake up, Elm," yelled Tiny. "Wake up."

Elmer opened his eyes, expecting to see the carnage of war, instead he only saw his wife leaning over him, shaking his shoulders.

"You were having a nightmare," said Tiny, laying back on her pillow, her belly swollen with child. "I swear if it ain't this baby girl keeping me awake, it's you. I can't remember the last time I had a decent night's sleep." She closed her eyes. "Jeepers, now I have to go to the bathroom."

Elmer watched Tiny put on her robe and slippers and leave the room. Waiting for her to return, drenched in sweat, he thought about his dream. Some parts were real, some were not. He was thankful he hadn't lost all of the soldiers who looked to him for guidance, but Thomas still haunted him.

He wondered if Thomas's family knew what happened to their son. Had his body been found and given back to his family? Or were they still wondering where their son was, like Evalyn still waited on word regarding Robert's whereabouts.

There had to be hundreds of soldiers still missing in action, but he could save one soldier's family the anguish of the unknown. The dream had brought it all back. Calmed now by his decision, Elmer knew what he had to do.

Tiny hurried back into bed, still wearing her housecoat. "It's colder than a polar bear's toenail out there. I tell you what, the first thing we need to get once our loan is paid off, is an indoor bathroom. Going to the outhouse is just uncivilized."

"Mary," Elmer said softly.

"I know it'll be a while until we can afford it since we just bought the butcher shop, and we're gonna have a baby in a few months, but let me tell you, as soon as we have the money, it's happening," said Tiny, pulling the covers to her chin.

"Mary, I have to tell you something," said Elmer.

"What?" Tiny sat up on her elbow. "What's wrong?"

"I don't deserve to be a father." Elmer's voice cracked.

"Nonsense," said Tiny, "you'll make a great daddy. I know you're scared. So am I, but thankfully, we have your entire family to make sure we don't mess this up."

"You don't understand," said Elmer.

"So help me understand," Tiny said. "I know something's been bothering you since we got back. Talk to me, Elm."

Elmer shook his head as he continued to look at the ceiling. "I promised I wouldn't leave him behind. I let him down. He was just a boy. If I couldn't take care of him, how can I take care of my own child?"

"Who?" asked Tiny.

"Thomas Pope. We were battle buddies, and I promised I'd protect him. He snuck off with some other men to steal a German tank. I woke up to find them gone. Before I could really look, we were told to advance. I followed orders, but I was really looking for Thomas." Elmer shook his head. "You can't imagine the chaos. There were soldiers coming at me from all directions, and I shot them like they were nothing more than a covey of quail."

"But you had to," said Tiny, "or they would have …"

Elmer nodded. "I know."

"So did you find Thomas?" asked Tiny, grabbing Elmer's hand.

"Yes." Elmer swallowed hard. "He had been hit in the leg by some shrapnel and couldn't walk. I tried to lead him to safety, but he kept falling. I knew I couldn't do it alone, so I rolled him into a trench. I thought he'd be safe there, but no sooner had I turned to run and get help, than an explosion hit the trench where I had just put Thomas. It knocked me to the ground hard and my ears rang something terrible. Everything was in slow motion. It took all the effort I had to crawl back to where I had left Thomas, but he was gone. The trench took a direct hit and there was nothing left."

Wiping the tears from his cheeks, Elmer turned on his side and looked at his wife. Tears wet both of her cheeks.

"The next thing I knew, two soldiers were picking me up and dragging me away as our retreat sounded," explained Elmer. "Thomas was listed missing in action because I couldn't tell them what happened. I don't know if it was the blow to the head I took, or that I just didn't want to remember. But I have to make it right. I have to tell the Army and his family, so they can lay him to rest."

Tiny nodded. "You go do what you have to do. We'll be waiting for you when you get back. Where do they live?"

"Down by Lubbock." Elmer kissed Tiny. "Mary, I don't want to leave you. We've already spent too much of our lives apart because of the war."

"You know I can't go," said Tiny, through her tears. "I get car sick when we drive down the road to Quail Crossings. I'll just slow you down. I'll see if Dovie and James will let me stay with them while you're away. You said you finished up the last of your weekly orders, so Jacob can run the shop until you get back." She kissed him. "You go and I'll be here waiting for you, just like when you went to war. I'll be here waiting and praying, hoping you find your peace and come back to me."

"Ellie talked to me," said Alice, after making sure Ellie was upstairs getting ready for bed after the dance.

"What did she say?" asked Dovie, coming closer, her eyes wide.

"She said she didn't start the fire at her last home," answered Alice.

"And what brought that subject up?" asked Dovie.

"Well," Alice looked at the floor and chewed her lip, "I guess it's kind of my fault. Lawrence Dodson asked me to dance, so I left Ellie alone with my friends. I thought she'd be fine, but then Shirley Manders opened her big mouth and spouted off that Ellie was gonna set us all on fire, so Ellie ran off. Took us a while to find her, but when I did, she told me she didn't do it."

"I should call Shirley Manders's momma right now," said Dovie, gritting her teeth. "The nerve of her daughter saying awful things like that."

"Don't think it'll do any good," said Alice. "First off, I'm certain they don't have a phone yet, and secondly, I'm pretty sure it was Shirley's momma who said the stuff in the first place."

"Well, I'll be," said Dovie, shaking her head, "and she calls herself a Christian woman."

Ellie came down the stairs and walked to the sink for a drink of water.

"Ellie, honey, are you okay?" asked Dovie. "Alice told me what happened."

Ellie shrugged before nodding.

"As I told Ellie in the truck, Shirley Manders is just a chicken with a loud cluck," said Alice.

Ellie placed her hand over her mouth to suppress her giggle. She walked over and gave Alice and Dovie a hug before going back upstairs.

Chapter Thirty-seven

Elmer sat in his truck in front of the Popes' residence and tried to work up the courage to go up the walk and knock on the door.

He knew he needed to get back to Mary, but first he needed to do what he had promised and let the Pope family know what had happened to Thomas. He felt fear and guilt. What if they hated him? What if he was doing the wrong thing by bringing Thomas up at all? It had been over a year since his death. He could just be bringing up bad memories. He had killed their son.

Taking another deep breath, he opened the door to his truck and got out. Without hesitation he walked to the Popes' pale yellow door and knocked.

Both of Thomas's parents answered the door.

"Mr. and Mrs. Pope?" Elmer asked. The couple nodded. "My name is Elmer Brewer, and I'm here to talk to you about your son and my friend, Thomas."

Mrs. Pope raised her hand to her heart. "You have information on our Thomas?"

"Please, come in," said Mr. Pope.

Elmer stepped in and followed Mrs. Pope into their kitchen. "I'll get us some coffee. Why don't you have a seat at the table?"

Mr. Pope gestured for Elmer to sit. Then took a seat across from Elmer. Mrs. Pope was quick with the coffee and sat beside her husband.

Elmer took a small sip, knowing he was stalling. "Thank you."

"So did you serve with our son?" asked Mrs. Pope.

Elmer nodded. "Yes, we were in the same platoon, and we were about the same age, so we became friends really quick."

"Worst thing I ever did was sign off on my boy joining the army at fourteen," said Mr. Pope. He looked at the table and frowned. "I knew he wasn't ready."

"None of us were," said Elmer. "But Thomas and I felt the same after Pearl Harbor. Nothing was gonna stop us from joining up. Even if my brother hadn't signed off, I would've found a way to join. I bet Thomas would've done the same."

"You know our Thomas, that's for sure," said Mrs. Pope.

"He did really great during basic and was one of the stars of our platoon," Elmer started. "I mean, he could run like the wind. I never saw a soldier more ready to fight for his country. He made friends with everyone almost instantly. Even our ol' Drill Sergeant wasn't sure how to deal with how likeable Thomas was. Everyone knew Thomas was going places. All you had to do was ask Thomas."

Elmer took another drink of his coffee feeling his throat go dry as he reached the most difficult part of his explanation. "Once we got into the heat of things, Thomas began to change. Some days he would be aggressive and on other days he was barely fighting off tears. I could tell he was scared. I mean, we were all terrified. I told him to keep close to me, that we'd be battle buddies. Truth be told, having him close by helped me as much as I helped him. I was honored to have Thomas fighting beside me. He saved my life a number of times, and I'm just so sorry I didn't return the favor."

Mr. Pope grabbed his wife's hand as tears fell on her cheeks.

"Please," said Mr. Pope, "tell us what happened to our son. They have him listed as missing in action."

"When we marched through the Ardennes Forest, something in him changed." Elmer took a deep breath. "He and some other soldiers thought they could steal a German tank that was pinning us in. They snuck out in the middle of the night while I was sleeping. I had told them it was a bad idea. I thought I'd convinced them not to go, but when I woke up, Thomas and four other men had left."

Mrs. Pope's hand flew to her mouth to stifle her cry.

"I looked for him in the trenches, hoping I was wrong about where he had gone, but then the advance sounded," explained Elmer. "I took off into battle hoping to find Thomas in the chaos, and by some miracle I did. But he had taken some shrapnel to his leg and couldn't walk. I tried to carry him out, but I wasn't strong enough. I knew if I didn't get help, we'd both be killed, so I put him in a trench where I thought he would be safe."

Elmer looked at his coffee mug and felt his tears drop on his hands. "I thought he would be safe," he repeated himself in a whisper.

Mrs. Pope reached over and grabbed his hand. "So he's ..."

Elmer nodded. "After leaving him in the trench, I turned to get help and there was an explosion. It knocked me to the ground, but I crawled back to the trench and Thomas was gone. He was just gone."

"So he didn't suffer," Mr. Pope said more than asked.

"No," Elmer whispered. "I'm sorry. I'm so sorry I left him in that trench. I thought he'd be safe."

Elmer knew he was repeating himself, but he didn't know what else to say. There were no words to comfort these parents who had lost their son because of a decision he had made.

Elmer felt a firm hand on his shoulder. He hadn't noticed Mr. Pope rising and walking around behind him.

"Thank you for being there for our boy," said Mr. Pope. "You did what you thought was right, and that's what matters. We know you were trying to save him."

"I came here not only to let you know what happened to your son but to ask for your forgiveness," said Elmer as he tried to clear his throat of sobs. "What I did killed him and I'm so sorry."

"You don't need our forgiveness," said Mrs. Pope as she cried softly, "because there is nothing to forgive. You needn't carry this burden any longer. You didn't kill him; the Germans did." She took a moment and cleared her throat. "Do you have a family, Mr. Brewer?"

Elmer nodded. "I just married my high school sweetheart back in August, and we're gonna have our first child here in a few months." Elmer smiled at the thought of his child.

"Then you can do something for us. Something that will help bring us all peace." Mrs. Pope returned a small smile. "You can have a lifetime of happiness with your wife and child, and in Thomas's name I hope you will continue to help your fellow man and lead a good, Christian life. Living your life in the shadow of grief and guilt is not what Thomas would've wanted for any of his friends, and it's certainly not what we want for you."

"I can do that," said Elmer, as he wiped his eyes. "I stopped at Amarillo Air Force Base on my way here. I told them everything."

"What did they say?" asked Mr. Pope, his brow furrowed as he sat back down in his seat at the table.

Elmer lifted his chin and looked Mr. Pope in the eyes. "They are going to start the process of declaring Thomas deceased. He'll have a proper burial with honors. Someone should be in touch with you soon."

"I think I've known for a while that he was gone," said Mrs. Pope in a small voice. "Thank you, Mr. Brewer. Thank you for having the courage to tell us what happened."

Mr. Pope patted Elmer on the back. "My son was lucky to have a friend like you."

Elmer felt like the world had been lifted off his shoulders. He looked at the Popes and felt their love, understanding, and even the forgiveness they said he didn't need. A wave of emotion overtook Elmer, and he laid his head on his arms at the Pope's kitchen's table and wept hard for the first time since returning home. He felt Mr. Pope's strong hand on his arm as Mrs. Pope took both of his hands in hers.

He wept for Thomas. He wept for Robert and Evalyn. He wept for the numerous soldiers he had called friends who didn't make it home. And with every tear that puddled onto the Popes' kitchen table, he felt his soul shake free of the chains of war.

Chapter Thirty-eight

March 1946

James stomped the mud and snow off his boots in the doorway before closing the large winter door and shedding his coat. "Got Bill home. Can't believe he walked over here. Told him not to worry about coming back today or even tomorrow. The snow's really blowing."

"I can't believe we're having a blizzard in March," said Dovie, taking James's coat and hanging it on a nail while he removed the rest of his winter clothing.

"It's gonna be a wet one too," said James. "Mostly sleeting out there now. Better get the kerosene lanterns and candles out. We'll lose power more than likely."

"Already done," said Dovie, "and I'm really thankful that Bill brought up all that firewood yesterday. I'll admit I thought y'all were being foolish, bringing up firewood in March."

"Felt it in my wrists yesterday," said James "and Bill was complaining about a twitch over his left eye."

Dovie put her hands on her hips. "So it had nothing to do with that article in the paper that told us the Weather Bureau was expecting us to have a late winter storm?"

James gave his daughter a wink. "The wrists never lie."

Dovie looked out the kitchen window. "I hope Evalyn and her children are doing okay. I hate them being at Rockwood all alone." She nodded at her father. "Your wrists should've told them to come over here to stay during the storm."

"Evie will be fine," said James. "Rockwood is stronger than ever, and Bill went over there yesterday evening and stocked up the firewood. If anything, she might get a little bored."

Tiny walked into the kitchen. "Looks like it's getting worse out there. I'm really glad Elmer closed the butcher shop."

"Too bad he couldn't talk Jacob into coming out here during the storm," said Dovie. "I hate him being all alone as well."

"He said he wanted to look after the shop during the storm, but to be honest," said Tiny, scratching her head, "I think he prefers it. I took him to the library, and we both got a stack of books, so he has them to read."

"They let him have a library card?" asked James, eyebrow raised.

Tiny shook her head. "No, not even after I hissed at Mrs. Spitzer like a wet cat. I couldn't believe the nerve of her, saying she couldn't issue him a library card on account he's colored. I thought Knollwood was past that." She sighed. "I checked all the books out under my name and then, right in front of her, I handed him his and told him to enjoy. Then I told Mrs. Spitzer we'd be back next week to check out some more."

"It's gonna take time for things to change," said James.

"Well, they need to change faster," said Tiny. "I can't imagine my baby girl growing up in a town where Jacob can't even check out a book."

Ellie walked into the kitchen and scanned all the faces. Dovie could tell by her frown that she didn't like what she was seeing. She got behind them and started pushing them all into parlor.

"What on earth are you doing, Ellie?" asked Dovie. "Pushing me out of my own kitchen."

Ellie pulled out a small notebook she had started carrying and drew a smiley face before pointing at the picture and then them. She then pointed to the parlor.

"I think she wants the kitchen to herself to do something to make us happy," said James.

Ellie pointed to James and then her nose.

"What are you up to, Ellie Brewer?" asked Dovie.

"Guess we'll just have to wait and see," said James.

"Momma," whined Joy, "there's nothing to do if I can't go outside and play. I was plannin' a big adventure today. I was gonna ride my pony, Prairie, over to Laura Ingalls Wilder's house."

Evalyn looked up from her sewing and cocked her head. "You don't have a pony named Prairie, and we're nowhere near the Wilder homestead."

"Momma, it's pretend," said Joy, placing her hands on her hips. "I was gonna pretend to ride my pretend pony to Laura's house."

"Too bad we didn't borrow Alice's books," said Evalyn before continuing her stitching. "Then we could've read together."

"Not like you'd stop sewing to read anything," complained Joy as she plopped herself down in a chair.

Evalyn paused her sewing and stared at her hands. She had to admit Joy had a point. She had been sewing nonstop since the news that the man in Paris wasn't Robert. She needed something to keep her mind off the knowledge she might never see him again, so she had turned to her trusty Singer sewing machine.

Evalyn finished her line and clipped it. "There, I'm done with this part. How about I take a break, and we do some things together while Caleb sleeps?"

Joy sat up. "Really, Momma?"

Standing, Evalyn smiled at her daughter. "I know I've been working hard lately, and it may seem like I don't have time for you anymore. I'm really sorry about that, so today is all about you and your brother. I won't sew another stitch until y'all are in bed. Promise."

Joy giggled. "So what should we do?"

"Wanna play dolls?" asked Evalyn.

"I do that all the time," said Joy, shaking her head. "I wanna do something new."

Evalyn looked around the house. "How 'bout we decorate the house?"

"What do you mean?" asked Joy.

"Well, we can make paper chains to hang on the walls and make snowflakes to hang from the ceiling. While we do that we can sing songs, and I can tell you stories about when I was younger. It'll be almost like *Little House on the Prairie*."

"That sounds like so much fun," said Joy, clapping her hands in delight.

Evalyn walked to a chest of drawers that sat in the parlor area and opened the top drawer. "I just bought this colored paper at Johnson's last week. I'm not sure why. I just liked the colors, and now we can make chains out of it."

Joy ran to Evalyn's sewing machine. "I'll get the scissors!"

"Joy Smith, you stop right there," said Evalyn. "You know we don't use Momma's fabric scissors on anything but fabric. I have some scissors for paper and paste, right here."

"But I like your fabric scissors," Joy said with a pout.

"So do I," said Evalyn, walking over with the supplies, "and I'd like them to stay nice and sharp for my work. But if you're really careful, I'll let you use these scissors."

Again Joy clapped her hands with delight.

"How 'bout a game of Go Fish?" asked Lou Anne, holding up a deck of cards. "It's something everyone can play by the fire."

"Rosey can't play," said Dean. "She's too little."

"Well, since she's asleep, it really doesn't matter does it?" Lou Anne raised an eyebrow at her son. "And if she wakes up while we're playing, she can be my partner. Who wants to play?"

"Yay, Go Fish," squealed Annabelle.

"I'll play," said Bill with a smile. "Maybe I'll actually be able to beat your momma at Go Fish since she always beats me at Rummy."

"Fat chance," said Lou Anne. "I'm a natural winner."

"Where we gonna fish, Momma?" asked Annabelle with wide eyes. "It's snowing outside."

"We ain't really gonna fish. It's a game," Dean said with a sigh. "Annabelle, you're so dumb."

"Billy Dean Brewer, you apologize to your sister right now!" ordered Bill. "Then you can go over and sit in that corner while the rest of us play cards. We don't need anyone ruining our fun."

Dean bowed his head as he walked to his sister. "I'm sorry I called you dumb, Annabelle." He turned to his dad. "Do I really have to sit in the corner?"

"For one game," said Bill.

"I was just teasin'," said Dean as he shuffled to the corner.

Bill walked over to his son. "I know that, Dean, but you're her older brother, and it's your job to look after her. If her own brother is callin' her dumb, who's gonna stand up for her if some mean boy calls her dumb?"

Dean puffed out his chest. "Nobody calls my sister dumb but me."

Bill tilted his head. "Well, that's kind of the spirit, but not even you should call your sister dumb. Treat your sister how you want to be treated." He ruffled his boy's hair. "Now sit here for one game while I beat your momma. Then you can come join us."

Dean slid down into the corner as Bill made his way back to Lou Anne. Annabelle had all the cards loose on the table and was swirling them around in an attempt to shuffle.

Lou Anne kissed him on the cheek.

Bill blushed. "What was that for?"

"You know one of the reasons I fell in love with you was because of the way you treated your siblings. Even as a young man, who should've been off starting your own life, you took care of your family. You showed such patience with Evalyn when she didn't deserve it, kindness with Alice who has a delicate soul, and understanding with Elmer. I knew that a man who treated his kin like you treated your brother and sisters would make the best kind of husband and father."

Chapter Thirty-nine

Dovie put down her book and sighed.

"What's wrong, Momma Dovie? Your book not good?" asked Alice, looking up from the notebook she'd been writing in since Ellie had shooed everyone out of the kitchen.

"The book is fine. It's just too quiet in here," said Dovie. "I'm used to the boys going in and out for chores, and kids screaming as they run from room to room. I want to hear you girls gabbin' about the latest movie stars, clothes, and boys"

Color flushed Alice's cheeks. "I've got no reason to talk about boys."

"Bill said you danced with that Lawrence Dodson boy three times at the dance," said Dovie with a wink.

Alice shrugged. "He's nice and all, but he's really into his schoolwork like I am. We're friends, but that's about it."

"Don't you want a boyfriend?" asked Tiny.

"Sure," said Alice, "but I don't see why I need one right now. When school's out, I'll be going to college.

It's not like I'm going to get married right after graduation."

"Yep, pretty soon, you will be leaving us too," said Dovie with a sigh. "Then it'll just be me, Dad and Ellie. I can't even begin to imagine how quiet that'll be. Makes my heart hurt just thinkin' about it."

"I won't be gone long," said Alice. "Just to college, and then I'll be back."

"What if you get a job someplace else?" asked Dovie. "You can't say you'll be back after school. You'll have to go where the work is or, if you're married, wherever your husband is."

"Well, if it's Lawrence Dobson, she'll be right here tending to the ol' grocery store right next to Lawrence and his father," said Tiny with a chuckle, nudging Elmer who was reading the newspaper beside her. "Isn't that right, Elm?"

"As far as I'm concerned she can be an ol' spinster," said Elmer as he gave Alice a wink. "No man will be good enough for my baby sister to marry."

"I think we're getting a little ahead of ourselves," said Alice.

"Just wait, Alice," said Dovie. "You'll find your callin', and it might not be Quail Crossings."

Alice shook her head. "I'm never leaving here, Momma Dovie. I promise. This is my home and Mrs. Spaulding thinks she can get me a job at the school once I finish my degree." She smiled at Dovie. "Quail Crossings is the first place that I ever felt warm, loved, and safe, and I don't ever want to leave. It's my forever place."

"Glad to hear that," said James, coming into the parlor, awake from his nap. "You and the rest of your family are always welcome here, whether you're sixteen or a hundred and sixteen, I want it to be your forever place."

The smell of freshly baked sugar and cinnamon wafted into the room as Ellie walked in carrying a plate of snickerdoodle cookies. She placed them on the table and looked around at all the smiling faces. She pulled out her notebook and pointed to the happy face she had drawn earlier.

"Well, Ellie, you did make us smile," said Dovie, grabbing a cookie.

Alice took a bite and let it melt in her mouth. "Yeah, you keep cooking like this, and you'll have to shove, or better yet, roll me out the door."

Lou Anne snuggled into the crook of Bill's arm and laid her head on his chest. She could feel his heart's steady beat as he slept. She closed her eyes and concentrated on matching her breathing with his. With every breath she fell more in love with her husband.

He squeezed her tightly. "I can't believe we're lying in bed in the middle of the day."

"I can't believe all the kids are taking a nap at the same time," said Lou Anne.

"Must've been all those riveting games of Go Fish," said Bill.

"Oh, you mean the games that I won?" asked Lou Anne playfully.

"I do believe Annabelle beat you a couple of times," Bill said with a smirk.

"Only 'cause I let her win," said Lou Anne.

Bill raised up on his elbow and leaned over his wife. "You mean to tell me you can let Annabelle win, but not your loving husband?"

"Annabelle is three years old. You are not," said Lou Anne playfully.

"Doesn't mean I don't like to win," said Bill.

Lou Anne gave him an ornery smile. "Why, Mr. Brewer, you've got me. You've already won."

Bill leaned down and kissed her as Lou Anne wrapped her arms around her husband. He broke from their kiss and looked at her, his eyes radiating love. "You've got that right."

Evalyn looked around the room and took a deep breath. She held Caleb in one arm, and Joy stood by her side. They had spent the greater part of the snowy afternoon hanging the colorful paper chains on the wall and snowflakes from the ceiling while singing every song they could remember by heart.

"It's perfect. Like it's just waiting for a party," she said, putting Caleb down and kneeling to give Joy a hug. "I'm so glad we did this. What kind of party should we throw?"

"How 'bout a cowboy and Indians party?" asked Joy. She grabbed a leftover paper chain and wrapped it around her little brother. "I've got you now, little brave."

Caleb patted his hand over his mouth and started to do an Indian chant, causing Evalyn to laugh out loud. He must have learned that from Dean. Evalyn stopped laughing as both kids stared at her.

"What's the matter?" she asked.

"Momma, we just haven't heard you laugh like that in a long time," Joy said with a smile. "I've missed it."

Evalyn gathered her children up in a group hug. "I've missed laughing too. I promise there will be more of it from now on."

"Even with Daddy gone?" asked Joy.

Evalyn nodded. "I'll be sad sometimes, as will you. But that doesn't mean we should stop laughing on the days we aren't so sad."

She squeezed her kids tightly, feeling their warmth and love. She would make it through this difficult time, because of them. She would learn to laugh again and have fun, even while her heart ached. At that moment Evalyn understood exactly what Dovie had meant about grief being like a pebble. They might not know it, but her children were helping her shoulder the grief.

A firm knock at the door caused Evalyn to let out a startled cry. "Who on earth could that be in this weather?" She looked at the kids. "Joy, you take your brother into your room and close the door. Don't come out until I tell you it's okay, understand?"

"Momma, just don't answer it," said Joy, fear in her eyes.

"I have too, Baby Girl," said Evalyn. "In weather like this I have to make sure it's not someone we know who needs help. Now go. I'll be all right."

Joy reluctantly led Caleb to her room and closed the door. The knock came again. Evalyn grabbed the shotgun off the wall and went to the door. She looked out the side window, but the man who had knocked, had his back to her. Probably trying to keep his face out of the fierce northern wind that had blown in with the storm.

Keeping the shotgun tight under her arm, she opened the door a crack. "Can I help you?"

The man turned and Evalyn screamed and dropped the gun.

Chapter Forty

The man stepped up just in time to catch Evalyn as she fainted. Swooping her up, he carried her to the sofa.

"Momma?" cried Joy from the crack in the bedroom door. She opened it wide and ran at the man, both hands raised in fists as she let out a warrior cry. She started beating on the back of the man's legs. "Let go of my momma!"

The man gently laid Evalyn on the sofa before kneeling in front of the ferocious little girl. He caught her little hands with one of his hands while pulling down his scarf with the other and dropped to his knees.

"Daddy?" whimpered Joy, standing in shock. Her little lips started to quiver.

"It's me, pun'kin," said Robert. "You don't have to be afraid. I would never hurt Momma."

Joy's eyes grew wide and tears formed as she pulled her hands away and threw them over Robert's shoulders. "Daddy!"

Robert wrapped his arms around his daughter and squeezed gently. "I've missed you so much."

"What took you so long, Daddy?" asked Joy. "Why didn't you come back with Uncle Elm and Mr. Pearce?"

"I just got a little caught up is all," said Robert. "But I'm back now, for good."

Joy squeezed her daddy's neck again.

"Is Momma okay?" asked Joy.

Robert turned and gently brushed Evalyn's hair away from her face. He could tell she was breathing and looked to be okay. "I think she was just overcome by the shock of seeing me. She'll wake up soon."

A cry came from Joy's room, and they both looked up.

"Is that Caleb?" asked Robert, eyes already wet with tears. "Is that my son?"

"Come on, Daddy" said Joy, pulling him towards her room.

Robert rose still holding Joy's hand, and they hurried to her room. Robert bent over and picked up the crying little boy in the doorway. "You are a handsome little fella." He bounced Caleb in his arms. "No need to be afraid. I'm your daddy. Sorry I wasn't here for you when you first arrived. But I'm here now, and I am so happy to see you."

Caleb continued to cry, so Robert started to sing his favorite hymn, *The Old Rugged Cross.* The little boy quieted. He stared at Robert and smiled as his daddy's warm baritone voice washed over him. Caleb laid his hand on one of Robert's cheeks.

"Caleb," said Joy, "this is our daddy, and he's the best daddy ever."

"He sure is," said Evalyn, looking over the back of the sofa at her small family.

Robert placed Caleb on the floor by his sister and rushed to her, kneeling by the sofa. "Are you okay?"

Tears fell onto Evalyn's cheeks as she gently caressed Robert's face. "Where have you been?"

"It's a very long story," said Robert.

"Joy," said Evalyn, with a smile, "go with your brother and get those cards we made for Daddy. It's been a while, so they're probably buried in the bottom of your art box."

As soon as the children vanished into Joy's room, Evalyn threw herself into Robert's arms. "You don't know how scared I was for you. I can't believe you're really here. I was so afraid you weren't coming back."

Robert hugged her tight. "I know. I'm so sorry I couldn't get word to you. I tried, but they wouldn't let me. I hated knowing what you were going through. I just hated it. I'm so sorry."

Evalyn pulled back, her face white with concern. "Who wouldn't let you? Were you held prisoner? Tell me you weren't in one of those awful camps."

"I was held prisoner but not like that," said Robert. "I'll tell you all about it, but first I need to do something I have been wanting to do for a very long time."

"What's that?" asked Evalyn.

Robert pulled Evalyn close and kissed her passionately.

Dovie helped herself to another cookie and listened to the chatter. Ellie's round of baked goods had put everyone in a good mood and started conversations. Tiny and Alice were discussing baby names, while Ellie, her hand on Tiny's stomach, sat on the floor next to them giggling every time she felt Tiny's baby move.

James and Elmer were talking about business and about how well Jacob was fitting in. Most of the town's people loved that Jacob had come back and given them a second chance to make things right. Business at the butcher shop was better than ever, and James figured Elmer was doing more business than even Butcher Davis had.

Dovie smiled at her family and their cheerful chatter. She remembered a time, right after Simon and Helen had died, when the silence had been so deafening it gave her headaches. She knew now that the headaches were caused by the grief of not hearing her daughter's happy squeal throughout the house. A few months after their deaths, she began to embrace the silence. Silence meant not having to pretend there was something to talk about and allowed her to wallow in her grief.

That all changed once the Brewers came to live at Quail Crossings, and the place hadn't been quiet since. Dovie wondered if she would retreat back into old habits of preferring silence when Alice was gone.

The back door suddenly burst open causing everyone to look up in surprise.

"What in the world?" exclaimed James, standing.

Elmer stood also and put a hand up towards James, stating that he would see to whatever was going on. But before he could even move, a man barreled into the parlor and marched right up to Dovie. He pulled her up from her chair and planted a kiss on her lips, right there in front of everyone.

Even under the heavy layers of clothing, Dovie knew instantly it was Gabe. She fell into his passionate embrace, forgetting her family, forgetting how hard she had once grieved, and forgetting all about embracing the silence.

Gabe was back, and he was never leaving again. Her heart was full, her mind was in agreement, and her entire soul knew she loved Gabe more than she ever thought possible. Gabe released Dovie and smiled. "I found him, and he's home right now. If there wasn't a blizzard outside right now, I'd march you to the church this instant and make you my wife."

"Robert's home?" Dovie questioned. "He's really home, safe and sound?"

"He really is," said Gabe, taking off his coat, hat, gloves, and scarf.

"I'll take those," said Alice, with a big smile on her face. "Warm up by the fire."

"So what happened?" asked Elmer, coming back in from securing the door.

Gabe pulled a wooden chair close to Dovie and sat directly in front of the fire. She sat back in her favorite blue chair.

"Thank you, Alice." Gabe said as Alice returned to the room. He looked at the group. "I have to admit, my hopes were pretty low when I traveled from Paris to London. You don't know how much I had hoped that Robert was in that Paris hospital. Once I got to London, I was told I had to go to the Royal Air Force base in Lakenheath to identify a man claiming to be Robert." Gabe smiled. "I swear I did a jig right there in the commander's office. That was the break I had been looking for since receiving news that Robert was missing."

"So if he knew who he was, why was he missing?" asked Tiny.

Gabe laughed and shook his head. "He got separated from his company and was actually captured by British troops over enemy lines. In order to fit in, he had traded his dirty uniform for some clothes with a nearby farmer. That farmer also wanted his I.D. tags. Robert knew the only way to get back into friendly territory was to look inconspicuous, so he agreed to the trade. He also knew that if the Germans found him with U.S. tags, he'd be sent to a camp."

"But the British troops didn't believe him?" asked Alice. "How could they not realize he was an American once he began talking?"

"The Brits had encountered a lot of German spies with impeccable American accents, and his name didn't help." Ellie brought Gabe a cup of coffee. He smiled at her. "You read my mind, Ellie. Thank you."

"I don't understand about his name," said James. "It's about as American as it gets."

"Exactly," said Gabe, taking a sip of coffee. "Robert and Smith are two of the most common names in America. Why wouldn't a German spy use them?"

"But you've been looking for him," said Dovie. "Why didn't someone contact you to verify his claim?"

Gabe sighed. "And there's where we get into the red tape involved in trading possible spies with different countries. Our military wasn't even notified of Robert's existence until the British had debriefed him and checked out his story. Thank goodness that farmer in Germany still had Robert's tags. But as you can imagine, it took a while for an investigator to get to Germany, locate the famer, and check out the tags. I'm just glad I was in Paris when the information came to light. Honestly, I wasn't sure where to go next."

"I'm so glad you found him," said Dovie, taking Gabe's free hand.

"I'm thankful I'm friends with a five-star general, or I would've been kicked out of this search months ago," said Gabe. "I didn't want to tell y'all this, but the military had given up looking for Robert. They were ready to list him killed in action before I even came home. If I hadn't had connections with the higher ups, Robert would've been listed as KIA officially and probably executed for being a German spy."

"You're friends with a five-star general?" Elmer's mouth dropped open. "That's impressive."

"He was the base commander at Rockwell in California where I learned to fly. My buddy Calvin was General Arnold's driver but failed to show up one day after a night of heavy drinking. I was in the right place at the right time and became his driver." Gabe swallowed hard. "I was also there when his two-year-old son, John, died. I'd never seen two parents more devastated than General Arnold and his wife. After that night, he kept me as his driver. He said he needed someone who had been there with him through difficult times."

Gabe finished his coffee. "Later, his recommendations got me into flight school and he's the one who called after Pearl Harbor asking if I would become a flight instructor and consultant."

"I still don't understand why Robert couldn't just have written home," said Alice. "Couldn't he have asked Evie to send help? Couldn't she go and claim him?"

Gabe smiled. "For all they knew, Evie was a spy too and would say whatever it took to get a fellow spy out of prison."

Dovie put her hand over her mouth. "Can you imagine, our Evie a spy?"

"Of course I can," said Alice. "Don't we all remember how she first acted when we got to Quail Crossings? She was sneakier than a fox hunting rabbits, but thankfully she's over that."

"We hope," laughed Elmer.

Chapter Forty-one

April 1946

James walked into the house and went to hang his hat on the nail before remembering he was wearing his dress hat, which he stored in a box in his room.

"That was a beautiful wedding," said Evalyn, walking in behind James. "Did you ever think you'd walk Dovie down the aisle again?"

James shook his head and gave Evalyn a small smile. "There was a time when I was afraid she'd never love again. It's not easy being widowed so young, but I'll admit I'm happier than a snail in a garden full of tomatoes."

Evalyn started pulling out leftovers from the ice box. "So why don't you look happy?"

James let out a small chuckle. "I thought I was hiding it better than that."

"I assure you no one noticed anything at the ceremony," said Evalyn. "It wasn't until we were in the truck that I noticed something was wrong. Are you feeling okay?"

James waved her off as he sat and placed his hat on his knee. "I'm a bit tired, but that's not it. I'm worried about Dovie."

"Dovie?" Evalyn raised her eyebrows. "Why? She's never been happier."

"Exactly," said James. "And now she's on a plane with a pilot flying to Hawaii."

Evalyn scratched her head. "I still don't understand."

James sighed. "Besides not liking the thought of her flying over the largest ocean on Earth to an island that was attacked not that long ago by the Japs, I'm worried that she's married to a man with a very dangerous job. If something happens to him, I'm not sure she'll make it through that kind of grief again. Especially since I don't know how much longer I have on Earth."

Evalyn clicked her tongue. "First of all, stop talkin' like that. You've got plenty of good years left with us. The doctor said so himself. Secondly, if something happened to Gabe, Lord forbid, and you weren't around, we would help Dovie through it. She's the strongest woman I know and she'd cope." She walked to James. "I love you and I love Dovie. Y'all are my family, and I would stop at nothing to help Dovie through any hard times. She's done the same for me numerous times. You don't ever have to worry about Dovie being lonely. I promise you that." She gave him a hug. "And you don't ever have to be lonely either, especially since I'm pretty sure I just heard the other cars pull up with loads of grandkids all full of wedding cake and cookies and ready to play."

"Where's Robert?" asked James.

"He had to run to the lumber yard and put in an order for our new barn," said Evalyn. "He'll be out here in a bit."

Evalyn turned and looked out the screen door expecting to see a gaggle of kids piling out of the truck. Instead she saw Elmer run around his truck and help Tiny out. Evalyn rushed out the door and down the stoop. "What's wrong?"

"My back hurts something terrible," said Tiny. "I'm afraid something's wrong with the baby. She shouldn't be coming yet."

"Get her inside, Elm," ordered Evalyn, "and take her to Dovie's room. Tiny, try not to worry. Concentrate on taking deep breaths; it'll help with the pain."

Bill and Lou Anne pulled in the drive with all of the kids. Ellie, Joy, Dean, and Annabelle sat in the back of their car. Caleb sat on Alice's lap in the front seat, between Bill and Lou Anne, who was holding Rose.

Lou Anne quickly got out with Rose and rushed to Evalyn. "What's wrong with Tiny?"

"She's having back pain," said Evalyn as they turned to go into the house.

"Is she in labor?" asked Lou Anne, with wide eyes. She turned to Alice before Evalyn could answer. "Alice, dear, would you and Ellie mind watching the children outside for a few minutes until we get Tiny settled?"

"But Momma, I'm starving," said Dean. "I thought we was gonna eat cold chicken and tater salad."

"You're always starving, Dean," said Bill, ruffling his son's hair. "But you'll live. Come help me brush the horses."

Ellie took Rose from Lou Anne, as Alice, still holding Caleb, corralled the other children, and they all started walking towards the pond.

Lou Anne and Evalyn hurried inside to Dovie's bedroom. They found Elmer kneeling before Tiny, holding her hand.

"Is she gonna have the baby?" he asked. "It's too soon."

"First babies can come at any time," said Lou Anne.

"Should I call for the doctor?" asked James.

"The pain is gone now," said Tiny.

Evalyn looked at James. "Not yet, it could be a false labor. We need to wait and see if her pains are consistent. If they are, then we'll need to get her to the hospital in Perry. The baby won't survive out here without medical help."

"I wish Dovie were here," said Elmer. "Maybe we should call the doctor anyway."

"Why don't you and James go into the kitchen and make us some coffee?" asked Lou Anne. "Remember, I've had three babies and Evie's had two. We'll see to Tiny."

The men reluctantly retreated to the kitchen. Lou Anne kneeled in front of Tiny. "Tiny, did your water break?"

"I don't know," said Tiny.

Evalyn smiled. "Then it didn't, because you would know."

"I wish my momma was here," said Tiny.

"I know, sweetie," said Evalyn. "If we need to, we'll send her a telegram and have her come up right away. But we don't want to worry her."

"So, no more pain?" asked Lou Anne.

Tiny shook her head.

"Good," said Lou Anne. "I remember I had some horrible back pain with Rosey. Started near the end of my sixth month." Lou Anne grabbed an extra pillow. "Try lying on your side, and I'll put this pillow under your belly. Then we'll get another one to put between your legs. It might help. I know it helped me."

Tiny winced. "The pain's back."

Lou Anne looked at Evalyn. "How long has it been?"

Evalyn looked at the clock on the wall. "About twelve minutes."

"Let us know when it eases up," said Lou Anne. "Until then just breath. Deep breathe in. Deep breathe out. Okay? I know it hurts but try moving to your side."

Tiny did as she was asked and Lou Anne put one pillow under her belly and another between her legs. Evalyn left and came back with another pillow and placed it against Tiny's back.

"How's that?' asked Lou Anne.

"Better," said Tiny. Suddenly tears began streaming down her face. "Is something wrong with the baby?"

Evalyn grabbed Tiny's hand, and Lou Anne pulled a chair up close.

"I don't think so," said Evalyn. "The baby could be sitting in a bad position, causing you pain, or you could be having early labor pains."

At the sound of a timid knock on the door, Lou Anne quickly pulled a sheet over Tiny's legs to give her privacy. "You can come in."

"I called the doctor," said James. "I know y'all have it handled, but I was worried. Unfortunately he can't come until morning. His nurse said to keep her in bed until he gets here."

"We don't think she's in labor," said Evalyn. "But it won't hurt to have the doctor come look at her. Why can't he come until the morning?"

"He rode in the ambulance to Amarillo with a young girl who was bitten on the face by a rattler over near Wilson. Apparently she fell right on the darn thing," said James.

"A rattler? Already?" gasped Lou Anne. "I didn't think we'd need to worry about snakes waking up until late May."

"With the exception of the blizzard, we've had a very mild winter," said James. "George Wheaton said he killed two by his grain bin the other day. The winter didn't kill many of them off since it didn't stay cold for long periods of time like it usually does."

"All right then," said Evalyn. "Tiny, you'll stay right here until the doctor says otherwise. We'll keep an eye on the pain. As long as there's not a pattern to it, it's probably just the baby playin' the fiddle with your nerves."

"Great," signed Tiny. "Would someone please tell her I'm more of a piano girl?"

Chapter Forty-two

"So, Dr. Hushton, how is she?" asked Elmer. "How's the baby?"

Dr. Huston gave Elmer a smile. "Your little lady is doing just fine, as is your baby. Some women, especially the more delicate varieties, have pain that closely resembles contractions in their last trimester. But because she is so fragile, I suggest she stay off her feet until the real labor begins."

Evalyn leaned into Lou Anne and whispered, "When have you ever heard Tiny being described as fragile?"

"Shhh," scolded Elmer. "I'm listening to the doctor."

Evalyn held up her hands. "I'm sorry, Doctor, but are you sure it's not just the baby sitting in an awkward position? Is it possible that if Tiny would take a short walk the baby would reposition itself?"

"Mr. Brewer told me that Mrs. Brewer hasn't been eating much and has had trouble keeping a lot of food down during this pregnancy," said Dr. Hushton. "Is that true?"

"Well, yes, at first," said Evalyn. "But Dovie was able to …"

"Mr. Brewer also said that Mrs. Brewer fainted in the very early days," said Dr. Hushton.

"She skipped breakfast that day, and it was very hot outside," said Evalyn. "She has been fine for months. Dovie helped get her stomach settled down, and she hasn't fainted since …"

The doctor held up his hand. "How about we let me give the medical advice and decide if Mrs. Brewer is fine?"

Evalyn clamped her mouth shut, but Elmer knew from the shade of red her cheeks were turning she had a lot more to say to the doctor. Elmer looked at Tiny, who just stared at the ceiling. He had never known her to be so quiet, especially when it came to her own body and well-being. He couldn't help but think she looked defeated.

"Mary," Elmer said softly. "What do you think about all this?"

"Whatever you decide is fine," she said softly.

The doctor stood. "You'll be just fine as long as you stay off your feet. You're only to walk when you need to relieve yourself, and make sure you have someone close by to help you in case you feel faint."

"I'll see you out," said Lou Anne, leading the doctor to the door. "Would you like a cup of coffee before you go?"

"I hope he burns his tongue," declared Evalyn once the doctor was out of sight.

"Evie, stop," said Elmer. "He's just doing his job. He wants what's best for Mary."

"That man may have delivered a lot of babies, but he's never birthed one," snapped Evalyn. "Moving around can help."

"Or it can hurt," Elmer snapped back.

"Elm, it's not like we're gonna ask her to chop wood," said Evalyn. "I just think it would be better for her to move around more. She's gonna stiffen up."

"I should've eaten more," said Tiny. "I should've done more to make sure my baby girl was safe. It was my job to create a safe place for her, and I've failed. I deserve to lay here like a bump on a log. At least that way I won't hurt her."

"Oh, sweetheart," said Elmer. "You didn't do anything wrong. This isn't your fault."

"It is!" cried Tiny, tears running down her face. "I'm her momma. It's my job to make sure she comes into this world healthy and happy."

"Okay," said Evalyn sitting on the bedside. "If you want to keep your baby safe, you have to calm down. If you think staying in bed until this baby comes is the right answer, that's fine. Whatever you want, we'll see to it, but you have to settle down. Now take a deep breath."

Tiny narrowed her eyes at Evalyn but did as she was told.

"Good," said Evalyn. "Now Elm, you and Alice go into town and check out some books from the library for Tiny to read. Then stop by Johnson's Drug and buy some of those crossword puzzle books."

"I don't even like crossword puzzles," said Tiny.

"Trust me, you're gonna want something to do while you're lying in this bed," said Evalyn. "Elmer, on your way back here, stop by your house and pick up your mending and Tiny's knitting needles and yarn."

"That's not necessary," said Tiny. "I'll just lay here."

"No, you won't," said Evalyn. "You're gonna keep busy. Who knows how long you'll be in this bed, six weeks, maybe eight. I'm hoping when Dovie gets back in a couple of weeks you'll feel like moving around, and she'll agree with me that it's okay."

"She needs to rest," said Elmer. "You can't be loading her up with things to do."

"She'll have plenty of time to rest," said Evalyn. "Trust me, Tiny, after a few days in this bed, you'll be thanking me for thinking of stuff you can do, and you'll still be bored."

Joy skipped through the orchard as Norman waddled by her side. Alice had told her there was treasure to be found in the orchard. That wild bandits had buried their money while running from the law.

Dean hadn't believed Alice and laughed when Joy said she was going to go to the orchard and find the treasure. But she would show him once she came back with piles and piles of gold.

Norman honked loudly at her as if telling her to slow down. Joy stopped her skipping and turned to marching. "Come on, Mr. Norman, we're soldiers and we're gonna find those evil outlaws' treasure. If you can't keep up, then fall behind, but I'm marching forward."

When Joy was just north of the orchard, she stopped and looked back. She had never ventured past the orchard by herself before. She wondered if she should tell Ellie where she was going or just turn back all together. She thought of Dean's laughter, then turned and stomped farther away.

"How dare he laugh at me," Joy said out loud. "Aunt Alice said there was treasure out here and she wouldn't lie. There's got to be …"

Joy stopped mid-stride as she heard the loud buzz where her left foot was about to fall. The snake curled its body and raised its head. It rattled its tail, warning Joy to stay back.

Joy slowly lowered her foot behind her as if she were going to back away, but once her foot hit the ground it refused to move further. The snake pulled its head back as if cocking a trigger, and Joy's lip began to tremble.

"Help," she squeaked barely above a whisper. Her heart raced and she desperately wanted to run, but she was rooted into place.

Norman waddled by, finally catching up.

"Mr. Norman, stay back," Joy whispered.

Norman stopped, looked down, and narrowed his eyes at the snake. He took a step in front of Joy and raised his wings. The snake jerked its head back even further as Norman hissed.

Joy watched as the snake decided to retreat rather than fight, and her rapidly beating heart started to slow its pace. She finally felt her legs start to move again as she ran back toward the house. She wasted no time in finding James who was saying his goodbyes to the doctor.

"Papa James, Mr. Norman just saved me from a rattler," she panted. "I was sure I was gonna get bit, but Mr. Norman stood right in front of it and hissed, and that snake decided he didn't want no trouble from Mr. Norman."

"You were lucky," said Dr. Hushton. "I took a little girl about your age who was bitten on her face, to the hospital yesterday. You better stay close to your parents."

"Momma's busy lookin' after Aunt Tiny, and Daddy's rebuilding our pig barn," said Joy.

Dr. Hushton narrowed his eyes. "Your parents should be looking after you." He looked to James. "I cannot stand people who think they know better than doctors while their children are out running God knows where. You had best get your family in line before something bad happens."

Before James could respond, Dr. Hushton got into his car and drove off.

"I don't like him," said Joy.

"You shouldn't say things like that, Joy. Dr. Hushton was just concerned for you," said James. "Now where were you that you almost stepped on a snake?"

"Just passed the orchard," said Joy in a small voice looking down and kicking dirt with her foot.

"Now Joy, you know better than to go that far from the house," scolded James. "What were you thinkin'?"

"I just wanted to find buried treasure," said Joy. "Aunt Alice said she used to look for it all the time."

"Did Aunt Alice also tell you she was almost bit by a rabid dog while looking for treasure in that orchard?" asked James. "Nothing good comes from trying to get money that doesn't belong to you."

Norman came waddling from the orchard. He walked by and honked at Joy, fully expressing his displeasure of being left all alone after saving her from a snake.

"I'm sorry, Mr. Norman," said Joy. Norman turned and headed toward the pond. He let out a small honk in response as if to tell her not to worry about it.

"I messed up bad, didn't I?" asked Joy.

"Well, it isn't your best day," said James. "I'm just glad the snake didn't get you. Joy, you have to be careful, and as the oldest of the cousins, you have to make sure your kin are careful. It's gonna be a bad snake year. Some years they just seem to come out of the woodwork, so you need to be watchful."

"Why?" asked Joy. "Even if I do die, I'd just go to Heaven and get to be with Jesus."

He kneeled down and hugged her. "Joy honey, your life is precious, and even though we have Heaven to look forward to, we need to cherish every moment we have before we go. Heaven will be glorious, but we have work to do here first. We have our family to love and the earth to tend to. God gives us our lives to live in His name, to show others through our lives and actions how to live a life of love and service, not to be in a hurry to go to our Heavenly home."

"So Jesus has a job for me?" asked Joy.

James nodded. "And right now that job is to love your family and stay safe. Do you think you can handle that job?"

"For you and Jesus, you betcha," said Joy, wrapping her arms around James's neck and giving him a tight hug.

Chapter Forty-three

May 1946

Ellie watched Dovie grab her basket and head to the door.

"Ellie, would you mind frying some bacon for me?" asked Dovie. "Everyone's coming over tomorrow for Sunday dinner, and I'm gonna make some baked beans to go with the tenderloins. They've been soaking for a while, so they should be ready for cookin'. Just fry the bacon we didn't cook this morning at breakfast."

Ellie pointed to herself.

Dovie shook her head and gave Ellie an ornery smile. "Oh no, dear, there is only one person in this house who makes baked beans and that is me. But you'll be helping me out a whole bunch if you'll fry up that bacon. I've got to go get Tiny some more yarn from her house. I swear by the time she has this baby that girl will have knitted herself to the moon and back."

Dovie then laughed. "One thing about it, we won't be needin' any sweaters this winter. If she asks, tell her we'll take our walk just before we start dinner. Gotta keep her movin' some, or she'll be stiff as a board when the baby's born. Gabe and Dad will be back from town soon. Don't let them eat any of that bacon. You tell them to keep their grimy hands off or no beans for them."

Ellie laughed silently at Dovie's statement. As if she would tell either man they couldn't have bacon. She walked to the ice box to get the bacon. Her smile remained even after Dovie had gone. She finally felt at home. Everyone knew she could talk, but not one person had tried to badger her into it. She loved how they constantly came together for each other. Nothing was too much to ask if you were family.

Ellie put the skillet on the burner and turned the heat to high, reminding herself to turn it down once the pan was good and hot. She then placed strips of bacon in the pan and listened to the sizzle. She loved the sound of bacon frying, mostly because it meant she'd get to eat it later. She wondered if Dovie would mind if she took just one piece to snack on while cooking the rest.

She flipped the bacon and walked over to the onion bin to grab a red onion. Dovie would need one finely chopped for her beans. Ellie had watched Dovie closely when she had made the beans for Christmas dinner. It was an art form, and Ellie hoped one day Dovie would allow her to do more than just watch.

A smell assaulted Ellie's nose and her eyes grew wide. She had forgotten to turn the heat down and the bacon was burning. Ellie quickly turned but accidently hit the skillet handle with her hand. Hot bacon grease poured over Ellie's hand and onto the rest of the stove. The flames from the burner caught the grease, and Ellie fell back as the fire *whooshed* over the stove and licked the wall.

Ignoring her burned hand, Ellie ran to the pantry. She grabbed the box of salt, ripped the top off, and threw the salt onto the fire. It helped, but the fire still wasn't out. The fire danced on the stove top and Ellie saw the wallpaper above start to bubble. She had to get the fire out before the whole wall went up. She grabbed a towel, quickly wet it in the sink, and then beat the rest of the fire out.

Her hand throbbed and sweat drenched her forehead. Ellie panted as tears took over and slid down her cheeks. "Not again," she whispered as she looked at the mess of the stove and the blackened walls. "Not again."

"Ellie," cried Tiny from the back of the house. "What's goin' on? I smell smoke."

Ellie glanced towards Tiny's voice, then looked back at the ruined stove and wall. She shook her head. They wouldn't understand. They would think the same as the last family. They would beat her. She had ruined everything she had come to love.

Letting out a wail, Ellie tore out the back door and ran.

Dovie exited her car and noticed the smell immediately. There had been a fire. Forgetting Tiny's yarn, she rushed up the steps and through the back door. Tiny stood by the kitchen table, hand resting protectively over her belly, staring at the stove. Dovie followed Tiny's eyes and gasped at the mess of salt, soot, and scorched walls.

"What happened?" asked Dovie.

Tiny shook her head. "I don't know. I smelled smoke and thought I heard a yell, but by the time I got in here all I found was this mess."

"Where's Ellie?" asked Dovie, stepping closer to examine the damage. "Was she hurt?" She looked around the room "Ellie, are you here? Come on out. It's okay."

"I don't know," said Tiny. "I haven't seen her."

Dovie reached down to turn off the burner knob and jerked her hand back. "It's still hot. This just happened. Ellie can't be far."

She wet a towel using it to turn the burner off, then bent below the stove and turned the main valve to shut off all the gas. "We've got to find Ellie. Tiny, please open all the windows and call Elmer to see if he can come home to help look. You stay here in case she comes back. If she does, you know the drill. Ring the dinner bell."

Tiny nodded as Dovie left the house. She called out for Ellie before jumping into her car and rushing down the road toward Bill's house.

Lou Anne met her on the porch. "What's wrong? Is it Tiny?"

Dovie shook her head. "No, there's been a fire and now we can't find Ellie. I need y'all to look around here and search your way over to Quail Crossings. Would one of you drive over to Rockwood? That way Evie and Robert can look to the south."

"Absolutely," said Lou Anne.

Dovie peeled out heading back towards Quail Crossings. Driving up to the house, she was relieved to see that Gabe and James had made it back from town. Gabe was unloading grain into the bin when Dovie pulled up.

"Girl," said James, narrowing his eyebrows, "you need to slow down. You know we got all sorts of children and animals running 'round here."

"Ellie's missing," said Dovie, getting out of the car. "There was a fire inside…"

"A fire?" Gabe's eyes grew wide. "Like before?"

Dovie shook her head. "I don't have details. All I know is I went to get Tiny some yarn from their house, and when I came back I could tell there had been a fire. She couldn't have gotten too far. The burner knob was still hot when I turned it off."

"She left the burner on?" asked James. "The whole house could've exploded."

"I know," snapped Dovie. "The important thing right now is to find Ellie. I'm afraid she's hurt, and I know she's scared."

Robert and Evalyn pulled up, and Dovie let out another sigh of relief. She ran to the truck. "How'd Lou Anne get to you so quickly?"

"Lou Anne?" said Evalyn as she helped Caleb out of the truck. "We were coming to visit. James asked Robert if he'd help unload a big grain shipment y'all were getting today. What's wrong?"

"Ellie's missing," said Dovie. "I don't have time to tell you everything, but I need you and Robert to search south. Gabe, can you go west? Dad and I will go north, and Lou Anne and Bill are searching from their house to here. So we've got all directions covered."

"I can't just leave the kids," said Evalyn. "I'm sure this is all just a big misunderstanding. Maybe Ellie just ran to Bill's to get help. I'm sure she'll be back in a moment."

"I would've seen her running across the pasture when I drove to Bill's," cried Dovie. "We're wasting time. Now take your children into the house where they can stay with Tiny and bring out the shotguns. Y'all know what to do. Fire two shots in the air if you find her."

"I wanna help," said Joy. "Ellie's my friend."

Dovie leaned down. "You can help, Joy. You can look around here, and if you find Ellie, run in and tell Aunt Tiny. Make sure to check all the best hiding places in every building, okay?"

Joy nodded and immediately ran toward the tool shed.

Evalyn took Caleb inside. Gabe placed a gentle hand on Dovie's shoulder. "It'll be okay."

Dovie turned and buried her head into his chest. "Oh, Gabe, I can't believe she's having to relive this nightmare. We have to find her. We just have to."

Evalyn came back out with the shotguns. "I saw the stove. Now I know why you're so worried. There's no way that happened without her getting burned." She handed the shotguns out and turned to Robert. "Let's go."

Gabe hurried to the west as Dovie and James started toward the orchard, everyone calling Ellie's name.

"Slow down, Dovie," said James.

"We have to find her, Dad," said Dovie. "She has to know it's okay. If I'm going too fast, give me the gun and go back to the house. I don't want you to have another spell."

"I want you to slow down, so we can really look for her," said James. "The speed you're going, we're gonna walk right past her."

Dovie sighed. "I don't know why she ran. It's not like when Alice ran away during Black Sunday. She was mad at Evalyn and me for fighting. But Ellie and I had a good conversation before I left. She seemed happy, other than the fact I wouldn't let her make the beans." Dovie's hand flew to her mouth. "Do you think that's why the fire happened? Because I wouldn't let her make the beans? Because she didn't get her way?"

James shook his head. "No, I don't. I think the fire was an accident, and we have a scared little girl to find. I don't think this was any of your fault, just like Alice running away during your fight with Evalyn wasn't your fault. We all have things we would do differently, Dovie, but this isn't one."

Dovie's eyes narrowed. "What's that?"

She started through a heavy portion of evergreens. "Ellie!"

"What?" asked a startled James. "Did you find her?"

Dovie dove through the thick brush, fighting her way to the patch of ivory among the green. She got to the small clearing and sank to the ground. There was no Ellie, just a pair of her unmentionables that Norman had stolen off the laundry line long ago.

Chapter Forty-four

"Ellie!" called Bill.

"Ellie!" cried Annabelle, mimicking her father.

"We've looked in our barn, the chicken house, and the tool shed," said Lou Anne walking up with Dean and Rose. "No Ellie."

"We need to make our way to Quail Crossings then," said Bill.

Bill's family started walking toward Quail Crossings. "Let's spread out a little," said Bill. "Dean you walk over by the south fence line. Lou Anne, since you're having to carry Rosey, you stay here in the middle, so you'll get to Quail Crossings faster. You can backtrack after leaving Rosey with Tiny, and Annabelle and I will walk a bit north of y'all. I want to check out the ol' dugout."

Lou Anne's hand flew up to her mouth. "Bill, you don't think she went in there do you? That place is a death trap. I'm surprised we made it out alive."

"Honestly," said Bill. "I have no idea where she could've run off to, but it's a place she could hide. I know James has told the kids a hundred times about saving us from there. I have to look, just to be sure."

Dean started toward the fence line.

"Watch for snakes," Bill yelled to his son, "and go straight to Quail Crossings when you're done walking the fence line. Don't go lookin' anywhere else."

"All right, Daddy," said Dean. "Don't worry, I'll find her."

"Our boy always wants to be the hero," said Bill.

Lou Anne smiled. "He's just like his daddy."

"What happened in the kitchen?" asked Alice as she walked into the parlor after school to find Tiny tending to Caleb. "And why aren't you in bed?"

"We think Ellie accidently started a fire," said Tiny. "Then she ran away. Evalyn asked me to take care of Caleb while she helps look."

"Where do I need to go look?" asked Alice, her eyes darting around the parlor as if already looking for Ellie.

"I think they've got everything covered," said Tiny as she winced a little.

"What's wrong?" asked Alice, hurrying over.

Tiny waved her off. "It's just a little pain."

"Like your back pain?" Alice grabbed Tiny's hand.

Tiny shook her head. "No, it's in the front this time, down low, but I'll be fine. Evalyn told me they were going south. Bill's family's searching from the east to here. Dovie and James went north and Gabe went west. Joy's lookin' around here. She's searched upstairs and in every room." Tiny forced a smile. "I think she thinks it's a very big game of hide and seek."

Alice slowly nodded as Tiny winced again and squeezed Alice's hand. "Okay, they have it handled. I think it's best I just stay here and wait for further instructions."

"You don't have to stay here on my account," said Tiny. "I'm fine."

"Of course you are," said Alice. "Now, why don't you put your feet up on the sofa while I see about cleaning up the stove?"

Alice decided she should phone the doctor regarding Tiny's new pain. She knew absolutely nothing about pregnancy, but a pain in the lower belly couldn't be good. Part of her wanted to go and find Dovie to send her back to the house while Alice searched with James, but she had no idea where exactly to look. "North" was too vague to just go looking, and if she left Tiny alone to find Dovie and something went wrong, she'd never forgive herself.

"Ellie Brewer!" Evalyn called out.

Robert raised an eyebrow. "Because there might be other Ellies hiding in the pasture?"

"Don't judge me," snapped Evalyn. "I haven't heard you call her name once."

"No you don't because evidently she doesn't want to be found. With everyone calling her name, she's going to hear us a mile away and find a new hiding spot."

"Why wouldn't she want to be found?" asked Evalyn.

"Evalyn, she has no idea what's gonna happen to her next," said Robert. "The last time she was involved with a fire, she ended up spending a week in the hospital."

"She knows we'd never do that to her," said Evalyn.

Robert shook his head. "Does she?"

Evalyn stopped and stared at her husband. "She's been with us for almost a year, and we've never once raised a hand to her."

"That's not what I meant," said Robert. "She might have been here for a year, but think of where she was the past twelve years. It's gonna take her a while to understand that forgiveness is something we practice."

Evalyn bowed her head. Robert was right. Ellie had no reason to believe that they wouldn't throw her to the wolves like all of the other families had. Tears slipped down her cheeks. "We have to find her. She can't run off without knowing we love her no matter what. I won't let my sister live a life without unconditional love."

Joy panted as she climbed the loft ladder. Normally she would have gotten into a barrel full of trouble climbing into the loft alone, but she figured her momma would allow this one exception. Dovie had told her to check all of the buildings for hiding spots. Arriving at the top, she sat on the hay stack and wiped the back of her hand over her forehead.

"This has been the hardest game of hide and seek ever," said Joy out loud. "Usually I find Dean and Annabelle within a minute."

She heard a movement in the hay and stood. She wondered if it was a rat, or maybe it was kittens. Joy remembered how her friend at Sunday school had talked about chasing her cat's litter through the hay bales.

"Here, kitty, kitty," called Joy softly as she looked through the slits in the hay bales. A flash of blue caught her eye, and Joy jumped back. "Ellie?"

A hay bale started to move forward and then fell to the ground exposing a large opening in the middle of the hay stack. And there in the hay, Ellie was scooted back to the corner and curled up into a ball.

"Wow, Ellie," said Joy, climbing inside. "This is the best hiding spot ever. I didn't think I was ever gonna find you. Whatcha doing?"

"Hiding," said Ellie, figuring it wouldn't hurt to talk now. She was already in trouble.

Joy pursed her lips. She had never heard her aunt speak before but figured she just hadn't had much to say. "Well, I knew that. I've been looking for you for hours."

Ellie didn't respond. She knew she hadn't been up in the loft for hours, even though it had been a while. She was beginning to think no one would find her, and she could sneak away after dark as planned.

"I guess the game's over," said Joy. "Do you want to go inside?"

Ellie shook her head.

Joy shrugged. "Okay."

She started to crawl out of the haystack. "Hey, Ellie, if it's okay with my momma, can I come up here and play with you some time?"

"I don't think I'll be around to use it," said Ellie. "You'll have to ask Alice. It's really her place."

"Okay," said Joy. "Shame you won't be around. I like you. You're my friend."

Joy jumped out and headed toward the ladder, a big smile on her face. Now all she had to do was tell Aunt Tiny that she had found Ellie and the game would be over. She had won, and she had even beaten all the grown-ups.

Ellie watched Joy leave wondering if she should run and find another hiding place, but she knew she had nowhere else to go. Even if she did try to run towards town, they'd find her. It was all fields and pastures with no place to hide.

Ellie heard the back door to the house open and knew it was Joy going inside. She would probably tell Tiny where she was hiding, so if she was going to run, now was the time. The tears falling on her cheeks surprised her. She thought she had cried every last drop she had in her body after the fire. Pretty soon it would all be over. She wished she hadn't taken Lovey inside. She could have really used her stuffed friend to talk to.

Her burned hand ached and had started to blister. Ellie knew that the wound needed treatment, or it would get infected. Of course, the last family hadn't cared if Ellie received treatment, or if she got an infection. That was clear as they had thrown her into the dirt after splitting her lip and cheek open.

She had tried to put out the fire then too, although they had never stopped to ask her what happened. It wasn't even her fault. She had told them their small daughter, Sloan, had been playing with the knobs on the stove. Ellie had just gone to the outhouse for a moment while the chicken was frying. She knew she'd be back in plenty of time not to burn it. But Sloan, who was supposed to be in the care of her mother, had toddled her four-year-old self into the kitchen and turned all the burners on high.

By the time Ellie returned, the pan was on fire. She got Sloan out of the house and called for Sloan's mother to come out, but by the time she returned inside after securing Sloan into a nearby car, the kitchen was fully ablaze and no amount of salt was gonna put it out.

Ellie ran through the house to find Sloan's mother, half drunk on moonshine. She grabbed the woman, who was twice her size, and pulled her to her feet. The woman barely knew what was going on, but thankfully she let herself be guided out of harm's way.

After laying Sloan's mother beside the car, Ellie ran to the pump and started filling a bucket with water. It was then that *he* and his brothers pulled up. She had been frying the chicken for their family dinner. He looked at his house on fire, his daughter screaming in the car, and his wife passed out against it, and Ellie could see his rage.

It took him only an instant to close the distance and hit her square in the jaw with his balled fist, and only moments later for his brothers to join in the beating. Had it not been for that one sweet cousin who had draped her body over Ellie's to stop the beating, Ellie was sure *he* and his brothers would have killed her and thrown her body into the fire.

Ellie knew that cousin had sacrificed her life with her family to save Ellie. The cousin had taken Ellie to the police station and told them everything she knew. She betrayed her family for a stranger and now Ellie had done it again. The cousin had destroyed her life for nothing.

Ellie sobbed. She had no right to be here. She had no right to this wonderful family. It was time for her to go for good. She got up and started towards the hole.

"Ellie?"

Ellie sat back. This time it was Alice's voice. Ellie flinched as the dinner bell rang through the air. They were all coming back. There was no cousin who would come to her defense this time. She was a goner.

Alice crawled into the opening. "I don't know why I didn't think to look in here. When Joy told us where she found you, I felt more stupid than a cat trying to climb a cactus. Are you okay?"

Ellie shrank away from Alice's outstretched hand.

"It's okay, Ellie," said Alice. "We know it was an accident. We're all just really worried about you."

"It was an accident before," Ellie cried, "and they beat me."

Alice's smile fell. "Ellie Brewer, we are nothing like that other family. Do you really think we're those kind of people?"

Ellie shook her head. "I don't want you to be."

"Well, we're not," said Alice. "And that dinner bell you just heard was Tiny telling everyone we had found you. You know you've got a mess of people searching for you right now? Every one of them is worried sick about you."

Ellie brushed her hair out of her face. "Really?"

"Really," said Alice. "Looks like a bad burn on your hand. Why don't you come down so we can tend to it? The doctor will be here soon."

"No." Ellie shook her head violently. "No doctor."

"Ellie, you're safe," said Alice, inching a little closer. "I know you don't like doctors, but we have to see to your hand. We're not gonna let anyone hurt you. I promise."

"I didn't mean to start the fire, but he won't believe me," said Ellie. "If you call the doctor, they'll take me away."

"No one is taking you away," came a voice from outside the loft. "Now, come on out."

Alice looked at Ellie. "You know we have to do what she says. Momma Dovie doesn't like to wait. Go ahead."

Alice gestured for Ellie to climb out of the hole first. She moved slowly, careful of her hand. The minute she was out of the hole, Dovie swooped her up and gave her a mighty squeeze. "Don't you ever do that again, you hear?"

"The fire?" asked Ellie. "I'm sorry."

"No, not the fire," said Dovie. "Run off like that. I was worried sick. Ellie, we don't care about the fire. We can fix all of that. In fact, the damage isn't even bad. We care about you. We love you, Ellie, and if anything would've happened to you, it would devastate us. Now come on down and let's get you looked after."

Ellie felt a warmth radiate through her body. It wasn't the heat that came from a fire, it was the warmth of knowing she was truly loved and finally had the family she had always longed for.

Chapter Forty-five

Dr. Hushton walked out of Dovie's room, his lips making a thin line across his face. Ellie cowered in the corner, hoping he wouldn't see her. She knew the doctor was not happy, and she was partially to blame. He had marched right into Quail Crossings and wouldn't let anyone in the room while he examined Tiny.

"How is she?" asked Elmer.

"She's gone into early labor," said the doctor. "Why don't you go on in and see her?"

Dr. Hushton waited until Elmer was in the other room before continuing. "She confessed to me that you have been taking her on short walks twice daily."

"Yes," said Dovie stepping forward. "She stayed off her feet completely while I was gone with Mr. Pearce after our wedding. Once I got back, she and I decided it would help her to get some fresh air, as long as we didn't go very far. We'd walk to the orchard where we have a little bench ..."

"I don't care about your bench, Mrs. Pearce," snapped the doctor. "You and your kin directly disobeyed my orders to keep Mrs. Brewer in bed, and now her baby is in grave danger. It is imperative that she remains in bed for the duration of her pregnancy, or she will have this child early. I will not have your hillbilly ways interfering with my work. You do anything like that again, Mrs. Pearce, and I will call the law on you."

"Leave her alone!" yelled Ellie.

"Ellie, it's okay," said Dovie in a controlled voice. Ellie could tell Dovie was holding back so she could get medical attention. "We'll just have the doctor look at your hand, and then he can be on his way. The others will be back from town soon and we don't want the little ones under foot." She motioned for Ellie to come closer. "Ellie burned herself cookin'. Would you be so kind as to look at it?"

Dr. Hushton took in the fire scene for the first time and his eyes narrowed. "Again, had you listened to me this wouldn't have happened. I told you that children like her ..." He pointed a sharp finger at Ellie. "... are not right in the head. If you think for one minute this fire was an accident then you are delusional."

Ellie wished Dovie hadn't sent everyone but Elmer into town for ice cream. She wished Mr. Gabe was there. He wouldn't allow the doctor to talk to Dovie like that. She wondered if she should call for Elmer, then changed her mind. Elmer had enough to worry about with Tiny.

"This is what happens when you let women folk run your households," snarled the doctor. "If you were my wife, I would have you in line with a firm regiment of discipline."

Ellie had heard enough and stormed out of the house. There was no way she was going to let that man see to her hand. It throbbed something fierce, but she would keep it clean and use Dovie's aloe plant to help it heal. She didn't want *him* to touch her.

"You get back here," the doctor called at her. "You're the cause of this family's troubles. You're nothing but a curse."

Ellie cringed and stopped near the doctor's car. She didn't want to face him. Fear raced through her body. She thought of her family, and how ugly he had been to Dovie, and forced herself to turn back to him.

Dovie was standing on the stoop, ready to intervene. That gave Ellie the courage she needed. She would not let *him* talk bad about her. She would not allow *him* another day to discipline anyone. She had seen *his* discipline tactics first hand.

She looked at Dovie. Every ounce of Ellie's being was telling her to run to Dovie. To hide behind her back and let Dovie handle the situation. But it wouldn't end there, and Ellie knew the doctor wouldn't think twice about striking Dovie.

She could stand up to him, but she had to know Dovie was out of harm's way. "I'm okay, Dovie. Please go inside and see to Tiny. I'll be right in." But Dovie remained on the stoop.

Dr. Hushton's eyes grew wide. "So you're talking now?"

"I only stopped talkin' because your family forced me to," said Ellie in a harsh whisper. Her legs trembled, and she wondered if she would melt to the ground like butter. "But I'm done with all that. I won't allow you to hurt my family."

The doctor laughed, and Ellie heard the evil in his voice. Dovie must have thought the laugh meant things were okay with the doctor because she stepped back inside.

"How are you going to stop me?" asked Dr. Hushton, his eyes narrowed.

"I feel like talkin' a lot," said Ellie, forcing her voice to stay steady. "I was thinkin' maybe I'd go chat with the sheriff. I think he'd be mighty interested in hearing about how your wife had to drink moonshine because you beat her almost daily. You know, he might even give Mrs. Waterman at the Children's Bureau a call. Does Sloan still like to play with the burners on the stove?"

"You little heathen," snarled the doctor. "You are the devil's child."

Ellie could see the shock in the doctor's eyes. His face grew red, but she kept going. She knew if she stopped talking for too long, she'd never continue. "While I'm at it, maybe I'll tell the county hospital board how you lost your job in Amarillo. I think they'd like to know how you "disciplined" your lady patients when they had the nerve to disagree with your treatment."

Dr. Hushton raised his hand.

"Go ahead," said Ellie, lifting her chin in defiance. "It's nothing you haven't done before."

The doctor lowered his hand and glanced toward the door. "No one will believe you. Just like they didn't believe you last time."

"Maybe not at first," said Ellie, fighting her tears. "But with everyone here at Quail Crossings on my side, the authorities will look into it and find the truth. This time I'm the one with the family who will back up my story, and you're the one who's all alone."

Dr. Hushton grabbed Ellie by her shoulders and started pulling her to the car. "I won't let you do this. I won't let you ruin my career a second time. I'll get rid of you once and for all!"

Ellie dug her heels in the dirt and tried to wrestle herself away from the doctor. Norman flew out of the barn and start honking at the doctor. Wings raised, he hissed.

The doctor's grip was so strong, Ellie could feel his short nails biting into her flesh through her shirt.

"You let her go!" ordered Dovie, barreling out the back door.

Dr. Hushton stopped as Dovie marched down the steps and walked toward them, pointing a shotgun at the doctor's chest. He let go of Ellie and raised his hands in the air.

"Come here, Ellie," said Dovie. Ellie did as she was told.

"Now, you need to be on your way," Dovie said to the doctor. "And be expecting a visit from the sheriff because you can bet your bottom dollar as soon as you hit the road, I'll be giving him a call."

"She's lying about me," said Dr. Hushton. "She'll ruin my career."

"Not if you ain't got nothing to hide," said Dovie, inching a little closer.

The doctor lowered his hands. "I told you she was trouble. Children like her are so bad that not even their own parents want them. Children like that are the devil's spawn."

"You just let me worry about that. I know Ellie a heck of a lot better than you do," said Dovie. "Besides, I think you have your own situation to worry about. Now you just get on out of here. Trust me, you don't want to be around when everyone else shows up and hears what you've done to our Ellie."

Ellie's heart swelled with love for Dovie. She knew instantly that this was what unconditional love felt like. It didn't matter what the doctor said. Dovie and the other family members would never let him hurt her ever again. She was safe. She was finally safe.

Dr. Hushton shook his head. "No. I won't let her ruin everything I've built."

"You don't have a choice," said Dovie, raising the gun.

"The hell I don't."

Before Ellie could blink, the doctor had ripped the shotgun out of Dovie's hands, thrust the butt of the gun up, and struck Dovie in the temple.

Ellie screamed as she watched Dovie wilt to the ground. "Dovie!"

The doctor turned and shot at Norman, barely missing. Norman half ran, half flew to the barn for safety.

Ellie looked up at Dr. Hushton. "You monster!"

She sprung herself at the doctor clawing at his face. She could feel his flesh under her fingernails as he cried out. His hands holding the gun, were pinned between their bodies. Ellie didn't care about the gun. She didn't care if she were hurt or even killed. Her rage was all that mattered. Protecting Dovie from further harm was all that mattered.

"What's going on out here?" yelled Elmer as he came out onto the stoop. Ellie glanced behind her, ready to yell for Elmer to watch out. Dr. Hushton took advantage of the distraction and threw Ellie to the ground. He took aim and fired the shotgun at Elmer.

Ellie watched in shock as Elmer's body was thrust back from the force of the gunshot.

Chapter Forty-six

Ellie covered her mouth in horror as she watched Elmer fall to the far side of the stoop. *He shot him. The doctor hit Dovie and shot Elmer. They could both be dead.* Ellie's mind turned to Tiny, lying helplessly on the bed and the innocent child in her belly. The child whose father now lay bleeding in the dirt.

She had to get the doctor away from Quail Crossings and away from Tiny and her baby. She scrambled to her feet and took off toward the orchard, hoping that Dr. Hushton would follow her. She had to distract the doctor and buy enough time for everyone else to get home and call the law.

"Get back here!" yelled Dr. Hushton. Ellie was relieved to hear his heavy footsteps behind her.

Her plan was simple, get through the orchard, and then head toward the thicket of sand plums. If she could lose the doctor among the thorny branches, she might be able to circle back and get help. She hoped Dovie would wake up in time to tend to Elmer, that is, if he weren't already dead.

As Ellie cleared the orchard, she picked up her speed. She would be out in the open for about a half mile until she reached the thicket. It would take a miracle to reach it before being shot.

Tiny walked through the kitchen slowly. She thought she heard a gunshot and yelling. She cradled her belly in her arms, hoping she wasn't doing any damage by checking things out.

Goose bumps covered her flesh. It was too quiet. Even with most of the family in town, there should've been birds chirping, cows mooing, and the sounds of conversation in the kitchen. After all, wasn't the doctor still tending to Ellie? He couldn't be done so soon.

Tiny approached the screen door and scanned the yard, her eyes falling on a heap of yellow near the doctor's car. She gasped as she realized the heap was Dovie. She hurried out the door and down the steps, her eyes locked on the limp body on the ground.

"Dovie? Oh my goodness, are you okay?" Tiny knelt beside Dovie and rolled her to her side. Tiny sucked in a breath as she saw blood flowing down Dovie's face from a wound on her temple. Dovie's eye was starting to swell shut. Tiny released a breath as she saw Dovie's chest rise and fall. At least she was still breathing. This was no accident. Someone had hit Dovie with something hard.

Tiny froze. Where was Elmer? Ellie? The doctor? Why would someone come to Quail Crossings and hurt

Dovie? Had Elmer and the doctor chased the man away? Was Ellie hiding somewhere away from harm?

Tiny wanted to call out for Ellie but didn't want whoever had hurt Dovie to know she was there. For all she knew, the assailant hadn't known she was in the house. She should go back inside and call the sheriff.

She searched the yard for signs of anyone else. It was so quiet, as if the whole world were hiding.

"I'll be right back, Dovie," said Tiny. "I'm gonna call for help."

Tiny turned and bit back her scream as she saw a brown work boot. It bore a hole in the sole that looked exactly like a crescent moon.

"Oh God, no! Elmer!" Tiny ran to her husband, skidding to a stop just before his crumpled body. Blood saturated the right side of his shirt. She fell to her knees and pressed her hands firmly against his wound.

A shot rang out and Tiny quickly covered Elmer's body with her own. Elmer groaned. "Elm," she whispered. "Elmer, it's Tiny, wake up."

Elmer's eyes fluttered open, and Tiny let out a cry of relief before clamping her mouth shut, so no one would hear. She whispered, "Elmer, what's going on?"

"Dr. Hushton shot me," Elmer said, his voice hoarse.

"What? The doctor? Why?" Tiny shook her head. "Can you walk?"

Elmer faded out of consciousness. Tiny gave him a firm pat on the cheek, leaving a smear of his own blood, and he opened his eyes. "Don't go to sleep,

Elmer. You have to stay awake. Now tell me what to do."

"Go inside," said Elmer. "Call the sheriff. Lock yourself in."

"I'm not gonna leave y'all out here," said Tiny, getting to her feet. "Let's get you inside, and then I'll see if I can't get Dovie to wake up. Where's Ellie?"

"No," snapped Elmer. "Forget us and get yourself and our baby inside."

"I can't do that," said Tiny as Elmer passed out again. She shook him. "Wake up, Elm! Wake up!"

Elmer's eyes remained shut. Tiny looked to the sky. "Help me."

Shaking her head, Tiny stood and hurried to Dovie. She was not going to fall apart now. She was not going to leave Dovie and Elmer to die in the dirt. She prayed Ellie was someplace safe and that she would stay in her hiding place until help came.

Tiny grabbed Dovie under both arms, leaving bloody hand prints on her shirt, and pulled her into a sitting position against the doctor's car. "Dovie, can you hear me?" She gave Dovie a little shake. "Dovie, you have to wake up. We have to get you and Elmer inside before the doctor comes back."

Dovie's right eye fluttered open. She winced as she tried to open her left eye and then delicately touched her left temple.

"Can you walk?" asked Tiny.

Dovie looked at Tiny, then at her feet. It was if she were trying to determine if anything else was hurt or broken. Then she looked at Tiny's blood-covered hands. "Where'd all that blood come from?"

"I know you're confused right now. This is Elmer's blood; he's been shot," said Tiny. "We have to hurry. We have to get you and Elmer in the house, and I can't pick up Elmer on my own."

Dovie's eyes fell on the stoop. "Okay," she said quietly. It reminded Tiny of a small child.

"Good," Tiny stood and helped Dovie get to her feet.

"The doctor shot him?" asked Dovie, still looking dazed.

"That's what Elm said before he passed out," cried Tiny, trying to hold back tears.

She kneeled over Elmer and prayed she could wake him long enough to get him in the house. "Elm, wake up." She tapped his cheek.

Elmer opened his eyes. "Go inside."

"We're all going inside," said Tiny. "Dovie, you get on his left side and I'll take the right, where he's shot. He'll need to lean on you more, is that okay?"

Dovie gave her a small nod as she moved to help Elmer up.

"You've got to help us," Tiny said to Elmer. "On the count of three we stand. One ... Two ... Three ..."

The women lifted as Elmer got his feet under him. He let out a loud groan as Tiny lifted his arm to get under his right shoulder and again as they walked up the steps. "We've got to move faster," said Tiny. "He could come back any minute."

Elmer supported most of his weight but still felt heavy to Tiny as she guided him. She wondered if she was doing harm to her baby by saving Elmer, and then she wondered if Elmer would ever see his child. She pushed the thought away.

Tiny reached for the screen door handle and yanked it open. Dovie turned slightly to go in first and after they all cleared the door, Tiny shut and locked it.

"What about Ellie?" asked Dovie. "Where is she?"

"I haven't seen her. I hope she's hiding somewhere," said Tiny as they walked Elmer to the sofa. "Lie down."

With Elmer on the sofa, Tiny hurried to the kitchen and grabbed a handful of towels. "Dovie, I know your head hurts something terrible, but can you keep pressure on Elmer's wound while I call the sheriff?"

Dovie looked at Elmer and took the towels. "Yes, I can do that."

Tiny ran to the phone and waited for the operator. The minute she heard the voice at the other end, she started rambling, "Operator, this is Mary Brewer. There's been a shooting at Quail Crossings. My husband's been shot, and Dovie Grant is badly wounded. We need all the deputies you have. Quickly. We believe it was Dr. Hushton who did the shootin'. Also, my sister-in-law is missing. We think the doctor's after her."

"Ma'am, did you say the doctor shot your husband?" asked the operator. "Dr. Hushton?"

"Yes, now get someone out here to Quail Crossings!" yelled Tiny before slamming the receiver down. "The nerve of that woman. I tell her I need help and she wants details." Tiny picked the receiver back up, and tried to calm herself, hoping she wouldn't get a bunch of questions from the next operator, "Johnson's Drug Store, please."

Tiny didn't know if James had taken the family to Johnson's or Annette's for ice cream, but she knew Johnson's had a phone, and if she got word there, someone would run to Annette's and find James and the others.

"This is Johnson's Drug," answered Mr. Johnson in his charming tenor voice.

"Mr. Johnson, it's Tiny. I need to speak to Elmer's family if they're in your store, right away."

"Sure, Evalyn's right here, will she do?" asked Mr. Johnson.

"Yes, please."

Even though Mr. Johnson had said Evalyn was right beside him, it felt like a lifetime before she finally came to the phone. "I've told you before Tiny, I can't bring you an ice cream cone. It'll just melt before we get there."

"Evalyn, Dr. Hushton shot Elmer and hit Dovie in the head something bad. She's got blood all over her face, and Elmer's bleeding badly, I don't know if we can stop it. And I don't know where Ellie or the doctor are now. I'm really scared, and I need y'all to come back here, right now. I called the sheriff, and they're on their way out here."

"Slow down," said Evalyn. "I can't understand you. It sounded like you said the doctor shot Elmer and that Dovie's bleeding from the head."

"'Cause I did!"

"Is he …?" asked Evalyn. Tiny could hear the catch in Evalyn's voice as she tried to remain calm.

"No …," Tiny answered. Tears that she had forbidden to fall no longer obeyed her as Tiny lost her voice. She took a deep breath, "… he's still alive. But Dovie is dazed, and she can't hardly remember her name much less how to tend to a gunshot wound. Please, come home. I'm so scared, Evie. I'm so scared that Elmer's gonna die."

Chapter Forty-seven

Ellie felt the shot whiz past her right ear but kept running. Apparently the doctor had a harder time hitting a running target than one just standing on the stoop. She thought about the way Elmer had fallen to the ground and the crack of the butt of the gun against Dovie's head.

Shaking the thoughts from her head, she concentrated on the sand plum thicket. Her sides cramped and her calves felt as if they'd fall right off at any moment, but she had to keep going. She had to keep the doctor busy until the rest of the family got back. She wondered how long it would take them. They were keeping the children busy for Tiny's sake and could be gone for hours.

She hoped she could run fast enough to lose the doctor in the thicket and then double back to Quail Crossings. Surely Dovie would have woken up and gotten Elmer inside. And if she hadn't, then there was a pretty good chance neither of them would wake up again.

Before Ellie could think any more about Dovie, her foot caught on something and she sailed through the air, landing hard on the ground. Pain shot through her wrists as she caught herself, and she could feel both knees being scratched open by the rough terrain of the plains.

She heard the heavy footsteps just before she saw his shadow. She tried to scramble to her feet, but it was too late. Dr. Hushton was on top of her.

She let out a scream as he pulled her to her feet by a fistful of her hair. "Why did you make me do that?" snarled the doctor, yanking her hair hard. "You made me shoot that boy. You should've just come with me and none of this would've happened. You ruined my career, and you cost that boy, and probably Mrs. Pearce, their lives."

He gave her hair another yank. "And now you will pay with yours."

Dr. Hushton let go of her hair and grabbed her arm. He placed the shotgun barrel under her chin as he pulled her toward some old boards lying in the grass. The boards had grown warped and rotted with time. Ellie realized the boards were what she had tripped over.

The doctor turned, keeping his grip firmly on Ellie and stomped his foot on one of the boards causing it to break. Ellie looked down into what looked to be an old dried up water well that was partially caved in. She thought she heard a series of buzzes as the board hit the ground, but the sound was quickly drowned out as

Dr. Hushton broke another board. As soon as the second board fell, Ellie heard it again.

After not talking for so many years, Ellie had grown very good at hearing little things. The small pop a skillet makes when it's the perfect temperature for frying, the click of a necklace when it's firmly latched, and the buzz that a rattlesnake makes when it's fully on alert.

She looked toward the bottom of the well and noticed the ground was moving. There wasn't just one snake down there, but hundreds. The old dried up water well had become a snake parlor.

"Please don't," said Ellie, her eyes growing wide.

"Oh, I'm not gonna shoot you," said Dr. Hushton. "I'm just gonna knock you out cold and then throw you in the well. By the time you wake up, they will have already searched high and low for you. They'll stop looking, thinking I've taken you somewhere. All the while you'll die a long slow death alone in the depths of the earth, close to Satan, which is where you belong."

"I'll go with you," Ellie said quickly. "I'll tell the law whatever you want. I'll admit to the fire. Just don't put me in there."

"Oh no, missy," the doctor said with a wicked grin. "I'm not taking any more chances with you. Since I shot that boy, they won't care who started a fire a year ago. They'll only care about that boy."

"Not if he dies." Ellie hated the taste of the sentence as it rolled off her tongue. She wanted nothing more than for both Dovie and Elmer to be alive and well. But if she could just buy some more time, then the others might arrive to help. "We'll go back, and I'll help you make sure both of them are dead."

"You are the devil's spawn," spat Dr. Hushton with wild eyes. "I'm doing the world a favor."

Dropping his weapon, Dr. Hushton spun Ellie around keeping a firm grip on her arm and raised his fist. "I'm gonna enjoy doing this."

Evalyn barreled out of the pickup and ran towards the back door of Quail Crossings.

"Evalyn, wait," yelled Robert. "We need to make sure it's safe."

She ignored her husband, threw open the screen door, and rushed through the back door.

"Why wasn't that door locked? Where's Elm?" asked Evalyn, as she ran through the kitchen not waiting for an answer. "Have you been keeping pressure on the wound?"

"Yes," said Tiny, as she kneeled in front of Elmer. "I've cut his shirt away, and I've been using Dovie's tweezers to pluck the buckshot that was closest to the skin. There's just so much."

Evalyn kneeled beside Elmer and examined the wound. "You've done good, Tiny."

"Where are the children?" asked Tiny.

"Mr. Johnson took them to the Spauldings," said Evalyn.

Lou Anne rushed in. "How is he?"

"Tiny managed to get a lot of the buckshot out, but there may be some deeper," said Evalyn.

"Half the town's on its way out here to see about the doctor." Lou Anne looked around the room. "Where's Dovie? You didn't let her lay down did you?"

Tiny looked around. "She was just here sitting in her chair. I … um …." Tiny put both hands on her forehead. "I'm sorry … I was trying to get the buckshot out of Elmer. I thought she was fine. I didn't even hear her get up."

Lou Anne ran to Dovie's room. As quickly as she went in, she came out shaking her head. She checked James's room and hurried upstairs before rushing down the stairs and out the back door. "Gabe, Dovie's missing too!"

Chapter Forty-eight

Ellie watched the doctor cock his fist back like a snake ready to strike. She heard the rattle below and could sense the movement of hundreds of snakes just below her. Everything seemed to stop as the sun peeked above a random cloud, basking her face in its rays. She felt the heat of the sun on her cheek.

She studied the doctor's face, so full of fury and anger. His eyes were hard and his nostrils flared. His cheeks were red with heat and anger, and his lips were curled into a cruel smile.

His face blurred as Ellie thought about her family. She pictured Alice's face full of faith as she believed Ellie's declaration about the fire and Elmer's pride as she spelled out "cat" for the first time. She remembered Bill standing guard at the dance, ready to be her knight in shining armor and Evalyn's compassion after Ellie had not been accepted at school. She saw James's joy after downing two plates of her biscuits and gravy, letting her know full well they were the best he'd ever had, and she felt Dovie's unconditional love as she recalled the way Dovie had believed her over the doctor. Ellie turned her face to the sun and soaked in the warmth of her family. A peacefulness she had never known settled over her.

She was finally home, and she was not going to let *him* take it from her.

With a sly smile, Ellie turned suddenly and kicked Dr. Hushton hard in the shin. Caught off guard by the blow, he bent over in pain. Ellie took advantage and brought her knee up into his chin. His head snapped back, and Ellie turned to run. The doctor's grip on her arm loosened as Ellie ran past him, pulling herself free. He spun around, lost his balance and fell through the rest of the boards right into the snake den.

Norman waddled around the yard honking his complaints to the family members who had just arrived.

"How should we handle this?" asked Gabe, ignoring the goose.

"We find the doctor, and then we shoot him just like he shot Elmer," Bill said through clenched teeth.

James put a firm hand on Bill's shoulder. "We're not shooting anyone unless we have to. We find him and bring him back for the sheriff to take care of."

Bill looked toward the house.

"Bill, if you want to stay with Elmer, we'll understand," said Gabe, loading his rifle.

Bill shook his head. "No I'm goin'."

"I'll stay," said Jacob, "and look after Elm and the others."

Lou Anne burst through the screen door. "Gabe, Dovie's gone!"

"Dovie?" James's face lost color. "I thought she was inside with Tiny."

"She wandered off while Tiny was taking buckshot out of Elmer," explained Lou Anne. "She didn't even hear Dovie leave. But Tiny told Evie on the phone that Dovie was confused after taking a blow to the head."

"So where do we look?" asked Gabe as he ran his hand through his hair. "They could've gone in any direction or in separate directions. Should we split up?"

James shook his head. "I think we better stay together, since we don't know what Hushton is liable to do." He looked around the farm. "I say we either go east or north. There's nothing but pasture west and south, I think we would've seen them as we came back from town."

Three sheriff's cars pulled into the yard, followed by two trucks of men from the town.

"Looks like we can head in all directions now," said Gabe.

James walked over to speak with the officers as Bill went to gather the town's people. After a few moments James walked back toward the house with an officer and three other men.

"Lou Anne," called James, "Officer Fields is going to take Elmer to the hospital in Perry. These folks will help get him in the car. Tiny can ride with him, and then y'all can follow in Elmer's truck. We'll meet you there with Dovie and Ellie as soon as we find them."

"I'll take you to Elmer," said Lou Anne. The men turned to follow Lou Anne when suddenly a cry of agony pierced the air. Everyone froze at the horrible sound.

"Was that Ellie?" asked Lou Anne.

"Miss Dovie?" Jacob wondered out loud.

"No," said Gabe, "that was a man's cry, and it came from the north!"

Chapter Forty-nine

Ellie froze as Dr. Hushton let out a blood-curdling scream. She could hear the buzz of the rattles and hiss of the snakes as they struck. The doctor let out a wail for every bite. Ellie covered her ears and began singing, "Jesus loves me this I know."

"Help!" cried the doctor, his voice was weak and pitiful. It bore no resemblance to the voice of the man who had just spat in her face and called her the devil's spawn. Ellie turned and looked toward the hole. Could the doctor be trying to trick her into coming back? She knew the hole would be too deep for her to reach the top, but maybe it wasn't for the doctor. She turned back around and took a few steps back towards Quail Crossings.

"Please help me," called the doctor. "Oh God, help me."

Ellie stopped again. Her head told her to race home and get whomever was there to go back and get the doctor. Her body shivered at the thought of all those snakes.

The sound of another rattle and hiss echoed out of the hole, followed by a cry from the doctor. How many times had he been bitten now? Half a dozen? A dozen? More?

Ellie remembered the way the ground had moved in the hole and fought the urge to vomit. She fell to her knees as the doctor cried out again. She couldn't leave him. She couldn't just let him die in that snake den. She wasn't the evil person he claimed her to be. She wasn't like him. If she left him there now, she would be doing to him what he had planned to do to her. She would be just like *him*.

Ellie slowly walked back toward the hole. Her heart was pounding, as if screaming … *Run away. Run away. Run away.*

She took a deep breath and then peered into the hole. The doctor faced the wall, his hands grabbing for anything to hold onto as he tried to climb out of the hole. Snakes slithered around his feet, several in their coiled positions, rattles up and shaking, heads back, ready to strike at any movement. Snakes lay on every ledge of the hole's wall. Ellie shivered. She had never seen so many snakes in one place. There was no way the doctor was getting out without disturbing the snakes on the ledges.

Hushton lifted his foot to climb and two rattlesnakes bit at his leg. One snake met his mark, and the doctor cried out again. He looked up and saw Ellie peering at him.

"Ellie, help me," he cried. "I think I broke some ribs, and I've been snake bit something terrible. Please don't leave me here to die."

Judging by the doctor's height she guessed the hole was about eight feet deep. Ellie turned and started searching the ground for the longest board she could find.

"Ellie!" shouted the doctor. "Where did you go? Come back! Don't give into the evil that grips your soul."

Ellie grabbed a board and got down on her belly.

"Watch out," she said to the doctor as she used the board to knock the snakes off the ledges as far down as she could reach. The doctor covered his head as Ellie tried to knock them away from him. As she stretched down to reach the last snake that lay between her and the doctor, a brown and tan blur struck her hand.

Ellie cried out and dropped the board. She looked at her hand and her breathing became labored as she noticed the two large puncture wounds on the back of her burnt hand.

"You'll be okay," said Dr. Hushton. "Get me out of here, and we'll get you to the hospital. I'm a doctor. I can help you."

Ellie worried that once he was out he would try to kill her again. She should run and get help, make sure her own bite was tended to.

Ellie shook her head. She would not be afraid any longer. She reached down and the doctor grabbed her wrists. He tightened his grip, and Ellie let out a scream as he squeezed her burnt hand. Digging his feet into the sides of the hole and using Ellie as a makeshift rope, he made his way out of the hole. She was surprised he had so much strength after being bit by multiple rattlesnakes, but figured he was fueled by the desire to get out of there. Using Ellie as a rope, he climbed up and out of the hole.

Ellie quickly got to her feet and then helped the doctor to his. She didn't want to be around the snakes any longer.

"Thank you, Ellie," he said, grabbing her shoulders firmly.

"What are you doing?" Ellie tried to fight as Dr. Hushton pushed her toward the snake parlor. "I helped you."

"Stupid girl," he snarled. "Did you really think I'd let the devil's spawn live to see another day? Your body will rot with the serpents of evil where you belong."

"No! Stop!" Ellie dug the toes of her shoes into the dirt but could feel herself being pulled towards the hole. She looked into her would-be grave, the ground still writhing with hundreds of snakes. She couldn't believe this was happening. She had helped him. She had put all her pain and anger aside and saved his life.

"May God have mercy on your soul, Ellie Brewer," spat Dr. Hushton as he went in for the final push.

Ellie heard a crack, and the doctor's eyes glazed over. His arms went limp, and he fell back into the hole.

"May God have mercy on yours," snarled Dovie, as she stood looking into the hole, the butt of the shotgun still raised.

"Dovie!" cried Ellie as she ran into her arms. "I thought I was never gonna see you again." Ellie cried into Dovie's shirt. "I was afraid you were dead."

Dovie cradled the girl's head. "No, sweetie, I'm okay. We're all okay."

Ellie's eyes shot open. "I've been snake bit."

"What?" cried Dovie. She stepped back and looked Ellie over.

"On my hand, when I was saving the doctor," said Ellie.

"Oh, Ellie, you kind soul you." Dovie shook her head. She ripped the bottom of her shirt into a strip and tied a tourniquet around Ellie's upper arm. "God love you. I don't know if I'm proud or upset that you were bitten saving that monster. I guess I'm both. Come on, let's get you to the hospital."

Chapter Fifty

Gabe paced the tiny waiting room at the small Perry hospital. The white room with three chairs and a row of overhead lights was crowded with people from Quail Crossings and Knollwood, leaving little room to get an actual good pace in.

"What's taking them so long?" he asked Evalyn.

"We brought in a shotgun wound, a snake bite, major burn, a blow to the head, and a pregnant woman with stomach pains," said Evalyn. "That's a lot for any hospital, much less a small one like this. Give them time."

"We've given them enough time," growled Gabe. "I'm going back there. I need to know what's happening with Dovie."

As he walked toward the white doors that led to the emergency rooms, he was met by the doctor.

"Mr. Pearce?" asked the doctor.

"Yes, how's my wife?" asked Gabe as James rushed to his side. Everyone else crowded closely in to hear what the doctor had to say. Gabe heard Evalyn suck in a breath and knew she probably wouldn't breathe again until they had an answer.

"She's got quite the nasty head wound," said the doctor. "We've stitched her up, but we'll need to monitor her for the next couple of days for any brain trauma. That way we can transport her to Amarillo quickly if needed."

"Does she need to go there?" asked Gabe. "I'll fly her there right now."

The doctor shook his head and smiled. "No, we feel pretty confident she'll make a full recovery right here. We're just playing it safe."

"Do you know about Elmer Brewer?" asked James.

The doctor flipped a couple of pages on a chart he held in his hand.

"We've removed all the buckshot, and he's resting comfortably," said the doctor. "We've put his wife in the same room. We'd also like to monitor her for the next couple of days. But both of them should be able to go home by the end of the week, as long as there are no complications. Again we're confident Mr. Brewer will make a full recovery and that Mrs. Brewer's baby is okay."

"And Ellie?" asked Alice.

The doctor shook his head, not even referring to his chart. "I'm afraid Miss Brewer is in a very critical condition. I've been working on her which is why it has taken me so long to come and give you an update. Between the burn and the snake bite, a lot of this is out of our hands. Her body is trying to fight off both injuries. We are doing everything in our power to help her. If y'all are praying folks, I suggest you do so."

"Can I see Dovie?" asked Gabe. He knew she'd want to know about Elmer, Tiny, and Ellie, and he felt he should be the one to tell her the news. "And the others?"

"I'll allow it," said the doctor. "But family only and one at a time. The rest of you should go on home."

"Thank you, doctor," said James as the folks of Knollwood started to file out of the hospital. Each stopped to give one of the Brewers or James a word of encouragement and to say they were praying for Ellie.

"Please, let Elmer and Miss. Tiny know I've got the butcher shop covered," Jacob said to Gabe. "They've got nothin' to worry 'bout, but gettin' better. Mr. Johnson's giving me a ride home, but I'll be checkin' in and tell them all I'm prayin' for 'em."

"Thank you, Jacob," said Gabe.

Gabe stayed rooted until everyone was gone except for the family and George and Kathleen Wheaton.

"I'll go in and see Ellie first," said Lou Anne. "I just want to tell her how much I love her, and then I'll head back and pick up the kids from the church and take them back to my place to sleep."

"We'll help you," said Kathleen. "In the morning I'll head over to Quail Crossings and see about cleanin' it up before Dovie and the others come home."

As the waiting room door opened, everyone turned to see the sheriff walk in. He took off his hat. "How are Mrs. Pearce and the rest?"

"Ellie's not doing so good," said James. "But the rest are expected to be fine. And Dr. Hushton?"

The sheriff sighed. "It took us a while to get to him. We had to get a few torches in there to clear out most of the snakes. I didn't want any of the men getting bitten. By the time we got to him, he was gone. He just had too much snake poison in his body. The deputies counted sixteen different sets of puncture wounds. Even if we had been able to get him out and here, I don't think he would've made it."

The room fell silent as everyone became lost in their own thoughts.

"I hate that it came to this," said Gabe and the others nodded in agreement.

For the next couple of days the family took turns sitting with Ellie, Elmer, Tiny, and Dovie. Dovie was the first to be released and took up residence at Ellie's bedside. The doctors and nurses urged her to go home and rest, but she continued to sit holding Ellie's unharmed hand.

As the doctor had predicted, both Elmer and Tiny went home at the end of the week. Tiny had strict instructions to continue her bed rest at home until the baby was born. Elmer hated to leave Ellie, but Evalyn convinced him to go home and rest so he'd be completely healed by the time the baby was born. He agreed only because he knew Tiny needed him by her side.

Dovie lost track of the days she sat by Ellie's bedside. If not for Ellie's bandaged hand and arm, Dovie would have thought Ellie was just in a deep sleep, instead of heavily medicated. When she did wake, it was usually with screams of pain and terror; which brought tears to Dovie's eyes every time.

"It's okay, Ellie," she'd coo. "You're safe. Dr. Hushton is gone for good."

Ellie would settle back into her sleep as Dovie wept into the sheet beside her.

The other family members rotated in and out. Alice came and read to them. Evalyn brought Ellie's doll, Lovey, along with a new doll to the hospital hoping they'd comfort Ellie. Bill told the same story every time he visited, about how brave and strong Ellie was, and he encouraged her to keep fighting. James prayed.

"Mrs. Pearce?" said the doctor, waking Dovie. She hadn't realized she had fallen asleep. "Mrs. Pearce, you really should go home. Two weeks have gone by, and Miss Brewer hasn't woken up in three days. Her body has suffered too much trauma from the snake venom and infection from her burn. It is most likely she will slip away in the next few days."

"No," said Dovie, shaking her head, tears stinging her eyes. "No. That isn't right."

"I'm very sorry for your loss," said the doctor.

Dovie bolted up. "Don't you say that! Don't you give me condolences for my girl when she's still lying here living and breathing. Just this morning her eyes fluttered, and I swear I heard her whisper my name. If you can't help her, then you get a doctor here that can because I am not giving up on her." Dovie wiped away her tears and pointed to Ellie. "Everyone in her life until now has given up on her. They have treated her no better than a piece of dirty newspaper lying in the street. They have walked on her, kicked her, and ripped her soul into pieces and do you know what she did?"

She stared at the doctor waiting for him to answer. He shook his head.

"She looked directly into the eyes of the one person who had hurt her the most, and she showed him kindness and compassion. I will never give up on her. Until my dying breath, I will believe in her. So don't expect me to sit here while you give me condolences for my ...," she looked at Ellie, then back at the doctor. She squared her shoulders and raised her chin. "... for my daughter."

"Momma?"

Dovie looked down, new tears falling as Ellie looked back at her with her bright green eyes. "Oh, Ellie, honey, we were so worried about you."

"Did you mean what you said?" asked Ellie, her voice hoarse. "You want me as your daughter?"

"Ellie honey, you became my daughter the moment you came to Quail Crossings," said Dovie. "I love you, sweet girl."

"I love you too, Momma."

Chapter Fifty-one

July 1946

Elmer gave Tiny a sly smile as they walked through the prairie back towards Quail Crossings. They had been at Bill's house, so Elmer could help Bill add on to his chicken coop, and Lou Anne and Annabelle could gush over the new baby.

"What?" asked Tiny.

"Oh, I was just thinking about how you called our baby a girl this entire time and then you had our little Benjamin Thomas here." Elmer softly tweaked the little boy's nose, receiving a smile in return.

"I knew he was a boy all along," said Tiny. "I was just messin' with you the whole time."

"Sure you were," said Elmer.

As they got closer to Quail Crossings they saw Ellie playing tag with Joy in the yard, while Evalyn and Dovie sat on the stoop with Caleb laughing at the fun and games.

"To watch her now, you'd think it had been years since her stay in the hospital instead of just a month," said Elmer.

Tiny looked at Ellie. "She sure is a miracle. The doctor still can't explain why she just woke up when she did."

"To hear Dovie tell it, it was because she found a reason to live," said Elmer. "She longed for a family, but specifically a mother. She's found that in Dovie."

"She does seem really happy," said Tiny. "And I'm so happy for her. I know she'll never have the kind of life that we have. Dovie doesn't think she'll ever be able to live on her own after everything that's happened to her."

"She'll always have a home here," said Elmer.

"If you think about it," said Tiny. "We've been through an awful lot this past year, and don't even get me started about you being away for the war."

"Yep," said Elmer. "But I do know one thing for sure."

"Oh yea?" Tiny cocked her head.

"This is our forever place." Elmer looked at Quail Crossings and then back at his loving wife and new child. "And I'll never again find myself missing Quail Crossings."

The Murphy Family

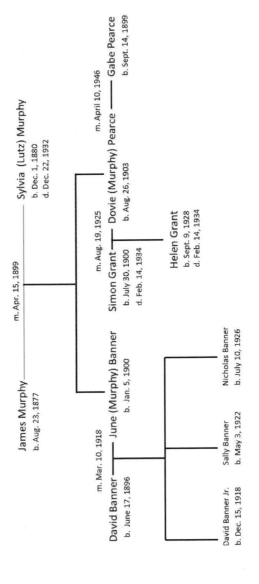

James Murphy
b. Aug. 23, 1877

m. Apr. 15, 1899

Sylvia (Lutz) Murphy
b. Dec. 1, 1880
d. Dec. 22, 1932

m. April 10, 1946

Dovie (Murphy) Pearce —— Gabe Pearce
b. Aug. 26, 1903   b. Sept. 14, 1899

m. Aug. 19, 1925

Simon Grant
b. July 30, 1900
d. Feb. 14, 1934

Helen Grant
b. Sept. 9, 1928
d. Feb. 14, 1934

m. Mar. 10, 1918

David Banner —— June (Murphy) Banner
b. June 17, 1896   b. Jan. 5, 1900

Nicholas Banner
b. July 10, 1926

Sally Banner
b. May 3, 1922

David Banner Jr.
b. Dec. 15, 1918

The Brewer Family

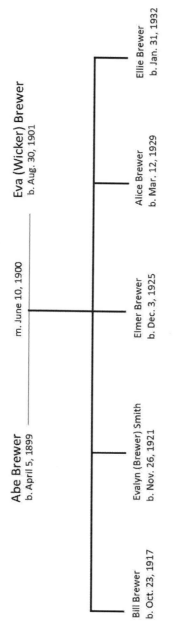

Abe Brewer
b. April 5, 1899

m. June 10, 1900

Eva (Wicker) Brewer
b. Aug. 30, 1901

Bill Brewer
b. Oct. 23, 1917

Evalyn (Brewer) Smith
b. Nov. 26, 1921

Elmer Brewer
b. Dec. 3, 1925

Alice Brewer
b. Mar. 12, 1929

Ellie Brewer
b. Jan. 31, 1932

Bill and Lou Anne Brewer

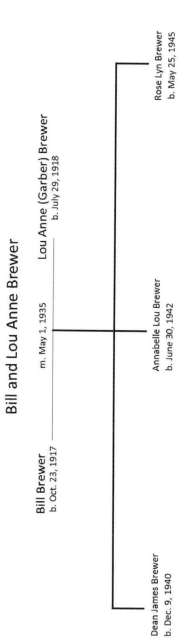

Bill Brewer
b. Oct. 23, 1917

m. May 1, 1935

Lou Anne (Garber) Brewer
b. July 29, 1918

Dean James Brewer
b. Dec. 9, 1940

Annabelle Lou Brewer
b. June 30, 1942

Rose Lyn Brewer
b. May 25, 1945

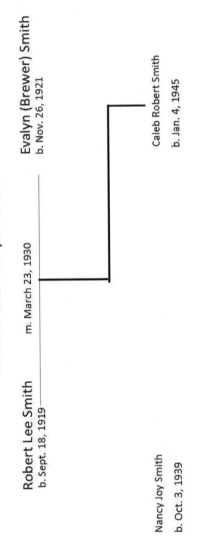

Robert and Evalyn Smith

Robert Lee Smith
b. Sept. 18, 1919

m. March 23, 1930

Evalyn (Brewer) Smith
b. Nov. 26, 1921

Caleb Robert Smith
b. Jan. 4, 1945

Nancy Joy Smith
b. Oct. 3, 1939

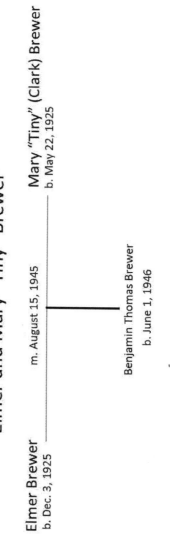

Elmer and Mary "Tiny" Brewer

Elmer Brewer
b. Dec. 3, 1925

m. August 15, 1945

Mary "Tiny" (Clark) Brewer
b. May 22, 1925

Benjamin Thomas Brewer
b. June 1, 1946

If you enjoyed *Missing Quail Crossings*
watch for *Summer's End*
coming May 2016

Enjoy an Excerpt from
Summer's End

Chapter One

"You can't surf in that." Sean pointed at Jessica's skimpy bikini. He gestured to the North Carolina waves coming on shore. "It'll come off with the first wipeout."

"Thought you'd prefer it that way." Jessica laughed, winking at Sean. "Besides, you know very well I don't surf, I tan."

Sean ran his hand along his red and yellow surfboard. "Well, since this is our last day together, I thought you might like to give it a try. You'll regret it if you don't."

Jessica threw her arms around his neck. "And I thought maybe since this was our last day together, you'd skip the surfing and cuddle on the beach with me."

Sean dropped the board, wrapped his arms around Jessica's waist and kissed her. "I guess I could surf tomorrow after you've gone back to Kansas."

She cringed and pushed him away. "We promised never to say the K word."

Sean turned around and picked up his board. "You know you don't have to go."

"You know I do." Jessica sighed, when he didn't turn around. "I have to finish my degree. I only have one semester left. It would be stupid for me not to finish at K

State. Just think, in six months I can come back here, get a job, and stick to you like glue until you're sick of me."

Sean's silence prompted another hug from Jessica. "I don't want to fight today, baby. Let's make a deal, you forget about me going back to ... well, you know where ... and I'll try to surf."

He looked over his shoulder. "Really, you'll try?"

Jessica eyed the board. "I don't see the appeal, but you love it, so I'll try it. But only because I love you."

He turned and kissed her hard. "I love you, too."

The couple spent the day playing and making out within the waves. As the sun drifted down into a beautiful Carolina sunset, Jessica paddled to catch one more wave. Sean cheered her on as she reached the crest and attempted to pop up. The wave crashed into her and everything went black, followed by a blinding white light.

"Jessica. Jessica, wake up."

Jessica felt a hand shaking her shoulder and reached up to grab it. "Sean?"

"No, it's not Sean." The hand jerked away. "It's your mother. It's three o'clock in the afternoon, and you've been sleeping all day. For the love of God, I thought you were going to look for a job today."

Jessica sat up and looked around the room. She was in her parents' house. She flopped back down.

"Look, I told you if you were going to move back in with us, you had to get your life together, find a job, and then an apartment. But no, you just sleep all day. I can't imagine why you'd want to sleep so much anyway."

Jessica stared out the window, taking in the horizon of sunflower fields blowing in the wind like ocean waves.

Wiping a tear from her eye, she whispered. "Because that's the only place where I can see him."

Her mother planted her hands on her hips. "For the love of God, Jessica, it's been three years. It's time to move on. Now get up and take a shower, you stink."

"Whatever Myra," Jessica muttered.

"And don't call me Myra. I don't care how old you are, I am your mother. You will call me Mom," Myra snapped back.

Jessica waited for her mother to close the door before exiting the bed. She shuffled to the desk at the far side of the room and took a small shoe box out of the bottom drawer. Inside were all her mementos from her summer interning in North Carolina.

She smiled at each memory, tracing the faces in the photos. At last she came to the bottom of the box where a single newspaper clipping lay open. Sean's obituary, dated two days after she returned to Kansas.

Returning the items to the box, she grabbed her teddy bear and returned to her bed. Jessica desperately wanted to return to her dream with Sean. She closed her eyes and listened to the rhythmic ocean waves washing over the shore in her head. Soon she was back at the beach where Sean stood scanning the water, panic plastered all over his face.

"Sean," said Jessica running to him. She was again in her bikini, the fields of sunflowers a distant memory.

Sean ran to her and wrapped her in a tight hug. "That was quite some wipe out. Are you okay?"

"I'm fine," said Jessica, realizing she was wet.

Sean picked a towel up off the sand and wrapped it around her shoulders. "How 'bout we call it a day. We'll have some dinner and then I'll help you pack."

"I've changed my mind," said Jessica, smiling. "I've decided to stay in North Carolina."

"Really?" Sean beamed. "You mean it? What about college?"

"I don't need it," said Jessica. "I'll get a job as a maid at one of the hotels if I have to. I just don't want to leave you again."

"Jessica!"

"Who's that?" asked Sean, looking around for the person who had just screamed Jessica's name.

"No one," answered Jessica, knowing full well it was her mother. "Just ignore her."

"Jessica Lyn Collins, you get up right this minute!" yelled Myra.

"I better go," said Sean.

"No," cried Jessica, "don't go. Please don't leave me."

Before she could hold him there, Jessica's mom dumped a cup of cold water over her.

"Mom!" Jessica screamed, stunned from the cold water. "What's the matter with you?"

"What's the matter with me?" Myra slammed the plastic K-State cup down on the bedside table. "What's the matter with you? I told you to get up and take a shower. I don't know how you can possibly go back to sleep after sleeping all day. This isn't healthy, Jessica. I'm taking you to Dr. Upton tomorrow and that's final."

"I don't need to see Dr. Upton," said Jessica, wiping her face with her bedspread. "I'm fine."

"There is nothing fine about what you're doing." Myra sighed. "This is my fault. I should've taken you to see Dr. Upton a while ago. Grief is hard and I guess I didn't think this fling was that serious."

"It wasn't a fling, Mom," retorted Jessica.

"You were only there for four months," said Myra. "That's not a very long time."

"I loved him, Mom," said Jessica, picking at the embroidered flowers on her bedspread, hoping she wouldn't cry again.

Myra sat on the bed next to Jessica and gently laid her hand on Jessica's shoulder. "I believe you, and that's why we're going to go see Dr. Upton. He can give you some medicine to help with your grief and to help get your sleep cycle back under control. What you're doing now, Hon, it just isn't healthy. Maybe he can recommend someone for you to talk to." Myra gave Jessica a little hug. "Now seriously, get up and take a shower before your father gets home. You really do stink."

Acknowledgments

I have so many people in my life who share their love and support with me and made this book possible. I am honored and blessed to have y'all in my life.

LilyBear House staff and author family – I call you family because that is what you are to me. It is an honor to work with you.

Christina Laurie and Cheryl Trenfield – I asked a lot of you with this book, and you jumped at the chance to help. I can't say thank you enough for pouring over my rough drafts and making them better than I ever thought possible.

C.D. Jarmola, Heather Davis, and Marilyn Boone – I've said it before. I'm not sure how I ever wrote a book without you guys, and a year later, I'm still not sure how I did it before you guys. This past year was crazy and you guys kept me sane. Thank you for being there for not only writing support, but emotional support. I am blessed to call y'all friends.

Brandy Walker –Thank you for being not only a fabulous cover designer, but for being a fantastic sister.

Randy and Cathy Collar – I'm going to pay you the highest compliment I know. I hope that one day Baby Girl looks at me the way I look at you. Thank you for everything. I am who I am today because of the two of you.

Anna Collar – I say it every day, "I miss you." But I know you're here. I know you're smiling down on me as I work my dream job. I know you weave yourself into my stories. I love you.

Claressa Carter and Rubina Ahmed – You girls. What can I say? We've been friends for a long time and I know no matter what, we'll be friends forever. Thanks for all the reads and encouragement. You two will move mountains, and I will happily push them with you.

Linda Boulanger and Darlene Shortridge – From the start you two have been there holding my hand, answering my questions, and letting me know I'm not alone in this crazy publishing world. I can't say thank you enough.

Lynn Endres, Steve Mathisen, and Jayleen Mayes – It takes a village to raise a child and publish a book. Thank you so much for your help and volunteering to be my BETA readers. You are my eagle eyes, and I appreciate your time and support. Thank you for not only being fans, but friends.

WordWeavers – I wouldn't be where I am today had I never met the WordWeavers. You guys keep me motivated, keep me encouraged, and are always quick to help me when needed. I am honored to call y'all my friends.

Extended Family – I wish I had the space to name each and every one of you. The support y'all offer is not forgotten or taken for granted. I appreciate it more than you will ever know. Thank you for loving me.

Baby Girl – Your Momma loves you more than you'll ever know. Each day you grow more intelligent and beautiful. I am proud to call you my daughter and know there are big things in store for you. Thank you for being patient when Mommy's working. You are my sunshine.

Mike McMurrain – Every morning I wake up and wonder how I got so lucky to have you in my life. You work so hard for this family and support me with your whole heart. To just say thank you and I love you seems poorly inadequate.

My Readers – I believe Janae Mitchell said it best, "Readers are often fans of authors, but I, myself, am a fan of readers. They are the ones who breathe life into the pages we give birth to, after all." I am thankful for each and every one of you who have taken the time to read my books and an extra thank you for those who have become my friends due to them.

About the Author

Having a great deal of wanderlust, author Jennifer McMurrain traveled the countryside working odd jobs before giving into her muse and becoming a full time writer. She's been everything from a "Potty Princess" in the wilds of Yellowstone National Park to a bear researcher in the mountains of New Mexico. After finally settling down, she received a Bachelor's Degree in Applied Arts and Science from Midwestern State University in Wichita Falls, Texas. She has won numerous awards for her short stories and novels. She lives in Bartlesville, Oklahoma, with her husband, daughter, two spoiled cats, and two goofy dogs.

Author photograph by Sister Sparrow Photography

Other works by

Jennifer McMurrain

Novels

Quail Crossings
Return to Quail Crossings
Winter Song

Novellas

The Divine Heart
Birdsong

Anthologies & Collaborations

Whispered Beginnings
Seasons Remembered
Amore
Chicken Soup for the Soul: The Dog Did What?
Seasons of Life
A Weekend with Effie

Short Stories by
Jennifer McMurrain

Thesis Revised
Emma's Walk
Footprints in the Snow
Finding Hope
Jar of Pickles
The Looking Glass

Friend Author Jennifer McMurrain on Facebook:
https://www.facebook.com/pages/Author-Jennifer-McMurrain

Follow Jennifer's tweets -
https://twitter.com/Deepbluejc

Visit her on her website:
http://www.jennifermcmurrain.com

Made in United States
Orlando, FL
24 July 2022

20125877R00245